A Pardon Too Few

By

Margaret Callow

A Pardon Too Few

By

Margaret Callow

*'. . . named himself John Mortimer, whose very true name
was Jack Cade, and he was an Irishman'*

From *Three Fifteenth Century Chronicles*

AUTHOR'S NOTE

The failure of the insurrection led by Jack Cade gave victory to supporters of Richard Plantagenet, the Duke of York, but England still struggled under a corrupt and unstable government. All around the country lawlessness and strife dominated life. Taxes still crippled, the simpleminded Henry was incapable of proper rule and controlled by his ambitious French wife, Margaret of Anjou. Wilful and strong-minded, in the end it was she alone left fighting to save the House of Lancaster. At times much maligned, she was both loyal and dedicated to England and the Crown.

Most of the heads of the other leaders in Cade's uprising were also displayed on London Bridge as a warning to others, but the desire for rebellion did not die down neither did the lot of the poor commons improve. The unlawful behaviour of later rebels was inspired by the flamboyant Irishman, Jack Cade.

There would be no rest in England. Henry lapsed into insanity again in 1453. In the same year, Margaret gave birth to their only son, Edward of Westminster. The Wars of the Roses would follow two years later and rage for thirty-two years. These violent civil wars were fought between the Houses of York and Lancaster for the English throne.

The wars eventually came to a close when Lancastrian Henry Tudor, later Henry VII, defeated and killed Richard III at the Battle of Bosworth in 1485. Through Henry's marriage to Elizabeth of York in 1486, the warring Houses were finally united.

Henry VI died in 1471, believed murdered during his imprisonment in the Tower of London.

Margaret of Anjou died in poverty in France in 1482. Whilst there was wide speculation she took lovers and her child was a bastard, there is no proof she was unfaithful to her husband.

***

In writing this novel, I have drawn on historical accounts at the time. These have been researched and reproduced as faithfully as lends itself to the story. Some is fiction which I have created to fulfil the purpose I set out to achieve – to tell of an ordinary man, Jack Cade who did extraordinary things.

At times in his head, he was motivated by the prospect of fame and fortune, but there is no doubt in his heart he cared about the lot of the common people . . . and like all rebellions lives were lost for the freedoms we enjoy today.

Margaret Callow, April 2013

Chapter One

Ireland
1417 AD

BREENA looked at the small boy sorrowfully. Poor wee man, he had a right to know, but how could she tell him when she didn't know herself. What she did remember seven long years ago was the time of the year she birthed him. So she waited until buds were bursting on the nut tree close by their ramshackle cottage. On a day when spring's elusive sun wove russet threads through his soft black curls she told him this was the month of his birthday. She was glad she did. He was so excited God love him, clapping his small bony hands and laughing.

"So Mammy, I was born in April," he said for the fourth time since she told him.

She tried to be patient. A knotted muscle under her thin cotton shift was hurting. Bent over the turves with one work-worn hand resting on her back she tried to ease the ache.

"Yes Jack that you were. Now no more chatter. We must finish the last of these before the rain comes," she told him, watching him balance another heap of damp peat in his arms to carry into the cottage. She was quick with the topping knife taking off as much moisture-laden soil as she could before adding to the pile stacked against one wall of their dwelling.

The hearth looked handsomely full with faggots of birch twigs, seaweed and peat laid out to dry. It would burn with speed and her frown acknowledged the wearisome task of collecting more. In their one room demands on the fire were many and it was never allowed to fail, but her boy worked willingly. With his help she always found the strength to collect what was needed from the seashore and the bog.

"Can I use the knife, Mammy?" he said wistfully as she cleaned the blade with a handful of straw.

"When you are grown, you know that. What would I do if you lost a finger or two? Clear this up for Mammy, there's a good boy and then I'll get you your dinner."

Touching the boy's shoulder to acknowledge his help, she could feel his bones sharp against her palm and it made her wince. He nodded obediently and struggled with more of the weighty turf.

Beaded along the skyline behind her the mountains of Connacht looked as if they climbed straight out of the sea. When she glanced up at them she could see their weak purple-grey wash. It was a colour of emptiness which didn't bode well, much like the contents of her larder. One meal a day and scraps were all she could afford and they were far from adequate for a growing child.

He rewarded her with a smile stretching the freckles on his angular cheeks. In a too thin a face, his pale skin was taut across his nose. She knew by his expression he saw distress in hers. Bless him, he knew what hunger was, yet made no complaint when she filled his bowl with watery stew, a pottage thickened with beans or cabbage. Not that she always had them to spare. Sometimes a shred of salt pork

6

might find its way into the pot if Maeve could get it, but not enough, never enough.

Looking into Jack's eyes, dark like the peat he carried, she was grateful to see a twinkle of mischief. He was growing up too quickly and she was sorry for that. Every night before climbing onto the lumpy pallet beside him she knelt for her prayers. Each time she asked the Holy Mother to keep her strong for him. She of all people would know the bond between mother and son and Breena took comfort from such a surety.

"Will we visit Maeve this afternoon?" she asked, watching the boy scour his bowl with his scrap of heavy rye bread. He made no apology for the loud sucking noise as he tried to draw out every last precious drop. She too scraped at her bowl tipping it away from his so he shouldn't see how little she allowed herself. He nodded, wiping his mouth with the back of his hand.

"It's raining," he said.

"We must go just the same. I've candles to make and need the cow suet, then there's the honey for the water." She pointed to the full bucket she'd recently drawn from the well. "I'll take Maeve the last of the onions and some beans, that's a fair trade then. So find your jerkin whilst I wash the pots."

That's how they lived, hand to hand, neighbour to neighbour, supporting one another for the essentials which made the difference between a little food in their bellies or starvation. Surviving on O'Neill land was an uneasy existence for the poor, him too mean to spare them an oyster from the Galway beds flourishing in the cold brutality of the

7

Atlantic Ocean. And harsh was his scolding should he find them trying to steal one.

Watching Jack poking his hand about to find the armhole in his tattered sheepskin jerkin, she noticed a fresh rip across the back. She sighed knowing it meant more stitching to be done. Sometimes she despaired as to whether it would hold another repair, but somehow managed a clumsy darn.

"I can tell Maeve I have a proper birthday now," he said, excited at the thought. Then his expression changed.

"What day is my birthday? You didn't tell me."

"Didn't I?" she said vaguely.

He locked his eyes on hers and the innocence she saw made her want to weep.

"Well then it was on a Tuesday on the very last day," she replied, turning to reach her worn woollen cape hanging from a crooked sliver of wood. She made it an extra minute before she turned back giving the flush of guilt in her cheeks time to fade.

It would take them an hour or more to walk to their neighbour. On a fine day they took a short cut and went along the seashore. It brought gladness to her heart to see Jack running and skipping just as any child should. More times than not he collected flotsam to add to his hoard which he kept tied up in an old kerchief. Today's rain meant the sea scud hung low wrapping itself round every visible landmark so foreshore and sea would become one and they'd like as lose their way.

"Will we have to go over the hill to Maeve's, it takes longer," he whined.

"The weather," she said, inclining her head towards the puddle forming outside the door and the noisy blobs of rain filling it.

It wasn't until they were well on their way across the empty waste of bleak moorland she noticed Jack's bare feet. She set down the basket of vegetables as rain drove her hair hard on her skin where it clung like a limpet to a rock face. Plodding through the peat, muddied wetness slithering over his toes and creeping up his stick-thin legs, he seemed unconcerned.

"Why aren't you wearing your boots?" she called out sharply.

"What's the point Mammy, they leak," he answered over his shoulder.

***

Later when the tallow was set, Breena lit a candle and the sheep's wool wick smouldered. It was a vile smelling smoke drifting about the room in idle curls before floating towards the hole in the thatch. It was always lazy on wet nights and she hated the stench, but she needed the extra light to mend Jack's jerkin. She drew the gut carefully through her bone bodkin and strained to see where to put the first stitch.

Jack slept soundly snuffling in his sleep like a small creature. As she studied his long feather-like lashes on his cheeks and the gentle curve of his child's lips she was thoughtful. Once she would have seen a mirror image of her own looks, but hardship and worry had erased any sign of her youthfulness long ago. When she was just turned sixteen and a beauty men lusted after, there were two things she was sure of. When O'Neill sent for her and forced himself on her, she was sure she'd get pregnant and secondly that he would never acknowledge the child. On both she was to be proved right.

At first it gave her glow, him being related to a long line of nobles in England so the gossip went. It was even whispered O'Neill had ties to the King. It made her feel special and she dreamt of riches for her boy when he was grown. Only as she got older did she understand. Bastard children were as common as tares in the barley field and just as unwelcome.

Chapter Two

Brigstowe (Bristol)
Spring 1447 AD

THE single-masted cog turned on her route into Brigstowe. With her burden of cargo her flat bottom lay low in the water. For the three passengers she carried travelling had been an uncomfortable journey from Dublin. Even at the harbour entrance the ship pitched in the swell and the sea slapped like the Devil's hand at her wooden hull.

Anxious for the first sight of land, their feet and legs were braced to stand upright under leaden skies. When a shrouded shape finally did appear it danced in their vision through a mist of sea spray and unbridled waves. They were a middle aged couple and a younger man who exchanged no more than the civil courtesy of a smile since leaving Ireland, yet were united in misery. Having suffered ferocious bouts of sea sickness, it left them pale and watery eyed. As the vessel plunged through the Irish Sea at its worst they held on with grim need to the rail.

None of their clothes hallmarked them as prosperous. The older couple might once have possessed better, indeed despite it being almost threadbare the fine wool of the woman's cloak was still evident. So too was her husband's in the weave of his breeches, but they were more patched than whole. In turn the younger man wore a poor quality linen shirt and worn hose with a dark mantle of rough, unbleached wool. All three of them were carrying no more baggage than a small satchel each. When the sea spray rose higher than a man and coated them in brine it leached out their colour leaving them white-ringed and stiff.

"Have you far to go when we reach Brigstowe?" the woman enquired in the soft brogue of the south. Fighting with the wind her cloak threatened to leave her body altogether and she dragged it closer. Her other hand repeatedly forced strands of her greying hair back under her bonnet so she could see him when she spoke. Her husband looked irritated.

"Can't you mind your business woman and come away from that rail 'afore you take leave of it." He made a noise of disapproval and raised an eyebrow of impatience in the younger man's direction.

"All the same aren't they, women? Tattle is more important than good sense, wouldn't you say? Cause you'd know that if you're married," he said, with a gruff laugh.

His wife sniffed loudly.

"Now who's being a poke-nose? Perhaps the young man has no wife."

Venturing to leave her cloak for a moment, she extended her liver-spotted hand to her fellow traveller.

"Moyna Cotter and this is Ahern, we come from Cork," she said pleasantly raising her voice as the wind attempted to gust her words away.

Their lean-faced companion looked at them briefly with granite eyes. Holding his hat firmly on his dark curls he moved back from the rail. Plucking at the stained sleeve of his shirt the wind exposed his elbow and Moyna's hawk-like eyes were drawn to the skin it revealed. She knew enough to recognise a lance wound and while half healed the puckered flesh made her flinch. In places it barely knit together and seeped spots of pus from under crimson edges. Quickly her eyes slid away before he should notice her dismay at the sight of it.

"Jack, Jack Cade," he replied the lilt in his voice unmistakable.

Moyna waited clearly expecting more, but she was to be disappointed. She tried again.

"So where is it you said you were going?"

"I didn't," Jack replied.

Hardly able to contain his glee, Ahern took his wife's arm and pulling her closer murmured.

"Mother of Mary, that told you. Now do you see? Stop meddling, will you?"

Not only brisk, the wind was cold too and it bleached every vestige of colour from their faces leaving a pale hint of blue in their pallor. Ahern's ancient felt cap lifted dangerously high as if about to leave his head and he clamped a heavy hand on it.

"I've had enough of this. Will you step over there woman, out of the wind," he instructed his wife, nodding towards the stack of crates above the hatches. They provided a small corner of shelter on the desolate deck. Below, bales of linen and sacks of barley were packed to capacity and the less savoury cargo left on top to offload its stench into the salty air. Sheltered together, the couple were grateful prevailing winds carried the vile odour of long dead fish and fresh animal hides away from them, yet both the stink of tar and the creak and grind of the cargo offered them no peace.

Amidst guttural shouts and muttered oaths the crew ran about their duties and soon the vessel lurched into position to approach the dock. The slack sea and the turning of the tide allowed them to slip into the fast running, but quieter waters. Here they rapidly traversed the narrow wooded gorge of the River Avon and then into the harbour.

"Anchor aweigh," someone shouted.

"At last we've arrived. I shall walk unsteady for a week just you see," Moyna said, when she and Ahern felt the motion stop beneath them. Back at the rail the wind had dropped and there was a smidgen of blue in the patchwork sky.

"The weather looks set fair," Ahern remarked, craning his neck to get his first sight of St. Augustine's Reach behind the row of grand merchant houses with their fine views over the water.

"Good, I shall be glad to see the back of the rain." Ahern frowned. "What for?" he said. "They'll be no time to enjoy it. I've work to look for."

"I know," Moyna said in a vague sort of way. She was more interested in looking about her, but search as she might she failed to see the man who sailed with them.

"Strange," she said. "You'd think he'd be here waiting to get off."

Ahern sighed heavily whilst never taking his eyes of the small gangway about to be dropped.

"Will you hush your breath, woman. It's no business of ours. You'd do better to worry about where we rest our heads tonight if that sister of yours can't take us in."

Still intent in finding their companion, Moyna didn't reply. Even when she and Ahern cautiously stepped onto the gangway and then took their first steps along the dockside, she was still searching.

Once she thought he stood ahead of them talking to another man, but when he turned it wasn't the right face. She was good at faces so she'd been told and the man she looked for was an image distinct in her mind.

"Now his was a face I won't forget in a hurry, that I won't," she would tell her sister later, but for now it seemed the man who called himself Jack Cade had vanished.

***

If it wasn't enough that Jack felt hemmed in by the dense buildings, the woman Moyna unsettled him.

"Wouldn't you know some meddlesome creature would be on the voyage?" he muttered. Morosely stuffing his hands deep in his pockets he tried to get his bearings. He'd slipped off the ship as they started unloading the cargo, but not before making sure Moyna and Ahern were well ahead of him on the dock. When he saw them turn left, he made a point of going to the right and so found himself in Redcliffe Street. Behind him was the harbour, the mansions of the rich and the smell of success. Here he was overshadowed by crumbling warehouses and squalid looking tenements. Wary of them he also took care to avoid the black poking fingers of the narrow alleyways and the wretches who propped them up.

Lost and disconsolate, he noticed the lengthening shadows. He must decide what was best to do. His sheepskin satchel would yield him nothing apart from a crust of rye bread long mouldered in the bottom. Then his fingers touched some coins in his pocket. He knew they didn't amount to more than a few groats and halfpennies, but

15

enough for a meal and bed as long as he chose with care. With his hat pulled well down so only someone of small stature might be able to look up and glimpse his face he started walking.

He hadn't known what to expect when he arrived in England, but it wasn't horse droppings ground thick between the cobbles or the baggy-eyed children dressed in such tatters it was hard to tell whether they be boy or girl. Nor was it beggars sat in plaintive worship of an empty alms bowl. Above all it wasn't the gut-churning stink of human excrement mingling with other putrid effluences which caught in his throat.

And where were the colours he grew up with? Gone were the pastel greens and fulsome ebony of the bogs or swathes of ochre as the grain ripened in the fields. The steely-blue contrast between sky and sea was missing too as was the mauve shading of mountains on the horizon. Instead he was surrounded by leaden greys like tombstones, drab streets and dark buildings which reeked of hopelessness.

Two horsemen passed close to him. Dressed in silk doublets with capes richly trimmed with squirrel fur and swords on their belts they rode with expressions of haughty disdain. One drove his black charger through a large stagnant puddle laughing loudly when the water flew up soaking Jack's legs. Now his hose would stink and clenching his jaw, Jack had trouble containing his anger. His hand hovered over his dagger which was tucked out of sight in his waistband then thinking better of it he let it drop again.

"Out of my way, swag-bellied oaf," the rider shouted over his shoulder. "Next time stay in the gutter where you belong."

Without saying a word, Jack pushed his sleeve up to keep it dry whilst he used his hand to rub down the front of his clothes. Aware eyes were on him he raised his head and met the gaze of the second rider. Jack saw his face bore a look of contempt as he leant down from his saddle. Lip curled, he spat out his scorn.

"Think you're someone of importance do you? Don't you know to stand back for the likes of us to pass? Vermin know their place. Best you learn quickly too if want to keep those pretty looks of yours, you loathsome churl." He paused, wheeled his horse and nodded at Jack's arm. "Nasty wound you have there. Looks like you've been branded. What did you do to earn that, eh peasant? "

Jack knew better than to respond although with his hasty temper it was tempting. Instead he hunched his shoulders further into his cloak and turned up the next alley. For a short way he was kept company by a pig snuffling its way through slops and twice he neatly sidestepped to avoid rats, but a gentle creaking noise of an inn sign drew him on.

Pained by his arm and indescribably tired, Jack pushed open the door of *The Crutched Friars* and stepped inside. It was crowded and noisy, but an atmosphere of spilt ale, sawdust and sweat was a slight improvement to his nose after the rancid air in the streets.

Being close to the port a stranger was commonplace amongst the comings and goings of sailors, watermen and dock workers so few gave him a second glance. He found himself a corner of a bench to sit on and wasted no time catching the eye of the alewife. Stifled by the sudden heat he put his rabbit skin satchel down on the floor beside him and laid his cloak and hat on it careful to avoid a slick of dried vomit.

The woman brought him a sort of fish stew, but the addition of actual fish would cost him more than he could afford so he made do with a bowl of pale stock and a crust of bread to eat it with. As he drew on the last of it he thought of Mammy. Now *she* knew how to make a fine dish with proper salted cod, onions and parsley, but he hastily shut out the picture in his memory and reached for his ale instead.

"Fresh from a ship?" the woman asked in a kindly way as she picked up the empty bowl.

He grunted and she looked hurt.

"Sorry," she said quickly. "I just thought I'd ask only you don't carry much baggage. No harm intended."

"No harm taken," he replied softly.

Brightening, she smiled with the glint of a gold tooth.

"I'd know that brogue anywhere. Irish isn't it?"

This time he didn't reply. She heaved her generous hips away from him then and disappeared in the crowd. His eyes felt heavy and he was only half aware of a change in the seating as someone moved away. Not bothering to look up, he continued staring into the beads of ale left at the bottom of his wooden flask.

The warmth of the thigh pressing against his startled him. As did the scent of lilies so heavy they managed to cut their way through the torpid air in the inn. Very slowly he looked sideways through narrowed eyes, but there was no mistake.

"Looking for company are you?" the girl said in a voice as thick and inviting as a pot of molasses.

Her smile was wide as the neckline of her dress was low. A pretty mouth, he thought, painted as it was with a red balm so it shone when her lips moved.

"I might be," he replied.

Her laughter was coarse, her eyes spoilt by too much charcoal and her hair overly streaked with henna, but when she took his hand and traced it along her chest nothing much mattered.

"That's good only I got a room not far from here and a mattress with a real bolster."

"How much?" he asked

He thought she seemed uncertain. "Is half a groat too much?" she said, her hand first resting and then pushing further up his thigh.

He shrugged. "What do they call you?"

The tip of her tongue playing on her upper lip was pink and moist.

"I'm Mary and you?"

"Too many questions," he muttered.

He pulled out a few coins from his pocket and searching through them, chose two which he slid under the flagon. Hardly were they there when the alewife pounced on them depositing them down her generous cleavage. She gave Mary a wink and shuffled off whilst Jack bent down for his belongings. He was annoyed to see most of his satchel was still covered in white stains. He thought he managed to clean the spray off before he left the dock. Needing to rid his possessions of flecks of sawdust and whatever else they may have laid in he shook them hard, but deep in the fur the salt crystals wouldn't move.

Depositing his satchel more firmly over his shoulder he moved to stand up, but Mary seemed to be more interested in fiddling with her hair. As she parted the dry strands, he could see the straw colour it had once been and stains on the skin at her hair line from colouring it. She buried her cheap comb into the depths of its unruly mass, humming to herself.

"Are we going or not," he said impatient now.

"In a hurry are we?" she said, with a suggestive snigger.

Following Mary's slight frame out of the door his only thought was one of slight annoyance. Such was the cheapness of his accommodation that night he could have asked for fish in his meal after all.

Chapter Three

Windsor Castle

SILENCE prevailed. Not the companionable sort, but a rather more awkward one. In such a spacious room with a lofty ceiling the strained atmosphere appeared to cling to the moulded architraves and hang from the heavy serge drapes. It seemed to repress all who sat in it except for the King who was cheerfully talking in endless riddles.

It was no coincidence that those present chose to sit facing one another on different sides of the room, but casting their differences aside all were more than a little downhearted. Seated side by side, Humphrey, Duke of Gloucester and Richard Plantagenet, Duke of York exchanged glances which spoke of their impatience whilst the expressions of the other three men opposite were more of sad resignation. It was clear to each of them no official business would be conducted today, but they could all agree on one thing. Without doubt their king was entering another period of madness.

"They become more frequent," whispered William, the Earl of Suffolk to his companion Edmund, Earl of Somerset. Lolled in his chair beside them Edmund's uncle, the elderly Cardinal Beaufort appeared to be dozing.

"Speak up William. I can't hear what you are saying. Have you thought up a new verse perhaps?" Henry said from the depths of a tall throne of a chair. One pale hand rested on his temple while the other traced patterns on his almost non-existent chin.

"Verse Sire, what sort of verse do you require?" William replied politely.

"One that speaks of beauty and love not the terrible tales of war and bloodshed, it's all you seem to talk about, you know I abhor such things."

"But it is of those we must speak of, Majesty," Humphrey said shortly. "There is growing disorder up and down the land and with the disasters in France . . ."

"Then we must pray," Henry interrupted reaching for a heavy gold Bible which lay on a pedestal beside him. "Come on, down on your knees all of you."

Before any of them could move the Bible flopped back on its place with a low thud and Henry sat still as if cast in stone. His gaze was vacant and his mouth went slack. As it did so, a slender spiral of spittle appeared from one corner and crept down his face. Richard leapt to his feet in consternation.

"God's blood, what's wrong with him?"

His raised voice woke the Cardinal with a start. Jerking upright, his lapful of papers slithered in a slow white rivulet onto the floor at his feet. Bemused and not a little embarrassed he hastily started gathering them up.

"I shall fetch the Queen," Humphrey said, laying a sedate hand on Richard's arm. Reaching across him he tugged hard on the silk bell-cord and sat with a smug smile at appearing so competent. Still trance-like Henry remained unmoving whilst the others collected themselves as well as their possessions ready to leave the room. It was William who was quick to reassure.

"There is no need to flee the room in such haste. This is not uncommon with His Majesty. Look, now he stirs. Soon he'll be quite recovered. We should continue as if nothing has happened."

Humphrey's pointed beard quivered with his indignation.

"Nothing has happened? Trust you to take such a casual stand. If things were left to you we should be more in a muddle than ever. Does he see the apothecary?"

"When we deem it necessary thank you my Lord Gloucester. His Majesty suffers from no more than nervous exhaustion at times," said a clipped female voice from the doorway and the air chilled like a wintery afternoon.

With a refined rustle of the finest silks the young Queen entered the room. Blonde hair elaborately twined under a jewelled coif and her grey dress exquisitely tailored and set with trails of seed pearls, she conveyed an elegance which the French excelled at. Indeed Margaret of Anjou carried herself with regal aplomb. No man should be fooled however since under her composed exterior there rested a woman both bold and high-spirited who would not be trifled with.

Showing the expected deference, Henry's advisors bowed in her presence remaining low until she had passed them. Choosing a matching but smaller chair next to the Henry, she stretched out her arm resting her hand on his. Stroking it gently up and down, she waited as he in turn blinked rapidly as if to assess his surroundings. Then looking more alert he smiled amiably before turning to his wife.

"Have you come to take me to dinner or shall we read a little, my love?"

"Come my Lord Husband, gather your wits. Do you see how the sun shines out there, it is barely past noon and we have business to attend to. Are we well enough for that? You know we rely on you for such things and why are you wearing clothes only fit for a yokel. We must get changed at once," Margaret chided, softly spoken, but firm with him.

He in turn was mild-mannered saying only, "Yes, my love."

It was more than his advisors would dare to mention. Despite their Court dress of well cut velvet with silken doublets and capes edged with furs, the King had taken to wearing breeches and tunics made from poorly dyed wool as befitted a peasant. Having dispensed with any apparel made from expensive cloth or trimmed with ermine, he explained it made him feel closer to his poorer subjects. Most simply took it as another sign of his deteriorating mental state.

***

All three of the King's most favoured nobles met later that day. After dining on capon, swan and game pie they gathered in William's chamber discussing the day's events. Stretched out in his chair, William toyed with his new acquisition recently bestowed on him by Henry. The Lord Chamberlain's chain hung from his neck. At its centre a perfect ruby rested in a gold wreath surrounded by small red roses and a gold bordure lying on his breastbone.

"So it is agreed then," he said sharply. "We must be rid of our so called friend the Duke of Gloucester. He causes much mischief and repeatedly calls for further attacks on France. Should we heed his words there will never be peace."

"Yet he is popular with the people who listen to him well. Then yet again thanks to Gloucester, it seems only a matter of time before we have to raise another army. However, I cannot agree to foul deeds if that is what you scheme," the Cardinal reminded quietly.

William immediately sat upright, his jaw set firm and his eyes icy to their depths. "If we wish to remain our king's favourites and fill our own coffers too then there must be no more war. The country cannot afford it, you and I certainly cannot afford it and since our monarch most fervently desires peace that is what he shall have. Make no mistake about this."

"Some might say you are greedy, dear William," the Cardinal remarked with a wry smile. "Of course, I myself know different."

The room rang with the sound of William's laughter.

"Indeed sir. Then you are the only one."

Fingering a bloom-blushed fig, he rubbed it against his fine lawn shirt and buried his teeth in its succulent rose coloured flesh. A tiny jet of juice spurted from it landing on his chin, but he appeared not to have felt it as he took another generous bite.

"I do hear tell 'tis Gloucester's wife who will be his undoing," Edmund murmured, one foot in the air to admire his new hand stitched fawn-skin boots. "Since her trial, more and more in the Court shun him or speak in whispers as he passes. They say it was quite a sight to see her parade the streets in a white sheet, but few believe she repents and there is much contempt abroad for such a disgrace."

Shaking his head, the Cardinal's tendrils of purest white hair brushed the fine lines criss-crossing his forehead.

"I'm old now and never did I think I should live long enough to see such wickedness. That the lady Eleanor should practice the sorcery of Satan against our king, her husband's own flesh and blood is too terrible to contemplate. She was lucky to escape with her head intact."

His rheumy blue eyes filled with the moisture of age and he sat dabbing at them several times with a shaky hand. Squeezing his arm, his nephew attempted to console him.

"You are a great strength to us Uncle, but neither of us will involve you in any of our plans to be rid of Gloucester. Isn't that right, William?"

William was up on his feet instantly and with a look bordering tenderness stretched out his hand to take one of the Cardinal's. It resembled a bird's frail claw resting in the expansive fleshiness of William's palm.

"Indeed not old man and I call you that with the greatest affection," William said with genuine warmth. "Edmund and I will take care of everything and I'm sure when the word *treason* is breathed in the king's ear it will bring the results we desire."

"Then you must be cautious for Gloucester is well thought of by the masses and he has Richard of York on his side," the Cardinal said shrewdly, whilst trying to conceal a yawn.

Always thoughtful, Edmund said. "It is even possible His Majesty may want to reward us for such loyalty to the Crown, What think you of that Uncle?"

But the Cardinal was beyond any waking thoughts, only those which might appear in his mind should he dream. His eyes were tightly closed and the even rhythm of his breath did no more than gently ruffle the cotton of his clerical collar.

Chapter Four

BEING both poorly lit and exceedingly cold the thin corridor offered no comfort to Humphrey, Lord Gloucester as he paced it with impatient steps. The more he thought of the cursory message he'd received, the more he bridled. Had his nephew the boy-king Henry, his own flesh and blood, so quickly forgotten the years he, Humphrey, had been his Lord Protector. Nursed him and nourished him to become a good monarch when he became of age. That it was apparent Henry was an unpopular king was through no fault of his. Yet many thought it so and he knew full well of their schemes to be rid of him.

Frowning darkly and mumbling under his breath, Humphrey's outrage continued. Impudent puppy, how dare he make him late for everything else that day? All he could hope for was the king had now passed beyond his recent madness and was restored to a more normal state of mind. Somehow, he doubted it. To those concerned about such things the episodes appeared closer together of late.

It took the page several minutes to summon the courage to approach the irate noble. Finally with a deep breath he stepped forward from the security of a curve in the panelling.

"His Majesty will see you now," he said, already turning to retreat.

"And about time," Humphrey replied, abrasive as usual.

Striding past with an icy glare he gave no more than a cursory tap before flinging open the door to the Royal

Receiving Room. He needed to look down to see his nephew. Henry sat cross-legged on the floor surrounded by books. Small, large, weighty and thin ones, all of them piled neatly in size by a methodical hand. Dressed completely in black, it was only the braiding of gold on his collar which relieved the mournful colour of Henry's robe, but Humphrey was pleased to see his nephew looked brighter than of late.

Waving limply, Henry directed him to sit whilst turning the pages of large tome absent-mindedly. Hardly stopping to look at it and without lifting his head, he said, "You see we wear black."

Another page turned with a noisy rustling. Puzzled, Humphrey was unsure of the remark, but he didn't allow his irritation to show.

"Indeed Majesty and I thought how fine you look," he said, seating himself.

The book shut abruptly.

"No, not fine, not fine at all," Henry said petulantly. "It is because we are in mourning."

Immediately concerned, Humphrey stood up, saying quickly, "Please accept my sympathy, Majesty. I had no idea. Just who is it who's died?"

Henry got to his feet. Then with slow precise steps he reached his wooden couch. Throwing himself on it heavily, he disturbed the fresh leaves scattered across the velvet cover and a pleasant aroma of lavender and thyme wafted across the room.

"Not exactly died, Uncle, but we have learned of a turncoat who plots against us and it pains us greatly. It is a dark hour, a very dark hour for such news about one we trusted." His melancholy sigh and grim expression sent shivers of alarm through Humphrey, but he managed to remain calm.

"Surely Sire, you are wrong," he said, with a ghost of a smile. "Who is this black heart for I shall stop at nothing until he is found and sent to the Tower?"

"Then we need look no further. They say 'tis you that plots an uprising against us, Uncle. It means you no longer care for us and for that we grieve," Henry said sadly.

Humphrey's cheeks drained of colour and he could feel the beads of cold sweat on his brow. Before he could gather his thoughts the door opened wide and Margaret swept into the room followed by her ladies-in-waiting. Rising as she entered, Henry bowed, but ignoring him she stood in front of Henry. Stretching out one heavily bejewelled hand, she waited for him to kiss it. Smiling up at her he brushed his lips against her cool palm.

"Have you told him we know of his scheming, my Lord Husband?" she asked in a brittle voice.

Then with a scornful look and a pretentious smile on her sharp little countenance, Margaret locked her gaze on Humphrey's bewildered face. Sensing spite in every inch of her frame, he knew at once who his enemy was. Refusing to meet her eyes, he sunk to his knees and appealed to Henry.

"What you tell me horrifies me, Your Grace. It is outrageous. Have you forgotten so easily that I acted as your Regent, your Lord Protector when you were no more than nine months old? I took care of you for many years, how can you think so badly of me? Ask the people, I seem to find favour with them."

"But not with us, my Lord Gloucester," Margaret said, her words as cold as hailstones.

With a sour look she wandered to the window where the late September sun cast multi-coloured spindles of light through the glass. It set the myriad of beads sparkling on her gown into a glitter of colour.

"This room is cold," she said, with an exaggerated shiver.

Henry looked surprised "I was only just thinking it is somewhat over warm."

"Do you take pleasure in disagreeing with me, my Lord?" Margaret said sharply.

"Certainly not, Lady Wife, the room is indeed cold. We shall have a fire," Henry said obediently.

Stunned by events, Humphrey stood silently beside Henry, but Margaret wasn't finished with him.

"You are not forgotten, my Lord Gloucester. What have you to say for yourself?"

Humphrey found his mouth and lips almost too dry to shape any words. Swallowing hard he tried to find a trace of saliva so he could reply.

"It's all lies and I can guess who is behind them," he croaked. "The Earl of Suffolk and his friends that's who it is, they have never liked me. I believe they give you false information in order to be rid of me. I pray you do not listen to them, Your Majesties. I am as loyal a subject as any you will ever find."

Margaret bent close to Henry and whispered something. Humphrey could see by his expression he was dithering. Fearing the strength of his wife's influence he watched anxiously as the King chewed on his finger nodding occasionally.

"We have thought about your plea, but we are not convinced. We believe you should be arrested on a charge of treason. Let the courts decide if you are innocent," Henry said with a trace of anguish in his voice. "However . . ."

"Do not waver, my Lord. It is agreed," Margaret interrupted curtly.

***

William's jubilation was hard to conceal and he was struggling not to laugh out loud. Few would notice since all who passed were servants who knew better than to raise their heads when notables were close. Less than a week after the accusation, it had gone exactly as he and Edmund planned.

He only found the frail Cardinal when he arrived at his friend's room. Sitting in a chair the old man was resting his swollen legs atop a stool. With his head hanging low on his chest, a string of drool dangled under his chin. William noticed when he raised his eyes his skin was so translucent his veins knotted together in threads of blue and without a hat his bald pate seemed shrunken onto his skull bones.

"You seem pleased with yourself, my son. Come sit by me and tell me the news," the Cardinal said, patting a stool with a skeletal hand.

William flinched at the sight of the bones through the white flesh and looked away. Perching gingerly on one corner of the wood, he spoke quietly.

"Do you expect Edmund soon? He should hear this too."

Shrugging, the cardinal's blade-edge shoulder bones jutted from his black silk gown which hung from his frame like a sail without a blow of wind to fill it.

"He left for London this morning on business for the king so he said. Tell me what news of Gloucester?"

William's smile was wide and his eyes glittering with triumph.

"It went as well as we hoped. It only took the court at Bury St Edmunds a few minutes to pass their verdict of High Treason and my Lord Gloucester was done for. He is to be held in their prison whilst they wait for the king to recover from his present malaise. The jailor knows what is to be done. Then it will be announced that poor Gloucester was taken by a seizure. By the end of the week we should have cause for celebration."

Racked by a bout of coughing, the Cardinal's face screwed up with pain and it was several seconds before he caught his breath. William watched in concern, but there was little he could do.

"This old chest of mine," the Cardinal rasped. "Gloucester will not be the only one in a winding sheet before too long."

"Hush, my Lord Cardinal, speak not of such things," William said in a low voice. "Edmund will take badly should anything happen to you."

With a ghost of a smile, the old man said.

"My nephew will manage well enough without me. These bones of mine tell me 'tis time. Don't begrudge an old man the chance for a long sleep. Now leave me if you will," he said, his eyelids beginning to droop.

As William tip-toed to the door, the old man spoke again.

"Remember what I said. The people will be disgruntled. Be ready for disturbances for it will take little for them to rise up you can be sure of that."

His words became indistinct and William strained to hear the last of them. With his eyes closed, the Cardinal lapsed back into the blur-edged world privy only to the dying.

Chapter Five

Brigstowe

WATCHING Mary reach for some soiled wadding, Jack slid up his sleeve.

"It's the best I have," she said apologetically.

Every day for over a month she performed the same ritual, and still the wound was refusing to heal properly. He sat watching her dabbing away and tried to decide which was dirtier, the piece of cloth or her hands. It was another reason for his growing dislike for her. Her sluttish ways now overcame his desire and were adding to his frustration.

Poverty was no stranger to him. Hadn't he and Mammy known it all their lives? Small as he was, he knew she saved food for him rather than herself, although she told him differently. But when it came to keeping a clean home then she was a zealot. Not a day passed that she didn't scatter fresh rushes on the floor, and regularly ask for clean straw from the stables at the Big House, so their pallets never smelt stale. The hearth was always trim too, and her few clay pots and her stirring stick kept scrupulously clean.

"There," Mary said emphatically, breaking in to his precious memories with her loud voice. She gave a final, heavy-handed thud on his tender skin. "I can't do no better than that. Perhaps it'll teach you not to get into fights."

He fought with his hasty breath, a warning to him of his temper.

"I've told you before, I got this in Gaul during the war," he said tightly.

"Ah, but whose side were you on, tell me that?" she said with a snort of laughter.

Looking into her black-smudged eyes he wished he'd never admitted he fought for the King of France or that they'd driven the English back to Calais which was where he received his wound. Once she knew she wouldn't let him forget it. Almost gloated over it, he thought as if it were a punishment for his supposed disloyalty. Reaching for his cap he was brusque.

"I'm going out."

Her face dropped. "Can't I go with you?" she whined.

"You need to empty the piss pot," he said, waving his hand at the pan brim-full, "and whilst you're about it we want more water or have you forgotten where the well is? Clothes want washing too," he said, nodding to the pile of dirty laundry heaped on the pallet.

"Anyone would think I charged you for staying here. Why, you don't even pay me for your treats," she snapped, her sulky expression swiftly changing to one of defiance.

"Is that what you call them," he said with a sarcastic smile, tucking the haft of his knife more securely into his waistband.

"Well I don't see you refuse them," she said, anger spots staining her sallow cheeks. "I've let you stay here all this time because I felt sorry for you, you being from across the water and all that with no home to go to."

"Perhaps I should leave," he murmured.

"Perhaps you should," she retorted, picking up the pot of urine with such ferocity it slopped over onto the boards.

"You disgust me, slattern." His cold voice jolted her.

"And I'm with child," she shouted. Then looking bleak her voice fell. "It's yours too not that I would expect you to care."

It stopped him in an instant and left no time for rational thought. Instead he said that which was uppermost in his mind as his anger took control of him.

"How many men have taken you, answer me that. And yet you expect me to believe it's mine?"

She flew at him then. Her small rough hands curling into fists and her eyes lit with a wild fury, she pummelled his chest screaming such a torrent of curses he could only guess at some of the words. Turning his forearms broadside he warded off the vicious blows and felt her nail gouging flesh out of his neck. Afterwards his recollection was that it was Mary's hand who found the knife first, that he had no choice but to prevent her sinking it into him. It happened so quickly he never could quite remember.

Bemused, he saw her eyes widen and the sudden spurt of red. It was the first of many which appeared through the slit in her dress turning it into a sodden swab. Her stricken face turned alabaster pale and he could feel her falling away from him. Then she hung from his arms, her sudden unexpected weight almost making him lose his footing in the slippery blood. He stepped back at the same time lowering her to the floor.

With her lying in a tangled heap with her skirt ridden up to her thighs, he could see the irritating blotches which patterned the skin on her legs. Bed bugs, he had them too and the thought sent his hand hurrying to the newest of them on his ankle. Scratching it he thought the drops of blood on his finger tips came from the bite until he was reminded of her nails buried in his neck. Touching the place gingerly he saw the scarlet stickiness on his fingers.

She was staring up at him milky eyed like a dead fish kept too long.

"Mary?"

The bitch is pretending, he thought bending to rest his hand on her cheek, but feeling the unexpected cool of her flesh made him flinch. Moving back he saw the knife and as if he'd been made rigid by the feel of her skin, his stiff fingers folded round the haft. Still disbelieving he cleaned the blade listening for anything in the dingy room which might break the dreadful silence. Her voice or even her ragged breathing was all he wanted. He tried again, louder this time.

"Mary, you can get up now."

But of course she didn't. The more he looked at her the more he thought he should feel sickened by the brutality of her death. Just like he did the first time he put a lance through a lad on the battlefield at Gaul and cut his throat to finish him. After that it became easier, drop by crimson drop, life juice shed because he could make it so. There was never any elation just mute acceptance. Then his emotions became cold as they were now.

A voice coming from somewhere deep in his mind spoke in harsh whispers. *But they weren't women, those were soldier boys. You have no right to kill a woman . . .* Shaking his head to clear it he stood looking down at his hands. Her blood smeared his palms. Once the sight would have repulsed him, instead he walked calmly to the bucket. Only a quarter full the torpid contents looked unappetising, but it served his purpose. He dried his hands as best he could on the corner of the stained bolster leaving a scum of pink froth on the water.

She's just told you she carries your child, Jack. What are you thinking now?

He heard the sudden whimpering noise and wondered it was her. But it couldn't be. So was it him? Reluctantly he crouched down beside her, running his hand over her dishevelled skirt trying to feel her belly through it. She was lying of course wasn't she? *You'll never know now, Jack.* Dear God, where was Mammy, she'd know how to help him.

Suddenly voices floated through the window slit startling him, but it was passers by talking to one another in the humid sunshine on the street outside. Normality stirred him and he knew what he must do. Careful to avoid the viscous puddle he moved about the room collecting up his few possessions. He wasn't going to bother about food. There was little enough anyway. But a square of cheese still sat on the table. Dry and cracked like parched earth it would suffice for now he thought dropping it into his satchel.

He needed to hunt for Mary's money box. He knew she hid it away changing the place from time to time so he wouldn't find it. He also knew she saw other men who paid her well. What did he expect? Once a doxy, always a doxy. It was stuffed well down her side of the stained mattress and the amount of groats took him by surprise. He imagined they felt hot to the touch as he emptied them out, as if Mammy was watching him and her displeasure heated up the silver.

"Jack, that's stealing," he heard her say. *What would the Holy Mother think?"*

"Sorry, Mammy," he said, like he always did when she caught him making mischief.

There was no time to question anything he did. Although Mary's sightless eyes focussed on the damp patches on the ceiling, he felt sure they were looking at him. Sudden unaccustomed distress thickened his throat when he looked at her body.

"By the Saints, would you stop your staring," he exclaimed, stifling a sob. "It was an accident. How did I know you would fall on the blade, you stupid whore."

One of her hands became flaccid and sliding across her chest, it fell onto the boards with a thud. It was enough. Feeling the hair standing up on his neck, he groaned under his breath and desperate to be rid of the sight of her he tossed one of her soiled dresses over her face.

There would be no particular surprise when she was found. Whores were discovered dead many a day, but he still didn't want to be caught with her body. Besides the room smelt more evil than it usually did. Like a butcher's slaughtering pit, he thought. Without a backward glance, he left the room shutting the door carefully behind him, but even the slightest shiver on the wormy frame shook flakes of damp lime off the walls.

Once in the street he breathed in deeply, suddenly grateful for the foetid street odours he'd grown used to. Above the rooftops dark clouds throbbed with fierce energy and the rain fell. Slowly at first in plump drops spinning off the cobbles and skittering across the top of puddles. There were always pools of water which never dried up no matter what time of the year. Then with determined intent the rain came down so hard he could hardly see where he was going, yet he kept his pace steady despite others hurrying to reach somewhere dry.

The downpour was timely so when he pulled his collar up high to conceal his injuries it didn't look out of place. When he reached High Cross he followed the city walls into Broad Street. He could just make out St. John's Gate in the distance made hazy by the cloudburst. Lengthening his stride it didn't take him long to walk through the simple arch and turn onto the road for London. Before long he vanished into the mingling travellers who frequented the highway in great numbers.

He left nothing to mark him by and nobody who cared if he did.

Chapter Six

WHEN Jack reached Southwark directly south of the River Thames and entered the City of London, he'd left some of his memories of Mary behind and all of his boot leather. With sores on his feet he was limping heavily as he crossed London Bridge. Pausing to look down onto the murky depths below, he was shocked. All he could remember were the wild waters of his childhood where rivers threaded their way down mountainsides and bounced over granite crags. When peat found its way into it the waters they turned dark and mysterious, but they were always singing of their purity.

The Thames ran fast and wide carrying with it the dregs of everyday life and death. As it trundled past he could make out what looked like a human arm caught up in a vast raft of vegetable and human waste and beside it a dog, its body inflated to grotesque proportions. Fast behind, timber planks fallen from a cargo ship travelled side by side with raw sewage and the unwanted trifles from a nearby slaughterhouse.

Others could see it too. Above the grey stone three human heads impaled on pikes watched the flow of the river. Blackened by the sun and rotting, theirs was a view seen only through black holes for eyes and when he noticed the vile tableau, Jack felt cold despite the warmth of an unclouded sky. With no wish to spend long in their company he resumed his journey across the bridge and through the South Gate into a maze of clay and timber tenements.

Such were the number of town folk hastening on their business he hardly had space to pass in the narrow mud lanes. The merchants and traders he saw looked anxious with hardship stamped into their expressions and poverty etched on their lean frames. No one spared him a glance. Behind stalls in the street market, peasants were offering up their crops for sale and he could see they fared no better. He expected more of a city like London. Instead he only saw pinched faces and weary acceptance and he found the dismal and odorous atmosphere oppressive.

Some of those who passed him carried their wealth in the arrogant tilt of their heads and the cut of their fine clothes. There were others made listless through hunger and hopelessness who wandered without purpose. And more than once he narrowly missed being pushed into a ditch where flies danced above fetid water. Occasionally his eyes met another traveller, but mostly he was ignored as he searched for somewhere where he could find victuals and rest his painful feet.

Spoilt for choice, he deliberated first in front of one inn and then another. Finally, it was the *White Hart* at the end of the High Street which drew him in. Pushing open the door he heard the hum of voices and felt eyes on him from dark corners, but here at least there felt an essence of life if only in the occasional outbursts of laughter and contented drone of conversations.

Partway through a trencher of mutton stew he ordered sweet ale. Before the alewife could bring it to him a voice said.

"I'll have the same as my acquaintance here."

At first Jack thought he'd misheard, but when two flasks of amber liquid were set down on the table beside him he looked up. Surprised by the silver coins he saw readily given in exchange he noticed the man's purse of softest leather was weighted by many more. The stranger smiled and Jack was even more perplexed for this didn't look a man who would seek out the likes of him. His manner and bearing set him apart as did the outfit he wore. Not for him the common man's jacket and breeches in coarse wool of a nondescript colour, but a rich grey cloth tailored with some refinement. Quality was also reflected in his velvet cap set with a feather, in his quietly spoken voice and the contours of his structured face.

"Richard de Courcy" he said, extending his hand to Jack. "Merchant and before you ask, I make my living from the sea. My ships trade far and wide, furs from Rus, spices from the east, horses and timber. If it can be loaded below deck I carry it."

Jack found it disconcerting that this was a man with money who owned more than one vessel. He wanted to feel impressed, but instead he felt he felt more of a pauper than ever. He hesitated reluctant to converse with a stranger, but Mammy disapproved of rudeness and taught him manners.

"John Mortimer," he murmured, feeling the firm grip of the man's fingers on his.

Sitting on the stool beside him, Richard took a long swallow of his drink and dabbed away any traces from his upper lip with a fine lawn kerchief. Jack saw his eyes resting on his satchel for a brief moment and he moved his foot to push it more firmly under the table.

"Don't let me disturb your meal, this inn serves some of the best food in Southwark," Richard said, watching Jack over the top of his flagon. "I don't recall seeing you in here before, on the road are you?"

Jack brooded as he ate the last of the stew. Questions were not what he wanted, yet the man appeared friendly enough and his appearance aroused his curiosity.

"You could say that," he replied, searching Richard's dark eyes.

If he hoped to find answers there he failed for in their depths there was no expression. It was odd he thought, for Richard's quick smile was warm and he gave no hint of hostility. Yet Jack knew he must take care and it pleased him his change of name slipped so easily off his tongue. He'd had long enough to rehearse it as he journeyed from Brigstowe, day after wearisome day. The thought revived the discomfort in his feet and the ache in his bones.

"It seems pleasant enough here. I shall take a room for a few days," he said.

As the door opened again the candles in the wall sconces quivered with the rush of dusk's cooler air and he yawned.

Richard nodded. "Good, then we shall meet again." He pushed back his stool and thoughtful said. "You're not by any chance looking for work?"

Laughing, Jack tapped the money in his pocket.

"Before too long I fear. Why do you ask?" He tried to sound casual, knowing very well one night at the *Hart* would be all he could afford.

"Be here tomorrow evening. I have something you might be interested in," Richard said. His hint of a smile looked mysterious, but his eyes remained unreadable. Intrigued, Jack barely noticed. A change of fortune was just what he sought.

Still puzzled by Richard's offer he took a room on the top floor of the inn. Accompanied by the alewife, he took stock of the garret chamber whilst she fussed, brushing imaginary specks of dust off the wooden sill.

"You look tired, dearie, have you come far?" she asked, looking hard at his drawn face and the charcoal smudges under his eyes.

It was said kindly and he had this strange notion he wanted her to fold her arms about him and hold him, like Mammy did when he worked extra hard at one chore or another so that tears welled with his weariness.

"It's a long walk from Brigstowe," he said without thinking.

"On the ships were you?"

When reality nudged him he was horrified. Why had he told her that? Why Brigstowe? His tongue was too free and he cursed himself. To make amends he shrugged in a vague sort of way and she didn't persist.

"Your business of course," she said amiably. "Are you sure this room is alright for you. It's the cheapest I do."

"Its fine," he mumbled, walking over to the window and raising his hand to wipe a circle of clean on it.

"Oh, my, that looks nasty," she said, nodding at his exposed arm.

"It's fine," he repeated.

It was the alewife's turn to shrug.

"I'll see you later then," she called cheerfully.

Pressing his nose to the tiny pane he didn't reply and he heard the door closing. Timbered balconies surrounded the inner cobblestone yard and his window three storeys up afforded a fine view of the wharf. He could see the boats ready loaded, waiting for a tide before they could sail. Behind them the marshes on the opposite bank stretched far into the distance seamlessly joining the sky. Reminding him of home, he turned away abruptly.

It wasn't a large room, but the pallet smelt clean and the reeds on the floor so fresh they still had the greenness in them. On a stool the candle in its holder was full length and its wick newly trimmed. It all added to Jack's satisfaction and he felt contented. More so than in fact he had for some while, he decided. Resting on the pallet he stared up at the lime washed ceiling and considered the recent events.

He had no fond memories of his journey across the sea from Dublin or his stay with the whore, Mary. As for his return home from Gaul a few weeks earlier he was filled with a deep melancholy. If only someone could have warned him it wouldn't have been such a shock. Of course there was no one and so nursing his lance wound, he'd arrived in Connacht unprepared.

There he found Mammy under a newly turned hillock in the green and their empty home already falling into disrepair. Hot tears drenching his cheeks he tramped the path to Maeve's home, but that too was deserted. Fearful of what he might find he cautiously searched behind the cottage, but there was no sign of a recent burial. Distraught, he went back the way he had come and knelt by the small wood cross. Then in a harsh voice he shouted her name. "Mammy . . ." It was so loud that the huge boulders and stony peaks received it and sent it bounding back to him in a gleeful, mocking echo.

Too vivid a memory to bear, Jack got up. Splashing his face with water from the earthenware jug he found in the corner, he used the chamber pot and went back downstairs. The inn was still crowded, but preferring his own company he took his flagon of ale outside. It wasn't particularly pleasant. A breeze blowing off the river carried with it a strange stench of rendered fat, strong fish and animal odours. Never had he smelt anything so vile. It made him feel queasy and yearning for the aroma of wet peat and salt blown in from the breakers of the ocean.

In his room later as he prepared to sleep he heard music, a plaintive air which drifted up and over his balcony and when he looked down a group of travelling minstrels entertained in the yard. He stayed at the window and rested his head on the wood frame, but his eyes were too heavy and his legs too weak to stay there for long.

Pulling the cover over his head he was asleep in minutes.

* * *

Since his new companion, Richard, made no mention of a meeting time Jack made a point of being down in the inn as the late afternoon light began fading. He avoided the soot-darkened corner used by the dice players and sought out a bench away from others where he settled down to wait. As usual the place was busy. Red-faced from the kitchen, the alewife carried plates of steaming eel stew back and forth and the serving girl, a buxom young woman with a mass of auburn hair and a coquettish smile, laboured with her jugs of ale. Admiring her passed the time for Jack and he didn't see Richard until his shadow fell across the wall light.

"I see you have an eye for a pretty vixen, John," he said, with a knowing nod. "Fancy a dalliance with her, do you? I'd say she's well used. Most of them are round these parts."

His remark made them both laugh and dispelled any awkwardness on Jack's part. A fresh jug of ale and another flask and they were comfortable in each other's company.

"So, how have you spent your first day in the city?"

"Little of interest except a lot of walking, trying to find my way around," Jack replied.

Pursing his lips, Richard's expression showed some curiosity and he leant forward.

"Forgive me if I'm mistaken, but your voice tells me you are not from around these parts."

"No," Jack said shortly.

There was a long moment of silence, both men locking on to each other's eyes. Richard looked away first and then with an easy laugh, said, "It's no matter to me, so to business." Drawing his stool closer to the table, his face grew more serious. "Since you are here it must mean you are interested in what I might have to say, so we'll waste no time. You are free to decide whether to accept my offer. Do I have your word you will mention this to no one?"

Jack nodded. "You have my word and my interest although I confess to be mystified."

"When I told you my living is in trade, there is a little more to it than that. Expenses can ruin business so I have another outlet for my goods. What the Customs Officers don't see can do them no harm, don't you agree? So from time to time, goods arrive – shall we say through a more uncertain route. Are you following me?" His voice was low and at times his words were delivered in little more than a whisper. Jack thought he stopped short of looking shifty, but only just. Tilting his head back, he observed Richard through half closed eyes. A ghost of a smile played on his lips as he felt a frisson of excitement. His feelings told him he might enjoy this offer of work.

"Smuggling?" he murmured. "Is that it?"

"I'm looking for someone who I can trust. The last fellow I employed was careless and sits out his time in the Clink. You will appreciate there are times when it is more prudent of me to not show myself at the docks when the goods arrive. It's a delicate matter which I'm sure you understand."

Jack wasn't exactly sure he did, but he nodded just the same. Money was far more interesting to him and he was anxious to get to the detail.

"What sort of goods might they be?"

Richard concentrated on filling the flasks up and then said.

"Mostly wool and liquor, wine from France, Italia perhaps. It just depends what's available. So what do you say?"

It was Jack's turn to be under the other's gaze.

"There'll be risks," he said slowly.

"For which you will be handsomely rewarded," Richard assured.

"Then I'm exactly who you are looking for," Jack said confidently.

Chapter Seven

The Tower of London
Winter 1448 AD

FIDGETING with her tapestry work until she found the light she needed, Margaret drove her needle through the canvas with determined intent. When her wools became tangled she finally lost patience and tossed the embroidery to one side. She threw a sideways glance at Henry. Irritated by his drab clothing and the pile of his books at his feet her waspish tongue refused to rest.

"Is my company so tedious my Lord Husband that you prefer to ignore me?"

It seemed to her there was some reluctance when Henry raised his eyes from the book. Not saying anything, his eyes travelled over his young wife. Her looks were breathtaking, he thought but so was the strength of her will. Peace must be quickly restored. Giving her an apologetic smile, he took one of her hands and pressed it to his lips.

"God forbid that should be so, sweet Lady Wife. What is it on your mind, my love?"

Her lips were set tight and her expression told him all. Unsmiling, she said.

"You have yet to satisfy me with your thoughts about Gloucester's death. It wounds me to think you would believe such evil gossip about William, the Earl of Suffolk. Since I took my first step on English soil it has been that dear man who has shown me so much kindness and become a trusted friend. What reason do you have to think he would play some part in such tromperie, such deceit?"

Uncomfortable under her penetrating glare, Henry shuffled awkwardly in his chair. At times his wife's imperious manner was an assault on his gentle nature, but anxious not to upset her further he felt obliged to mollify her.

"So ma petite oiseau, my turtle dove, how would you like me to make amends? I merely listen to the Privy Council who tell me the populace are most displeased by Humphrey of Gloucester's sudden demise. Not only that, but there are mutterings throughout Court that Suffolk played a large part in his death. After all no one is quite sure who bribed the jailor to poison his food."

For a moment he thought Margaret was about to explode. Her pale complexion darkened and her eyes glittered dangerously.

"Trop cher! Outrageous," she snapped, stalking to the window and slamming it shut to close out the sudden sound of high spirits from somewhere in the garden. As she did so a tracery of frost on the glass crumbled and fell on the sill. She blew on the tips of her fingers before resuming her tirade.

"Whoever speaks such wickedness should lose their head and if you wish to please me, give my Lord Suffolk the Dukedom of Suffolk at once and perhaps dear Edmund Beaufort should be raised to a Duke too. He is deeply grieved by the death of his uncle, the wise Cardinal Beaufort and this may go some way to help him in his loss."

"But my dear, these elevations are usually reserved for close relatives of mine. It will be difficult . . ."

"No Henry, it's not difficult at all. You are the King. And another thing, you are much too trusting. You are too easily influenced by those in Parliament who seek only to line their own pockets. They give no thought of your well being and the people sense this. That is the reason for their dissatisfaction. I know they love both William and Edmund as we do and will be pleased you favour them so."

He watched Margaret's hands jabbing the air to emphasise her words. It grieved him that at times her belligerent expression stole her youthfulness. If only she would fulfil her duty, he reflected. Her purpose was to give him an heir, yet she remained as barren as the atmosphere in the room. Resting his head in his hands, Henry sighed heavily. Is being honest and well meaning so wrong in a man, he said to himself, for if it was then he was guilty. Still feeling the strength of Margaret's gaze on him, he rocked in the chair trying to decide how best to reply. His wife's quickness of mind frequently left him disadvantaged, and she often mocked him because he always sought peaceful solutions when confronted by problems. Taking the silence as another of his dithering moments, she said icily.

"Well? What of my request?"

"You are usually right, my Lady Wife," he conceded "I shall make them both Dukes if that will bring a smile to your face."

Now her expression was kittenish and bending to him she brushed her lips over his cheek.

"My dear sweet Lord," she murmured. "I shall find them and tell them at once."

With a whirl of her skirts and a cold draught of air, Margaret was gone and Henry pressed his hand to the pain throbbing in his temple. Ferreting up his sleeve, he pulled out a lace edged kerchief and sniffed hard at the lavender water sprinkled liberally on the material. Slowly his eyes closed. With no idea whether it was minutes or an hour he was somewhat befuddled and barely heard the urgent knock on the door. He only opened his eyes when he sensed someone entering the room.

With a deferential bow, William looked concerned. Even though he knew it was Henry's bold wife who was behind his new honour, he held Henry in some esteem and was as concerned about his health as any other.

"You look pale, Sire. Are you unwell? Shall I send for the apothecary?"

Waving a feeble hand, Henry inhaled the lavender again. This time when he lifted his head his eyes were watering.

"It's not necessary, a simple ache of the head that's all. The Queen can be very forceful when she wants," he said, blinking several times.

He tried to laugh as if it was a joke, but he knew William would know exactly what he meant. Indeed William's smile was one of sympathy. Henry was no fool. He knew behind closed doors the opinion was without his Queen, he would fall from power in an instant such was his inept ability to govern. Looking closely at William's face, he saw no betrayal of his thoughts. And he must have thoughts aplenty. The gossip had failed to stop in time although Henry wasn't sure how close William was to his wife. Too close, some said emphatically.

"I come to thank you, your Majesty for the great honour you have given me," William said. "That I am now the Duke of Suffolk is an accolade I did not expect and I shall serve you with even more devotion if that were possible."

Henry looked thoughtful. "I have never questioned your loyalty or that of Edmund Beaufort. You both attend me well and I have need of your wise words. What should I do Suffolk, for at times I feel I cannot gather my wits together? The Lady Queen needs to conceive a child or Richard of York will take the crown. The people call for less taxation, yet our coffers are drained with the expense of our struggle to hold France. Now I hear there is growing disorder here on our streets. Yet all I want is that we secure peace. Is that too much to ask?"

His sadness was accompanied by a single tear which unable to stop it, he hastily dabbed away on the sleeve of his simple woollen shirt. William's grunt sounded loud in the room and focused Henry's attention. His hand went to his head again as if to push away the obscuring darkness which threatened to envelop his mind.

"I have no control," he whispered, his eyes blinking rapidly.

Hands behind his back, William walked to the window. In a chill February sky a vivid sunset was turning the grey into gun-metal blue. Threading it with streaks of crimson and orange it looked as if the horizon set fire to itself. He shivered as if it were a portent.

"You fret too much, Sire. Our possible defeat at Formigny and therefore the loss of Normandy is a grievous setback, but all is not lost yet. As for our impoverished state, we must simply exhort more money from the populace. It is for their good after all," he said levelly as he turned back.

Henry's face brightening, his chuckling was unnerving.

"Do you think so, Suffolk, do you really think so. Your words console me. Then we must celebrate. Shall we have a feast?" His brow furrowed. "No, not a feast, we shall have entertainment instead. What say you to that? No, that's not enough. We shall have a dinner too. A hundred oxen, swan, capon, venison, all shall be used. We must inform the kitchens."

Clapping his hands, a light akin to madness illuminated his eyes. He jigged up and down in his chair. Oblivious to the look of anxiety on William's face, he seized the Bible and turned the pages with feverish haste.

"Majesty, I fear you have over done things, perhaps if you rest," William said.

"Rest, how can I possibly rest? There is so much to read. I *must* read, I *must . . . I must . . .*"

He jerked his head up and although he looked straight at William there was blankness in his eyes. Lips moving soundlessly he followed the text on the page with one slow moving finger. Then no longer able to resist he allowed the demons to take him into their familiar world. In a stride, William wrenched open the door and beckoned to a uniformed guard in the corridor.

"Find the apothecary and make haste. Tell him the king is deranged again, but don't speak of it to anyone else. Is that understood?"

When he turned back, his expression was a mix of sympathy for his feeble and compliant monarch and elation which marked his position as the power behind the throne.

Chapter Eight

Late Winter
1450 AD

PRETENDING to kiss his palm, Jack blew his affection towards the woman who stood watching him depart. Theirs was a comfortable house in Kent, modest to some, but in his eyes the social status he craved. In the two years since he arrived in England, he had not only worked hard to improve his standing, but done well for himself. He'd much enhanced his own financial state thanks to Richard de Courcy, and found a good woman to be wedded to albeit one he cared little for. She raised her hand to acknowledge his gesture and disappeared from the window.

Mariamne was a little older and more portly than he might have desired but as the daughter of a wealthy mercer, she brought with her a most pleasant house, money and a discreet tongue. Moreover she adored him, reminding him a little of Mammy in her ways when it came to forgiving his fiery temper. Sadly her father had been less enamoured with his prospective son-in-law and Jack smiled wryly at the thought. But Mariamne was nothing if not determined and the consideration of keeping an ageing unmarried daughter worked wonders in her father's mind.

Jack stepped back and took a moment to scan his eyes over the fine timbered hall house with its three-light casements. Its hearty thatch never so much as allowed a raindrop to penetrate. The stout front door boasted an impressive brass door knocker which Mariamne never neglected whilst in summer a climbing rose close to it overpowered the senses with its perfume.

With a satisfied sigh he went in search of his horse. His destination was the *White Hart* in Southwark. He rode fast and hard taking his mount through frozen mud and pools of water made brittle by a thin covering of ice. Contented at the prospect of a new year ahead he enjoyed the ride arriving at the *Hart* scarlet-cheeked and enveloped in a miasma of his own breath.

From the bright light of a late day in January he was forced to blink when confronted by the poorly lit interior of the inn, but he knew the way to his usual secluded corner and those who waited for him at the table. Pushing a full flagon of ale towards him, Richard kept his voice low as he greeted Jack.

"Good morrow my friend, I have someone I should like you to meet. May I introduce Simon of Kent, Simon this is John Mortimer. I trust him like a brother so you may talk without fear."

The stranger who emerged from the shadows stayed long enough to extend a plump hand in Jack's direction before moving back into them again without a word spoken. Jack got the impression he was a short, bulky man with a sallow complexion and eyes almost concealed by heavy lids. Since entering into business with Richard no one he met surprised him for smugglers came in all shapes and sizes.

As he reached to take a drink, Jack noticed his sleeve slipped back revealing the livid scar on his arm. Under his breath he swore and hastily fiddled with the cuff of his shirt. It was a mark of his identity he preferred others not to see.

"So Simon, what is your trade? Is it wool or hides?" he asked pleasantly.

"Neither," Richard said smoothly. "Our friend here comes on another matter."

For a moment Jack was uneasy. He doubted Richard would be foolhardy enough to bring a stranger to the table. Certainly not one who might jeopardize their nefarious activities, yet what place had Simon here? Was the man a mute, he wondered, but then finally Simon spoke. Leaning forward just enough to allow the flickering flame of a wall sconce to illuminate his features, he said.

"I am not here to waste your time so I shall come straight to the point. I am a man who is disturbed by the disorder in our country. The time for protest has come and I'm looking for someone to raise a following. The government take us for fools. Our sovereign is inept and his advisors corrupt for they think only to line their own purses. Now we have lost the good Duke Humphrey whilst my Lord Suffolk grows richer and I'm told that his friend Edmund prepares to flee to Calais where he can indulge in a more indolent way of life. What think you of that, Master Mortimer?

When Jack didn't reply, Simon looked a trifle exasperated.

"Come sir, you can be frank with me. Surely you must have some thoughts on the state of our fine land. There are issues which must be brought to the attention of our government and what better way than a march of protest? Richard speaks very highly of you and tells me you might be the man I seek."

59

Jack noticed when mentioning nobility, Simon's lip curled and he spoke so softly he needed to strain to catch his words. Startled by what he considered to be dangerous talk, Jack sat silent. It was true he and Richard shared the same thoughts echoed by many about the growing dissatisfaction with the country's leadership and the need for reform, but 'twas only in passing over a jar of ale after their plans were made for another shipment of illegal cargo.

"I can see by your expression you care little for our problems," Simon said curtly withdrawing into the half-light again.

"Not so hasty, my friend," Richard said anxiously. "I had no time to speak to John and he is taken by surprise. Isn't that right, John?" He laid a reassuring hand on Jack's arm. "Think on it. Have we not often talked about our poor government and those who strangle us with heavy taxation? You seemed to feel as strongly as I do, but perhaps I was mistaken."

Indignant at being misunderstood by both of them, Jack looked first at one and then the other.

"Forsooth, you give me no chance to consider this. Should I be willing I have much to lose . . ."

Perturbed by Jack's reaction, Richard raised his voice as he interrupted.

"God's blood, John, you have your head to lose if we are found by a ship one night as its being loaded."

"Keep your talk low lest you are overheard," Simon hissed. "Master Mortimer, I hear you are well thought of in Kent. Intelligent and capable, they say. Not only that I hear you have a high degree of military ability too, just the sort of person I'm looking for. Will you at least give this some thought?"

Dark-browed, Jack shot an angry glance at Richard. Clearly he had disclosed all that was told in confidence, yet Simon's description of him was gratifying and he mellowed a little.

"Perhaps," he said softly.

The *Hart* was becoming more crowded and Simon seemed ill at ease as people pushed nearer their table.

"You must excuse me, 'tis time I was gone," he said finally. "I hope I shall hear from you 'ere long, Master Mortimer. Farewell to you both." He scuttled for the door like an awkward scarab beetle and without a backward glance, hurried out onto the street. Waiting until their jug was replenished, Jack could hardly contain his curiosity.

"Strange fellow," he muttered. "I don't understand why he can't get his own followers. What say you, Richard?"

Shaking his head, Richard ran his fingers his thick beard and leant closer.

"Simon of Kent is a mystery to me too. I'm grateful for the work he brings my way, and I ask no questions. As for his connections, it is said he is some distant cousin of Richard of York, but that's only a dark rumour. If he is, now do you see why he can't be seen to lead a rebellion? The Houses of Lancaster and York are at an impasse; it would be impossible. Still you must decide. Meanwhile we have a full jug in front of us and the *Blithe* waits for us to deliver her fresh cargo of hides. She sails on the morning tide so we should waste no more time."

Later with his wife gone to her chamber, Jack mused as he looked out at the landscape. The sky and land merged into an indefinable mass like a black blanket. He could just make out dotted skeins of light as stars pushed aside their veil of clouds. Since leaving Southwark he'd felt discomforted by the turn of conversation. Perhaps he'd been too busy with his own good fortune to think about the general discontent which rustled its way through England. Certainly he shared the view of others that poor leadership by the king and his close advisors was slowly dragging the land into the mire of disorganised mayhem, yet he'd never once thought about doing anything about it.

Pouring out a beaker of mead he watched as the swirl of honeyed liquid settled to become an oasis of tawny gold. The first sip dribbled over his tongue and he closed his eyes savouring it, but the question bedevilled his brain.

Why did the stranger who called himself Simon pick him out to lead an uprising? Long after all that remained of the mead was a thick circle of residue which clung to the sides of the beaker, he was still pondering.

Chapter Nine

The Tower of London

WITH a faint *hiss* the silk sheet embroidered with gold emblems slithered off the bed and lay rumpled on the floor. It was accompanied by a throaty laugh and one slim arm reaching through the hangings to retrieve it.

"*Mon Dieu*, it has legs," a woman said, as she flung it back to cover their nakedness.

"You spoil my fun, madam. Now I can't see you," a male voice complained.

"No sirrah, you have seen more than enough for one night," she reprimanded.

He loved it when she giggled and she was giggling now. It was in answer to William's hand as he ran it over the outline of her lissom form. Then the richly hued tapestry bed-hangings parted and with a sigh of regret he clambered reluctantly from the four- poster bed.

"And where are you going?" she asked.

"Ah, I mourn 'tis time. Soon the cock will crow and . . ."

Her sharp voice quickly interrupted.

"I, sir, am Margaret of Anjou. I shall tell you when you may leave my chamber."

William's smile faded instantly at the imperious manner which she adopted.

"Your Grace, best you remember discretion is better than the executioner's block," he said tartly. "Should the

King get to hear of our dalliance, neither of us will be spared, is that what you want?"

Wriggling to the side of the feather mattress she sat on the edge with her legs dangling. As quickly as sun may follow rain her mood sweetened. Her unrestrained corn coloured hair fell over her face and childlike her lips were fashioned into a pout. She held out her hand and smiled, but he was quick to notice the gesture didn't travel to her cobalt blue eyes. Hers were soulless which showed nothing of her inner mind, not her pleasures, her pain, or her gladness.

"Forgive me my silly ways. I need you *mon petit lapin,* for where else would I find such satisfaction?"

He laughed at her term of endearment, grateful that the last time he looked he didn't actually resemble a rabbit.

"You honour me, dear Lady Queen," he murmured.

Her face took on a mournful expression.

"My Lord Husband regrets I don't quicken with child and says I must be barren, but he rarely feels the need such is his illness. He requires a mother to look after him not a lover." She tossed her hair away from her face and licked her lips so he had an urge to nibble the tip of her small pink tongue. His willpower almost weakened, but despite her pleas to stay he dressed with speed.

"Will I see you later?" she called, resting one slender hand on a richly carved oak post.

Next to the great standing bed, wearing a transparent shift, she looked so fragile, he thought. Yet her beauty was mesmerising, and despite the splendour of the counterpane of gold cloth and the costly Eastern silk drapes, they dulled in comparison.

"I have to meet with the Privy Council. There is much to discuss and who knows how long it will take. There is a wish from some to make Richard the rightful heir now we are rid of Gloucester," he explained.

Margaret's haughty expression rapidly returned.

"Preposterous," she said curtly.

"Exactly my thoughts, my Lady, but there are others who point out the King's derangement makes him unfit."

"Then I shall reign for him," she rattled back. "Tell them I am the Queen and my wishes must be obeyed. Now leave me. All this treasonous talk you tell me puts me in a bad humour. I shall find you afterwards, and William, I shall ask the King to appoint you his Chief Minister. You deserve no less. Would that sit well with you?" she asked.

"If he agrees," he replied.

They both knew he would of course. The hapless King was too gullible to do otherwise. William's courtly bow was small but neat.

"Most gracious Queen, I am forever in your debt."

Margaret's delightful laughter rang in his ears long after he returned to his own chamber.

* * *

Looking round the table, William took stock of those present. Already bored with their dull faces, he was looking forward to the end of the meeting. As usual George, Duke of Cornwall was in a heated argument with Anthony, Earl of Chester and they snapped angrily at one another.

"Gentlemen," William called to the end of the table. "It would help if we could have your attention. We should move on to business matters."

"Which one had you in mind, my Lord Suffolk, there seem to be many," Thomas Howard, Earl of Surrey replied in his falsetto voice.

William sighed. His loathing of the Council Chamber and the tedious discussions which took place in it were widely known at Court and some felt they made better progress without his attendance. So most of the time he appeared just to irritate them.

The burnished mahogany table top was littered with papers, yet no one looked at them and with an impatient hand he swept them away. When the sun ray's suddenly appeared through the window, warmth invaded the room on a chilly March morning. Loosening the collar of his pale blue grosgrain jacket, William relaxed back in his chair. In need of a nap to compensate for his somewhat disturbed night, he yawned loudly.

"Perhaps I could speak?" Sir Edward Hastings said in his perfectly modulated voice.

Tall and dignified, his white hair framed ageing aristocratic features which at that moment were set in a grim expression. Waving vaguely, William forced himself to pay attention. It took little of his imagination to anticipate what was to come. It would be money. It was nothing but these days. Hastings was the one always anxious to discuss it, as if he didn't fill his own pockets full from time to time, William reflected. Hastings stood up, nervously fiddling with the button on his sleeve.

"Thank you, my Lord. Once again I must remind you all how grave financial matters are for both the government and the country. I would not be exaggerating to say the Crown is all but bankrupt." He looked at each of them in turn, but no one spoke. When his eyes locked on William's, William gave him a disarming smile. They both knew each of them was as dishonest as the other although no one would admit it.

"Then there's our hostilities with France," Hastings continued in a troubled voice. "Men grow weary of fighting and few are prepared to enlist. Without fresh forces we will shortly be on the brink of surrendering our French territories. What the people will think of this shameful situation is beyond me, but there is sure to be a backlash. We must either find new reinforcements to send across the sea and the money to do so or we must abandon our desire to conquer France."

Sitting down again, Hastings mopped his brow with a flowery silk kerchief whilst the others fidgeted uncomfortably in their seats. The blunt summing up of the truth left them all somewhat chastened. It was William who replied.

"You spare nothing in your assessment of the situation, Sir Edward. Quite what the King will make of it troubles me."

"It's all right for you, Suffolk. You have the King's ear rather more than most of us," Sir John Stanley commented brusquely.

"Perhaps it is Margaret's he prefers," the Earl of Chester sniggered behind his hand.

Receiving a withering look from William, he resorted to the occasional snort.

"My Lord Suffolk, as far as the King is concerned, all you must do is be firm with him. Please impress upon him the gravity of the situation," the Duke of Cornwall said pointedly.

"I'll do my best," William replied trying to conceal his impatience. "But you all know His Majesty has trouble being positive. He immerses himself in his devotions . . ."

"And day dreams his life away. Meanwhile the 'French woman' interferes in state matters which do not concern her," Hastings said bitingly.

Through narrowed hostile-filled eyes, William looked at Hastings trying to decide whether he deliberately enjoyed making offensive comments about the Queen. He bit back his anger since it wouldn't do to provoke more from Hastings in view of the circumstances surrounding him and Margaret's relationship. *One day . . .* he thought.

"Has anyone anything else to say?" he asked with cold indifference.

At the far end of the table, the Earl of Chester leant forward.

"Perhaps we should look at the Treasure's report." William tapped the table with irritated fingers.

"Not now, Chester, not now. I have to be somewhere else. You may be interested to know I am now the King's Chief Minister and I cannot delay offering him my gratitude." The others exchanged knowing looks, but no one wished to upset Suffolk further. His elevation at the behest of the King made him a man not to be crossed although some silently vowed his day of reckoning would come.

"Well if there's nothing more," William said, getting to his feet. He waited long enough to adjust his jacket and smooth down his dark beard. It was beginning to show a fine web of silver, but Margaret swore it made him even more handsome. The room was hushed as he strode to the door.

A Pardon Too Few

"I wonder what title my Lord will award himself next," the Earl of Chester murmured as the door closed behind William with an abrupt bang.

Chapter Ten

PICKING up his cape, Jack went in search of Mariamne and found her spinning flax in front of the vast hearth. Beneath a haze of gossamer smoke the light from the wall sconce bathed her in a lemony glow. It was unflattering as the misplaced shadows accentuated her blunt features. Beneath her coif her mousy coloured hair was lacking in curl or wave and her heavy bosom struggled to contain itself within the stiff material of her navy gown. Whilst he saw some of his mother's traits in her, she certainly did not have her crow's-wing black hair and a winsome smile set in a perfect oval face as Mammy did, nor Mammy's lightly freckled nose and ready wit. In fact at times he wondered why he'd married such a drab-looking woman. Then the jingle of coins in his pocket reminded him. Yet of late it wasn't enough and he was becoming bored with such domesticity.

Looking at her he knew what her first remark would be. It was written in her expression. Pointing out the state of his hair and beard was a preoccupation of hers. On his arrival in London it served him well to allow both to grow long and now untamed curls and a wiry growth on his chin suggested to Mariamne she must remark on it.

"If you are intending to go out, should I take these to tidy things up a little? One day someone will mistake you for a beggar." Sniffing disdainfully, she waved her scissors at him.

"You worry about your own appearance, wife, and take no note of mine," he said coldly.

She bowed her head over her work, sniffing again. In her fingers the spindle flashed back and forth with fierce direction through the hessian and for a moment he was mesmerised by its speed.

Despite a mild winter as spring was approaching, the weather turned particularly unseasonal as if to make amends for being tardy. The room with its high brick and stone walls and oak-beamed ceiling cushioned little heat and he felt the chill of it. He didn't need to look round it to know everything they owned belonged to her, brought with her on their wedding day. The dark oak dresser, table, stern-looking carved chairs, even the pewter pitchers and platters were as austere as Mariamne and lent no homeliness to the room.

"Have we no more wood for the fire?" he asked, indicating the smouldering remnants of a log with a point of his boot.

"I thought it better to be more prudent under the circumstances," she replied, looking up at him with a semblance of a smile on her plain face.

"So how long does your father intend to withhold your allowance?"

"I'm sorry he doesn't say." Her voice had an edge of regret. "It displeases him to hear rumours about your business matters and he tells me he intends to make more enquiries. Until then . . ."

He could see her struggling with her loyalties and his hasty Irish spirit instantly surfaced. Feeling the sudden flush of anger suffuse his cheeks, he clenched his fists behind his back.

"Meanwhile we are left in dire circumstances and expected to freeze with the cold because the old goat wants to poke his nose into my affairs," he snapped.

She reached out to pull the iron candlestick closer to light her work and as the melted wax fell it pitted the metal. It was then he noticed her fingers were blue-tinged. Losing its calm her face assumed a stony expression.

"My father's a good man, John. He wants only the best for me. You mustn't blame him for being concerned. After all *even* I have no idea what it is you do. He worries for me that's all," she said tightly.

"And me, what about me? Am I not your husband? Do I not deserve some respect?" he said raising his voice, his quick temper firing his words.

He made no apology when he saw her lip quivering and the sudden glisten of tears in her listless blue eyes. Perhaps had they children things might have been better. As the mother of his child he might have felt more obligated to her. He serviced her regularly, yet nothing.

"I'm going out," he snapped.

"Is it more business?" she ventured to ask.

"As it happens, no, I have a meeting to attend, but I'll thank you to consider your place. I'm the master of this house. You'd do well to remember that."

He closed the door with such vehemence that the sword and shield hanging over the chimney breast rattled in metallic unison.

* * *

Once out of the house the journey to Southwark was more pleasant than Jack was expecting. His property was within easy riding distance of London and Fireflanel, his excellent stallion, gave him a comfortable ride. As slow as the warmth was in coming, the thorn hedgerows caught his eye. They were sprinkled with tiny white flower buds as if a sudden flurry of snow had caught them unawares. Before long the brisk wind flooded high colour into his cheeks and his mood improved. Exhilarated by the ride he found himself laughing. He couldn't remember when he last felt so light hearted. There was no point in brooding over Mariamne and her father. He had more important things to occupy his mind as his mount rapidly covered the miles.

In the yard at the *White Hart* he slid from his horse and handing the reins to a stable lad he gave him a coin for his trouble.

"Thank you master," the boy called after him with a grin.

Above the door the painted sign groaned as the restless air tugged it. His cape of middling quality barely kept him warm, but once inside the inn the heaped logs were blazing on the hearth. Throwing out great heat he found he was sweating in moments and flung the cape over his arm.

He made his way through the throng of men towards Richard and the bland expression of Simon of Kent. At first he thought the crowd were there for a drink or two until he realised they were gathering in their numbers round Richard's table. Were they part of the meeting, he wondered? If they were he was surprised by the number of well clad gentry. Standing with the simple peasants and labourers there were many whose social positions would normally have made them step back from such mixings. They too must be rallying to the call.

A Venerable Prior in a brown wool robe, gold plaited cord about his waist and with a heavy hooded cloak was in earnest conversation with a man wearing the uniform of a warrior. The olive skinned man was dressed in a white tabard richly embroidered with a red and white Maltese cross. His tunic was girded by a black sash and he wore gloves of chainmail. Standing nearby was a wealthy landowner Jack was used to seeing with Richard and several merchants in bespoke worsted jackets and breeches.

"There you are, John," Richard called cheerfully from the corner. Seeing his beckoning wave and wide smile, Jack was pleased to see he seemed in high spirits. "We wait on you. Now the meeting can begin."

In contrast Simon's greeting was no more than a nod which Jack acknowledged with his own curt bob of his head.

"Sit my friend, sit," Richard said sending the ale jug sliding toward Jack with a sharp flip of his hand. "Would you believe so many would come? An excellent start, don't you think? We must thank Simon for most of this is his doing."

Jack was taken aback. To think someone like Simon would know so many made him begin to wonder. Perhaps he'd made a mistake and there was truth in a royal connection after all. His brief smile across the table to the man was tight and begrudging. It would seem Simon preferred wine to ale and raising his glass of the amber liquid, he looked at Jack over its rim. From their dark depths his eyes conveyed no emotion. Then sliding his gaze away, he turned to speak to a man close by. Getting to his feet, Richard had everyone's attention immediately.

"May I welcome you here for this is a significant day, 'tis the day we must stand together to send word to our king that we have no faith in our country's leaders. We want an end to poor government and reforms to benefit us. What say you all?"

The throng replied with strident voices confirming their unity to a man. Bouncing up to the oak beams the sound vibrated off the smoke-stained lime washed walls and crept away under the hard earth. Such a response was exactly what was hoped for and Jack saw satisfaction on Richard and Simon's watchful faces.

"So who will be leading us?" a rough voice asked from somewhere in the room.

"That has yet to be decided and one reason I called this meeting," Richard replied.

As he hauled himself upright, Simon's stool groaned under his weight leaving furrows in the earth floor. The room was hushed.

"We have amongst us someone who I recognise as a leader of men. However I think he may need some persuading so I introduce you to Master John Mortimer." Caught unawares, Jack shifted uneasily. He knew by the feel of the heat his cheeks were burning. Conscious eyes were on him, he swallowed hard.

"Speak, speak," they chorused.

Jack felt Richard's boot nudging his leg and felt the power of Simon's inscrutable look from under his heavy brow. Holding his hand half concealing his mouth, Simon leant closer.

"There is nothing for you to do except lead these men and many more still expected. You will be told the details in good time. There are several hundred marks in this for you if all goes well. You'll not regret your decision, John, I can promise you," he breathed in the hushed tones of a conspirator.

Still doubtful, Jack got to his feet reluctantly. His forehead felt moist and he struggled to find his voice.

"I am honoured by such faith in me, but I fear I'm not your man. I am a sympathiser to our problems 'tis true and I begin to be sickened by the failure of this government, but I'm no leader of assemblies such as this."

"You disappoint me, Master Mortimer," Simon said quietly. "If my instincts serve me right, there is an adventurer under your quiet demeanour. You are educated and what's more a soldier of repute, so I'm told. What more could we want?"

Jack's smile hid his nervousness. Educated – if only they knew how hard he worked at learning. His blessed Mammy taught him at first in the language of Ireland, but he was a quick learner. The king's forces in France helped and then on his marriage to the well placed Mariamne, he'd watched and listened, picking up every refinement she offered. Even the lilt of his brogue was barely discernible. He wondered if the enigma that was Simon, would pay him such compliments had he known he was the low born son of a young unmarried woman from the Bogs of Eire and a murderer to boot.

He could feel Richard's eyes on him, Simon's too, and the others in the room waiting in tense silence for what would happen next. He saw Mammy telling him what the future held. His destiny she called it. They were sitting together at the hearth, she holding him close, both of them sharing the warmth of a meagre fire. That's when she knew, she said. Growing up into a fine young man with his birthright due, with the blood of an important man in his veins, she whispered. By the Virgin Mary, wasn't she always right? Now these strangers were offering him an escape from his boring wife and mediocre existence. He would have wealth at last, if it pleased God and at the time of his birthday too. How hard could it be to lead a willing army? Hadn't it been worse on the windswept wasteland in France?

More ale was poured. His glass topped up, he drank it eagerly enjoying the taste easing his parched throat. Another swallow and another then the ale started running through his body with abandonment, but it would take more than sweet ale to destroy his dreams.

A sharp bow of his head to the assembled throng, and the deed was done.

Chapter Eleven

Tower of London
Late spring 1450 AD

WILLIAM could hardly call it a welcome. Sitting at his desk, holding a quill, Henry appeared vague. Giving him no more than a glance, his head dropped back to the pages in front of him, sheets of them covered in his careful slanting script. Margaret's heart shaped face looked brighter, yet her greeting too was lacking the warmth of their usual encounters and William sensed tension in the air.

At Margaret's insistence the window was open despite the chill of the early morning. On the earth below beneath the frame, bowls of flowers were arranged so their perfumes wafted upwards. Cultivated at her request before their season, roses, lilies, ox-eye daisies, blue iris and violets were brought fresh every day for Margaret to constantly admire. Not today. Instead she pulled the window tight and wafting her hand in front of her nose declared, "It is too much. The gardeners must attend to it for we swear the smell makes us feel unwell. So my Lord Suffolk you finally grace us with your presence, yet we sent for you some time ago. Why were you delayed?"

Seeing her eyes lacking kindness and her manner so haughty, William was careful with his choice of words and his manner of address. Despite their relationship, it was unwise to overstep the mark where Margaret was concerned.

"My apologies, gracious Majesties, I was called to the Council chamber. It seems there is poor news from France."

"Poor, is that what you call it?" Margaret retorted. "A strange choice of words considering the importance of the message, a disaster is what I would name it."

With a hideous scratching noise the Henry's pen raced across a sheet of vellum and quickly copious writing flowed onto the cream paper.

"Must we do that now, my Lord Husband? Surely our plans can wait," Margaret said, frowning.

Obediently Henry laid down his pen, but his expression was pained. Lying back in his chair he closed his eyes. "I am listening," he said feebly.

Trying to diffuse the taut atmosphere, William made an effort to appear interested despite Margaret's irritation.

"Plans, Majesty? What is it you are planning, if I may ask? Is it another charitable trust perhaps?"

So often jaded, enthusiasm brightened Henry's expression and he answered with strength in his voice which was refreshing.

"How nice of you to ask, William, I am reconsidering the building works of my foundation at Windsor. Our Lady of Eton School whilst open to scholars is not yet finished. I intend for the church to be pulled down and we shall have another much grander than the first, I think," he paused, staring thoughtfully over William's head at the panelling on the far wall. Then he said enthusiastically. "The almshouse could do with some improvement too, what do you think of that, William?"

As William was about to reply, Margaret started pacing across the room. As her steps became more rapid so the extravagant beadwork on her glittering gown swung about her in a kaleidoscope of colour.

"Mon Dieu! Sacrebleu!" she muttered. "Have I only idiots for company?" Finally standing still, she threw her up arms in fury. "How can you waste time on such frippery, don't either of you realise we have lost all our dominions in the north of France. Charles has seen to it that all but Calais are lost to us. My Lord Somerset has failed dismally. Everywhere else has surrendered and that, my Lord Suffolk is what you refer to as *poor* news. And you, my Lord Husband care only to prattle on about your wretched school."

Knowing better than to interrupt Margaret at such times, William said nothing. Playing with his marriage ring, Henry looked bewildered.

"Normandy has gone?"

"Yes, do you not listen, almost all of it apart from Guienne and the Calais Pale," Margaret said sharply. "I notice you say nothing, my Lord," she snapped at William. "Who do you think will get the blame for this?"

The ring continued twirling until moving so fast it flew off the Henry's finger and landed on the floor.

"But I don't understand," he said, his voice muffled as he crawled under the desk. "Edmund, Duke of Somerset was sent to France to command the army, what's happened to him?"

"I'm told his troops were overwhelmed, Sire," William said quietly trying to calm the situation.

Margaret swept up to him until there was barely an inch between them. Compared to his tall figure she was diminutive, but he felt the chill of her look as if she had grouts of ice in place of eyes. Certainly a lesser man would have weakened under her wilting stare.

"I'll answer our question, shall I? I'll tell you who will be blamed by the people when this news gets out. Whilst Somerset hides in Calais, it will be you, Suffolk, and I who will suffer, make no mistake about that." Moving to stand beside Henry she laid one hand gently on his arm. "If only you were well, my Lord Husband. If only you could attend to affairs of state then perhaps things would have been different," she said in a softer voice.

His eyes glistening with tears he took her hand and softly brushed his lips against it.

"I'm so sorry, my sweet Lady Wife, but you do see how important it is that I finish my plans for the new church. Later we shall talk of France, I promise."

* * *

For one of the few times in his adult life, William felt shaken and it wasn't a pleasant feeling. He should have gone home to Alice, but he was in no mood for her wifely ministrations. Having left the royal chamber he retreated to the room on a lower floor which he used when attending late functions at the Tower. It was furnished simply, but expensively and a much loved retreat after a difficult day.

Sitting down heavily in his chair his usual habit was to trace the scenes of hawking and hunting which were embroidered in silver on the arm cushion. He found it soothing, but this time he was dismayed to see his fingers trembling. Unable to settle he moved to his table where a servant left his customary flask of mead. As he released the stopper it wavered and drops of liquid pooled on the polished wood.

Things were going wrong, horribly wrong, he thought and news of their defeat at the hands of the French was as Margaret had said a complete disaster. But what was deeply worrying was her stark warning as to who would be held responsible. Wandering to the window he took a thoughtful sip of his drink. In the distance a multitude of moving lights shone from the craft moored on the river as they bobbed up and down with the stroke of the water. Fairy jewels, he told his children when they visited.

Less attractive was the view almost immediately under his window. Lit by meagre-flamed wall sconces, Traitors Gate cast elongated shadows on the damp stone walls. It was not a sight which usually troubled him, but tonight . . . God's blood, it wasn't all his fault. Politically he'd enriched himself, 'tis true, both in prestige and wealth, but hadn't he earned it? Wasn't much asked of him and didn't he take pains to ensure things ran smoothly.

Arranging the marriage between Henry and Margaret took all his efforts. It was an important alliance which was a delicate matter requiring both tact and discipline, he recalled. If he'd rewarded himself with a few thousand marks, he felt he earned it. There was the cost of keeping his household, Alice liked nice things and then there were his young ones . . . And if some complained of his contempt for others at times, it came with his position. He had no need of their friendship, he thought scornfully.

So immersed in his deliberations, William didn't hear the first soft tapping on the door. Only when it opened in a hasty rush did he turn to face it. Margaret had changed into a fine cream silk nightgown and robe which draped itself round her feet and he heard it swish when she moved. With the tortoiseshell pins taken out of her hair her lustrous locks fell about her face in fat ringlets making her look like a vulnerable child and he felt his breath catching in his throat.

Bowing low he waited. When she came close enough he reached out to pull at the satin ribbon of the robe, but her hand flew up to prevent him undoing it.

"No," she said harshly, moving away from him. "I'm not here to play games. You and I must speak. The court talks of nothing, but how badly you have conducted government affairs and in the matter of France some say your behaviour is nothing short of scandalous." She paused and William saw the mist of tears on her cheeks.

"Who told you?" he said fiercely.

"My Lady of the Bedchamber, Catherine, she is most loyal and hears things I may not. It was she who whispered in my ear."

"Gracious lady, you must not heed such nonsense. I shall speak in the Council chamber in the morning."

He hoped to reassure her, but her grim expression didn't alter. Throwing herself down in a chair she was plucking at her gown with nervous fingers, repeatedly bunching and releasing the material.

"I don't think you understand. Such is the dis-satisfaction of the country. They demand an explanation and I'm told you have many enemies at court, my Lord. So grave is the matter some say they will sign a petition to impeach you," Margaret said, lowering her voice.

A tightness gripped William's chest and he could feel his heart thudding with extra beats. He swallowed hard, but still his voice sounded thick.

"I shall deny all the allegations against me and what of you, my Lady Queen, what do they say of you?"

She dropped her head quickly, but not before he saw her lips trembling.

"They also blame me for they say I am responsible for your favoured position, but 'tis you I fear for, sweet Suffolk, 'tis you," she whispered.

Chapter Twelve

The Palace of Westminster

THE nobles stood with Ralph, Lord Cromwell in a dimly lit passage close to the cellars. It wasn't a favourable place for a meeting, but they hoped they were out of earshot of both servants and those less favoured of their cause. The need for secrecy was paramount. Suffolk's enemies had much to discuss and it was Cromwell who led them.

"So it is agreed?" he said in his deep voice. "We must find more charges lest our plan fails. As it is, Suffolk is hardly deprived. There is talk he receives wine with every meal and his food is served on a silver tray."

"Not the usual fare for the Tower dungeons either, but handpicked delicacies his gaoler fetches from the kitchens," Sir John Stanley said morosely.

"The man is artful and dismisses every allegation. It is more serious a matter I think than discussing his menus," the elderly William Hastings remarked impatient at the trivial chat. "I thought we meet to decide a course that disposes of Suffolk once and for all."

Handsome and smartly dressed, Cromwell was held in high regard by those who sought the downfall of William, Earl of Suffolk. His hand laid gently on Hastings arm was accompanied by a smile intended to pacify the ruffled man.

"Patience, my dear Hastings. This time we must not fail, but it means very careful plans and proof of our allegations too. Evidence is what is needed which is why we are here."

Hastings didn't look convinced. "We have only a week," he muttered with a heavy sigh.

"How many truly believed Suffolk conspired with France to invade England? At best it was flimsy evidence if I may say so," Stanley piped up.

"Did you think of anything better? It sent him to the Tower," Cromwell retorted sharply. "We have the commons on our side. They care even less for Suffolk and as for that French woman, they are more than happy to blame her too. Worse the public's dissatisfaction with Suffolk's rule reflects on the government too, but 'tis hardly enough to accuse him of treason, mores the pity,"

Somewhere in the corridors above them there was the sound of heavy footsteps and voices. Slipping back further into the shadows the three men waited in silence.

"We should leave, 'tis dangerous being seen together, especially down here," Stanley breathed when the echoes were fading.

Cromwell nodded. "Just remember when the date of Suffolk's trial is set, we must be ready. I trust you both to find enough to condemn him before then; and not a word to his friends."

As they emerged onto the corridor and walked in the direction of The Common House, Stanley said.

"Does he have any friends?"

Cromwell frowned. "Keep your voice down, there are peers who still hold Suffolk in good regard and he also has friends on and behind the throne as you well know." He went first to check there would be no witnesses to their collusion. The Long Hall was deserted. "I suggest we go in separate directions since I suspect at times even the portraits have ears."

Smiling wryly, he waved at the panelled wall where past illustrious offered a frozen stare from behind their mask of oil paint.

Grief did not sit well with Margaret. It marked her face with tears she shed in an unstoppable flood, pinched her full lips and bowed her shoulders with the weight of her sorrow. Unsteady through lack of sleep she stopped her constant pacing and threw herself down on a chair in her private chamber.

"My sweet lady is there anything more I can do to comfort you?" Henry asked, closing his book. "I can only reassure you, Suffolk wants for nothing despite his confinement in a cell, I made sure of that."

Stifling a sob, Margaret whispered, "I can't understand why William is there at all. Surely you could have stopped it, my Lord."

Henry sighed. "I have told you. I sent him there on good advice. For his safety you understand until this whole sorry business is cleared up. The allegations against him are serious."

"He is *not* safe there my Lord, and every minute he spends in that vile place is another reason for my distress," Margaret replied, tugging impatiently at a loose thread on her gown. "He deserves better than rats for company and as for those who conspire against him, I cannot bear to think what might happen."

Another rush of tears welled in her red-rimmed eyes and Henry wriggled uncomfortably in his seat.

"Then what would you suggest?" he murmured, his hand edging toward his book again.

With a loud sniff, Margaret toyed with the double strand of pearls knotted on her breast which were reflecting iridescent shades of cream and pink in her fingers. It was clear she was deep in thought. Suddenly she gave a little grunt as if she were pleased with herself.

"Those intent in destroying him will stop at nothing, of that I'm sure. So my Lord Husband, can you not order he be brought here to Westminster in your custody? In a few short weeks he will stand trial, what harm can there be in offering him your protection?"

Her suggestion sounded straightforward, but inwardly she was struggling to keep the artfulness out of her voice. If Henry so much as suspected anymore to her request than simple concern she knew she might lose. Whilst he was so biddable and his will weak, she still never dare underestimate him. Henry's fingers drummed lightly on the book cover.

"Very well, I shall send word to the Chief Justice and have William moved if that pleases you, but there is one thing that troubles me."

Concealing a smile, Margaret leant forward as if to show her concern.

"What might that be, my caring Lord Husband?"

"They all know I am a merciful man and I wish to look kindly on Suffolk. Although I think the case against him is poor, there may be things revealed which we don't know about. You *will* instruct me as to what I should say at his trial."

Rising quickly from her chair, Margaret knelt at Henry's knee. Gathering his hand in hers she laid it to her forehead.

"By whatever scruple it takes our friend Lord Suffolk must live, for without him we shall be lost so do not fret, my Lord, I shall tell you exactly what you must say," she said, scarcely bothering to conceal her triumph.

* * *

The air was more inclement than usual and the early morning brought with it a keen wind. In Henry's inner chamber cold air seeped through the sides of the casements ruffling the silk drapes. Standing close to one of the windows, Margaret shivered, yet her palms felt damp. It was not often she was troubled by nerves, but there was much at stake and her fitful sleep didn't help her mood.

She was also striving to contain her annoyance with Henry, who refused to clothe himself in appropriate kingly garments that morning, despite her orders to a servant to lay out his court dress. But she kept closed lips for fear of upsetting him on this an important day.

At his desk, Henry played with a button on his brown wool jerkin. He was repeatedly mouthing words he rehearsed for when the time came. Watching him Margaret felt satisfied he'd been well instructed and could only pray William too would remember his part in the coming hours. His move to the palace had been timely allowing her to make frequent visits to the room he was confined to. Confident he would do and say exactly as she had coached him, she turned her attention back to the moment.

"At what time did we instruct the Lords to arrive, my Husband?" she asked at her most imperious.

Easing the chafe of his coarse breeches, Henry deliberated for a moment. It seemed a struggle and an impatient hiss from Margaret only appeared to confuse him more. He rubbed his brow with sharp, agitated movements.

"I confess I wasn't paying attention, sometime soon I think. Pray don't distract me for I must remember what it is you want me to announce for Suffolk and his perceived misdemeanours," he muttered.

Anxious not to muddle him further, Margaret remained calm.

"Then I shall leave you, my Lord, but I shall be close by," she said evenly.

With a rustle of taffeta she curtsied by way of her allegiance to Henry and disappeared into the adjoining chamber closing the door quietly behind her. Moving with stealth, she removed two leather- bound books from the oak shelving. Behind them a square of wood slipped out with ease and with her eye to the aperture she could view every inch of the inner chamber. As she did so she heard the knock announcing the first arrival.

A few minutes later six senior Lords' were assembled in front of their king. Every one, William's enemies, she knew that. Elegant in their silks and braids their faces were expressionless when they saw Henry's thrifty attire. His frugality was no longer a talking point around the court and they kept their thoughts to themselves. In reply to their short bow he inclined his head at each of them murmuring their name. Then he settled back in his chair with a benign look on his face.

"I believe we are all ready. My Lord Cromwell would you bring William, Lord Suffolk before me," he instructed.

Even the sight of Cromwell's back stirred Margaret's loathing. His power was unrivalled at court apart from her dear Suffolk, and she thought him monstrous. I wouldn't insult hogs by comparing him, she thought as she listened to his smooth reply.

"Indeed, Sire," he said.

Looking relaxed the remaining nobles exchanged complacent smiles and Margaret's lip curled at their arrogance. When William entered the room, her breath caught in her throat and she was sure the noisy thud of her heartbeat would be heard. In his stiff new court dress with his back held straight, his jaw set and paler than usual, she thought how beautiful he looked, painfully so. A deep sigh escaped her. It was a dark time, but there was nothing more she could do.

Everything depended on him now.

Chapter Thirteen

MARGARET need not have worried. It was William who forgot nothing and unwittingly prompted Henry. To her delight they conducted themselves in harmony during the proceedings and she felt her spirits rising. With abject deference William went down on bended knee in front of Henry kissing his outstretched hand.

"Gracious Majesty, I am and always will be your most humble servant," he murmured.

Grave faced, Henry motioned him to stand and Margaret smiled from her hiding place.

"My Lord Suffolk," he said. "The charges brought against you are very serious, to say the least. What have you to say for yourself?"

"I am most mortified to find myself the subject of scurrilous accusations which I heartily refute," William replied. "I stand in front of you today in the hope you will be merciful for I am not guilty of such wicked attacks as have been made against me."

Sliding her eyes from one face to another, Margaret saw by the lord's expressions they condemned him to a man. Lord Cromwell in particular looked coldly infuriated.

"Guilty or innocent, that is my dilemma," Henry said thoughtfully.

Cromwell cleared his throat. "Majesty if I might . . ."

Holding her breath, Margaret waited, but Henry didn't fail her. He raised his hand and the gold and sapphire signet ring he wore dwarfed his thin fingers.

"No my Lord Cromwell, you may not," he said sternly. "We request you to remain silent."

Margaret would have chuckled if she had been sure she wouldn't be overheard. Instead she pressed her hand to her mouth to suppress any noise. Half-turned in the chamber, Cromwell's incensed face was visible. It amused her even more and this time she bit her lip to prevent laughter escaping her.

Henry acted his part well and she prayed his indecision wouldn't surface. But he seemed confident. Remaining quiet, his hands forming a steeple over which he looked into the distance. The tension in the room was so intense she could almost feel it trickling through the small grille in front of her and for a moment she felt faint.

"So my Lord Suffolk, is there anything else you would like to say to me in your defence?" Henry said finally. Margaret sighed softly with relief. For an awful moment she thought he might have forgotten what came next. Will he manage to remain sensible?

"Only that I swear my innocence and beg you to forgive me any minor indiscretions," William said contritely. "I have only ever served you and my country with respect and humility therefore I ask you to spare me a harsh punishment for something I have not done." His low anxious voice with his words practiced so thoroughly, caught at Henry's emotions as she thought it would. The tears rushed readily to Henry's eyes which he sat dabbing with the rough edge of his sleeve.

Exchanging uneasy glances the lords waited and Cromwell clenched his hands whilst rage bleached his already sallow complexion. On the wall a solitary flame burnt low in the sconce. In contact with the remaining oil the flame was impaired and its flicker only provided dim lighting over the assembly. Yet it was just bright enough for Margaret to see the glint of inhumanity in Cromwell's hard eyes and the lines of bitterness marking his mouth.

Resting his head in his hands, Henry shuffled his buttocks in his chair and closed his eyes. He was still for so long, Margaret wondered if he was dozing. Suddenly Lord Hastings suffered a prolonged and noisy coughing fit and Henry was instantly alert.

"We have come to our decision," he said in a measured voice, looking at each face carefully. "I am a compassionate man and you have indeed served us well, Lord Suffolk so we are in a mind to be lenient. We find no evidence of treason despite the allegations. Neither is there any proof you conspired with our enemies in France to betray us. That you embezzled money for your own needs may have some truth in it, but there again without proper evidence it will be difficult to prove." He paused and Margaret felt a rush of unladylike sweat dampen her forehead.

"Therefore your punishment is this; William de La Pole, Lord High Chamberlain, Admiral of England, Earl of Pembroke and first Duke of Suffolk. I banish you from all England and her Realms for a period of five years. You are to be gone on the first day of May in this year of our Lord 1450," Henry intoned in a sombre voice.

Those not privy to the endless rehearsals would think their monarch's relieved smile at the end looked slightly out of place and in the stillness in the chamber no one moved. To Margaret's keen eyes, the expressions of William's enemies reflected a mixture of cruelty and hatred as they digested the King's words. Then Henry stood up and laid his hand briefly on William's shoulder. No one in the room missed the gesture.

"I must protest, Sire," Cromwell said angrily.

"Perhaps you may wish to, but the matter is closed," Henry said mildly.

A shade of pink was returning to William's face and bowing low he said.

"Most generous Majesty, you find me your penitent and grateful servant, Sire. I shall make arrangements immediately."

Stiff from bending so long, Margaret stepped back from the shelving stretching one leg after the other to relieve her discomfort. Then with absolute care she replaced the wood square and the books.

If William's enemies thought his banishment signalled a lean time for him, they were mistaken she mused. They spent hours discussing his plans. First he would sail to Calais where his old friend Humphrey Stafford was Captain. William himself mooted the idea he might feel inclined to join the remaining English troops in France under Somerset's command. Then there was Charles, Duke of Orleans and a comrade of long standing Philip-the-Good, Duke of Burgundy who she knew would offer him work.

No, whatever happened her dearest lover would never be poor or friendless and he wouldn't be gone forever. That her secret scheming had suffered a setback was something she and only she must deliberate. For now it was difficult to stop grinning at how well her plan had gone. She needed to remain hidden until the chamber emptied and as she waited she gripped her wrist so tightly to prevent herself clapping, her nails punctured her flesh.

* * *

Cromwell stormed from the chamber seething. Waiting for the other nobles to join him, he gnawed at a fingernail with a surly expression. But they offered him one excuse or another and departed leaving him and Lord Hastings to walk the corridor together.

"A sorry business if you ask me. The Duke of York will not be best pleased when he hears the King's trusted favourite has managed to escape yet again," Hastings said, adjusting the ruby clasp on his cape.

"Not here," Cromwell snarled. "Come to my chamber." Sparsely furnished the room was cold and stern, symbolic of the man who used it. A large four-post bed took up most of the space, its counterpane monastic in its severity. The only relief was a pewter jug which stood atop a dark oak armour chest. By the window there were two chairs. Both upright and heavy armed they were cushioned by padded needlepoint covers, too small to offer any comfort.

Waiting while his servant brought in a flask of fine wine; poured it out and departed, Cromwell left it a moment then opened the door again. He looked up and down the length of the corridor. Satisfied they would not be overheard he threw himself down in one of the chairs.

"Sit, sit," he said to Hastings indicating the chair opposite him. "Perhaps you think that's the end of it, but you'd be wrong," he said darkly.

Intrigued, Hastings sat forward whilst Cromwell tilted his head back and looked at him through narrowed eyes. He saw advancing years leaving their mark of pouches and lines on the other's face and the blue veins which laced his skin. On removing his hat, Hastings revealed his pale pink pate owned very few white hairs and the rest round his face were thin and skimpy. But Cromwell knew he was a capable statesman with a sharp mind. Like them all he was at times a little too keen to dip his fingers into the government coffers, but trust mattered and he trusted him.

"May I ask what you have in mind, my Lord?" Hastings enquired.

"You may indeed ask, but plans are not yet complete. Suffice it to say Lord Suffolk is finished, you can be sure of that," Cromwell said ingesting a large mouthful of wine, savouring it on his tongue for a moment and then swallowing it noisily.

Hastings laughed.

"Now I'm even more curious." He wiped his chin free of a wine dribble with a hand speckled with brown age-stains.

"I must confess when Suffolk was arrested I thought it the end of the man, but it seems I was wrong."

Cromwell's eyebrows rose in an arch and his eyes shone like bright pebbles bursting with colour, but empty of warmth.

"Merely a delay, I promise you that," he said, with a sinister smile.

Chapter Fourteen

Southwark
April

IT was the talk in every door way, on street corners and wherever people gathered. Already horrified at the disasters in France and the impoverished state of England the citizen's of London were now outraged at Suffolk's light sentence. To them banishment was nothing, merely a short period before the man favoured by the King's grace returned to send their country into further decline.

In the *Hart* conversation was no less heated. At their usual corner bench Richard and Jack sat discussing what others already raged about.

"They say there's not a person in the land who sheds a tear for Suffolk leaving," said Jack.

"Apart from the Queen," Richard said sagely. "He'll be gone by the end of the week. I hear he sails from Ipswich on the first tide, although the winds of the North Sea are fickle maidens and he may find a delay, let's hope not." Tipping up the ale jug to refill their flasks he watched a few indolent bubbles slithering their way to the lip.

"Your turn to buy the next one," he said.

Jack made a great effort searching his pockets patting them and fumbling on the inside. He knew even if he turned them back to front they would yield nothing. Mariamne's allowance from her father was restored, but much reduced and she'd taken to hiding it from him. His own wife; it left a bitter taste in his mouth.

As for his once lucrative income from smuggling, that too was temporarily stopped. Since the unexpected arrival of Custom Collectors late one night on the wharf at Rotherhithe, only a speedy run and good fortune saved him from the rope. So Richard insisted they lay low until it was safe to start activities again.

"No, no," he said. "I don't seem to have a groat about me, wrong jerkin you see."

Leaning close, Richard said, "Listen, you don't have to explain to me, I understand. All the more reason for you to tell Simon you are ready to bring sympathisers together so the protest can begin. There is no better time than now, England thirsts for some action and since Suffolk will be back before we know it someone will take matters into their own hands 'ere long," his arm waving for a fresh jug.

Jack looked awkward. It was evident from his appearance things were difficult. The worn collar on his shirt, the fray of his cuff and the scruffy pair of breeches he wore told their own story. His companion's enviable clothing both in costly cloth and excellent cut left him disconsolate.

Simon's promise of money should he care to lead an uprising would give him wealth beyond his imagination, but then Mammy had foretold of such things. Had Richard looked closer he would have seen the lust in Jack's eyes, but the noisy conversation around them was distracting. Words were drifting across from the tables, *Somerset-Margaret and her foreign ways - Henry the imbecile, country-revolution - Suffolk the swindler - French disaster* - whilst Richard was still having difficulty attracting the serving wench for fresh ale.

"Does no one speak of anything else?" Jack asked, as finally the flasks brimmed with ale.

A grimace from Richard was answer enough. He beckoned Jack to turn his ear closer.

"What I would say is I hope you don't have second thoughts, after all you did agree. When I saw Simon last week he told me all is almost in readiness. They were waiting for Suffolk's sentence. Now the mood seems right, people are angry that he hasn't lost his head."

Hoping it would conceal his apprehension, Jack managed a smile. There was much to lose. Disappointed in Mariamne, his affection for her amounted to nothing, but it was consoling she at least prepared his meals, cleaned their home and gave him a pale air of respectability. There again more than a hundred marks was a fortune . . . The ugly scar on his arm gave a sudden throb. After France did he really want to march again? Yet somewhere deep inside the spirit of Jack stirred. Despite all his efforts to change who he was, his heart beat true to the Irish in his veins. He used to be bold and daring, an adventurer by nature with a lust for excitement, yet grown a dullard wrapped in Mariamne's homespun blanket of feigned good breeding. Was he even master in his own home, he wondered? Richard's voice seemed far away.

"Come John, instead of day dreaming let me hear your thoughts. Will you or will you not lead an uprising so our wishes and hopes may be heard?"

Straightening his shoulders, he looked across at him and grinned. It was boyish, reckless and utterly charming.

"God's blood, I said I would do it and of course I will," he said, striking the table with an emphatic thump of his fist.

"You can't blame me for hesitating, there is much at stake. But you can tell your friend Simon, I am ready and will lead a force so robust a government, even a king will shrink from it. Then they will listen, I can promise you that."

Delighted, Richard filled the flasks again. Over the rim of the flask his eyes were lit with excitement.

"Simon will not be found wanting in showing you his gratitude when he hears this. I shall find him and give him the good news though 'tis a shame to waste this good ale," he laughed.

The ride home was exciting. Jack rode fast so the wind tugged at his hair and brought tears on his cheeks. Even the start of rain falling in jagged lines didn't slow him. If he closed his eyes he was reminded of his wild bare back rides as a child across the bogs near his home, ploughing ankle deep through bog rush and pipewort, then chided by Mammy in her soft voice when she caught sight of stains on his clothes from one fall or another.

Caught by a rut in the road his horse stumbled, but as much a master of balance as his rider was of good horsemanship, neither of them came to harm. Reaching the lane to his home he found himself slowing reluctantly. Preparing himself for Mariamne's company stole his good humour; it always did.

* * *

Not far from the *Hart* the narrow confines of an alleyway trapped the stink of fouled drains and human effluence. Nosing through the piles of rotting waste, a hog disturbed another creature with its snuffling snout. Shrilling with fear a fully grown black rat ran in a haphazard fashion towards its hole at the base of one of the tenement walls.

Because of the passageway's thin angles, the closeness of the damp flint stone threw obscure shadows on the two men walking in single file. Water dripping from somewhere above them brought with it thick slime which slopped onto Richard's sleeve and he felt unseen garbage sliding under his foot. When Simon stopped, they stood close their head's bent in whispered conversation.

"Why must we meet here?" Richard asked, wrinkling his nose as the rodent passed them.

"Because I have no wish to be overheard," Simon said shortly. "So are you sure your friend Mortimer won't change his mind? I shall be passing this information to certain friends who in turn will send word to Richard, Duke of York. He tires of his exile in Ireland and is anxious for the uprising to begin."

Flicking imaginary specks distastefully from his braided serge jacket, Simon's eyes were piercing as they locked onto his companion's. Richard shook off the vegetable waste from under his boot.

"You do realise John Mortimer doesn't know the true purpose for this uprising? He is a man of the people, of the common folk and may think differently if he learns what lies behind this," he pointed out.

"I've thought of that," Simon said curtly. "We must give them a social reason for their rebellion and it will be this. They have not been content since the government tried to pull them into line sixty years ago when that fool Wat Tyler with his unruly rabble tried to bargain for all the labourers. What better time for the commons to try again? Surely that will attract sufficient numbers to fall behind Mortimer whilst in truth they will also attempt to bring down Suffolk and

Somerset. Their administration is incompetent at the very least and when that dolt of a king of ours finally loses his wits, Richard will be waiting to step up to the throne."

A woman appeared with a child at her breast. Shaking her lank hair away from her gaunt face she looked at them curiously as she threw out a bowl of slops. They narrowly missed Simon's black hose and he snorted angrily.

"What of Margaret? They say she is a force to be reckoned with," Richard said quietly when the tenement door closed again.

"When things come to pass a place will be found for her, you have no need to worry about that. The people dislike her as much as they do Suffolk. There'll be no tears shed for a woman of her sort." Simon grunted in contempt. He glanced up at the light uneasily. "It's time I was gone before we are seen. Tell Mortimer to be ready, I shall be in touch shortly."

Richard watched Simon's portly shape squeeze itself between the dank slabs as he hurried to the end of the passage way as fast as his small booted feet would carry him. On seeing him turning left into the main street, Richard sauntered to the right whilst pondering on his words.

Chapter Fifteen

The Palace of Westminster

ON the way to the Royal Apartments, Cromwell spoke severely to himself, commanding his body to relax. Not only that, but knowing how his news would be received he must compose his features in order to look sufficiently upset. For the last few paces he slowed his step and with a deep intake of breath raised his hand and knocked on the oak door. A Lady-in-Waiting opened the door to him.

"Are both their Majesties present?" he asked.

"Yes, my Lord," the woman assured him.

As was usual, Henry was reading. He looked up and Cromwell was taken aback by his pale complexion and his hollow eyes which showed so little perception. He did however manage a vestige of a nod on recognising his visitor before returning to the page in his book. Near the window, Margaret sat looking out with her embroidery discarded in her lap.

"Why, Lord Cromwell, we were not expecting a visit from you." Her eyes missed nothing as she scrutinised Cromwell's face. "I fear you look uncommonly solemn. Is it bad news you bring us?"

Cromwell's bow swept him low to the floor and when he straightened his expression was one of deepest misery.

"I regret so, Majesty. It pains me greatly to inform you, Lord Suffolk has met with an accident."

As he supposed, Margaret's face darkened with apprehension and he saw how she gripped her hands together, forcing her knuckles to protrude white through her skin.

"What sort of accident?"

He could hear the fear in her voice. Had he an ounce of kindness in him he might have felt sorry for her, but he hadn't so he didn't. Instead holding his grave expression, he said.

"A serious one, Majesty," he said, keeping the lines round his mouth taut as he felt his triumph at her visible distress.

"Oh dear Lord, I must go to him," she said, in a quavering voice. Her sewing tumbled to the floor in a flash of coloured wools as she sprang to her feet. "He sailed from Ipswich no more than a few hours ago. Where is he?" Henry marked the page in his book with his finger and then enquiring in a vague manner said.

"Has something happened?"

"Yes Lord Husband, did you not hear Lord Cromwell? William has met with an accident. I must leave at once." Her slender frame shook uncontrollably as tears coursed down her cheeks

"Oh, how tiresome," Henry said, his gaze back to his reading.

As Margaret passed him, Cromwell's hand came out to stay her.

"I don't think you quite understand, Your Grace."

"Understand? What is there to understand? Get out of my way," she hissed through sobs.

"Perhaps, my dear, you should let my Lord Cromwell finish," Henry ventured meekly.

Cromwell nodded. It was more difficult than he anticipated.

"Thank you, Majesty," he murmured. "I take no pleasure in being the bearer of such dreadful tidings; nonetheless you should know Lord Suffolk is dead."

Margaret shook her head. "He can't be . . . it's not possible," she said incredulously.

Dashing away fresh tears she swayed visibly. Cromwell was quick to steady her or she would have fallen. When she clutched at his sleeve he was surprised how small her hands were. For one so forceful and determined she was indeed amazingly diminutive.

"Please sit, Your Grace," he urged her, putting his hand under her elbow to guide her back to her chair.

"Now you must tell us," she breathed her face the colour of alabaster and her eyelashes clung with teardrops. Cromwell was quite enjoying the royal discomfort and his idea to wring his hands together he thought quite masterly. Anything which would avert suspicion away from him was wise so he also added a loud sniff to mark his concern.

"It would appear his vessel was approached off Dover and he was summoned to board the *Nicholas of the Tower*," he explained.

"She's a fine ship, one of my largest," Henry said affably.

Gulping back her distress, Margaret sat smoothing her skirt over and over in her turmoil.

"Please my Husband," she whispered. "Pray let Lord Cromwell continue."

Cromwell inclined his head. "They tell me there was some sort of trial, but apart from denying he was a traitor, Lord Suffolk refused to speak. They took him to the edge of the ship and bent him over the gunwale.

Her white lips quivering, Margaret had difficulty forming the words.

"What then?"

"He was executed with a cutlass, Your Grace."

A look of revulsion crumpled Margaret's face and from behind her, Henry made a retching noise. Springing out of his chair his book fell off his knees landing with a resounding thump on the floor. Then he ran from the chamber without looking back. Margaret gave no reaction to his sudden departure and for a long moment there was silence. Then barely audible she spoke again.

"What has become of him? We command you to find his body so he may have a proper burial."

Cromwell stared far over her head towards the sparkling water of the Thames.

"He has been found, Majesty. His corpse lay on the sands at Dover."

"Then bring him to us so we can bid him into God's arms for safekeeping," she replied, suddenly cold and distant.

Still without looking in her direction, Cromwell cleared his throat.

"That will be difficult, Majesty. Lord Suffolk is without his head."

Hard as he was, Cromwell was unprepared for the keening noise which rose from Margaret's throat and engulfed the chamber. Having kept a discreet distance throughout, Catherine, Lady of the Bedchamber rushed to her mistress, but was repelled by Margaret's flailing arms. She finally managed to grasp one of her hands, but out of control Margaret howled even more desperately whilst kicking her away.

Wishing to escape the chamber, but unsure how appropriate it would be, Cromwell turned to look down from the window. Henry was sitting below. His crown lay abandoned beside him and he wore on his head a daisy chain plucked from flowers in the grass. Appalled, yet fascinated Cromwell watched him rocking back and forth in silent mirth.

* * *

Each morning a fresh outfit was presented to Margaret. Each was dismissed with more tears and eerie wailing that carried along the corridors and clawed at windows to be released. Gone were the rich silks, satins and brocades; the shimmering gowns and ropes of lustrous pearls, gone too the coronets of fresh blooms bedecked with tiny diamonds and exquisite hand-sewn gem-encrusted girdles which looped around the waist.

When, after a week of mourning, Margaret did eventually appear she was barely recognisable. Bending forward when she walked it was as if grief loaded her back like a peasant might carry a heavy bundle of wood. Her face was masked by black veils draped from her hat. More of them swaddled her neck. With regular monotony she paced the corridors with a faint rustle of silk emanating from her black unadorned gown. Some said she took exercise, others said she was too distraught to know what she was doing, but whatever the reason she never strayed far from her bedchamber.

It was several days before she emerged back before the Court. Walking through a corridor which led to the Council Chamber she was met by smiles of sympathy. Some were forced. Words when murmured were supposed to comfort, but were often hollow. She ignored them all preferring to rest listless and red-eyed on a seat in the garden. Then one morning almost two weeks after she was given news of William's death she allowed Catherine to relieve her austere dress with an extravagant opal necklace. Each gemstone twining through the gold was a meld of emerald, amethyst and violet coming together in a fiery rainbow of glittering colours. Catherine took it as an encouraging omen. Later when she overheard two minor attendants spitefully murmuring Margaret only wore it when meeting with William Suffolk, she boxed their ears. Fastening the gold clasp she smiled at the memory.

"There Your Majesty. It does my heart good to think you might be feeling a little better," she ventured.

Margaret gave a dismal nod.

"I shall visit my Lord Husband today. How is he?" she asked in a dejected voice.

There was a moment of hesitation before a reply.

"He doesn't fare well, Your Grace. He refuses to leave his bed and speaks to no one although he asks after you from time to time," the woman replied, adjusting the hang of the jewellery with a capable hand.

"Oh my dear husband, you are truly a helpless man," Margaret whispered under her breath.

"Shall Your Grace have need of the veils today?" asked Catherine.

Margaret turned stern-faced.

"Would you think I would dispense with them so soon after the loss of such a dear friend?" she said sharply.

* * *

Dwarfed by his enormous four-post bed, Henry sat huddled in bed linen staring up at the painted ceiling. Unmoved despite the sound of Margaret's voice, he mumbled constantly to himself.

"Henry?" she repeated, throwing her veil away from her face as she approached the bed. "It is I, Margaret, your Queen."

Very slowly Henry lowered his head and moved it a fraction until his eyes were resting on her. Hesitating, she was shocked by the state of him. Was this her husband, the King of all England huddled into a rough shawl? He showed no more than a passing interest when she lifted his limp hand. His nightcap pulled down on his brow accentuated his sunken eye pits and gaunt features and she stifled a groan at the fresh blood smears which decorated his linen chemise.

Two of the King's attendants stood at the foot of the bed with their heads bents together. Margaret spun round to them looking appalled.

"What is the meaning of this that I find His Majesty soiled by his own blood?" she demanded.

The older of the two and less nervous than his companion hurriedly explained. "The apothecary calls twice a day, Your Grace. On each visit he applies leeches and has only just departed. His Majesty will be changed shortly, we didn't expect . . ." His words ended abruptly as Margaret interrupted.

"Didn't expect I should visit, is that it? What sort of wife should I be called who cared not for her Lord Husband when he ails so? Take care you don't anger me with such a careless remark." Her grief forgotten for a moment, her expression was fierce and her words biting.

Seemingly more alert in the knowledge his Queen spoke for him, Henry gave a relieved smile and gripped her hand more tightly.

"Fetch someone to refresh the King at once and whilst you are doing so summon Lord Hastings as well," Margaret instructed, gently stroking Henry's cheek.

"At once Your Grace," the man replied, departing from the chamber speedily.

Leaving Henry with his servant closing the hangings round his bed, Margaret seated herself at the far end of the chamber to await Hastings. Arriving short of breath it took him a minute or two of puffing and snorting to recover. Any other time, Margaret would have been amused today it was all she could do to speak without crying.

Bending with his black hat sweeping low to the floor, Hastings then stood up unsteadily. The hand he held out to Margaret was thin-skinned and its joints knobbly and bent out of shape by the nodules of age.

"May I say how pained I was to hear of Lord Suffolk's untimely demise, Your Grace," he said seriously.

Fighting the threatening tears, she looked steadily at the ageing man. "Please sit, my Lord," she said faintly. "There are arrangements to be made."

"Yes, Majesty, what is it you wish to arrange?" he asked, some of the flustered colour receding from his face.

"Lord Suffolk's burial of course," she replied, dabbing her eyes with a flimsy kerchief. "Since my Lord Husband is unable to advise I must see to it myself."

Hastings fiddled with a silver thread come loose from the embroidered cuff of his black padded shirt. Puzzled by his expression, Margaret frowned. His was a face she wanted to trust, but she also knew of his close friendship with Cromwell and had learnt to be wary.

"You seem perplexed my Lord. Is there something you wish me to know?" she enquired, drawing herself up straight.

"I'm sorry Your Grace, it seems Alice the Duchess of Suffolk has already taken care of her husband's remains." Ignoring the sharp gasp of Margaret's breath he continued, "She accompanies him to Wingfield where he will shortly be buried at Collegiate Church, the family's house of worship."

Margaret's shoulders slumped and the delicate lawn kerchief scrunched together as her fingers shut round it in a tight fist. "I see," she said tightly. "Then there is nothing more to be said. Tell me, my Lord, do we have word as to who might be responsible for such a heinous act as has befallen Lord Suffolk?" Her voice kept even, but her full lips were compressed together into a thin line.

Hastings was quick to shake his head, too quick she thought. In a gesture of uncertainty he spread his hands wide and she noticed their tremor.

"You may rest assured Majesty, everything possible is being done to apprehend the felons responsible."

Margaret's laughter was as brittle as a sliver of ice.

"Perhaps you need not look too far from home, my Lord. Methinks Richard Duke of York, may be able to assist in the enquiries."

It was Hastings turn to catch his breath and his face paled accentuating the purplish veins running close to his skin.

"As you are aware Your Grace, the Duke is in Ireland besides it would be unthinkable . . ."

"That will be all, thank you my Lord," Margaret replied stony faced. "As soon as my husband recovers we travel to Leicester, until then I have much to occupy my mind, not least how to protect my Lord Husband from his enemies." He had the grace to blush before he turned away and absented himself from the chamber.

After Hastings left, Margaret stood beside Henry's bed. He lay sleeping, his eyelashes softly feathering his wan cheeks and his occasional snuffling wrinkling his nose. She had never held her own child, but looking at her husband now she might as well gather him up in her arms and know how it was. She desired a man, not a helpless infant.

A shiver went down her spine and piteous tears came. *My dear, dear sweet Suffolk . . .*

Chapter Sixteen

Tonbridge
Kent
Late May

AS a manor house Penhurst Place was not only baronial and ornate, but of massive proportions set in a thousand acres. When the stones of the house were warmed they turned a mellow pink-grey like the breast feathers of a pigeon and gigantic shadows were cast on the land from numerous chimneys and turreted roofs. Dark amidst the lightness the high arched front entrance stood firm hinged and embellished in heavy brass with an enormous door knocker fashioned in the shape of a monstrous jaw.

The two men who emerged appeared from a smaller door in the west wing of the house were deep in conversation. They made an odd looking pair. Simon of Kent was both short and of a bullish build whilst his companion, Sir John de Pultenery, Squire of Penhurst, stood lofty and willow stripling thin. A good head and a half taller he needed to stoop to hear Simon. When he did so his shoulder blades protruded from his feather trimmed gown as if he wore conical moulds under the black velvet.

The path they took led them past a circular pond. The arching fountains plundered the stillness of the water and sent the lily pads gently dancing under the sparkling water drops. Then beyond the water gardens guarded by long neatly clipped yew hedges, they crossed trim green sward edged by vast stone urns and ornate statues. Finally Pultenery led Simon through an opening in the square of copper beech into the Flag Garden. Each massive bed was filled with iris blooms in blocks of colours; mauve, gold and magenta in an eye-watering display of perfection. It seemed only here in this secluded place some distance from the house did Pultenery feel it was safe enough to talk of confidential matters.

Reclining on a stone seat, one of several placed about the garden, he stretched out his long legs and removed his velveteen hat. His was a cool gaze from his calm blue eyes encompassing Simon, who slightly out of breath took a seat beside him.

"Not a bad place, eh for a country residence?" Pultenery said with a casual wave towards the building blocks of the grand house. "Being a good trader is all it takes, that and a diligence for work. You should try it sometime. But then I forget, you make your fortune from rather more dubious means, do you not?"

Discomforted by his remark, Simon grimaced and having to sit forward so his feet reached the ground, eased himself into a more comfortable position.

"Not entirely. Kindly remember I own several properties and a considerable acreage of land too. But much as I enjoy such a pleasurable walk through your grounds, I'm sure we didn't walk all this way to discuss one another's monetary affairs," he said shortly. His exertions left a shine of sweat on his forehead which he wiped away with dabs of his kerchief.

"No, indeed you are right though it makes entertaining thought," Pultenery said his smile a trifle smug. "So how go our plans?"

Prepared to overlook Pultenery's overbearing manner, Simon nodded enthusiastically. Now they were out of earshot of others he could relax. Being proud of his role in the forthcoming uprising he was anxious to impress the likes of Pultenary. Preening his expensive, but somewhat flamboyant tunic with a self-satisfied touch he said.

"They go well, well indeed and whilst not wishing to boast, I think you'll find your trust in me was more than justified."

Shielding his eyes from the sun he slid a quick glance sideways to see Pultenery's expression. It was hard to judge, he thought, disappointed that his companion seemed content to gaze over the multitude of pots on the roof top. Simon wondered if he should repeat himself in case Pultenery didn't quite catch his remark, but before he could do so, his companion spoke.

"I think others will be the judge of your efficiency, for now I'm only interested on a favourable report on your progress which I can send to the *Falcon* in Ireland." Reaching for some heads of lavender close to the end of the seat, Pultenery snapped them off and carried them up to his nose. He inhaled their perfume with an intense sniff and let out a deep sigh of appreciation.

"Such an exquisite smell from something so small," he murmured, looking at the collection of pale purple flowers in his palm before he tossed them away with disinterest.

Watching him, Simon agonised as to whether he dare show his ignorance since he had no idea who Pultenery spoke of when he referred to the *Falcon*.

"The *Falcon*?" he asked timidly.

Wary, Pultenery looked about him before he answered.

"It is too dangerous for anyone to mention the Duke of York's name and unwise of you should you speak of it to others. It must never be disclosed until he has claimed his rightful place on the throne. Therefore he is known as the *Falcon* by those most loyal to him," he explained gravely Impressed he'd been privy to this information Simon smirked with pride.

"I can assure you nothing you tell me shall go further than this garden," he said importantly.

"You would do well to remember that. So who is it who will lead the uprising and when will he be ready?"

"Very shortly," Simon assured. "A trusted friend of mine, Richard de Courcy is a man most loyal to the cause. He uses the *White Hart* in Southwark and 'twas there he encountered a Master John Mortimer. He too tires of all the ineptitude shown by our present government and has agreed to gather sufficient forces in order to take these grievances to the Crown."

Crossing one leg over the other, Pultenery blew a minute speck of dust off the toe of one of his black leather boots.

"Umm, and what do we know of this man? Is he a Mortimer related to the Duke of Clarence because if he is it will cause great offence to the *Falcon*?"

His own ideas about John Mortimer were not something he wished to share, at least not until he made more enquiries so Simon shook his head vehemently.

"On the contrary, he is not of high-status, but has married well and lives here in Kent. Those who know him say he shows admirable powers of intelligence and considerable military abilities in the battlefield, yet I feel he is likely dull witted enough to believe this uprising is all about reforms for the commons. When it comes to matters close to the heart of those of us who wish to see the rightful monarch return from Ireland, he will not be told. And I can vouch for de Courcy, he would make no mistake I can assure you."

"And you are sure this man is the right person, willing to undertake such a task?"

"He was reluctant at first perhaps, but I have some powers of persuasion," Simon said unusually modest, but desperate to impress.

Nodding contentedly, Pultenery got to his feet flapping his hand at a bumble bee flying dangerously close to his face.

"Good. Then I can leave everything to you and your friend. I find it a great relief Suffolk is dead. We no longer need worry about his influence over our imbecile king nor his penchant for increasing his own personal wealth at the expense of others," he said briskly as he and Simon began their trek back to the house.

"There are some who say Queen Margaret may be stronger than she appears," Simon ventured as he struggled to keep up with Pultenery.

The noise of Pultenery's scoffing laughter seemed offensive in the tranquil air of the gardens.

"Nonsense, without Suffolk's help she is nought but a troublesome woman and a French one at that who will soon see her proper place. She has neither the courage nor skill to fight off the king's enemies and there are plenty. If some had their way they would see her in a nunnery, best place for her if you ask me. No, all will be well if we are staunch in purpose," Pultenery said with a confident smile.

Feeling the collar of his tunic sticking to his neck in the heat, Simon was grateful to see the pebbled drive at last. It had been a long wearisome afternoon and he was anxious to be gone. Pultenery caught his arm with one final thought.

"You say Mortimer lives near here?"

"A very small house and belonging to his wife by all accounts," Simon replied, edging ever closer to the stable block.

"Then perhaps you should tell him he may assemble his troops in the parkland before he marches on London. I should like to meet this Master Mortimer," Pultenery said. He flourished his ivory topped cane in the direction of a rolling expanse of grass and glade next to the formal gardens. Stopping in front of a wrought iron gate he called over his shoulder. "You do understand there is to be no mention of my name in all of this."

Trying to minimise the noise his boots made on the pebbles, Simon raised a hand.

"Of course Squire Pultenery, I can be most trusted I assure you," he said with forced servility.

Chapter Seventeen

June

IN the parkland alongside the gardens at Penhurst the gathering crowd of Kentish men grew ever larger. Despite the earliness of the hour an expectant atmosphere prevailed and talk was noisy and amiable. Falling through the hours of darkness a shower of warm rain left the air fresh and a pewter coloured gloss on the stones.

From a first floor window, Pultenery cast an eye over the proceedings. He could see his herd of black deer were keeping far away from the activity. They shifted uneasily as the smell of humans wafted their way then stood watchful and mistrusting. Hastily he counted them. Relieved none had vanished he turned his attention to the gathering.

Anxious to see who he might recognise, he leant forward to get a better view and picked out Simon of Kent at once. There was no mistaking the squat and gaudily dressed man waving his hands about as he spoke. Recognising some of the men talking to Simon he was pleased there were several he mixed with on social occasions. Sir Horace Feltwell was well connected as were the Rector Edmund of Mayfield and with him Prior Henry Fairfax of St. Pancras, and Alderman Coldham from Sevenoaks. They were minor gentry perhaps, but all with standing, property and land and exactly who he needed on this uprising. Satisfied, he didn't bother to suppress his smile.

Closer to the house the vocal crowd standing with Richard de Courcy brought a frown to his face. One very tall and another too short, several extremely young and the wizened faced too weak to be useful. All of them were drably dressed and pinched featured as is the way of the poor. Low born all of them he thought, his expression dismissive, yet one stood out above the rest both by his upright bearing and his appearance. Pultenery scrutinised him closely. Was this John Mortimer? Wearing clothing a shade smarter than the poorly clad commons, the man stood at ease with them. One thing for certain, Pultenery thought as he watched the man's animated face, he seemed popular enough.

For a moment he mused on the man's features. Stray black curls were escaping from under his hood. They lingered on his fair-skinned brow above dark eyes and strong-boned, heavily freckled cheeks. Should he be fond of a wager, he'd be happy to toss down a groat or two on his conviction John Mortimer hailed from Ireland. Still no matter to him where the fellow came from just as long as he played his part. Certainly by the looks of him, Mortimer didn't stand true to peasant stock, yet not of gentility either, perhaps an artisan or a minor tradesman he decided thoughtfully stroking the bristles above his lip. He would make a point of finding out.

Slipping the catch, he opened the window leaving it a little ajar so he could hear some of the conversations, but more often than not they were lost in outbursts of ribald laughter. What did carry clearly was the sound of iron wheels from the carts crunching up his freshly raked stones. Scowling, he debated whether to knock on the glass then noticing the collection of hollow-cheeked women and boisterous children who travelled on foot behind, he thought better of it. After all large numbers of poor commons were needed to detract from the true purpose of the uprising so he snapped the casement shut and prepared to meet the assembly.

* * *

As the wicker weave door in the wall slowly opened, Simon moved swiftly.

"Master Pultenery, what a pleasure and such a fine day promised, it must be an omen," he said, swinging his arm in an expansive gesture towards the parkland. "Already a sizable gathering and more to come I can assure you."

"Most pleasing," Pultenery said shortly. "Perhaps you would be good enough to take me to Master Mortimer, I'm anxious to meet him."

Walking side by side, Simon's showy beading on his tunic glinted fiercely in sharp contrast to Pultenery's sombre outfit which was only relieved by a whispering of tawny fox fur round his collar and cuffs. Watching them, Jack found it hard to conceal his smile at the sight of Simon with a servile smile prancing beside the decorous Pultenery. It was a side of Simon he hadn't seen before and it amused him. Throwing his hand on Jack's arm, Simon tugged him forward.

"John, this is Squire Pultenery, a distinguished gentleman of this fine county and by whose kind permission we meet here on his property. Squire Pultenery, this is John Mortimer or as some would call him, 'The Captain of Kent'. He is our man who has volunteered to lead the Kentish protestors."

Making sure the sleeve of his shirt sat at the cuff on his wrist so his scar couldn't be seen, Jack took Pultenery's thin hand which showed every bony protuberance through the soft skin. Such was the brevity of the shake Jack could only recall a peculiar dryness of Pultenery's palm before the hand dropped to grip the cane again.

"Squire Pultenery, 'tis a pleasure," Jack murmured.

"And you, Master Mortimer. You do well, well indeed to gather such numbers already. Perhaps you and I could walk a little. I'm most interested to hear of your plans, but first I have made some arrangements for you," Pentenery said suavely.

Jack felt himself steered away. Pultenery, raising his cane occasionally to acknowledge someone he knew, led him towards a shady corner under a mature willow with whispering leaves.

"I have an old and trusted friend, Lord Saye. He is loyal to our cause and a good man. If you can reach Knole Park by nightfall, he is happy for you strike camp there," he said softly.

"That is most kind, sir. I have every intention in us reaching Seven Oaks before last light."

"Good. So tell me Master Mortimer, I hear you live nearby, so are you a Kentish man?"

"For most of my life," Jack said brightly, taking care with his voice.

Curiously he glanced sideways at Pultenery's profile noticing it was made even sharper by his prominent nose. From what he'd seen so far it seemed to him Pultenery was a most unlikely supporter of the poor commons and their troubles. Why would he concern himself about the fortunes of the common people? Did he spend a sleepless night worrying about those less fortunate. Or struggle for the next groat. So what was his place in this uprising?

Before Jack could think any further, Pentenery asked his next question.

"Do you have employment?"

"Richard de Courcy gives me work."

"Honest employment is what I ask, Master Mortimer," Pultenery said tightly.

Jack hesitated and then saw his opportunity to justify his presence.

"You could moot I seek an honourable trade, but with forced labour and such heavy taxes thanks to our greedy government, I say 'tis time for a change."

His companion persisted.

"Are you an adventurer?"

"No more than the next man," Jack replied evenly.

"And your allegiance lies where?" Bending forward, fixing him with the cold eye of a cobra and breathing very slowly, Pultenery seemed intent on the answer.

Jack replied easily. "Certainly not with our slow-witted king and his corrupt advisers, thieves the lot of them. I told you before 'tis time for a change.

Richard had coached him well and when Pultenery nodded he knew his place was secure in the uprising. But Pultenery wanted more. He leant his head close so Jack could feel the warmth of his breath and see the suspicion in his granite gaze.

"I'm not afraid to say you are somewhat of an enigma to me, Master Mortimer, but we have a common cause so do your job well and there could be certain rewards for you. It takes a brave man to face the possible consequences of an uprising so I applaud your courage. However should I find you stray from the path as it were, the outcome would be serious. Now I'll leave you for we should waste no more time. Good day to you."

Watching the straight back and stiff gait of Pultenery walking away, Jack sighed with relief, yet he would no more underestimate the man than he would an irate ox.

* * *

As Richard and Simon were attempting to count by heads the assembled crowd, Jack took the time to consider some he might call to the front as his henchmen. Three quickly caught his eye and he approached each in turn.

Merek the Brave stood taller than any other. Built broad and strong, he handled a weighty longbow as if it were a catapult and whilst he spoke little, his high brow and perceptive gaze marked him a man of intelligence. As small as Merek was lofty, Walter de Gray amused Jack. When he needed a lean weasel and one who would run at speed, de Gray would seem his man and the third to impress him, Barda the Bald offered quiet maturity and a wise head. With a satisfied nod, Jack touched each on the shoulder and they took their place beside him.

His chest heaving with his physical effort, Simon sought out Jack.

"Richard and I met at the bottom of the park. He's still counting, but we reckon there is nigh on two to three thousand ready to stand with us," he grunted. "We plan to ride ahead. There are things to be seen to so we'll both meet you at Black Heath."

Gratified by the numbers, Jack nodded and then looking up at the position of the sun he called to those closest.

"We should start out soon before any more of the day slips past. I plan we reach Seven Oaks by nightfall, but we must keep up a good pace. We make shall camp near Knole Park. Squire Pultenery tells me word has been sent to Lord Saye and we are expected."

Merek pulled a face. "That'll not be popular. The king's treasurer is no friend of the men of Kent."

Cuffing him gently on the arm, Jack laughed at Merek's expression.

"Fret not, 'tis but one night. Tomorrow we shall be in London. Spread the word we depart, and let the uprising begin, my friends."

* * *

Concealed in his arbour, Pultenery watched the long snake of men, the rumbling carts and the assortment of women, children and dogs setting off towards the main highway to London. Beside him an anxious-looking, nondescript fellow wearing Pultenery's colours kept tight hold of the reins of his horse. Keeping his voice low, Pultenery said to his man-at-arms, "Bailey, as soon as it's safe to do so ride fast to Charing. Lord Cromwell will be waiting for you. It isn't wise to carry a missive so you must remember the message. *The Falcon will soon be home for the birds of deliverance have taken flight.* Is that clear? He will know what you mean. Now be gone and stop for no one."

"Understood, master," John Bailey said, touching his cap.

He led his horse in the opposite direction to the marchers. Using a mounting block, he was soon astride the horse and turning the corner. Beside the stable block a bridleway would take him across country and onwards to the capitol.

Content he could do no more, Pultenery bent low putting his eye to a dislodged flint. It afforded him a small but effective view of the procession of people. Still they kept coming, wending their way from the park and out onto the highway. Finally the last of the supply carts and water carriers creaked past him and he watched them until they were dwindling shadows. Giving a soft snort of pleasure, Pultenery replaced the flint and then flicking at stones in his path with his cane he strolled back to the house.

Chapter Eighteen

Leicestershire
Melton Mowbray Castle

MARGARET found the view from the narrow casement soothing. In contrast to the dingy grey stone and unappealing dwellings she left in London, the Castle offered her a balm of greens and browns. She could see beyond the undulating countryside and then to the tranquillity of the river. To her left the watercourse of the Wreake sparkled below in the valley with its gently sloping sides. On the horizon her eyes were drawn to bleak high ridges which were so daunting in winter. In the summer light their wide expanse offered peace and freedom luring her to escape and climb them.

Her husband's outraged voice from behind the closed drapes distracted her and whilst it pleased her he sounded stronger and more sensible, she wished he would stop arguing with the physician.

"God's bones, am I surrounded by nincompoops? First the apothecary and now you, we have told you we are recovered. My sweet Lady Margaret tends me well although like a child at times, but neither she nor you need worry further. We are well again. Now take your pills and potions and leave us in peace."

His recent incoherence tired her and she turned for another look at the fresh countryside. Pressing closer to the glass she looked to her right. This time she found a water mill close to the steady flow of the river. Entranced by its huge wheel threshing the water into a froth of white her tense expression slipped away replaced by the enthusiastic innocence of a child. She sighed deeply. The panorama reminded her of Anjou left behind when she said farewell to France to marry the king of England. That Henry was at times a disappointment to her was a miserable secret she kept close to her heart and now her title and wealth were so priceless to her she would never relinquish either. But she had compassion too and bitter that at times she was much maligned. The wellbeing of her new country never left her mind, yet she knew what people thought of her. It made her distrustful, but not without cause.

"We are pleased to see you have abandoned your mourning clothes, sweet wife," Henry said from the depths of his chair, his page tucking a rug about his knees. "The dress you wear is most becoming, what colour should we call that?"

"They tell me its lavender, my Lord," she answered in a disinterested voice. She fanned her face with a slender hand. "I feel the need for air. Perhaps I shall ask them to saddle me a horse so I may take a short ride if you will permit it?"

Already thumbing through the pages of a book, Henry looked up. With the colour returned to his face and his eyes unfettered by illness, his smile was boyish and innocent. She loved him for that.

"Of course you may. In a few days we will join you, but the damnable physician tells us we must rest."

Irritable at the thought he snorted impatiently and beckoned to her. "Sit with me for awhile first. I grieve you feel unwell," he said patting the cushion beside him.

"Not unwell my Lord, merely in need of a fresh breeze and the balm of the summer sun," she said tersely with a graceful dip and swish of her silk gown.

"A tisane might help," he offered.

"Thank you, but no."

"Then what is it? Do you still pine for dear Suffolk?" Her lie was convincing as she shook her head so firmly the crystals threaded through her hair jigged among the gold strands. How could she tell him the truth?

"No my Lord, I do not, although it saddens me he is gone and I'm fearful without his protection."

Waving an airy hand, Henry hastened to correct her.

"He was our friend, I grant you, but at times we felt he sought not only our benevolence, but a great deal of our wealth which I found unbecoming. In other words he relied on us too much for his position at court and as you well know we admire meekness in a man. That was not something William was familiar with so we shall manage well enough without him." Henry's hand gently stroked the back of hers and she resisted the urge to snatch it away.

How dare he be so harsh as to speak ill of a man so lately lost to her, murdered in cold blood. Her memories of William Suffolk's strength and passion were still unbearable and Henry didn't miss the rush of tears. At once he was concerned. Looking hard at her, he gently traced her high cheekbone with his finger.

"Dearest Lady Wife, could we dare to hope we have a woman's condition which makes us a little weak and tearful?" he asked tenderly.

Under the pretext of wiping her eyes she turned away. When William took her and she soared out of reach of any human but him, she prayed for a child. Her weak dreamer of a husband would have known no different. Yet her soul remained unfulfilled and her womb empty and now it was too late. Numbly she shook her head.

"Then we must try again. We shall come to your chamber tonight. Have your ladies leave your hair free but trouble not with a modest nightgown, you will have no need of it," Henry said amiably.

Restless, she stood again and felt herself pulled back by his hand. With a quizzical look he said, "I see sorrow in your eyes. Are you not pleased your husband is well again?"

"It brightens my spirit to see you recovered and I thank God for it," she said with a poor attempt at a smile.

He let her go then and she walked slowly back to the casement. A track from the river wound its way across water meadows and a moving shape caught her attention. As it came closer she recognised the small windswept Royal pennant being carried quickly toward the castle by a horse and its rider. Craning her neck she watched until the rider crossed the bridge over the moat and disappeared.

* * *

Thwarted in her plan to ride out through the countryside, Margaret acknowledged Henry's envoy, Sir Richard Basset with a curt nod and little graciousness. Henry however greeted him cheerily.

"My dear friend, what brings you to Leicester and in a hurry by the looks of you?" he enthused.

Basset pulled a wry face.

"My humble apologies, Majesties, 'tis remiss of me to appear thus dressed, but I carry an important message from London."

Margaret Callow

"Then get on with it," Margaret said bluntly, frowning at Basset's mud-splattered hat in his hand and his dusty boots.

"Perhaps we should be a little more understanding, Margaret. It's a long ride from the capital and dear Basset is looking exhausted," Henry said with a sympathetic smile.

Margaret's curtsey was no more than a brisk bob. Then in a swirl of silk, lace and impatience she went back to the window.

"Of course, Lord Husband, my mistake that I needed reminding about the length of the journey from London," she said, her fingers tapping the window sill.

If Henry didn't detect the scorn in her voice, Bassett certainly did. All of Court knew what to expect from the King's consort, the determined, opinionated and unstoppable Margaret of Anjou. But the citizens were right their king was a weak ineffectual monarch. Did he deserve the derision heaped on him? Basset was unsure.

"I come to report unfortunate news," he said, conscious of Margaret's cold gaze. "Yesterday a large number of commoners gathered in Kent and they are at this moment marching to Seven Oaks and then on to Black Heath where they will be joined by more."

Reaching into a silver bowl, Henry selected a honeyed fig.

"What purpose do they have?" he asked, his mild tone showing no concern as he inspected the fruit.

"It seems they are discontented and wish to present a list of grievances, Sire."

Margaret's snort was not only loud, but unladylike and her expression pained. Her eyes narrowing into glittering slits she said, "What is it these poor commons want? They do nothing but whine, yet seem unable to help themselves. Spare me some sad tale. Our coffers are as empty as theirs." Henry laughter echoed through the chamber. "Not exactly true is it, sweet wife? So tell me Basset, is it only peasants who complain? If so, we should do all we can to help them."

"There you go again, my Lord Husband, always worrying about one problem or another when it comes to poor people," Margaret retorted.

"Since you ask, Majesty, they are joined by others of higher status. They include artisans, merchants, several squires, even two members of parliament and some are men of the church."

"You haven't answered our question, my Lord Basset. What is it they seek?" Margaret said tartly.

Bassett cleared his throat, tried to steady his nerves and taking a deep breath said, "They talk of deception and incompetence, of mismanagement by the government and one or two even suggest His Majesty should step down from the throne."

"I knew it!" Margaret raged. "They plot again. All they ever do is scheme, ungrateful wretches the lot of them. We are betrayed and Richard York has much to answer for. Henry, I beg you to deal with them once and for all. You are too soft. These people must be kept submissive. Punish them and then we shall see how many are still dissatisfied."

At times her anger at the situation seemed to bewilder her and she found herself trembling. Basset noticed it and in the tense atmosphere, he felt the sweat run from his armpits. More leaked onto his forehead, cold clammy perspiration measuring his discomfort. Hissing and muttering under her breath, Margaret paced in front of him.

"Who leads this rabble?" she demanded.

Henry, brooding over Basset's words said nothing. Shifting uncomfortably the envoy was hesitant.

"I command you to tell us or you too will feel the scrape of a rope around your neck," she insisted.

"He goes by the name of John Mortimer, Your Grace," Basset said reluctantly. "He seems most organised, has a pleasing personality and when last seen he and his followers marched with a light step and in high spirits."

"Am I interested as to how you see this man? Kindly refrain from making out this enemy of ours is everyone's friend. High spirits, indeed. Let us see how high his spirits go when he faces the noose."

"Mortimer, Mortimer, not one of the Plantagenet Mortimer's surely?" Henry said, his fingers round a plum this time.

Basset shook his head. "Not to any one's knowledge, an ally perhaps. There are rumours of course. Some say he could be related to nobility, others murmur Mortimer is not his name at all, but it is Simon of Kent who vouches for him."

"Do we know this person, Simon of Kent?" enquired Henry.

"Minor nobility twice removed, so I'm told Sire," Basset replied.

"What of his allegiance?" Margaret asked abruptly. "Does he support the House of Lancaster?"

"I'm afraid I have no knowledge of that, Your Grace."

Thoughtfully touching the pearls knotted and looped round her neck, Margaret stared hard into Basset's eyes. She knew shiftiness when she saw it and would wager he lied. But proof, proof; never did she have proof of such things.

She knew in waiting for his orders Basset would expect them to come from her. She wouldn't disappoint him. A quick look at Henry and she saw he was eating more fruit and already turning the pages of a book. Straightening her shoulders and resolute, she spoke to Basset.

"We have decided. Send Government troops to Seven Oaks at once. Sir Humphrey Stafford of Grafton would do well enough to lead them. These rebels must go no further. Stop them and disperse them or do whatever you must to crush them. Is that understood?"

Looking up from the page, Henry frowned.

"Tell Stafford to send them back to their homes Basset, if he can. I don't like the thought of bloodshed. After all we do have a duty to our people. We should find a way to appease them. And are we safe here? Should we go to Kenilworth until they are dealt with?" he asked, sucking one sticky finger after another.

"Is that really necessary, my Lord Husband? I'm sure Mowbray will see we come to no harm."

His voice trembling at a rare attempt to defy his wife, Henry's lips were set in a stubborn line.

"Basset, be so kind as to inform Lord Mowbray we intend to leave immediately. Warwickshire suits us better and the castle more robust should my Lady Wife be in need of protection."

"I? Will you not come with me?" Margaret enquired with an incredulous expression.

Taking her hand, Henry gently pressed it to his lips. "Come, don't be vexed. I shall ride out with my troops, the people will expect it. After all that is what kings' do," he told her. "Basset, be good enough to advise Humphrey of Grafton he is to lead the force."

What little colour Margaret had in her cheeks faded and she looked aghast.

"Is that wise? You are hardly recovered from your illness."

Throwing his knee rug aside, Henry stood up. His was a frail figure compared with Basset, but his voice was strong and his intention firm.

"There is no need for further discussion, my sweet Lady Queen. I intend to lead my soldiers so let that be the end of it."

Deliberately avoiding meeting Margaret's eyes, Basset bowed low.

"It shall be done, Majesty." Leaving the room he heard Margaret's voice and interested, loitered a little longer.

"Since you have had your way and we must move, allow me to have mine. You must command every man who raises his hand against us is to be hoisted on the gibbet and we shall settle for nothing less. Promise me that, my Lord Husband, lest you find my bedchamber less than welcoming when next you visit. In fact so cold the spittle will freeze in your mouth," she said icily.

Chapter Nineteen

THEIR walk on the road to Seven Oaks took the marchers past fields of grain already about to turn into ripening swathes of ochre; and along tracks segmented by dry stone walls sprouting thin rooted ivy-leafed toad flax in purple drapes. A dense sweetness wafting from dog roses and wild honeysuckle perfumed the air had the men the inclination to smell it. But theirs was a march of purpose with no time to notice such things.

Spirits were flagging as the loads they carried began to feel heavy. With longbows pressing hard into aching flesh, they were bemoaning the state of their boots as flints ripped into leather and dust turned them a shade of sullen grey. At the very end of the procession children's laughter was changing into incessant whining as hunger bit their bellies and tiredness bowed their thin legs. Only the wealthy landowners, squires and shop owners carried plenty of sustenance in their pouches and enough ale to wash it down.

Once they reached Seven Oaks, they would find Knole Park close by and Jack was anxious to reach there before dusk. He was struggling with an unfamiliar mount after his went lame and this was a white beast with spirit. The horse preferred to prance sideways, rolling its eyes and huffing wild snorts of breath. When not trying to control the animal, the passing of mile after steady mile afforded him time to contemplate his affairs at home.

He recalled Mariamne's displeasure when she learnt of his departure with a measure of distaste. He wasn't surprised when he saw the distrust on her face once he told her he was leaving. Going away to seek work, he told her. Her father should be pleased that he was a good husband trying to provide for her. They couldn't exist on the pittance he gave his daughter. Was nothing he did ever right?

Begrudgingly he admired her attempt to try what ploy she might to stop him going. First she spat angrily at him then fawned over him with pitiful entreaties and finally wept so loudly he covered his ears. He felt no shame that nothing she did moved him and even wondered if she might have lanced Fireflanel's leg with some dirty implement in order to render him unfit to ride. If his last image of her, red-eyed and distraught, was meant to weaken him it failed. Riding away from the house all he could think was how old she looked.

When his horse suddenly skittered and its hoof caught the edge of a rabbit hole, it jolted him out of his thoughts. Only his excellent horsemanship saved him from a fall.

"God's bones, you hairy beast, you nearly took me down," he exclaimed loudly, red-faced with the effort of tugging at the reins trying to guide the horse straight. Those riding just ahead of him turned and made no effort to suppress their amusement.

"Come Captain, be firm, handle her as you would a reluctant virgin," Marek shouted back to him amidst ribald laughter.

Somewhere amongst the male voices Jack heard the sound of girlish giggles. Nonplussed he looked about him. There was a girl walking on the track close to the hedgerow watching him with wide-set saucy eyes. Her sun-touched face was framed by a mop of unrestrained light brown curls with a battered wide-brimmed hat atop them.

"I could have fallen," he said by way of explanation, but it sounded weak and abashed he concentrated on looking ahead.

When a few moments later he gave a sideways glance he saw her running fast between the hawthorn and briar. Looking round, he shouted.

"What do they call you?"

She didn't look back and then she vanished. He could see no sign of her among those on foot trooping doggedly behind so shrugging he rode on.

They entered Seven Oaks quietly. First the riders, then those on foot and at the rear the supply carts. Despite the main highway to London being at the end of the street, they were surprised how deserted the market place looked. Even the usual pilgrims and travellers were missing, doors were firmly closed and shutters swung idly at dark windows. Walter de Gray cantered up beside Jack.

"Odd don't you think, 'tis too quiet for my liking. Where is everyone?"

Passing empty stalls they saw wares lay unattended. There were black rye loaves drying in the last of the sun and bundles of lavender scattered by a breeze out to make mischief. The same fickle wind swept through the open slaughter house doors carrying the reek of rotting entrails and stale blood, yet even the last bellows of a beast were absent.

Growing evermore uneasy, Jack turned to Walter and beckoning Merek and Barda to join them said in a concerned voice.

"I smell something amiss. Ride down the ranks, tell them all to be careful lest there is a trap. Call the carts forward. The women and children travel on them so I want them close and it will be costly if we lose our supplies. Barda, we need you at the back of the column, take others on horseback with you and keep good watch."

Raising his hand, Barda turned about and made for the rear. Once the word was passed the atmosphere immediately changed and the marchers fell silent. Better armed than the peasants, the squires kept one hand on their swords, the Friar fumbled for his Rosary with agitated fingers and the commons grasped their longbows more tightly. As if his bible would offer divine protection the Rector of Mayfield brandished it aloft whilst muttering under his breath. In different circumstances he made a comical figure, but this was no time for laughter.

They passed the last house in the row, larger and smarter than its neighbours. It looked newly built and its timbered gables and air of affluence set it apart from the impoverished dwellings around it. Without a word, Merek pulled at Jack's sleeve and nodded towards a side wall. Against the lime wash the figure stood tall. He held a mace that threw black orbs of shadow onto the brickwork as it swung from his hand. Then it moved quickly and they heard the sound of a door closing.

"I began to think everyone got carried off by the pestilence. Now we know they hide behind their doors, but why?" Jack said quietly. "Can word have spread so quickly of our march and they are afeard of us?"

"Things don't bode well," Merek whispered uneasily. "Why was he armed?"

At the turn of the road they passed the gallows. It stood empty with the hemp noose swinging each time the humid air collected enough strength to tug at it. Entering Knole Park through an avenue of trees they could see for the first time the deer park, rolling greens and in the distance the grey turrets of the house.

Wary as he was, Jack couldn't have known what lay ahead. All he could hear were the trudging steps of thousands behind him, all he could smell was their rank body odour and the dusty earth now parched for want of rain. All he could see was their stopping place a short way ahead.

When the word *"Fire"* clattered through the trees, lines of arrows were already airborne and whistling towards them.

Uttering bellows of intent, The King's force of foot soldiers sprang out from their hiding place behind the leafy boles of the chestnut trees. In an instant the orderly march disintegrated into chaos. Jack's shock was momentary. Rearing up, his horse gave an unnatural scream of fear, but Jack, pulling out his broadsword and shouting angrily plunged it between the soldiers hacking his way forward.

Though outnumbered, the king's pike men were better armed. Steel clanged on steel and heavy breaths mingled with shouts and screams from both sides. The women joined in hurling clods of earth and flints which darkened the air. Hand-to-hand fighting demands concentration and when Jack glanced round him he was impressed by the strength and tenacity of the peasants. Longbows flung aside they wielded knives, axes and pitchforks with jaw-clenched determination and the soldiers fell.

Scared and excited, Jack heard the rebel's cries.

"For Mortimer, for Mortimer!" they screamed.

Then he felt his boot tugged and a soldier jabbed up at him with a spear which slid through the leather and then his breeches with a flash of silvery blade. Closing his eyes, Jack waited for more. It didn't come. Roaring in rage he spun his axe round slicing across the man's brow so his helmet flew off. His skull cracked and opened like the top of an egg.

Hacking and stabbing, Walter and Barda fought alongside the lofty figure of Merek. Amidst screams and shrieks they all gave good account of themselves. A blade to an unprotected throat, a turn of a finger to oust an eyeball or a vicious blow with an axe to cleave a skull in two, their fighting skills were untutored, but deadly. Soon the troops began to edge back and sensing an advantage Jack stood up in his stirrups and waving his sword yelled.

"Keep going, brave men. By God we shall win this so no time for faint hearts, do you hear me?"

When of one accord the soldiers started running, Jack led the final charge through the park. Nostrils flaring, the terrified deer thundered as one for cover in the trees where they stood flanks quivering and their eyes rolled into corners.

Shattered by the sounds of battle the tranquil parkland air took on a macabre atmosphere of menace as Jack's men chased the fleeing enemy and turned the soft green sward into a broad scarlet lake. It amounted to no more than crude butchery as the soldiers were brought down without compassion and with no one to weep for them.

As the fighting became sporadic, Jack attempted to count those lost from his followers, but it was hard to be sure when so many bodies littered the ground. In the park, Barda rested on his sword in an effort to catch his breath, whilst Walter, like a bright eyed rodent, scuttled from one fallen soldier to another dispatching them quickly should they still have a vestige of life. Only Merek still fought. Determination etched on his face by blood and sweat, he grappled with a boyish faced soldier.

Down on his knees, the lad held up his hands. He looked puny and vulnerable as he pleaded for his life, but the tall man towering over him was unmoved. With a vicious twist of his hand, Merek's dagger drew a thin red line with its honed tip from one ear to another and the young soldier swayed wide-eyed. As the grotesque mouth of his throat wound gaped so his bright blood arced and splattered onto Merek's distorted countenance.

"Son of a whore," he snarled with a grimace, scrubbing his hand across his eyes.

Raising the dagger again, he was about to strike, but with an imperceptible shudder the lad pitched forward and with a final spasm lay still. Merek bent his sinewy frame to clean his blade on the lad's ill fitting uniform, spat vile phlegm on his prostrate body and casually stepped over it to join Barda and Walter. Suddenly a great cheer went up with the realisation the battle was over. Fatigue forced them to sit down heavily along with others scattered about the park. It was where Jack found them.

"Methinks we did well," he said cheerfully, sheathing his sword.

Seeing the sun slipping quietly towards the horizon and shadows about to darken the light, he gave his orders.

"Time to rest when we've struck camp, eh my friends? We should build the fires high tonight just in case the king's forces need another lesson. Barda, I need you to tend to the wounded and get some to bury our dead. Look out for the women and children too. Tomorrow we march to Black Heath."

Anxiety flickered across Jack's tired face and he looked into the dusk uneasily. Wherever he turned his head a backdrop the colour of pitch seemed ever enveloping, but distant and unpredictable it told him nothing. Peaceful enough, he thought, yet all the same he felt himself shivering.

Chapter Twenty

IN a sky coddled by an ebony blanket, the new moon looked no more than a thin brushstroke of silver. Its spindly beam journeying earthwards would do little for a traveller, but it served the king well. At the top of a steep incline above Seven Oaks he was safe from detection and able to look down in dismay at the sprawling camp in the park. Flanked by his trusted aides, Sir William Stafford of Grafton and Sir William Stafford of Somerset, they were a group of three although the occasional jingle of a harness marked a dozen or more of his personal bodyguards concealed amongst the trees.

Roaring log fires below them blazed long into the night and it wasn't hard for the watchers to see there were still those active in the camp. When the faint, but distinct sounds of roistering drifted their way Henry pulled a face.

"Drunkards the lot of them I don't doubt," he remarked quietly. "Such are the sort of men who rise up to protest, 'tis sad we lose good men by the hand of poor misguided wastrels."

Henry's genuine distress came as no surprise to his companions. He would grieve for his dead soldiers and the poor commons in equal proportion because that was the man he was. If he happened to notice William of Grafton exchanging a look of hopelessness with William of Somerset, he ignored it. He was well aware of what others thought of his sensitive and gentle manner. Some said it weakened the firm hand of a ruler. How deflated they became because his was a nature more suited to a dreamer than a monarch. His God wouldn't have him any other way, but he doubted they would understand.

Known to be an outspoken critic, William of Grafton sighed loudly. Henry heard him, but didn't heed him. He almost pitied him. Staring hard at the landscape, he remained pious. I only answer to my Maker, he happily told himself.

"We should leave Sire, lest we are seen," William of Somerset ventured, softly spoken and less forceful than his cousin.

"How many of my soldiers lost their lives today?" Henry asked ignoring the suggestion.

"There has been no final count Majesty, but it seems all but a few."

"And what was the fate of Humphrey of Grafton, did he fall too?"

"Regrettably his body was found amongst the dead, Sire."

"Then it seems these ignorant men will stop at nothing and wish to speak with their arrows as much as their mouths. Perhaps things would have gone better had I been amongst our troops. We must be better prepared next time," Henry said sadly.

"I doubt it, Sire. We should have sent a bigger force. The ambush worked well, we were let down with too few fighting men," William of Grafton said firmly. "These serfs are not organised, they are nought but a rabble with few weapons and even less skill. Today they were fortunate."

Henry's horse snickered restlessly setting off the other two. Shifting with a rattle of bridles and a series of snorts the noise carried in the still air. Looking pained, William of Somerset whispered.

"They will hear those damnable beasts. We shouldn't tarry here any longer."

Henry appeared unconcerned and continued.

"Fortunate perhaps, but don't underestimate this Mortimer fellow, whoever he is. I'm told he distinguished himself in France and is a more than capable soldier."

Dogged as usual, William of Grafton said, "Rumour Sire, that's all it is. Our forces are well trained and better equipped. He'll not get the better of your royal army again."

Henry yawned and hunched himself down into the depths of his ceremonial jacket for warmth. Turning his horse he moved it gently off the incline and onto flatter ground.

"There is nothing more for us here. Tomorrow we ride to Kenilworth, the Lady Queen is there alone," he said. Spurring his horse into a fast gallop the ground suddenly shuddered as the rest of entourage raced to keep up. If anyone in the camp heard their departure they were to drunk or too tired to be troubled.

* * *

On the flat land below and unaware of the royal visitor, Jack was tearing more strips from a piece of cotton. Wrapping them round his shin he attempted to sop up the blood still trickling down his leg. Then he laid his hand over it to ease the throbbing. The skirmish was short but brutal and he muttered his thanks for receiving a wound which whilst painful hadn't done serious damage. Barda's report about the injured marchers he found more troubling.

"More than a hundred dead and some with terrible injuries, probably won't last the night," he told him gravely. "I've got the womenfolk tending them. They'll do what they can. Those with scratches and the like should be ready to march come the morning. I fancy the Rector is likely to lose a leg. He's lying there cussing at the top of his voice and him being a Holy man too."

With a final pull at the crude bandage, Jack felt Barda's eyes on him. He was staring at the scar on Jack's arm.

"That was a nasty one, a lance by the look of it, where did you get that?"

"It was an accident," Jack mumbled.

Cursing inwardly at sight of the ugly knotted skin, he wished he had a finer badge of courage to identify him. He grunted and pulling his cape closer around him, shifted about on the hard ground to find a more comfortable place. Dead leaves bundled up in a spare shirt served as a pillow of sorts which crunched in his ear as he fidgeted. Finally, despite the moans from the wounded disturbing the silence he closed his eyes and fell into an uneasy sleep.

Chapter Twenty-One

BLACK Heath looked extraordinary. Whilst grasses of the nearby meadows at Greenwich were scorched and next to them the River Thames flowed at half its usual depth, the high point of the land on the Heath remained a leaden green covered by furze bushes. These were broken by masses of acerbic yellow flowers which washed their thorny evergreen with a buttery glaze. Underfoot bell heather sprigs clung close to the brittle earth, bare rooted trees were turned to dwarves by the constant bleak wind in winter and frail slithers of brown, Heath butterflies spiralled into flickering circles above the vegetation.

But on this day, it was neither leaf or flower nor the heath's resistance to the sun that made it a spectacle. Midway across the heath the stony soil gave way to a steep sandy plateau devoid of everything apart from a few stunted shrubs and a circle of large stones. They knew it as *Gorsedd,* the Great Seat and it was here people were gathering when word spread of Jack's arrival with his rebels from Kent. With a sight of Essex, Kent and Surrey spread out below them they drifted in their thousands anxious to catch sight of the man they heard tell would be their saviour.

Set apart from the masses, Richard and Simon were also waiting. Seeking shade for their horses they stood under the protection of a gnarled and deformed Scots Pine on the edge of the plateau. Such were the winds which lashed the heath it was unable to grow strong and tall so it threw out its needle-clad arms in tortuous shapes.

Suddenly they saw the crowds press forward to surround an upright figure on horseback carrying a standard. The small pennant fluttered defiantly in blue and gold picked up from the fallen at Knole Park.

"So Mortimer arrives," Simon stated, watching the long procession following Jack surge onto the plateau.

"John's victory at Seven Oaks has been well received and now every man wants to be associated with him. It will serve us well when we march on London," Richard said, with a satisfied smile.

Urging their horses forward they left their position and rode toward the centre of the plateau, where Jack reigned in his mount. Flushed and elated he looked every inch the hero the crowds wanted. Standing proudly beside him Barda, Walter de Gray and Merek pushed back those too eager to be close to Jack and all the while voices swelled expressing their admiration.

Simon kept his distance, unwilling it seemed to risk spoiling his clothes by mingling with the commons. Waving a fastidious hand at Richard he pointed into the heart of the melee.

"Tell him we need to speak to him. It's not safe for him to linger here too long. The King's advisors will be more than a little displeased by the rout at Seven Oaks. Revenge will be sweet for them if they can bring Master Mortimer before the courts. Besides we have much to discuss so I can prepare the proclamation of grievances." Gently fingering the gold chain which acted as a closure for his crimson velvet cape, he rested back in the saddle.

It took Richard several moments to break his way through to reach Jack. Hoping the crowd would open a passageway for him he guided his steed carefully through them, but he was largely ignored as the excitement mounted. Finally Jack and his henchmen caught sight of him and it was Merek who used his height and strength to hold the eager crowd at bay.

"Back, back, the lot of you. Can't you see there are others who wish to speak to your Captain," he roared, holding his lance above his head to make his point.

"Greetings, my friend, 'tis good to see you," Richard enthused when he reached Jack's side. Then seeing the torn and bloodied leg of Jack's breeches, he frowned. "You are hurt?"

Dismissing his concern with a grin, Jack said.

"Pay no heed. It's no more than a flea bite." His expression changed. "But we lost good men and that troubles me."

He was indeed remorseful. Whilst he felt cold indifference to the death of an enemy, he was beginning to respect the men he lead and he felt their loss keenly. Richard threw out his arm in an expansive gesture behind him.

"Look how many have gathered here, we think some five thousand. Those brave warriors would be proud," he reassured. "Simon waits for us, we should go to him. He's found a quiet place where we can work on the complaints to be sent to the King."

Seeking out Merek, Jack gave his instructions.

"Find the others and make some order. We must be ready for anything, but remember this is a march of protest. Set some to dig the fire pits and see everyone is fed. Whilst I am gone you must lead like the good men you are."

* * *

Following Simon and Richard, Jack was beginning to wonder where exactly they were going. Two muscular henchmen rode either side of Simon, both carrying lances and dressed similarly in coarse brown serge doublets. Circling the Point, Simon led them on to a place where several flat grey stones of large proportions half concealed a black gape in a rock. Thorny shrub grew wantonly alongside the stones and it seemed nothing recent had passed. Despite the dusty ground there wasn't a print of either man or animal underfoot and the place looked desolate.

With his torch lit, Simon slid from his horse beckoning them to follow. All three needed to squeeze through an opening he indicated and found themselves at the top of a roughly hewn flight of narrow steps. Close to them on either side the walls rippled moisture running slowly drop by drop, pooling on the treads. Halfway down a wave of fusty air rose up to meet them and the smell of cold and damp chilled them after the warmth above ground. The only natural light came from above where slivers of pale daylight wormed their way through cracks in the vaulted stone roof.

"What in God's name is this place?" Jack murmured as they reached the bottom.

"Remarkable isn't it?" Simon replied picking a shred of cobweb off his cape with a delicate pincer movement of his thumb and forefinger. "A well preserved secret I might tell you," he said in hushed tones, leading the way through a short tunnel and into a wide cavern.

Head flung back in order to stare up into the looming space above them Richard was as surprised as Jack. "I had no idea this was here?" he whispered.

Shadows cast by their torch flame made bold corners from insignificant turns in the stone and created giants from the three men's shapes. Somewhere more water was dripping. This time the sound was audible, regular and unthreatened as it must have been for hundreds of years. Jack was overawed by the enormity of it all.

"Not this but these, follow me," Simon said secretively as if he were leading them to a horde of precious gold. A long winding passage led them into a further two equally spacious caverns all with the same similarity of workmanship. Crude tools chipping and knapping the stone and flint walls made them into sizeable rooms and still Simon showed them more. Striding importantly down a further few feet he revealed a well topped by a pool of placid water. Swooping low, he cupped his hand bringing it up to his mouth with a grand gesture so water flooded through his fingers.

"Sweet as a honeyed fruit," he warbled, dabbing his chin with a silk kerchief. Then beckoning them he led them round a sharp corner. It was little more than a niche in the wall, but it made Jack and Richard freeze their steps. Above a stone slab alter in a curve of hollowed out stone the wooden effigy stared directly at them. The man's head was large and his features crudely hewn. Green leaves streamed from his ears, nostrils and bulbous mouth and he was crowned with a fearsome set of antlers.

"The Hunter, what good fortune we find him here," Richard whispered.

Unprepared to find the Horned God displayed in such a place, Jack was finding it difficult to voice his thoughts. Swallowing hard, he tried sweeping away the images of

Mammy. On her knees at the time of the full moon she would ask that energy be delivered or meditate on the eve of a Sabbat so they should both be attuned to Nature's flow of harmony or so she told him. But the Green Man, Herne the Hunter here in the caverns stole his breath away. Seeing Richard about to show his respect, he too moved forward.

Simon observed his companion's genuflection before the deity with a serious expression waiting until they rose again before saying.

"Herne will oversee our journey and we shall sacrifice to him on the eve before we leave for London."

Keeping their eyes lowered the three backed away from the place only looking up again when they were back in the chamber beyond the well. Each lost in the power of the moment there was silence until Simon coughed gently and tapping his satchel said, "I have with me writing materials and intend to address the matters which bring us here. When our grievances are set out, I shall send word to the Court to send an embassy to us. Until then this is where we shall stay until you leave for London, Master Mortimer."

"Me? Are you both not travelling with us?" Jack asked, hesitant after the sight of the effigy.

"I have yet to decide," Simon replied, opening his satchel.

Setting out his writing requisites, he started writing. It took several hours until he was satisfied the proclamation matched his thoughts and could be presented to the monarch. Every so often he consulted Richard and occasionally Jack. With laborious care and his quill scratching noisily across the sheets of vellum he laboured until finally he set his pen down and slumped wearily back on his stool to peruse his work.

Anxious how the camp was faring, Jack said, "Until you need me, I have much to do and the camp requires my attention. The King's forces will not want to be beaten again so I must be sure we are fighting company if needs be."

He kept his voice low, but still it bounced against the stone and echoed through the emptiness. Richard and Simon had their heads together over the proclamation and merely nodded.

With Merek and his two companions, Jack walked the length of the camp spread across the plateau. They were met by several crackling fires and at the largest the women were tending to an ox revolving on a spit. Fed by dripping fat globules the flames stirred into a frenzy of reds and blue which leapt through the brushwood sending odours of roasting meat drifting across the plateau.

"Seems a week since I last tasted a good meal," Merek grumbled.

It was easy for Jack to see how efficient his henchmen were. Divided into cohorts of foot soldiers, the numbers were huge. Then in a separate area of ground, those of higher status with their attendants made more comfortable arrangements. Each set up a shelter with their personal bedding and tethered their horses close by. On the edge of the camp the carts were turned broadside for protection and here the women and children organised themselves. Jack's trained eye moved swiftly over the order which now existed. For a moment he thought he recognised the laughing girl he'd seen earlier, but when he focussed properly it wasn't her after all. It surprised him he felt disappointed.

"You've done well," he told his companions, bringing a grin to their dusty and tired faces. "They look like a proper army now. We are well placed here to repel all who attempt to thwart our purpose."

Leaving his horse in Barda's care and carrying his few possessions, Jack returned to the caverns. In the largest of them more torches added extra light sending quavering silhouettes to prance their shapes on the walls. Beneath them, Richard still squatted on the floor watching with weary patience as Simon muttered the words he'd written quietly to himself. He'd taken off his hat and resting his head on his hand one finger absentmindedly twisted a curl of hair. Once dark it now showed a heavy lacing of silver whilst his bushy eyebrows remained a startling ebon black. Hearing Jack's step he quickly looked up.

"Ah, John, the complaints are ready, but I need to read them to you and Richard. It may well be what we ask is not suffice though I think 'tis little I've forgotten. It would have been easier for me to write it in French, but there are some who would not understand." His lip curled very slightly. "And as for those who cannot read . . ." His voice tailed away and he shrugged. "So I shall be mindful of your thoughts when I have finished."

Clearing his throat before picking up the sheet of vellum he twisted until sufficient light fell on the words.

"These be the points, cause and mischiefs of gathering and assembling of us, the King's liege men of Kent, the fourth day of June the year of our Lord 1450, the reign of our sovereign Lord the King XX1X, which we trust to Almighty God to remedy, with the help and grace of God and of our

sovereign Lord the King, and the poor commons of England, and else we shall die therefore.

We, considering that the King our sovereign Lord, by insatiable, covetous, malicious persons that daily and nightly are about his Highness, and daily inform him that good is evil and evil is good."

It was a strong start and Simon paused to take breath before he droned the next portion.

"Item. They say that our sovereign is above his laws to his pleasure, and he may make it and break it as he pleases, without any distinction. The contrary is true, or else he should not have sworn to keep it.

Item. They say that the commons of England would first destroy the king's friends and afterward himself, and then bring the Duke of York to be king so that by their false means and lies they may make him to hate and destroy his friends, and cherish his false traitors. They call themselves his friends, and if there were no more reason in the world to know, he may know they be not his friends by their covetousness.

Item. They say that it were great reproof to the king to take again what he has given, so that they will not suffer him to have his own good, nor land, nor forfeiture, nor any other good but they ask it from him, or else they take bribes of others to get it for him.

Item. It is to be remedied that the false traitors will suffer no man to come into the king's presence for no cause without bribes where none ought to be had. Any man might have his coming to him to ask him grace or judgment in such case as the king may give.

Item. They say that whom the king wills shall be traitor, and whom he wills shall be not, and that appears hitherto, for if any of the traitors about him would malign against any person, high or low, they would find false many that should die a traitor for to have his lands and his goods, but they will suffer the king neither to pay his debts withal, nor pay for his victuals nor be the richer of one penny.

Item. The law serves of nought else in these days but for to do wrong, for nothing is spread almost but false matters by colour of the law for reward, dread and favour and so no remedy is had in the Court of Equity in any way.

Item. We say our sovereign Lord may understand that his false council has lost his law, his merchandise is lost, his common people is destroyed, the sea is lost, France is lost, the king himself is so set that he may not pay for his meat nor drink, and he owes more than ever any King of England ought, for daily his traitors about him where anything should come to him by his laws, anon they take it from him.

Item. They ask gentlemen's goods and lands in Kent and call them rioters, and traitors and the king's enemies, but they shall be found the king's true liege men and best friends with the help of Jesus, to whom we cry day and night with many thousand more that God of His grace and righteousness shall take vengeance and destroy the false governors of his realm that has brought us to naught and into much sorrow and misery.

Item. We will that all men know we blame not all the Lords, nor all those that are about the king's person, nor all gentlemen nor yeomen, nor all men of law, nor all bishops, nor all priests, but all such as may be found guilty by just and true inquiry and by the law.

Item. We will that it be known we will not rob, nor plunder, nor steal, but that these defaults be amended, and then we will go home; wherefore we exhort all the king's true liege men to help us, to support us, for whatsoever he be that will not that these defaults be amended, he his falser than a Jew or Saracen.

Item. His true commons desire that he will remove from him all the false progeny and affinity of the Duke of Suffolk and to take about his noble person his true blood of his royal realm, that is to say, the high and mighty prince the Duke of York, exiled from our sovereign Lord's person by the noising of the false traitor, the Duke of Suffolk, and his affinity. Also to take about his person the mighty prince, the Duke of Exeter, the Duke of Buckingham, the Duke of Norfolk, and his true earls and barons of his land, and he shall be the richest king Christian . . ."

Struggling to follow the list of complaints, Jack almost missed Simon's hesitation as he came to the penultimate item. Not sure he was hearing right he looked first at Richard, but he was staring up at the lofty space above them. Then glancing at Simon again he said, "My pardon for interrupting you, but are we, the poor commons asking for a new king? If so 'tis the first I've heard of it. It is those who surround him are to blame. They offer cruel oppression and rule like tyrants and the king is too weak to control them. It is them we must thank for our poor conditions and the insufferable burden of taxes that are forced upon us. But for all the people's disappointment with King Henry, I doubt they feel the need to be rid of him in favour of Richard, Duke of York."

"Enough," Simon said angrily. "I conceal nothing. We come together to support the commons not mislead them. It is just a matter of words, now pray may I continue?"

Jack looked again at Richard, but still he avoided his eye. Awful images flashed through Jack's mind. He knew well enough there would be no mercy spared on traitors and for a terrible moment he wondered if he'd been cuckolded. Puzzled, he barely heard Simon reading aloud the next item.

"Item. Where we move and pray that some true justice with certain true Lords and knights may be sent into Kent for to inquire of all such traitors and bribers, and that the justice may do upon our sovereign Lord *direct his letters patent to all the people there universal openly to be read and cried, that it is our sovereign Lord's will and prayer of all his people truly to inquire of every man's government and of defaults that reign, neither for love, favour, dread, nor hate, and that due judgment shall be forthwith and thereupon."*

John Mortimer
Simon of Kent

Signed for and on behalf of the good men of Kent

* * *

At first, Simon was unsure whether to put his name to the paper. It might not look well should the rebellion fail. There again assuming it would be successful he could benefit handsomely if it were seen that he played a major part in events. Lost in thought he nibbled the end of his quill then modesty not being second to his nature he added his signature. He rolled the vellum up with slow precise movements and looked expectantly at Jack and Richard.

"I have signed this too on behalf of the men of Kent?" he said waving his quill to demonstrate how he executed the signature which was small and pedantic, much like Simon himself. "And I don't believe Squire Pultenery could have done better." Reaching for his ring he carefully impressed a crossed sword seal.

"It reads well," Richard observed, nodding thoughtfully. Still uneasy, Jack gnawed a finger nail. Tapping the quill on his knee, Simon looked expectantly at him.

"Well, Master Mortimer, what think you?" he asked impatiently.

"I believe you will find the commons still disappointed. They have needs and I hear no mention of them," Jack replied firmly.

"And what might they be?" Simon enquired curtly. Seeing the look of concern on Jack's face, Richard gave Simon a meaningful look.

"Come Simon, you know well enough," he said quietly. "Their conditions are harsh and many struggle with arduous labour and poor working conditions. Most I spoke to have asked that the Statute of Labourers be repealed for their lords and masters make it intolerable for them as things stand. Why else do you think so many join the uprising? After all 'tis their social welfare they complain of and it must be included in these grievances."

"I insist you include mention of reform and name such men as are false to our well being in Kent," Jack persisted.

For a long moment silence prevailed. A puce colour seeped up from Simon's collar and flooded his cheeks as he fought to control his annoyance.

"You, Master Mortimer forget yourself. You were asked to lead this uprising on behalf of the commons that's all. I am following instructions which I intend to do."

His temper bettering him, Jack clenched his fists.

"And methinks you sir, have fanciful notions which I am not privy too," he retorted. Then he felt a slight pressure on his arm as Richard moved closer.

Suddenly the cavern echoed with loud laughter which penetrated the heavy stone surrounding them and turned it hollow. As indeed was Simon's attempt to pacify the situation.

"Fie Master Mortimer, we are on the same side remember," he said, forcing a more amiable expression. "Very well, I shall draft your requests at the bottom if that suits you, else I shall need more paper," he said evenly. "Go both of you. I'm in need of victuals so make sure a tasty slice of meat or two comes my way."

Watching Jack and Richard disappear up the steps, Simon smiled again, but it reflected no good humour. Fools he thought, still it would be prudent of him to keep up the pretence with the gullible commons. Pultenery as much as said his instructions were from Richard, Duke of York and as his loyal liege man he would never disobey. Perhaps Mortimer and Richard were right though, he reflected. The commons would soon lose interest in an uprising if there was nothing in it for them. With a heavy sigh he stretched out the vellum, reached for the quill and after considering for a moment, started writing.

"Requests:

Item, taking of wheat and other grains, beef, mutton, and other victual, the which is importable hurt to the commons, without provision of our sovereign Lord and his true council, for his commons may no longer bear it.

Item, the Statute upon labourers, and the great extortioners of Kent, that is to say Baron Saye and Sele, Slegge, William Crowmer, Isle and Robert Est.

Item, they say that the King should live upon his commons, and that their bodies and goods be the King's; the contrary is true, for then needeth he never Parliament to sit to ask good of his commons."

Signed
John Mortimer

The King's liege man and Captain of Ye Rebels in Kent.

Paying particular attention to the second signature, Simon's close set eyes searched the words he'd added and then he nodded. Smiling complacently, he rolled up the vellum and resealed it to await the arrival of the King's embassy. Thoughtful, he sat for awhile considering the man they called John Mortimer. He was undoubtedly intelligent and astute too, but quite how much so had now become clear when he challenged him over the mention of the Duke of York. What else might he suspect? Could he be dangerous if he thought he was being used? Was it folly to run the risk of going to the Tower because their hopes were carried by nothing more than a swashbuckling adventurer?

A ridge of sweat sat on Simon's brow and he sat fiddling with his quill pen so violently that it suddenly bent in two. Feverishly he searched through the oddments of unused vellum until he found an adequate sheet, but then he had rendered his pen almost unusable. It was a delay he didn't want and haste sent him ferreting through his satchel until his fingers closed round another quill.

Taking a series of deep breaths, he attempted to calm himself whilst an idea became clearer in his mind. Then pulling the paper closer he started writing.

Chapter Twenty-Two

Kenilworth
Warwickshire

LIKE an inland sea the waters of the Great Mere concentrated the eye. Today its usual placid surface was puckered as the breeze swept back and forth over it. A pair of black swans allowed the ripples to carry them effortlessly across the brooding olive coloured water. Otherwise the expansive surface was without any sign of life.

At the window of one of the state apartments, Margaret's expression was as dark as the bird's plumage as she too brooded. Things were not going well, not well at all. Her displeasure cast a pall over the chamber and the embassy shuffled his feet nervously.

"Has the King seen this?" she asked tightly, tapping the roll of vellum against the casement frame.

Taking a breath to steady his voice, the flushed embassy replied.

"No Majesty, he has not yet returned from hunting."

"I suppose as usual it will be my decision that my Lord Husband will depend up on," Margaret said impatiently, pressing her fingers to her temple.

She recoiled from the pain. Sometimes I fear a seizure when the pain comes, she thought, fighting to stay calm. The apothecary assured her it was no more than an irritable nerve which jigged in her head when she was tired, but she often questioned his abilities. Her face remained impassive as she gestured to the embassy.

"Very well you may go," she told him, turning to scan the horizon for any sign of the hunting party returning. He bowed low and she only waited long enough to hear the door closing behind him before reaching for her vial of floral water. Pouring it liberally onto a wisp of a lace kerchief the aroma of peppermint and feverfew filled the room. Pressing the kerchief close to her forehead she inhaled deeply until the vapours stung in her nostrils and brought tears to her eyes. Attacked by a violent fit of coughing she swayed on her feet groping for the casement for support.

Catherine, the most trusted of her ladies and confidant, hurried forward. With a gentle hand she guided Margaret to a chair with soft murmurings of comfort.

"There, there my Lady Queen, you take too much upon yourself and you, little more than a child yourself. Let Cat soothe that poor head of yours," she said.

With a plump-fingered hand she stroked the cascade of bright hair which tumbled from under Margaret's three-cornered silk coif.

"Do you think I go mad as does my Lord Husband at times?" Margaret asked fearfully, her shoulders slumped and her hand gripped tightly round Catherine's.

"You, Your Grace, never. Whatever gave you such a foolish notion? Your pretty head is both wise and strong let no one tell you different. So is it those which upset you?" she asked, pointing to the rolls of vellum lying on the crushed blue silk of the royal lap.

Margaret's vitality was never far away. Straightening her back, her expression quickly changed.

"You may well ask is it these," she said scornfully, holding up the cream sheets. "The Complaints of the Poor Commons of Kent, that's what they call them. Look, see how many they write. Impossible, they are all impossible," she fumed, her hands quivering with anger so the paper rattled.

Catherine stood quietly with her hands held crossed against the skirt of her gown as was her place. Since it was unthinkable to enquire who might be responsible for her mistress's ire, she could only wait. Twice Margaret returned to the window, the hem of her gown swishing noisily in time with her ill-tempered steps. Craning her neck to look for Henry, she could be heard muttering. She even went to the top of the grand staircase. Holding tightly to the golden-grained oak banister, her pale fingers strummed the burnished wood as her face became increasingly dour.

"What keeps him," she asked Catherine impatiently. "Sometimes I think he cares more for a stag than he does running the country."

"Perhaps if Your Grace rested it would improve the pain," Catherine ventured.

"My head is quite perfect. It is my mind which aches on receiving this," Margaret said, waving the rolls of vellum with ferocity. "Who are these men of Kent who think they can demand such things. It is my opinion they are nothing more than wretches who should be treated as such."

She paced the chamber. The darkness in her blue eyes and pursed lips were a clear indication of her mood. Suddenly, as if she came to a satisfactory decision the furrows on her brow eased.

"I can wait no longer. Find someone to fetch me Thomas, Lord Scales, he will know what to do and make haste, dear Cat," she said firmly.

* * *

Thomas de Scales took Margaret by surprise or rather his eyes did. Perhaps she never looked closely enough, but she couldn't recall seeing such fervour in their brown depths before. He stood tall and strong- shouldered and when she invited him to sit he kept up his bearing even in the chair. Upright and military like the professional soldier he was, he waited for his orders.

"So my Lord Scales," Margaret said sweetly. "You are back from France at last. So many months since we last met. How was my homeland?"

"Battle weary as is all of the north, Your Majesty," he replied his words clipped as if even so much as one extra breath would be too precious to waste on a battlefield.

"But triumphant surely?" she countered."Now all of England's possessions are lost."

"Indeed, Your Grace, but it must test you sorely to see your country in such turmoil."

Margaret's laugh was brittle. "*Au contraire,* my Lord, this is our motherland now. Why should we mourn when we have all this," she said, with a nonchalant raise of one eyebrow.

His face expressionless, Scales stroked his neatly clipped beard thoughtfully.

"Yes indeed, Your Grace," he murmured. "My apologies if I am late. I intended arriving last evening, but the ride from Norfolk took me longer than expected. But now I am home at Scales Hall and once my affairs are in order, I intend to visit the Court more regularly. Your messenger said it was important I come to Kenilworth, so how may I be of service?"

Dipping her fingers into a platter of sweetmeats, Margaret selected a biscuit of marchpane decorated with gold leaf. Her small teeth nibbled the edge before discarding it to seek out another. Then she pushed the dish towards Scales who politely declined.

"Does the King join us?" he enquired, crossing one immaculately tailored leg over the other.

"His Majesty tired himself travelling back from London then insisted he go out hunting. Now he lies abed late," Margaret said, dabbing at biscuit crumbs on the dark pewter silk of her gown and then at a small piece lodged at the edge of a glowing emerald in her necklace. "I fear he often overdoes things, but he should be joining us at any moment. To save time, I shall enlighten you on the purpose of our request. I'm afraid my Lord, should you have hung up your sword, I must ask you to gird it again and raise a force of soldiers. We have insurgents presently camped at Black Heath and a man called Mortimer is their ringleader. He and his rebellious army must be dealt with once and for all."

She searched Scales face for a reaction, but there was none. Damnable man, he seems without emotion she thought. His credentials were impeccable she knew that, and his skill as a warrior second to none. He was loyal to the House of Lancaster too. She made sure of such in her enquiries. Before Scales thought to speak the door opened and Henry drifted in. In a long black gown dragging on the floor and nothing to lighten it except a small gold button at the neck, he looked as drab as his wife was gilded. A thick tome of a book, his constant companion of late, was tucked securely under his arm and a page hovering behind him carried his silk knee rug. Margaret rose immediately and bobbed.

"My Lord Husband," she said quietly.

Scales stood stiffly to attention.

"Good day, Sire."

Acknowledging them both with a gentle smile, Henry made straight for his favourite chair beside the window. Surprisingly he didn't open his book and was looking more animated than of late.

"You look well, Sire," Scales said warmly.

Not so Margaret, he thought, who he fancied looked pale and tired. Was it still Suffolk she mourned for or some fresh concern? She gave little away hiding all behind her intelligent forehead and uncommunicative eyes.

"Thank you, Scales," Henry replied. "I feel well although a trifle concerned that my Lady Wife has required you to lead an army so soon after the disasters in France. Have we men enough for such a task?"

"It will not be easy, but I will do my best, Majesty. Since a standard of rebellion has been raised it would appear we have no other choice. There are soldiers recently returned from France, but they seem to think that earns them the right to become idle and dissolute. I need better," Scales replied with a disarming smile.

Lingering beside Henry, Margaret emanated a subtle but forceful air. She was a powerful lady and not one to show any weakness.

"Nothing worthwhile is easy, my Lord which is why we have sent for you. You come with the highest of recommendations," she said with the ghost of a smile. Scales could have hardly stood taller. "Then I must do my utmost to justify such praise," he said levelly.

"So it is agreed, prepare for battle. Oh and my Lord Scales this time I shall ride out with you," Henry said in good voice.

Laying down her embroidery, Margaret looked aghast. "Will that be necessary, my Lord Husband? I fear for your health at such times."

Henry smiled fondly. "You worry too much. Lord Scales will protect me, won't you dear man?"

Scales swept the floor low with his hat.

"Sire, I am your liege man. Should so much as a thorn prick draw your blood, I will offer you my life," he said firmly, without a hint of expression in his eyes or the move of a muscle.

"There, my dear Lady, you see how well I shall be looked after. Besides I shall hope to offer some clemency to these poor people when we meet them," Henry said, compassionate as always.

Looking as if she were about to speak, Margaret frowned. Then thinking better of it she pursued a line of silk stitches. Watching the crewel needle plunging deftly through the canvas, Scales winced.

Chapter Twenty-Three

PULTENERY reached Bromley Common before Simon, but it was a well-used thoroughfare and much too exposed for a private meeting. Leaving his retinue, all members of his household including John Bailey, to wait by the roadside, Pultenery rode away in search of somewhere more secluded. He found it in a copse of birch trees where he could see his men and watch the road to London.

Simon approached badly dressed. His tastes in fashion were as usual most unfortunate, Pultenery thought, running a critical eye of his garments. A gaudy red neckerchief pushed up his extra chins, his coat was too tight and his black breeches touched in the wrong places. Greeting him with a disdainful sniff, he led him into the thicket.

"You're letter told me little. I hope it is important that you bring me all this way."

"I thought half way would suit us both, Squire Pultenery," Simon said, smarting from Pultenery's curt greeting. "There is an urgent matter I must discuss with you."

"Then I can only assume you have problems for why else would I be here?" Pultenery observed, reaching for his flask. Taking a quick swallow he shook his head as if to clear it. "Dust in my throat," he explained. "So go on man, I have no wish to linger all day."

Simon could see Pultenery seemed ill at ease, glancing round every time there was a rustling noise or the shiver of leaves disturbed the silence.

"It's John Mortimer. I think he may cause us trouble," Simon said hesitantly.

Pultenery uttered an exclamation of impatience.

"I thought you told me he was the right person. What is it, is he a poor leader?"

Shaking his head, Simon shuffled awkwardly in his saddle. Why did he think he could get the better of the Squire? The hawkish eyes held Devil lights in them and beneath the strangely bulbous nose were thin hard lips which were a straight as a rod. He even imagined the bony hands curled round the leather reign looked like talons. Pultenery's harsh voice put a stop to his mental images.

"I said can he lead the rebellion?"

"Indeed he can. He's proving to be an accomplished leader well liked by the men. We are in the thousands and yet they follow him to a man. No, I think it a little more serious," replied Simon struggling to keep the quaver out of his voice. "I believe he suspects we are using him in our quest to bring the Duke of York to his rightful place on the throne."

The relief he felt having announced such a thing showed clearly on his face. Pultenery's eyes looking at him from under their baggy lids held a cold glitter.

"I see," he said slowly. "Could he have found out your allegiance to the House of York?"

A look of astonishment registered on Simon's face. He took off his hat, fingering it with agitated movements of his hands.

"It is impossible, he cannot know that," he said vehemently. "I should lay down my life first should it be known abroad."

"That may well be the case should this uprising fail," Pultenery said in a humourless voice. "How much do you know about the man, Mortimer?"

"Almost nothing, I relied on his friend Richard de Courcy. He assured me Mortimer was the man to lead the rebellion," Simon said.

"But you met him before the start of the uprising?" Pultenery enquired, his eyes following a butterfly dancing in the sunlight.

"Indeed I did, several times. I thought him a likeable fellow if not a little brash. When the matter of a reward was mentioned he took little persuading," Simon remarked with a taut smile.

"Perhaps you might remember a man who can be bought is not always an honest one," Pulternery replied tightly.

Simon's nervous giggle received a severe frown and he quickly composed himself.

"I want you to speak to de Courcy, see if he can tell us more. I shall task my man, Bailey to see what he can learn. He's a good man and remarkably adept at pursuing the truth," Pultenery continued. "You do realise Lord Cromwell will permit no interference in his plans and I hope you have taken the necessary steps to reassure Mortimer."

Beginning to feel he was on safer ground, Simon relaxed, even allowing a pale smile to linger on his lips.

"I think you will approve of my actions, Master Pultenery. Mortimer wanted his own requests to be included on the proclamation. They are merely ideas these rebels have got in their heads. Men of some standing in Kent who they belittle and want rid of. Naturally I added them at the last and made sure his name was clear."

Constantly watching the road, Pultenery seemed only half aware of what Simon was saying. A cautious man he trusted few and if he were to have been followed it could have grave consequences. The thoroughfare was never quiet as travellers made their way back and forth between Kent and the capitol. Having seen nothing untoward, he was anxious to be on his way.

"Then that seems satisfactory and I'm sure Lord Cromwell will agree. Now if there is nothing else 'tis time I started back," he said, still somewhat distracted. Seeking reassurance, Simon persisted.

"So there is nothing more you would suggest I do if Mortimer becomes difficult?"

"No and don't summon me again. It's too dangerous now the rebellion has started. We shall not speak again until the *Falcon* is safely back where he belongs. The O'Neills are his kin and look after him well, but he wishes to leave Ireland as soon as he can. You do understand should anything go wrong, I shall not be able to protect you," Pultenery said severely.

Then with nothing more he departed leaving Simon bemused and not a little fearful.

* * *

Jack couldn't account for how many bows were lost as he ordered more to be made. Just as quickly as fresh yew staves were found so they were fashioned into longbows. Working through the night, the Fletcher's grumbled quietly the wood was too green, demanding ash for the arrows and goose feathers to fletch. Some thought Jack too fussy, but as a military man he knew the importance of good weaponry and none were prepared to complain openly.

"So did Simon say where he was going in such a hurry," Jack asked as he and Richard sat with the sheaves of arrow in need of straightening.

Driving the wood into the heel of his hand, Richard applied pressure to the slender shafts whilst Jack felt the tension of the flax. Stabbing arrows into the earth as they were finished was Merek's job and he was counting them carefully. Concentrating, Richard didn't answer until he was satisfied with his work and then he said in a low voice.

"Simon keeps his own counsel and what he does is his business. You would do well to remember that, John. I met him some years ago when he had need of one of my ships to carry some cargo to Ireland. I was told then to ask him no questions and nor would I today. It would be wise if you did the same."

It wasn't an answer Jack was expecting and served only deepen his doubt about Simon of Kent and the true purpose of the rebellion. Yet hadn't Mammy made it clear. What lay ahead was his destiny. Wealth, influence and fame, they were too potent a mix to jeopardize. Laughing, he got to his feet.

"Then I shall bind my tongue. There will be time enough when we are victorious, for now there is work to be done."

* * *

No one expected Simon to return with a fair face. They had learnt to accept his brooding frowns and morose look. But when he found Jack and Richard, he seemed even more discontented.

"All is not well," he said abruptly. "We met a traveller on our way back here. He was in London two days ago and it seems by all accounts the king has managed to assemble a force and is travelling here to Black Heath. He rides with Lord Scales and two Royal commanders, Stafford of Somerset and his mealy-mouthed cousin, Stafford of Grafton. Are we properly prepared?"

"Perhaps they only come to talk through the list of complaints, Simon," Richard said brightly. "There may even be good news before the day is done. Is it wise to welcome them with bows and maces?"

Rarely did anyone see Simon laugh, so the guffaw he uttered was both loud and unexpected.

"What good news is brought by a man who speaks from inside a visor? They say the force is not large, but heavily armed and the sun itself shields its eyes from the glare of full armour. No my friends, the only words it seems to me will be spoken by the end of a sword blade," he said dryly.

All around them the camp carried on its day. The air clattered with the sound of men sharpening blades and the tines of pitchforks, women with babes on their breast ministering to children, youngsters oblivious to danger inventing games with anything which came to hand. At first glance it might have looked harmonious, but word travelled quickly. Now the air held no innocence just the smell of sweat, tension and not a little foreboding. With barely a moment of thought, Jack's instincts told him what must be done.

"Then we have no time to spare. Merek, find Barda and Walter. We move to the Great Park. They'll never find us there, but we must go quickly." His dark eyes lit with merriment he continued. "Perhaps we play the king's men at their own game and take them by surprise as they did us at Knole."

"You mean a trap?" Richard said warming to the idea.

"Exactly," Jack said enjoying the respect the others were showing at his plan.

Within the hour they were gone. As if spirited away into the ether people and carts were nowhere to be seen and the empty camp silent. A few rags used as shelters from the elements hung forlornly from thorn bushes. The fires were no more than grey shale and dropped in haste on the track a solitary wooden stirring spoon was rapidly being overrun by ants in search of sustenance.

Chapter Twenty-Four

The Weald of Kent

AS they arrived at the last of the marshes and reached safer ground the quiet splashing noises were gradually dying away. Accompanied by his chosen trusted Thomas Scales, William of Grafton, William of Somerset, Henry headed the cohort. Knights, squires and men-at-arms followed close to their monarch. In their heavy armour they were unable to travel at any speed, but were picking their way carefully through the uncertain ground where water and coarse grasses could easily confuse the eye.

In their wet hose and sodden boots, discontented foot soldiers focussed their eyes on the miles of dark trees in the distance. All that separated them from their protective cover was an open plateau of hard sandstone and then undulating grass land which promised easier going. Reaching this renewed their vigour and soon they could be heard exchanging banter again.

Their long journey to Black Heath only to find the camp deserted had left the nobility arguing and indecisive. Scales and William of Grafton were ready to return to London, but determined they would not be outwitted, Henry, supported by William of Somerset insisted the rebels were in hiding and must be pursued. It left them all in sour moods.

"Are we sure they have taken refuge in the Great Park, Sire?" Scales persisted.

"It's obvious isn't it? These are poor commons. They will flee without thought and where better than the Park. They'll have not gone far, you see," Henry replied complacently. Dropping his visor, he urged his horse in a gallop leading the royal army towards the open land. Beyond it the shadow-freckled ground gave way to the dense foliage of a mighty forest.

* * *

With every intention of returning to Black Heath Jack ordered just enough food be cooked to keep the gripes at bay. Then armed with their longbows, maces and full bellies, he and his force settled down to wait.

"Are you sure they will follow us into the Park," Simon said with trepidation in his voice. Unaccustomed to the cut and thrust of battles he was beginning to look alarmed. Jack and Merek worked on stabbing their arrows upright into the soft loam of the forest floor.

"We've left enough tracks, they'll know where we are and I'll wager they'll be here before long," Jack told him. At first glance the thicket they were hiding in looked impenetrable. Years earlier a flood had cleansed the ground and as generations passed so the thicket was born. The tangle of thick vines and briars made it almost impossible to reach the middle of it, but being men of the land the rebels soon found the concealment they needed.

Stealthy and sure footed, they broke away into smaller groups and the forest sunk back into its undisturbed reverie. The sun at its zenith would provide the contrast they needed and when the king's forces first entered the forest the sudden shade would disorientate. That was the hope.

A short distance away, Barda and Walter made their own preparations as did the appointed leaders of the thousands of men in the forest. With no more than a hint of a rustle, arrowheads rested in the notches made by branches. Close up it looked as if the greenery carried misshapen iron fruits.

Jack sensed the king's army were coming before many of the others. It was a weird sensation that made his spine tingle and the hairs rise on the back of the neck. He was annoyed to see his hand trembling, but time was too short for him to dwell on it. There was already a faint rattling of spurs and an occasional voice, the owner too tardy to bother to lower it. Then their enemy burst through the trees bending holm oaks and striplings of hazel as if they were brushwood.

* * *

Sent ahead by the mounted force these were hard fighting men-at-arms streaming forward without any true idea of where the enemy might be, let alone they were heading into a trap.

With the sun at their backs they blinked hard adjusting their eyes to the dim interior of the forest. There was no time to waste and Jack's arm raised once. Singing a whining dirge, rebel arrows fell heavily. Searching for a weakness in an exposed neck, a tender thigh or a niche in a chest with remorseless ferocity, they ripped apart muscle and tendons, pinioned blood vessels and left behind the seeds of rampant infection.

Gaining a footing, the soldiers surged forward and for awhile the rebels were forced into a savage fight. Watching from a safe distance, Henry was appalled. When he saw his two Royal commanders, William of Grafton and William of Somerset fall almost simultaneously he thrust his hand to his mouth. With horrified eyes he searched for Thomas Scales in the melee. When he spotted him he saw him bringing his sword down with such force, the rebel lost his head in one blow. Glancing at the fallen in front of him, Henry wanted no more of it.

"Lord Scales! Enough!" Muffled by his visor, his harsh cry had little impact.

Growing more concerned, Henry edged his horse forward, but he stopped short of the first bodies. Scales must have seen the movement because he immediately turned broadside against the rush of rebels and brought his horse level with Henry's stallion.

"Go back, Sire 'tis too dangerous," he screeched. Responding to his remark with a wave of his mail gauntlet, Henry shook his head.

"Enough, Scales. Enough I say. Call our force off. Leave this rabble to enjoy their victory – this time. We are in a bad place. A very bad place and they come at us like rabid dogs. We have lost two good knights and who knows how many more."

"I saw the cousins' fall, Majesty, but I have avenged their deaths," Scales chuckled bitterly.

The trumpeter's resonant command brought with it a sudden lull. Bewildered, the men-at-arms fell back and the rebels were left swinging their maces into empty air. It was impossible to ignore the repulsive results of the slaughter. Severed limbs defiled the soft green moss, fragments of chain mail snagged on the gently unfurling emerald ferns and leaves were speckled red. Not content with that a river of carmine snaked its way through the crunchy brown pine needles underfoot.

Turning toward the freedom of the grassland, Henry saw a horseman on a distinctive white horse break from the cover of the thicket. The cut of his clothes didn't denote him as a serf, but neither did he have the bearing of a nobleman. With breathtaking bravado Jack rode straight towards Henry. With a toss of his untamed dark hair and a smile to melt hoar frost he acknowledged his monarch with a flourish of his battle club before wheeling his horse and racing back into the forest. Far from alarmed, Henry seemed bemused.

"Impudent dog," Scales shouted after Jack. "Your liver streaked guts should hang on a bush should I catch you."

Taken aback, Henry turned to the knight.

"You are too hasty, my Lord. After all he is one of my people."

"That Sire, is the man they call John Mortimer, Captain of Kent and the man who leads the rebellion."

"He has pluck, I'll give him that," Henry replied and the admiration in his voice caused Scales to despair.

* * *

No more than twenty five souls were lost that day. The soft forest floor made for easy digging and after ten of the rebels were accounted for they were hastily buried in shallow graves. No such decency was permitted for the king's forces. They were left for scavengers to dispose of, but not until they were relieved of anything of value.

Jack wasn't averse to looting. He slid from his horse whilst Simon and Richard waited impatiently and approached William of Somerset. He was lying on his side in a bed of pink-tinged forest flotsam, the arrow at the base of his neck propping him up off the ground. Jack carelessly tossed him onto his back with his booted foot and as he did so Somerset's livery collar sprang free. It was bloodied and black earth besmirched the delicate silver links. About to bend down to it, Jack heard Richard's warning.

"Leave it, John. The King bestows it on those he wishes to honour. It will not go well for you if you are found with it. Best you send it to Hell with its owner."

"Then he shall bequeath me this," Jack called, recklessly tugging the armour off the corpse.

The glower on Simon's face said more than any words. Ignoring him, Jack quickly stripped the body of its sword, silver mail, hose and breastplate. Getting the dented bowl helmet off was more difficult. It needed several moments to free it, but finally with the gauntlets stuffed in his belt he loaded everything onto his horse.

Mammy had no time for the *wanderers*, the so called occasional aimless travellers and their ways. She told him they were not to be trusted, take anything so they would. The blush of his conscience stained his cheeks when he whispered. "Hush Mammy," under his breath, but it went unnoticed as they called in the rebels and made haste back to Black Heath.

Chapter Twenty-Five

The Palace of Westminster

RALPH, Lord Cromwell wasted no time on fripperies and his bed chamber was like the man himself. What little furniture there was numbered among them a canopied four-post bed with drapes of a sullen blue, a heavy oak chest its dark exterior relieved by piece of pewter and a few carved chairs with hard straight backs. Designed to be functional rather than comfortable, Edward Hastings in particular found his particularly uncomfortable under his skinny buttocks. Sir John Stanley, being rather more generously endowed in his posterior area was more troubled by the carved acorns which protruded into his shoulder blades.

"So, what is the mood of the Chamber today now they have had time to consider events in the Great Park?" Cromwell asked in clipped tones.

"A second defeat is worrying," Hastings ventured.

Grim faced, Cromwell swung round to Stanley. "Perhaps you would care to be bolder, Sir. Are the good men of the Chamber merely *worried* because I find that a ridiculous understatement."

Shuffling on his chair, Hastings looked apologetic. "What I meant was . . ."

Rudely interrupting, Cromwell glared at Stanley.

"Well?"

"There are differing opinions, my Lord, but what is generally acknowledged is that the man Mortimer and his demands are in part worth considering. Some now say openly that if civil disorder becomes widespread the streets will run with blood. Without doubt they are fearful of this rebellion. Whether we like it or not the populace blame His Majesty and his advisors for much of the present ills. Perhaps we should appease them in some way."

Nodding, Cromwell looked thoughtful. "Thank you. A most helpful resume, Stanley, I fear Hastings, you are do not grasp the nettle in this matter," he said scathingly.

The elderly Hastings sat tight-lipped with an expression of weary resignation on his lined face. "My apologies, my Lord," he murmured.

"I shall speak with the King this afternoon," Cromwell said firmly. "First I shall have to get through that belligerent wife of his. She is a tiresome creature. We should do well to be rid of her."

* * *

"Two hours, two hours you have sat there, my Lord Husband and still you come to no decision," Margaret ranted. "Until you do so, what shall we tell Lord Cromwell who we are to expect at any time. Only this morning we hear from Lord Scales the rebels plan marching on London and our army threatens mutiny. Then there is Richard of York waiting to pounce on the throne. It is a scurrilous state of affairs and one we must deal with."

"Shouldn't you be in Kenilworth, Margaret, my sweetheart?" Henry asked mildly with a benevolent smile.

Margaret gave him a suspicious look. She was pleased he remained well of late, but his bouts of mental frailty were never far from her mind. He looked bright-eyed enough if a trifle pale, yet it seemed odd he was so unperturbed by the trouncing they received at the Great Park.

"If you remember I was, until I received word of our defeat. Now that same army, *our* army is in disarray and I am here to see what can be done," she said, strutting across the chamber in a swirl of brown satin.

Henry laid his hand to his head as if thinking was too much of a burden.

"You will have to help, sweet Lady Wife, for my mind is unclear."

"Then first we must hear what Lord Cromwell has to say," Margaret said crisply.

To pass the time she took up her embroidery frame and holding up the colour swatches she unravelled her next choice of silk. Sewing soothed her or so those who watched her said. But accompanying every stitch were her thoughts embroidering themselves in her brain as surely as the silk on her sampler. And these days there was much to think about. She knew exactly what it was people wanted. To force her Lord Husband to abdicate and she would go with him. Her sigh was loud enough for Henry to hear.

"That is a sorrowful sound. Are you ailing?" he enquired solicitously, his fingers ever busy pleating his silk knee rug.

"Not at all, my Lord, I have never been better," she replied emphatically.

It wasn't true of course. She ached. Ached for William's soft touch, ached for his love and companionship, ached for his allegiance and most importantly she was tired of carrying pain instead of a child. Her hand surreptitiously bunched up her gown behind her sewing. Making a fist she drove into her belly until she was sure she must have bruised herself.

Glancing sideways under her eyelids she stole a look at Henry. His eyes were closed and his face the shade of a waning moon. In repose he looked no more than an innocent young boy. Perhaps his loins were as weak as his willpower and he would never give her a child. His visits to her bedchamber were more frequent of late, yet his virility was sorely lacking. No matter, with or without Henry's seed she would fight until her last breath to keep the House of York off the throne.

Casting aside her threads she stood in front of the window. Although her reflection was hazy she could see sufficiently. Spanning her waist with her hands it still felt slender, her arms were shapely, her pert breasts desirable and her hair the colour of sun-ripened rye. She of all people knew beauty and power make a deadly combination in Court circles.

Fingering the heavy gold chain round her neck she smiled to herself for she knew with certainty there wasn't a man she needed to do more than crook a finger at who wouldn't bed her with vigour. Taking a breath she contemplated such a man. He must be able to express gratitude for her favour and she should see it amongst the flush of passion suffusing his cheeks. Someone who could match her desires, yet remember his place. A man both discreet and loyal and not with the physique of an oxen, rather more lithe and graceful, she fancied. Feeling her heart beat a little faster, she hastily tried to extinguish the image of William which so readily came to mind. She thought she had found it in him, but that wasn't to be and it was a loss still hard to bear. So who, who would she want to sire the next king of England?

At the sound of knocking her guilt made her jump. It woke Henry too and he hastily wiped away a trickle of drool left on his chin as he slept. Bracing herself, Margaret was at her most haughty when Cromwell entered the room.

"Majesties," he said tersely, bowing low. Margaret's nod was far from cordial. It was Henry who extended his hand for Cromwell's kiss of allegiance.

"So my Lord, what news do you bring us?" he asked pleasantly.

Having taken her seat again, Margaret's expression was frosty and her mouth set in rigid lines. Unperturbed by her obvious displeasure, Cromwell addressed Henry.

"It is not good news, Sire," he said. "The Council has certain suggestions which I am asked to urge you to consider. Mortimer and his rebel following are already approaching London. There is cause for us to be concerned and the Council are united in their recommendations." Henry seemed nonplussed and seizing the moment, Margaret leapt to her feet.

"Have you forgotten we have an army, my Lord? What are they doing whilst these troublemakers advance on our city?"

Cromwell swung round adroitly. "They threaten mutiny, Your Grace," he said calmly. "It seems their commanders can no longer control them and we would suggest they are disbanded."

"*Mon Dieu! Quelle horreur!* We have such weak soldiers? It is an outrage," Margaret said savagely. "Why has this happened?"

"Many are fearful, others weary from fighting in France and there is a feeling that Mortimer and his complaints may have some substance. He promises them such good things when we agree to his requests. So we suggest you should meet some of his demands. I'm told he and his men are prepared to lay down their arms once certain punishments have been carried out. The soldiers too bay for blood, we must listen to them."

"No never!" Margaret stormed.

Somewhere below in the garden the sounds of laughter floated through the window. She raced across the chamber and slammed the casement shut with a venomous hissing noise. Alarmed, Henry waved his hand at her.

"Hush, my Lady Wife. Calm yourself. We must be advised by our good lord here. So Cromwell, what would you say we should do?"

"Mortimer names men who are highly unpopular particularly in Kent, Baron Fiennes of Saye and Sele and his son-in-law, William Crowmer are but two. It would do no harm to be rid of them," Cromwell replied.

"They are nobodies, take their heads off if that pleases you," Margaret snapped.

"James Fiennes is the Lord High Treasurer and I should greatly miss his company, the other, Crowmer was until recently the Under-Sheriff of Kent, they are hardly nobodies my sweet Lady," Henry reproved. "Besides we are all one in God's eyes," he said piously.

He may not have heard his wife's sharp intake of breath, but Cromwell did. She knew it when he swung his eyes to her and she met his hard gaze. She returned it without a flicker of an eyelash and it was he who finally looked away.

"Yes, my Lord, were you about to say something?" she asked him sharply, fanning the warm air around her with brusque flips of her hand. She could see the loathing in his eyes, yet he remained expressionless.

"No, Your Grace," he said through gritted teeth. Henry's benign laughter startled them both. Then clapping his hands he said.

"Forsooth, you remind me of two children bickering. What troubles you both, that you have such glum faces? Whilst you play games, I have made my decision. My Lord Cromwell, would you see that Lord Saye and the man Crowmer are taken to the Tower. Ask Lord Scales to accompany them so that they come to no harm. I intend to protect them, but we shall tell the people they are to stand trial for their crimes. That should satisfy the rebels and my army will be at peace. Is that not a fair idea my Lady Wife?"

Smoothing a wayward lock of her hair back under her coif, Margaret nodded.

"It pleases me you have made such an effort, my Lord," she said approvingly, casting a cold glance at Cromwell. He in turn was tempted to ignore her, but good sense prevailed at the last moment. Bowing stiffly, he murmured.

"Very well, Your Majesties, I shall see to it, but should the army not accept such a decision, what then?" Shrugging, Henry held out his hand to Margaret with a sweet smile.

"Then tell Scales to disband them if he must. My dear Lady Wife and I are leaving London. We shall retire to Kenilworth until order is restored. You can manage well enough, I'm sure," he said cheerfully.

Pausing at the door, Cromwell was about to speak.

"That will be all, thank you my Lord," Margaret said decisively, turning her back on him.

The door closed and alone with Henry, Margaret knelt at his feet. Stroking one of his hands she was at her sweetest.

"Perhaps it is not my place to say, my Lord Husband, but was that wise? Should not the King and his consort stay here in London and resist these insurgents? There must still be many prepared to stand up to them despite what Cromwell says."

Making a conscious effort to appear submissive she blinked fawn-like eyes at him, then resting her head on his knee, allowed his hand to fumble though her hair while she struggled to control her desire to order him to make a different decision.

"Sweet Lady Wife, you are my heart's delight, my precious sunshine on these days of grey, but no. We shall go to Warwickshire where it is safe. There I shall show you just how much you mean to me," Henry told her. "Now we shall say no more about it. There are preparations to be made."

Pretending to busy herself at the end of the chamber, Margaret's favourite, Catherine heard it all. What a minx her little Margaret of Anjou could be, first one ploy and then another. Reaching for their travelling bags, she lowered her head behind her sleeve so no one would see her smiling.

Chapter Twenty-Six

HAVING declared it a rest day, Jack took the opportunity to walk the length of the camp on Black Heath. It was then he saw her again, the bright-eyed girl he first encountered at Knole. It was possible she was a moor he thought, but on closer inspection her face was simply darkened by being outside so much and her glossy hair highlighted by the constant sun on it.

She was crouching in the grass by the supply carts with some of the smaller children showing them a cricket in the palm of her hand. Unaware she was being watched she sat down cross-legged bunching up her skirts and gathering her slender brown legs under her. Her sudden movement disturbed the insect who took off in a mighty bound.

"There, do you see how high he jumps?" she burbled to the small beings gazing at her with owl-like eyes.

A thin blond-haired urchin boy sprang up. Unwilling to lose sight of the creature he went to step out after it.

"Catch it again, Aditha, catch it again," he implored.

Putting her arm out to restrain him, she looked up straight into the admiring eyes of Jack.

"Aditha, that's a pretty name to be sure," he said with a broad grin.

She had the grace to blush, but she was far from tongue-tied. "Why Captain, how kind," she replied, smiling back. He wasn't to know her heart lurched uncomfortably in her chest as she looked him over. Her father kept fine horses and she was a good judge of horseflesh, but nothing to

193

compare with the broad-shouldered strength and lean muscle of this man. Such a handsome face, she thought yearning to reach over and touch every freckle on his high cheek bones.

"How old are you, Aditha?" he asked disturbing her reverie.

"Turned sixteen, Captain," she said, the look in her green eyes as provocative as the fullness of her lips.

"And what are you doing here?"

"I travel with my mother. Her sweetheart marches with you, Captain."

"John, the name is John," he said. He swallowed hard unused to such a dry mouth. Uninterested in their conversation, the children began wandering off and he dropped down onto the grass beside her. God's blood, she thought, those freckles are even nearer now. She was inclined to sit on her hands to keep them in order. Before she could, he reached out and took one of them, turning it over and examining it carefully.

"What is it you see in my hand," she asked curiously. Sometimes Mammy looked at palms, consulted the runes too he recalled although she refused to be called a *user.* Her readings were favoured and much in demand as were her potions for all manner of ailments. She taught him too, pointing out the meaning of the lines, but he was out of practice and Aditha's grubby palm was just squiggles and marks to him. Even so it didn't stop him enjoying the pulsating warmth under his fingers.

"There's nought there," he said dismissively, but chuckling just the same. Moving closer he could smell the musky scent of her and glimpse down between the sweet bulges of her breasts. "So, little Aditha, tell me more about yourself," he said softly, his dark eyes brimming with desire.

* * *

Striving to rest in the shade drove most of the rebels under whatever tree or ledge they could find. There was no such worry for Richard and Simon several feet down in the caverns. They relaxed resting their backs against the damp walls breathing in the cooling air.

"So John has told you we leave for London on the morrow?" Simon enquired of Richard, who sat with his eyes closed enjoying the quiet.

He nodded in reply and deeming it a good moment, Simon embarked on his questions. "Tell me, Richard. Our fine leader Mortimer, what do you know of him?" he asked.

"Very little as it happens," Richard replied, without opening his eyes. "I met him in the *White Hart* when he first arrived in London. He was a stranger to the city looking for a bed. It seemed likely he was in need of work too judging by the few groats he carried."

Feeling the stickiness of sweat on his palms, Simon made sure his voice was level.

"So he arrived from somewhere else. Where was that, do you know?"

"He might have mentioned somewhere or other. I can't recall although I could swear he must have been close to the sea. I do remember noticing white streaks embedded in the fur of his satchel. They are not difficult to recognise, the damnable salt lays thick on the cargo when my ships tie up after a rough crossing, but why all these questions?" Richard asked, finally opening his eyes.

Simon watched him carefully wondering if there was more. Damn the fellow. Squire Pultenery wasn't going to be much impressed with so little.

He tried again. "You will have seen the wound on his arm then?"

Feeling his shirt absorbing the moisture from the stone at his back, Richard scrambled to his feet.

"I said, why all the questions?"

"Just trying to get to know the man, that's all," Simon replied huffily.

"Yes, as it happens I have seen his arm. It's a bad wound which doesn't heal properly. He doesn't speak about it. Now I must prepare for this evening so pray forgive me, but I'm going to the camp."

"Of course," Simon said tightly, forcing a thin smile which wilted almost as quickly as it arrived.

* * *

On the Alter, the point of the torch flame darted over the stones poking at them like playful fingers. Surrounded by damp sullen walls it was hard to imagine where the draught came from or that it carried enough energy to feed them. But they stayed faithful in tune with the ritual being played out in front of them.

Below the top slab on a stool a freshly severed young buck's head still dripped lethargic ruby beads of blood whilst the beast's empty eyes stared ahead of it. Simon, Richard and Jack each wearing a stag's skin attached at their shoulders and a crown of antlers, supplicated to the God of the Hunt in silent prayer as all hunters do.

Getting to his feet, Simon's squat shape was dwarfed by the animal pelt so he looked like a cumbersome toad with a leaf caught on its back. Bringing out a red woollen pouch from inside his jerkin, he carefully took out three sprigs of sage. Waved through the flame of one of the torches the dry leaves ignited into acrid smoke. With no air to disturb it, it hovered in a grey ball. Anticipation mounting, Simon bowed his head and began chanting the Prayer of Protection in his usual colourless tone.

"Great God Herne, mighty hunter, hear our prayer
We dwell in the bright divine light
All goodness is attracted to us for our highest good
We are attuned with divine love and divine goodness
We give thanks for the divine light . . . Grant us our victory"

His voice came back to them in a low rolling echo followed by silence. Holding up his sword, he turned to Jack and said in a mysterious whisper.

"You will be anointed by the Horned God himself so you shall have his strength when the battle comes. Get down on your knees."

The air was thick with the sickly sweet smell of blood and charged with unseen spirits. Jack caught his breath as a surge of excitement sent his heart racing. His headdress felt like a heavy crown, but there was no cheering, no jubilation only the eerie emptiness of cold stone. Casting a glance he saw Richard's eyes were glazed and his face illuminated by the intensity of the moment. Beginning to sweat, Jack turned his attention to Simon again.

Carefully reaching above the alter Simon lifted down Herne's magnificent antlers. From a Monarch stag each antler bears eight points and was so weighty even Simon's big hands had trouble turning it. Eventually he managed to dip one of the points into the pool of blood under the head on the stool. Beckoning, he waited whilst Jack shuffled forward. Making a strange guttural noise, Simon anointed Jack's forehead with a scarlet slash before almost staggering under his burden, he managed to replace the crown back on the effigy. Richard nodded approvingly.

"There, John 'tis a good omen that Herne the Hunter gives you," he said, wiping his damp face.

It was in the blackness of night when Jack finally left the caverns. He gulped in the chilled fresh air eagerly, grateful to rid his nostrils of the oppressive odours. Walking silently and only guided by a sickle moon he returned to check the dark mass of the sleeping camp.

* * *

In a few short hours the Heath was alive again. Despite even more rebels joining the march, they were remarkably organised and before dawn they were already assembled in long segments. No one bothered to count them anymore, but the force ran into many thousands.

For a moment the man emerging from the caverns was unrecognisable. Somerset's suit of armour wasn't familiar apparel for Jack and he swerved a little under its weight. His mischievous eyes laughed at his own ineptitude as he clanked his way to his horse. With Merek and Walter wide-eyed beside him, he cast a satisfied glance over the gathering.

"Where are Richard and Simon?" he asked.

"At the back, Captain, they ride with the women and children," Merek replied, giving him an odd look.

Deciding to ignore their sniggers he smiled to himself. Aditha, his woman, for she was now his, would be there somewhere with them and he felt no guilt about Mariamne.

She would know no different. Besides when victory was theirs and he was wealthy he would pay her well to keep a good home. There would be something smaller for Aditha, but he would look after her nicely. Just like Mammy always did for him. "*Gach ag dul go maith,* all is going well," he thought he heard her whisper and contentment warmed him like a sheepskin jerkin.

Having sent Barda and three others ahead the evening before, Jack knew London would be expecting them. They were to make arrangements for the *White Hart* to become their temporary headquarters so everything was in place when they arrived. Snapping down his visor, he raised his arm. Just as apricot tinted clouds were crowding out the last of the night's tombstone grey, the rebels rose up behind him and swept away off the Heath making their way to Southwark.

On the dry road the long column sent the dust puffing upwards in small sandy clouds behind them, yet before long they saw the same ahead of them too. Merek stood tall in his saddle.

"It looks like Barda," he called out as the horseman drew nearer.

His horse was lathered in sweat and Barda's face shone like a newly picked apple by the time he arrived in front of them. Jack looked at him anxiously.

"You would wait for us in Southwark. Why such haste, are you being followed?"

Drawing heavily on his water skin, Barda quenched his thirst. Then wiping the droplets off his beard and lips with his hand, he shook his head.

"We saw no riders, only a few travellers on foot. I thought you would want the news."

"Go on," Jack said, keeping his horse steady.

"There is nothing to stop us advancing at all speed into London. Everywhere is in disorder. The soldiers have risen up in mutiny. They have your name on their lips and some wait to join us. When their commanders found them looting they disbanded them instantly. The King and Queen have left for Kenilworth, too frightened to stay some say and there are whispers Richard of York may sail from Ireland. Now is the time, Captain. London has been abandoned to its fate."

Chapter Twenty-Seven

Kent

BEING Squire Pultenery's man was a position John Bailey revelled in. He did his job well, could keep his mouth shut when he had to and was for the most part loyal to his master. In return, Pultenery allowed him to take game, fish from the nearby river and wood for his fire.

Much of his work involved carrying messages, running errands for Pultenery and exhorting money from those who owed it to his master and were slow to pay. His newest quest was more taxing for his small brain and Pultenery noticed his close-set eyes dulling when he gave him his instructions.

"Why do you look so perplexed, 'tis a little different to your usual tasks, I grant you, so if it is too difficult I shall need to look elsewhere," Pultenery said diffidently.

Bailey's untidy beard fringed his narrow face from under his ears, ending up in a droopy point beneath his chin. He scratched it with some agitation. Then rolling his eyes as if some good would come of it, he gave the matter a moment of thought. An end to his privileges was too awful to contemplate. So was the image of his ten children with no food in their bellies. His decision was almost immediate.

"Not at all, Squire. I'm sure I can find you the information you need. A mariner, you say? If there is travel it may take me some time."

Quivering with impatience, Pultenery grabbed Bailey's thin arm, dragging him towards him.

"Firstly there is no time and secondly, I didn't say he was from the sea, only that when he arrived at the *Hart* in Southwark someone saw traces of salt on his belongings. So make sure your miserable wit is fit for this mission and report back to me when you have news. Remember he calls himself John Mortimer. I trust you to find out the rest, do you understand?"

Mortified at his rough handling, Bailey scrabbled at his hole-ridden sleeves to straighten them then backing towards the door said.

"Is there nothing else you can tell me, 'tis difficult to know where to start, Squire."

The whine in his voice incensed Pultenery who laid his hand on his ink pot. Tempted to throw it he hesitated. It was a costly object. Instead he reached over, wrenched at the door knob and shoved Bailey into the corridor.

"By the all that's Holy, are you such a dolt? I thought better of you. Go to Southwark, see if any one remembers him and see to it you mention he's marked with a wound on his arm," he snapped.

Slamming the door closed behind him, Pultenery hastily threw open the casement to rid the room of the fusty smell emanating from Bailey's wretched excuse for a jerkin.

* * *

Whilst Bailey lacked intelligence, he wasn't short of cunning or money which he hoarded in a box under his earth floor. Nor did he lack so-called friends who living on their wits were always ready to exchange information for a bottle or two of liquor. He even amazed himself when he found with his persuasive tongue, the alewife at the *Hart* was willing to remember in exchange for three silver groats.

"You'll have to do better," she told him on his first enquiry when he offered her a solitary coin. But her hand, shiny with eel slime, shot out when another coin appeared. He thought it was probably the mention of Jack's damaged arm which tipped the scales.

"Now I do remember that wound, such a good looking boy too and brave if you ask me. A horrible thing it was, but he never did say how he come by it," she wittered, reaching for her cutting knife.

The eel's head shot off her chopping board in speckles of scarlet and slid in its own juices across the floor. Bailey didn't flinch.

"Was it Brigstowe or Bath he said he'd come from? I see so many travellers in here, hard to remember all their tales," she said, her eye moving rapidly from the board to Bailey's money bag. Shaking her head she reached into the wooden bucket. "No, I don't rightly know."

Bailey reluctantly slid another groat out into his palm.

"It's coming back to me now, Brigstowe. I could swear that's what he said," she announced, as the blade sliced down again with a loud *thwacking* noise.

With the coin on the board she concentrated on skinning the eel.

"You'll be stopping will you? I'll do you a nice trencher of stewed eels."

When there was no reply she looked over her shoulder, Bailey was gone. Already on board a passing ox-cart, he was on his way to Brigstowe.

* * *

Bailey's search was proving fruitless in the maze of vile-smelling alleyways and seedy hovels. The truth was he had no idea where to start once he reached Brigstowe. Having never been in the area before he got lost countless times so finally despondent, he fortified himself with ale at a hostelry close to the dock and finding a pile of old rags under an arch fell asleep.

When he woke dusk was approaching. Wandering back towards the town he noticed passers-by had changed. Gone were the traders and stall holders, strolling merchants and raw-boned women. Instead the beggars, dissolute and feckless prowled in the shadows and an occasional wretch of an urchin thrust an alms bowl at him. None of them bothered Bailey, in fact he was more at home in their company.

Then he noticed the ladies of the street. More loose women than he thought ever existed except of course down at Wapping where they waited for the boats to dock. They smiled at him. Then tugging at his sleeve if they were close enough, they offered their services for a half penny or a farthing if pickings were thin. At first he dodged out of their way, but a man has needs and when a slip of a girl with generous breasts stood hesitantly in front of him he couldn't resist.

Nodding at her, she led him behind a pile of cargo on the quay. It was quiet, desolate he thought as he looked about with nothing to disturb them, but he was wary. He knew how some of these slatterns carried on. Caught up in the nefarious ways of thieves and water-front rogues, these voluptuous creatures enticed and you knew they would take your very clothes if they could. His hand closed tightly round his fat money purse.

Fresh from the waterfront the wind whined round them seeking out corners and piles of cargo bringing with it the sour smell of rotting hides and boiled blubber.

"Are you on your own?" he whispered, looking around him nervously.

Her tufts of wispy hair bounced as she nodded and in the shadow he couldn't read her dark dulled eyes.

"You better be telling the truth. I'm not afraid to use my knife," he growled, his hand resting on his dagger. Her expression changed. Drawing back toward the cargo she gave a little whimper.

"I'm good, Master. I'll do anything you want. I swear you won't need to use it. Mercy on us, you're not one of those madmen that attack girls' like me? Don't hurt me, sir, please."

He saw her eyes then; wide, staring and terrified. Troubled by her pathetic plea he thought about it. She couldn't be much older than his eldest girl by the looks of her. He wasn't so inhuman as to not recognize fear. It tugged at her fading childlike features turning them into an ugly grimace. Putting out his hand he touched her gently on her bare arm. It was bony and dry under his fingers and the skin trembled.

Sobered by her plaintive voice, he asked the question kindly.

"Have you been attacked?"

"No, not me, Master, but you can't be too careful. My sister, Mary . . . a man . . . few years ago . . . she were killed," her words ending in a sob, she scrubbed at the tears leaving thin clean tracks down her dirty cheeks.

He felt his urges diminish. Instead he experienced a frisson of excitement at her words. It could be something, yet it could mean nothing. But then he had nothing so something, anything just might be useful and he had a nose for such things. That was why Pultenery depended on him.

"What do they call you?" he asked gently.

"Matilda, Master," she replied.

He ferreted in his purse and held out a silver groat. "Well Matilda, this is for you."

Fearful again, she rolled her eyes.

"I can't take it. I haven't pleasured you, Master."

"No matter about that," he said his voice gruff with the sudden tightness in his throat. "Sit with me awhile and tell me about your sister, Mary, God rest her soul."

* * *

He found the Squire in his stables watching the boy saddle up his horse. Bailey hadn't advanced two steps when Pultenery swung round.

"God's teeth I thought it was you. I could smell you," he said with a pained expression.

"My apologies, Squire," Bailey replied with no sincerity in his voice. "I've not been long off the road, but I thought it best to come straight here."

"Well in that case you must have news for me," Pultenery replied, looking slightly less offended. "I hope it's useful for I have no time to waste. It seems the march will shortly arrive in London so tell me what you found out and quickly."

They walked the length of the yard whilst Bailey recounted his tale. Surprising to Bailey, Pultenery listened intently although issuing a hiss of breath when Bailey told him how he encountered Matilda.

"Of course, Squire, I can't tell you for sure the man who done for the whore Mary was John Mortimer, but accounts have it he left Brigstowe sharply afterwards," Bailey concluded.

Disappointment clouded Pultenery's face.

"So we still don't know for certain if this is the man who is leading the rebels. Think hard man, have you any more proof? The woman's sister, did she ever see him?" Bailey's nod was jubilant and his wide grin showed all his blackened teeth in one go.

"Just the once when she visited her sister, a handsome young man, she said. She recognised his voice too, her offering her trade to newly arrived seaman. He was an Irishman, she would swear to it. She thought he told Mary near Connacht, but the girl wasn't sure. She did say she wouldn't forget his wound on his arm in a hurry, vile it was, she said, didn't know how her sister could bear to touch it." Frowning, Pultenery repeatedly tapped his cane thoughtfully on the stone wall.

"John Mortimer? Would you call that an Irish name?" he muttered half under his breath.

Bailey danced ahead of him still smiling broadly. He was enjoying keeping the best until last. Pirouetting to a halt, he looked as if he might burst with excitement.

"But that's it, Master," he exclaimed. "Matilda said she didn't know a John Mortimer. The man who killed her sister called himself Jack Cade."

Margaret Callow

Chapter Twenty-Eight

London

July

THEY were close enough to see the village of Deptford on the edge of the river. In the noon sun fishing boats lay idle draped in nets still beaded with glistening green drops. Lumbering through the blackish mud on the banks, a trio of hogs were turning up the ground faster than a man could till. After a heavy rain shower vapour still shrouded the wooden dwellings and cloaked the people gathering to watch their passing. Villagers ran up to meet the marchers who in turn rewarded their greetings with cheery grins. Jack's smile was broad despite the discomfort of his suit which he began to wish he hadn't worn.

All their spirits were high now London was within their sights and they poured over the bridge in such numbers the stout timbers quivered in response. Following the pilgrim's way there were still some miles to go. When eventually they turned north-east into the valley of the Walbrook, crossed the stream and started climbing the higher ground towards Ludgate Hill there was relief and anticipation on their tired faces. Their route was already lined with people curious at the sight of such a mighty force. Some ran alongside, others joined in at the back of the march. Advancing on the City, Jack didn't hesitate to force his way across London Bridge.

"Now they'll know I've come to stay," he shouted wildly, laughing into the breeze as he slashed the ropes of the drawbridge with an impressive flourishing of his sword. The opaque river water beneath them resolutely rippled past unmindful of the drama above it. Following its course into Candlewick Street, the column marched resolutely onwards.

Having availed themselves of some loose horses they found on the way, Merek and Barda flanked Jack as they approached The London Stone. He, sensing the importance of the moment, lifted his visor as they rode steadily towards the massive limestone boulder which stopped them in their path.

"This is where it starts," Jack murmured. "Since they fail to answer our demands they will soon see our discontent. Perhaps then they will listen to our requests with sharper ears," he said, dismounting.

Swinging his sword high over his head, he brought it down again striking the ancient stone with a forceful blow.

"Now is Mortimer rightful Lord of London," he roared. "Down with the policies of our king. It is I, *Lord* Mortimer who you will thank for your freedom."

The crowd were ecstatic. What had been a calm air was turned into a cacophony of clapping, cheering and bellows of approval. A small group of men-at-arms nearby stepped forward in defiance, but as quickly as they did so, they were dragged out of sight by some of the populace.

"Onward to Southwark," Jack called out.

Remounting he waved his sword at the marchers. He saw the scudding clouds overhead and felt the rain. Too elated he didn't stop to think it might be an omen. Lazy irregular drops came first then faster; slanting and needle-like. These tiny daggers were too sharp on his skin, so he hastily closed his visor and fumbled with his gauntlets.

* * *

Later, in his new headquarters at the *White Hart,* the ale wife showed him to his room. This time there was no poky garret, but a well appointed spacious chamber waiting for him. The woman fussed round him directing her serving wenches to bring trenchers of fresh bread, cheese and jugs of sweet ale. Hampered by the armour he wished she would leave.

"There Captain Mortimer, are you comfortable?" she asked, with a wide smile, arms on her hips and her greying hair adrift from her coif.

"It'll do me well enough," he said with a nonchalant smile.

This time the window was large and looked out onto the road. Standing at it he was amazed at the crowds who must have followed. Others pushed through the doorway of the inn in a steady stream.

"You're good for business," the alewife said, looking over his shoulder.

When her steps faded on the stairs he heaved his way out of the cumbersome armour and stretched out on the feather-filled pallet. Raised up from the boards, it offered comfort he'd long forgotten. He couldn't remember when he last felt so light-hearted despite his weariness. Later he would send for Aditha, but he was in no hurry.

Gazing up at the timbered beam he saw how notched and gnarled it was yet the dark oak was solid. As stout and lasting as his surety that this endeavour would have a happy ending, he was convinced of that. Then momentary doubt touched his thoughts. It was a bold thing he was doing, too bold perhaps? He needed his Mammy's reassurance. Just like she all gave it when he had a childish mishap.

"There do you see, Mammy? It's all coming true. Power and riches, that's what you said . . . You'll protect me . . ." He would have talked longer to her if Richard hadn't burst open the door. If he'd heard Jack's mumblings he didn't comment. Instead he leant casually on the door frame.

"So Master Mortimer, how does it feel to be a lord of the great city of London?"

Were his eyes mocking, Jack couldn't be sure. "Comfortable thank you," he replied lazily.

"Well now 'tis time you played your part. The Lord Mayor Wyfold and some of his Aldermen are waiting below. They wish to speak to you urgently."

Jack stretched first one arm and then the other. "I'm in no haste to speak to them," he said, smiling, but he swung his legs off the pallet just the same. Unhurriedly he opened his hose and aimed a long stream of urine into the chamber pot. "What do we know about the Mayor? Is he likely to be difficult?"

Richard shrugged. "All I know is he is the Mayor of London and a grocer by trade. He looks a bit uneasy though."

* * *

Nicholas Wyfold nervously refused to sit. Occasionally fingering his badge of office dangling on an absurdly large chain he continued his agitated pacing. His three companions did differently. They relaxed round a table in the corner of the pub supping ale. Smartly dressed in the official silk robes of city Aldermen trimmed at cuffs and hem with squirrel fur, they watched bemused at Wyfold rid himself of heat on his pale brow with hasty dabs of his large blue kerchief.

"God's blood, Wyfold, what are you so worried about? Mortimer is likely no more than a rebel out to make a name for himself," mercer William Dere said scornfully.

Still restless, Wyfold hovered over the table. "It's alright for you, but I'm the Mayor and greatly responsible for all that happens in the city," he hissed.

"That isn't to say I don't think the fellow should be resisted," Dere said, with an emphatic thump so forceful the ale flasks jigged on the wood.

"I disagree," John Gedney announced.

As the local draper he never appeared without pins and threads of cotton on his dapper clothing. His thin features almost hidden behind a profuse growth of greying hair, his insipid blue eyes were hard-edged. Strumming the table top with finely cut nails, he continued. "We should listen to what he has to say. I for one have some sympathy with the man. Not one of us here can say our king rules well and as for those he seeks advice from . . . greedy fools the lot of them." Dere turned on him immediately.

"You would say that. We all know where your loyalties lie. We have no guarantee the Duke of York would do better. Besides I thought Mortimer is championing the lot of the poor commons."

"Indeed he is, but there are others marching with him whose thoughts are in higher places," Gedney replied tightly.

Timid, mouse-like John Middleton with no trade, but impeccable connections, coughed gently and running a finger round his collar to ease it, said in his effeminate voice.

"Pardon me for interrupting, but I think we should all be agreed before we meet Master Mortimer. What say you, Mayor Wyfold?"

Before he could reply, Wyfold suddenly tipped back his head. Then they all heard the heavy tread on the narrow staircase. With a quick stride, Jack was standing before them. His dark curls were uncontrolled, his smile disarming and his demeanour one of a man both unconcerned and assured.

"Good day to you, sirs. I'm honoured you should think to greet me," he said amiably, his hand resting lightly on his broadsword.

"Upstart," Dere muttered.

Drawing himself up to his full height, Wyfold smoothed down his tunic and adjusting his brown beaver hat, said, "And a very good day to you too, Master Mortimer, as the Lord Mayor may I say how impressed we are with the great gathering you have with you." Only those closest to him might have detected the slight trembling in his voice as he continued. "Whilst we have no reason to doubt their good intentions do we have your assurance that such a crowd will behave themselves?"

"Fie, sir what do you take us for?" Jack replied robustly. "We come here in peace and I have good men like Richard here who will make sure there is discipline in the ranks."

"Perhaps introductions would be in order," Middleton warbled. "John Middleton, Alderman of the city at your service, sir," he said, barely raising his small-boned hand in Jack's direction before dropping it to his side again.

Gedney gave him a withering glance. Although suspecting greater forces at work, he for one would not seek to ingratiate himself with leader of such a rabble. Instead he hardly nodded whilst taking a long drink from his flask. He seemed to hold it awkwardly and Jack noticed he had two fingers missing. Reminding him of his arm, he felt for his cuff making sure it covered the distinctive scar. Anxious to avoid any bad feeling, Wyfold was more forthcoming. His courage returning, he forced a smile.

"Pay no mind to Master Gedney. He is a man of few words, but a stalwart of the city and this is Master William Dere, also a most respected Alderman."

Dere's expression was clearly suspicious and unwelcoming. He growled his words.

"You should know, Master Mortimer I am not one who takes pleasure from uprisings. If it was left to me I should ask you to take your rebels elsewhere."

Trying to make his laughter light-hearted, Wyfold only managed to sound a trifle hysterical.

"Goodness me, that is a poor welcome. What Master Dere means is there are some a little discomforted by the arrival of so many in Southwark."

"I didn't mean that at all, Wyfold," Dere said, scowling. Taking stock of the tense situation, Richard stepped forward.

"I'm Richard de Courcy and you have my assurance too there will be nothing to fear from us. As soon as our requests are granted we shall lay down our arms, depart your city and return to Kent. Is that not right, Captain Mortimer?" he said pleasantly.

Jack nodded whilst not missing Wyfold's attempt to stifle a giggle at the mention of his new title. Dere was less polite.

"Captain is it? I should think that an odd rank for one who is no more than a leader of insurgents. Strange, very strange," he commented to the room in general.

"Merely a title of affection by his followers," murmured Richard.

Such a trite conversation was beginning to bore Jack. Locking his gaze on Wyfold, he said.

"So, there is the matter of our demands. Do we take it you are able to speak for the king, Master Mayor?" Looking aghast, Wyfold took a step back.

"Oh no," he said emphatically. "We merely came in advance to welcome you so to speak. It is Lord Scales who will be here shortly. He is the man who speaks for His Majesty and 'tis he who will answer your questions."

As if with perfect timing, he had barely finished speaking when the door swung wide. The military presence striding towards them diminished the four poorly attired Men-at-Arms following behind. With an implacable expression, Scales did not hesitate until he halted only inches from Jack and Richard. Brushing the latter aside he addressed Jack.

"I take it you are the man they are calling the Captain of Kent," he said curtly, appraising Jack with his cool gaze.

"I am that person," Jack returned.

Unwilling to admit he found Scales somewhat disconcerting, Jack's smile was brazen and his look little less than insolent. Scales seemed to ignore both.

"His Majesty thanks you for your list of requests and asks me to enquire of you exactly what it is that will satisfy you and your followers?" he said without a flicker of emotion.

Realising Scales was not a man easy to deal with, Richard looked uncomfortable. Any dialogue with an envoy of the king and Jack's inexperience could cost them dear. Thinking the uprising might be over when it had barely begun, he tried to convey the need for caution by attracting Jack's attention with a gentle cough, but his companion was already about to speak. Tossing his curls away from his brow, Jack didn't hesitate.

"Heads I think. Lord Saye and William Crowmer to start with, but I should tell you we will not be thwarted. If it becomes necessary, we shall march to the Tower and help ourselves."

His audacity brought unmistakable gasps from those listening. All eyes were now on Scales as they waited for his response. They were unprepared for his smile. It was a weak affair which didn't reach his eyes, but nonetheless it played faintly on his lips in the nest of his black moustache. Despite the concerned looks of Wyfold and the Aldermen, Scales nodded slowly.

"Very well, but if I agree to this have I your word you will keep a firm hand on the thousands of your followers who fill our streets and ask them to refrain from pillage?"

At his most charming, Jack bowed. "Of course," he replied. "You can be sure they will give you no trouble. And when these two evil men have been punished, we shall hope to lay down our arms."

"Then you shall have what you ask for. I shall arrange for Fiennes and Crowmer to be brought here first thing in the morning," Scales said, his jaw set and his eyes emotionless.

Richard's sigh of relief was faint, but audible.

Chapter Twenty-Nine

OUTRAGED, the Lord Saye, James Fiennes struggled against his chains. His once neatly pointed beard had grown straggly since his incarceration, but it still managed to quiver with his indignation. His words spat into the face of the corpulent Constable of the Tower.

"What do you mean I am to be taken to Southwark? I was assured safety here, I had the King's word," he raged. Out of breath and sweating heavily, the Constable shrugged.

"Those are my orders."

Having just returned from taking delivery of a half-drowned ox fallen off London Bridge and one whose strength returned rapidly once it was landed, the Constable was in no mood for a further battle. He turned to a squire on horseback wearing Scale's colours, his eye wandering over the escort of a motley collection of six Men-at-Arms dressed in mail over drab serge.

"Where's Master Crowmer?" he demanded. "He's wanted too."

"They are bringing him now," someone called.

Looking equally indignant, Crowmer emerged from a door of the White Tower on the other side of the green. There had been no time for him to collect his hat and his powdery fair hair floated in the wind. Like his father-in-law, he was marched across the grass in chains. His resentment vanished when he saw the formality of the gathering and fear grew in his narrow blue eyes.

"What does this mean?" he whispered warily. Scornful of his son-in-law's obvious alarm, Fiennes gave him a withering look.

"By the Virgin's bones, you take fright easily. There's been a mistake, that's all. It will soon be sorted out. Now straighten yourself and walk with pride, no son-in-law of mine will be called a coward."

With peach fingers of light overcoming the dark, the procession emerged from Tower Green. Walking between two Men-at-Arms, the short and sinewy Fiennes tried to stalk ahead of Crowmer, but each time he ventured too far he was jerked back by the iron girdle around his waist. Ahead of them rode the squire and following behind the remaining four of the escort. Word quickly spread and as if summoned by an imaginary bell onlookers could be seen scrambling for places to watch the procession pass. Pressing forward curiously they all shared the same expression. It was one of ghoulish fascination as if they already sensed what was to come. Ignoring them, Fiennes looked stony keeping his eyes fixed ahead whilst the terrified Crowmer made small plaintive noises.

* * *

Jack was impressed. He would never admit he was beginning to admire Scales. Every inch of him a military man and a man of his word, a man he would be proud to serve with. Waiting outside the *Hart*, they watched the procession appear. Scales stepped forward from the shadow of the inn sign. Keeping close, Jack joined him followed by a large gathering led by Mayor Wyfold, Richard and the Aldermen.

"Halt them there," Scales authoritative voice called out pointing to the road in front of them.

Seeing the congestion, Wyfold hurried forward flapping his hands at the people who spilled across the thoroughfare.

"Make way, make way."

Few bothered to move and it was the broad chest of the squire's horse who managed to scatter them. There were sounds of disorder as the two prisoners with their escort quickly moved into the space in front of the *Hart.*

"So Master Mortimer, there we have it." Scales said, ignoring the noisy onlookers. "Lord Saye and Master Crowmer as you requested. They are now surrendered to you. What is it you wish to do with them?"

At first it didn't seem to dawn on Fiennes and Crowmer they were being offered up to the rebellion. Instead Fiennes started blustering, but the crowd were chanting, "God save the King, God save the King," forcing him to raise his voice.

"Now listen here, Scales," he shouted. "When the King comes to know of this you will rue the day. We were guaranteed his protection and this is an outrage. Release us at once."

His demand was met with a scathing look from Jack and the crowd, so united in their loathing of the two men, mumbled their displeasure. It began softly, but rapidly rose until the air was filled with an impossibly noisy clamouring. Showing his annoyance at the disturbance, Scales stepped forward briskly. Hand hovering over his sword, he whispered something to Wyfold. For a moment, Wyfold looked scared, but a dark look by Scales sent him scuttling into the road.

"I'm instructed to tell you by Lord Scales that any who persist in making such an ungodly noise will be arrested."

"On what grounds, I was just spitting out dust," someone called out impudently.

Wyfold looked flustered then said quickly. "Oh, I don't know, for causing an affray I suppose. Anyway be quiet, the lot of you or you will be thrown into gaol."

Beckoning Jack, Scales called out to the prisoners. "It seems you are not popular and there are grievous charges brought about you both. I have agreed to Master Mortimer's request that you answer these charges to him."

Wasting no more time, Jack approached the surly Fiennes and the tearful Crowmer. At the sight of him, Fiennes still managed a flicker of fury to lighten his eyes, but it was the quietly snivelling Crowmer who spoke first.

"I know who you are, Master Mortimer and whatever it is you want for from me, I beg you to be reasonable. Your cause is worthy, nay more than worthy, 'tis a fine thing you do in supporting the less fortunate and if I can help in anyway, you have only to ask."

Fiennes could hardly believe what he was hearing. Pale with anger he turned on his son-in-law.

"You scurrilous dog, I should have you flogged myself. Where's your honour and since when have you been bothered with the lot of the poor commons?"

Such hostility quickly brought an amused smile to Jack's face, but Crowmer's grovelling would have no effect.

"Lord Fiennes, Master William Crowmer, you are both required to answer these charges," he said.

"Then I insist there is a trial," Fiennes snapped back.

* * *

There was to be no proper hearing, Jack had already decided that. Fiennes and Cowmer were destined for Cheapside. Their brief stop at Guildhall was no more than a sham as the elated crowd whistling, jeering and clapping seized every possible space to witness their humiliation.

Standing next to one another the two men waited expectantly. When it became clear they were no more than a spectacle, Fiennes was fast becoming exasperated.

"I demand a trial. What are we waiting for? Scales, I insist you see to it," he demanded boldly.

"And who would you expect to try you?" Scales enquired smoothly.

"I want those who are decent men, not this band of rogues and half-wits who Mortimer calls his army." Half-smiling, Scales shook his head.

"Did you not listen to what I said yesterday? You are now the property of Master Mortimer. He will decide your fate. And it seems there will be no trial."

Fiennes gave an incredulous laugh while listening nervously, Crowmer grabbed at the arm of his soldier escort dragging at the material of his sleeve.

"For God's pity, find someone to help us," he whimpered.

The man roughly disentangled Crowmer's fingers with a grimace. "I can do nothing for you," he said in a guttural voice.

Impatient at the time wasting, Jack cut short the proceedings. "The Lord Saye, James Fiennes and William Crowmer, you are both charged with extorting money improperly from the people of Kent by way of unfair taxes and unreasonable payments of tithes," he announced dramatically. "How do you plead?"

Crowmer appeared to have lost the power of speech, but his companion proclaimed loudly.

"Not guilty."

"We say differently and for that you shall be taken from this place and meet your executioner, whereby your heads will be severed as a proper penalty for your crimes," Jack replied harshly.

Not a muscle twitched in Fiennes's white face as he listened to the verdict. Crowmer, equally blanched, was less stoic and when he all but fell to the ground and a dark stain appeared on his crotch, the crowd were ecstatic. Stamping their feet they joyously proclaimed their hatred at the tops of their voices whilst spite etched itself firmly on their faces.

"Guilty, guilty," they screamed in unison.

Once down from the steps in front of the building, Jack exchanged a glance with Richard. It had gone well, very well in fact, he thought. Richard had coached him late into the night as to how things should go and what to say. As quick to memorise as he was impulsive, Jack enjoyed his position as judge and the rebels loved him for it. So when he turned to them and raised his arm in a salute of triumph, they shouted out his name in a wild fervour.

"Mortimer, Mortimer, Captain of Kent. Our saviour, the man who will deliver us . . ."

Watchful in the crowd, Pultenery's man, John Bailey, clenched his hands in his pockets. He was struggling to remain silent whilst he watched Jack's posturing behaviour. This was not the time to unmask the man with a false name, yet he dearly wanted to. But he would not, dare not until he was given his instructions. As the walk began to the place of execution he slipped silently out of the crowd and vanished down a dark uninviting alleyway.

Scales, Wyfold and several of the Aldermen kept their distance. As the vast crowd of onlookers streamed along the street behind the slower paced escort there was a festive air about them. For Fiennes and Crowmer it was more shocking. His head bowed, Crowmer mumbled fervent prayers whilst walking stiffly, Fiennes looked dismally ahead. This time they were flanked by four garrison soldiers wearing embroidered tunics, dark hose and iron skull caps. They kept close to the prisoners occasionally jabbing them with their long handled axe heads with side hooks.

Merek was waiting for them on the scaffold. He was scattering handfuls of straw roughly around the block as the procession approached. It was close to sunset and whilst the air was humid, clouds threatened by releasing silent slivers of rain every so often. Hardly enough of them fell to dampen the dust, but they added to the melancholy atmosphere.

Emerging from behind the scaffold, a Franciscan friar of an undetermined age was ready to receive the prisoners. In his hand he held a Bible and a large gold crucifix dangled on his scrawny chest. A sudden wind gathered up his robe in puffballs of brown serge exposing the wrappings round his legs and some in the crowd tittered. With a sombre face and stern intent he positioned himself in front of Fiennes and Crowmer. Speaking softly, he bent attentively towards the prisoners waiting for their reply.

"I ask you, sirs, are you ready to denounce your traitorous ways and repent?"

Sobbing loudly, Crowmer waved a distracted hand at the friar. It could have meant anything. However his companion's defiance made up for Crowmer's inability to find any words.

"You are wasting your time. I have nothing to say except I am no traitor so be off with you and take your Popish drivel with you," Fiennes snarled.

As the rain fell more heavily the crowd grew impatient and started taunting. Jack raised his hand. Stationing himself close to the block, Merek covered his face with a black mask and picked up his axe. It was a signal to the escort. He took Fiennes first. Having loosened his collar the leading soldier tied a kerchief over his eyes and leading him towards the steps of the scaffold carefully guided him up them. Trembling with fear, Crowner hands gripped the rail so tightly his skin drove the knuckle bones outwards like the spine of a starved animal.

There was movement in the crowd and they pressed forward closer to the scaffold. Beside it, Scales sat impassively on his horse, Wyfold veiled his face with his cloak, but Jack and Richard gazed on. Holding out his hand to feel for the block, Fiennes bowed his head and called out emphatically.

"I have been wronged, may my enemies burn in the flames of Hell. God take my spirit."

The axe rose and the dull thud on the boards of the scaffold raised a noisy cheer from the onlookers. It was Crowmer's turn. Unable to mount the steps without assistance he was half-pulled, half-dragged up them. He gibbered something, but it was incomprehensible, then he promptly vomited. Soiled and shaking, he was led to the block. This time as the axe lifted the crowd roared their scorn at the sight of him.

The expression on the faces of the dead was trapped forever. Forced to look on one another from the straw their blood dripped silently off the block and more decked them in crimson collars. Slowly the crowd fell silent and with nothing more to witness they started drifting away. His work done, Merek hefted the bodies into the waiting cart. It was an undignified end for the Lord High Treasurer, Fiennes and his son-in-law, but there were no tears shed. Engulfed by his feelings of power Jack heard the crowd's jubilation. For a moment, he wondered if Mammy would have anything to say about the executions then dismissed his thoughts. She may have spoken of his destiny, but never how he might achieve it.

"We've made a start," he said, grinning at Richard. "There's nothing to stop us now."

Less certain, Richard was about to caution, but Jack was already speaking to Merek and the moment passed.

"Amen to that," Richard said under his breath. With his duty done, Scales left the place behind the death-cart. He was followed by Wyfold and the city Aldermen whilst with no more excitement the rebels set off along the street laughing and joking among themselves. Nodding to the disappearing cart, Jack instructed Merek with a sarcastic smile.

"See they get a decent pit to rest in. Where are Barda and William? Find them and tell them I want the heads of those two on poles. Take them through the streets to London Bridge so all can see we are rid of them at last. Then find the girl, Aditha and send her to the *Hart,* I have need of her."

"Aye, Captain," Merek replied simply.

Chapter Thirty

Warwickshire

IN London the Court was transfixed by events at Cheapside. Whilst the general agreement was that two heads were better than a city ravaged by rebels, there were mutterings about the Royal absence. A little under a hundred miles away at Kenilworth, Henry and Margaret gave London no thought as they enjoyed some courtly entertainment.

The jousting tournament was well attended and sitting side by side on their flower decked dais the couple were engrossed in one of the knights presently in the arena. Behind them nobles and their ladies relaxed in the warmth of the July afternoon. Attentive servants passed titbits amongst them and the talk was light-hearted and comfortable.

Both Destrier stallions were fine beasts. The one beneath Henry's half-brother, Jasper Tudor was an enviably fast and agile equine. Protected by armour, it was only the occasional movement of the plates where they met which revealed the beast to be the colour of glossy pitch. A light ornamental cloth covering its body carried the heraldic symbols of the King and the animal's armoured face shield threw points of silvery lights when it moved. To those who might not know, the richly embroidered pennant fluttering behind Jasper and the flash of scarlet on his arm revealed his identity. With his full helmet and plate steel armour, he could be seen spurring his horse to great speed. The stallion pounded towards its opponent and the young man's lance was raised at a formidable angle. With an imperceptible inward rush of air the audience held its breath.

Skilfully rising and falling, the lance plucked Jasper's opponent from the back of his horse as delicately as the dandelion releases its floating seeds and the audience roared their approval. Even Henry, usually lethargic in such an activity, felt compelled to stand and applaud the victor. Margaret was more restrained, but just as tempted. Sure her flushed features would be noticed, she sat fanning herself with one hand. Holding a snippet of Brussels lace in the other she gave a delicate wave.

"The boy is a master. Did you ever see such a fine performance?" Henry murmured as he seated himself. "Of course Owen, my step- father never lost at a tournament as far as I recall. It is high time I rewarded Jasper for he is fast showing great ability. He might enjoy being the Earl of Pembroke and the dukedom of Bedford too? What do you think, Lady Wife?"

Lost in her thoughts, Margaret didn't reply. Puzzled by her silence, Henry turned to his wife.

"Dear one, are you overheated? You look remarkably pink or is it you are unwell? Perhaps you flush due to a certain condition?"

His concern and hope were touching, but only managed to irritate her. Shaking her head, she stifled her desire to be abrupt with him and managed a faint smile.

"Forgive me. I too was admiring Jasper's prowess so not concentrating on your words. But of course he deserves such accolades. As always you are most thoughtful, dearest Husband."

Knowing Henry's hopes were always raised in matters concerning her barren state, she watched him carefully, but concealing his disappointment was not difficult for him. Patting her lap he said, "Good, that's settled then. I shall tell him when he joins us later."

Managing to get to his knees, the knight unseated by Jasper looked dazed. Still shaking his head, he allowed himself to be helped to his feet. Lying close by his lance was snapped in two and his horse stood apart snorting out noisy breaths. The minstrels fell quiet and the audience craned their necks for a better view.

"I do hope he's not hurt," Margaret said in a faint voice.

"Do you mean the horse or its rider?" Henry quipped, but his attempt at wit fell on fallow ground.

"Both I suppose," she replied vaguely, allowing Catherine to apply drops of rose perfumed water to her brow and points on her wrists.

It was Jasper's turn to command attention. To a loud outburst of clapping, Jasper removed his helmet and bowed first to Henry and Margaret and then to the crowd. Fearful Henry might hear the thudding of her heart, Margaret delicately edged her way a little apart from him. She mustn't allow anyone to see the effect Jasper had on her. Watching him through half-closed eyes she saw the softness of his dark hair as it curled at the nape of his neck and his aquiline nose which some might find unattractive, but which to her was an admirable characteristic of the House of Lancaster.

When their eyes met briefly she was sure he would see how much she adored him. Yet he might see uncertainty there too for she was still unsure whether he returned her affections. Leaving the groom to take his horse, he was walking towards them now with the token she gave him at the start fluttering defiantly from his upper arm. Even now she could still feel the taut flesh under her fingers when she tied the scarlet sash in place. Now she must clench her hands to prevent them reaching for him.

She felt herself wilting at his eager to please smile and his touching deference to Henry. Yet for him it hadn't always been so. Her beloved William Suffolk's sister, Katherine raised the boy and his older brother, Edmund at her nunnery in Barking. Such was the quality of her care it enabled them to slip into their life at Court with barely a glance. She knew Henry was genuinely fond of both boys, but somehow Jasper won over hearts with his charming manners and self-effacing ways.

I must be cautious, she thought appraising the figure in front of them. He was slender, but not too thin, tall, yet not lofty, a little on the youthful side, but so much the better for his virility would unquestionable she told herself. Now all she had to do was make him want her as much as she desired his presence in her bed. For unbeknown to Jasper Tudor, soon to be Earl of Pembroke and the first Duke of Bedford, Margaret had chosen him to sire the next King of England.

* * *

Disgruntled at being kept waiting, Scales paced the Long Gallery. Good at hiding his emotions, no one seeing him would guess his displeasure. When finally one of Henry's attendants arrived to escort him to the Royal Chamber, he conducted himself with his usual aplomb. "Majesties," he said, bowing to the floor.

After such a pleasant afternoon at the tournament, Henry was relaxed and in good humour. His hair and small beard were neatly trimmed and his eyes had lost their usual dreamy look, replaced with an unexpected brightness. Laying aside his red leather book with its exquisite gold tooling, he smiled broadly at their visitor.

"Scales, my good fellow, it is always a pleasure to see you. What brings you to Kenilworth?"

"I'm greatly concerned about events in London with the Kentish uprising, Sire."

Raising her head a fraction from her crewel work, Margaret's eyes travelled the length of the smartly attired military man. Once she might have considered him a suitable replacement for William, but it was only a passing thought, a moment of whimsy on her part.

"Are you not able to control matters, Lord Scales," she enquired. "For we have no intention of returning until you can assure us it is safe to do so."

Detecting some dislike when Scales looked at her, a weaker woman might have retreated. Not Margaret of Anjou. Instead she was enjoying seeing him thinking such things, yet unable to articulate them. Tightening his lips, he gave a quick bob of his head.

"Of course, Your Majesty, but despite us agreeing to the disposal of two of Kent's most despised men, the rebels still insist their demands are unanswered. Now they have added another complaint, bemoaning the fact that our loss of French land has severely affected trade in Kent with the foreigners and livelihoods are threatened. Perhaps, Majesty, if these people were to speak to the King himself . . ."

"Unthinkable!" Margaret snapped.

Usually slow at noticing tension, Henry felt forced to answer for his wife's somewhat churlish manner.

"I don't think my good Lady Wife meant that as it sounds. I fear she is not quite herself. The heat this afternoon may well have taxed her."

Margaret's hard expression didn't alter. "I am perfectly well, thank you. Pray continue, Lord Scales."

Once again the neatly trimmed hair barely moved as his head was inclined in her direction. Repressing an urge to shake him if only to rid the man of what she perceived to be a natural pomposity, Margaret gave up. Certain Jasper would be more entertaining she folded her work and stood.

"You are right, dear Husband, I do have the beginnings of a head pain. If you will excuse me, I shall retire. Perhaps a rest will cure me."

With her tiny girth, no more than a man's hand span, enclosed within a cream fitted Cote Hardie, Margaret's appearance was breathtaking. Low at the waist the bodice slipped without sight of a seam into her full damask skirt enhanced by a dazzling display of embroidered flowers each intended to replicate her natural colouring in tawny gold, bronze, rust and her pale complexion. Over it her Burgundy Garnache, a mantle of the finest wool, swished gently behind her as she bobbed to Henry brushing his knees with the length of her cape-like sleeves. Then ignoring Scales, she swept from the room.

"Women at certain times," Henry laughed fondly. "Do you have a wife, Lord Scales? If so you will understand such things. Now, where were we?"

Raising one eyebrow, Scales merely smiled.

"It is the matter of the Kentish uprising, Sire. We gave their leader Mortimer, the two men he asked for, Lord Fiennes and his son-in-law, and their heads now sit atop London Bridge, yet Mortimer has not kept his promise." Listening attentively, Henry said adjusted the silk coverlet about to slip from his knees.

"Which was what?"

"He gave his word to lay down his arms and keep his rebels in order. Already they have become undisciplined and are looting and brawling. Now I'm told there are more of them on their way from Essex this time. My informant says they intend to take the Tower and as if that weren't enough, disorder is spreading in the countryside. Only yesterday in Wiltshire, Bishop Ainscough of Salisbury was dragged from his alter and stoned to death."

Good humour deserted Henry in an instant. Instead his eyes grew dark as he looked at Scales.

"It can't be true. The good Bishop officiated at my marriage. My sweet Lady Wife will be distraught at the news. Did the Wiltshire men give reason for such a cruel act?"

It was rare for Scales to look awkward, but on this occasion he hesitated.

"Well?" Henry demanded.

"I'm sorry, Sire it concerns the Queen," Scales said in a low voice. "It would appear Her Majesty is not popular and they say the blame lies with the Bishop for approving your marriage to a . . ." he faltered.

Henry leant forward. His fingers were taut round the arms of his chair whilst a red flush travelling up from his collar swamped his usual pallor.

"Go on, to a what, what is it they call my wife? I demand you tell me."

"That 'uppity French woman', Sire," Scales said reluctantly.

A small moan escaped Henry and rubbing his hand distractedly across his forehead he lay back in his chair closing his eyes.

"Leave me, Scales. Do whatever you think best to repress the violence and rid the city of these tiresome commons. I thought I had some sympathy with their complaints, but now I'm not so sure. My dear Lady Wife is staunch in her belief our Lancastrian dynasty must be protected. Is that so wrong?"

It might have been a question to him, but Scales could only guess Henry asked it of himself. Seemingly oblivious of anyone else in the room Henry's head nodded onto his chest and his hands started twitching feebly on his lap.

Retrieving his hat and sword, Scales quietly left the chamber.

* * *

Henry had no idea how long he slept only that when he woke purple shadows inched their way into corners of the chamber. A servant must have entered because the wall sconces were lit sending a trembling lemony glow to relieve the imminence of dusk. Looking pensively at Margaret's empty chair, Henry sighed. Sometimes he wished she wasn't so headstrong, so determined, so wilful at times. If she had her way she would rule forever, he thought with a wry smile.

And where was the child they both desired so desperately? Visiting her bedchamber at regular intervals brought no success despite him consulting the apothecary.

Now he tired of hearing his virility was not in question. The man postured well enough, but he was incompetent and his pills and potions useless. A sudden heat seared his face as he thought about such an intimate matter and tears welled without warning.

He would go now he decided, wiping his cheeks dry. Demand Margaret should use all her tricks to rouse him. She was good at such things and he wasn't without manly feelings. Getting to his feet he straightened his crown. Concentrating hard on her feminine form he was grateful the corridors were deserted as he made his way to Margaret's chamber. Such was his arousal by the time he reached her door it was clearly obvious beneath his robe. Tapping, he waited impatiently. The steps he could hear seemed impossibly slow and this time he rapped firmly and called again.

"Hurry, dear Lady Wife, 'tis I your husband, do not tease me, my little cuckoo. Open the door."

It wasn't the sweetly arranged features of his wife who faced him when the door swung wide, but an older, coarser looking woman with several black hairs sprouting from her chin.

"Your Majesty," Catherine, the Lady of the Bedchamber said, in some surprise, "Is there something wrong?"

"I'm looking for my wife. She retired some time ago. Is she within?"

He thought a look of embarrassment flitted across Catherine's face, yet it was so fleeting he couldn't be sure.

"A walk Sire, that's it. Her Majesty thought taking the air would be beneficial."

"She is out walking, at this time of the day?"

"Or perhaps she went to the kitchens. She likes to supervise the catering from time to time. When there is a banquet that is," Catherine said lamely, flustered now.

Henry could feel his desire slipping away. A feeling of dejection washed over him.

"There is no banquet tonight. No matter, it is no longer important," he said quietly, swinging round from the room.

When he heard the door shut he set off down the corridor. Turning a corner he stopped a few paces down at another door and listened. Jasper's hearty and boyish laughter was unmistakable. Equally recognisable was the throaty feminine response.

Minutes before his step had been sprightly. Returning the way he came he walked with his head bowed in the shuffling manner of an old man.

Chapter Thirty-One

Southwark

SPREAD out on the sagging bolster their hair tumbled extravagantly in a wild mix of raven and sun-streaked brown. Heads close, their limbs were tangled in the coarse woollen blanket and both were slumbering. Rarely did Richard need to raise his voice, but seeing Jack and Aditha still abed he added urgency to his second attempt to wake them.

"Forsooth, Jack, rouse your selves. The cock has crowed and more. You are needed. Kentish men are raging through the streets. There is talk they attack women and worse. Some of the houses have been fired and there is a crowd of them on their way to Marshalsea. You must speak to them for they will listen to no one but you."

Slowly Jack's dark eyelashes quivered and opening his eyes, he struggled to sit up. In his moving the blanket fell away and Aditha lay sprawled in her nakedness. Jack had indeed found himself a beauty, Richard thought. He swallowed hard feeling sure he should look away, yet unable to do so. Watching her through half-closed eyes he saw her nubile body wriggle and then her eyes shot open.

"By my maidenhead, Sirrah, let me cover myself," angry, she clawed at the blanket.

Her outrage was met by a slap on her rump from Jack and his ribald laughter.

"Up wench and leave us. There is work to be done." Scowling at Richard, she collected her dress and left the room. Both men listened to the pad of her bare feet on the stairs until she vanished into the tavern below them.

"She's an attractive wench, John I'll give you that," Richard observed drily.

In the middle of yawning, Jack didn't reply, but the look on his face left Richard in no doubt this was a woman he cared a great deal for. Still this was no time for such ponderings, not when the uprising had lurched into mayhem with so much at stake. Gathering up the heap of Jack's clothes, he hurled them at him.

"I'll order us some food, but there is no time to waste," he said.

Jack grunted his reply.

Later, with a trencher of mutton inside them they saddled their horses and turned out into the High Street. The cool morning air enlivened their senses and it would have been a pleasant ride had it not been for the sound of shouting ahead of them and the sight of trails of surly smoke drifting above the tenements. As the clamouring grew nearer so did the stench of burning wood.

Drawing well ahead of Jack, Richard was the first to turn into Lant Street. In front of him the building blocks of the church of St. George the Martyr were struck golden by the sun ray's sneaking between the ragged rooftops. The street seemed undisturbed. Yet, waiting for Jack to catch up, he could hear the rallying cries of the Kentish men coming from the rear of the church.

"God's bones, they must be attacking the gaol," Richard said with an anxious frown when Jack joined him. "It won't go well for us unless you curb their behaviour. You gave your word to Scales there would be no pillage or have you forgotten?"

Unperturbed, Jack's smile was casual.

"Marshalsea is no place for a decent man, 'tis time they tasted freedom. Perhaps our men are a little reckless, but they grow bored waiting for our masters to agree to our requests. What matter if they pass the time amusing themselves."

"What matter? Have you lost your senses, John? Have you thought how quickly the people of this city will turn against us if we become lawless?"

"You worry too much, my friend," Jack replied. Laughing heartily he raced toward Angel Alley and the depressingly high wall embellished with spikes. Behind it lay the entrance door to Marshalsea. There was no time for more discussion when they confronted the wild scene in front of the gaol. Forced open with bars of iron, the door hung from a few bent rivets. Every dreg of impoverished and debt-ridden humanity was surging out of it in a stream of little more than skin and bones. Crowding onto the street most looked dazed, blinking in the sudden light. Others too starved and weak to run stretched out under the wall where they had fallen.

One end of the building was made up of a row of squalid houses. Scorched wood bore testimony to an earlier fire. Now too lazy to burn it simply issued the occasional puff of acrid smoke. Two drably dressed gaolers with bunches of keys dangling from their belts like grapes might hang from a vine, paid no attention to the escape of criminals and debtors. Talking together they were ignoring the wretches who managed to summon enough strength to run for their lives. Some turned away from the gaol and bolted for the nearby passage ways. A few ran farther passing Jack and Richard. In their grey bony faces, their hollow eyes rolled into the corners and their skinny hands clawed at the air as if attempting to part it.

"It seems we come just in time. Those poor devils don't look long for this world," Jack commented.

There was no reply from Richard. When Jack cast a sideling glance he could see the other's jaw set and his lips pursed in a thin line.

"Methinks you have no approval of setting them free, eh Richard?"

"It's not what we came for," Richard muttered.

"Maybe not," Jack mused. "But it's a good day for the poor just the same."

A noisy group of Kentish rebels came strolling towards them. Their faces were rosy with effort and they talked excitedly. Recognising Jack they swaggered up to him. Raising his hand in greeting, Jack said.

"You look pleased with yourselves, masters. Have you freed all the prisoners in that rancid place?"

"Aye, that we have, Captain and let the air into it, stinks it does. We saw more rats and dead bodies than we did living."

"So where are you off to now," Richard enquired, tight lipped.

"King's Bench Gaol," one replied. "There's plenty there who need our help."

"Then to Fleet," said another.

"Good for you, be on your way then," Jack called recklessly.

"John, be careful," Richard cautioned. His words tumbled onto the baked dirt beneath him. Watching Jack already ahead urging his horse into a gallop along the street, he gnawed hard on his lip. His opinion of Jack had changed. There would be unease when people in high places learnt of the rebels actions. He wanted no part in it and must make his position safe. Without doubt their chosen leader was an enigma and a perhaps a dangerous one. Resolving to speak to Simon of Kent, Richard disconsolately followed Jack.

* * *

When Richard sent word, so important was the meeting that Pultenery had ridden hard from Knole, Simon of Kent travelled from Court and Ralph, Lord Cromwell sent his representative, a heavily-bearded knight they called Sir John Fastolf who wore his colours. The gathering both small and select sat in a gloomy corner of the *Ship* tavern some distance from the *Hart*. Richard beckoned for the serving girl whilst Pultenery seated himself so as to preside over them all.

"So Master Pultenery, what is so urgent that my Lord Cromwell has been disturbed? I think we all believe the rebel leader may not be who he says he is. Plenty of people masquerade under a different name. Do you know more?" enquired Fastolf, his arrogant manner adding tension to the meeting.

"I do, sir. Now Richard and Simon have confided in me of their concerns about him, my informant has been finding out more."

"Is this man of yours reliable?" Fastolf asked, his suspicious eyes wandering across the other's face.

"I can assure you there comes no better than John Bailey," Pultenery replied tartly.

Simon sniffed. "I know the man and I think him a bit of a weasel."

"So much the better, it means he is familiar with the stench of black holes for that is where he must go to gather his information," Pultenery said, permitting himself a tight smile. "We are sure the man is Jack Cade, but who calls himself Mortimer. He is thought to have left Brigstowe in a hurry after killing a woman, a woman of the streets I might add."

There was a moment of silence as they considered his words and then a shrugging of shoulders.

"Go on," Fastolf said.

Enjoying the fact all eyes were on him, Pultenery looked smug as he said, "I took it upon myself to send Bailey back to Brigstowe and thence on a ship to Ireland. What he learnt will, I think, interest you all," he continued.

His companions leant forward in anticipation. The air was taut. Pausing to wait for the serving girl to replenish the jug of sweet ale, Pultenery slowly fiddled with a loose thread in his cape sleeve as if he was enjoying taking his time with the words.

"Bailey took great trouble, but even so he had difficulty in finding anything out. Methinks he's more a terrier than a weasel at times for he's hard to shake off when he gets a scent," he said finally.

Pleased with his little joke, he looked round for appreciation. There was none only rigid expressions and a stony silence.

"I'm beginning to wonder if you appreciate the seriousness of the situation, Pultenery. Lord Cromwell however will not be amused. Have you more to tell us or not?" Fastolf said grimly.

Exchanging glances, Richard and Simon could feel the animosity growing between Cromwell's man and Pultenery.

"It will be of great interest to us all should you care to tell us. I myself thank you for your diligence," Simon said pleasantly, anxious to mollify Pultenery.

It worked. Giving Simon a grateful look, Pultenery said.

"By all accounts our young hothead, Mortimer, may well be the spawn of Conall O'Neill and we all know the *Falcon* and O'Neill are almost as one. Mind you, 'twill be hard to prove . . ."

Fastolf, his expression a mix of anger and dismay, brought his fist down hard on the table top. "Kindly stop there if you will," he said. "This must never be known. If the commons learn of such a thing our cause will be lost. They must continue to believe Mortimer leads them in protest of their unfortunate lot and for no other reason."

Swivelling in his chair, Falstolf locked eyes with Richard. "Should Mortimer ever hear of his connection to the throne of York however vague, you will see to it he does not live long enough to act on it. Is that understood?"

There were sharp intakes of breath as Falstof spat out his words in fury. His cold grey gaze lingered on each of his companion's faces daring them to question his instructions. Only Simon defied his assumed authority.

"Are you in a position to make such a statement, Sir?"

"If these wishes are not carried out, 'twill not be me you answer to, I can assure you of that. It is Lord Cromwell himself who issues this command. Does that satisfy you, Sir?"

Chapter Thirty-Two

TOSSING the remains of his meal into the slop bucket, Jack sat on the edge of his rumpled pallet. Another day almost passed and as more news reached him of the rebel's wild antics on the city streets he grew ever more uneasy. *What should I do, Mammy? Things get out of hand. They say we grow unpopular with the people and no one seems willing to give us what we want. Have I been misadvised?*

He would have liked to hear her answer, but all he could make out was the random creak of the stair timbers and whispers of wind in the eaves. Striding to the window he pressed his face to the solitary pane of glass. Close to the *Hart,* all he could make out were bulky shadows cast by a watery moon and on occasions a glimmer from a torch. In the distance a different sight greeted him. The west of the city bled a crimson stain onto the horizon rising further and further skywards. Had he not realised what it was, he might have been perplexed, but he recognised a great burning when he saw it. The rebels were firing buildings again despite his reluctant orders earlier in the day.

Where were Richard and Simon when he needed them? He hadn't seen them for some time. Why did he feel troubled? What must they do next to make sure the King was listening to them? His hand reached for his temple kneading it as if that would make the answers appear. But they didn't.

Deciding he wanted company he reached for his boots. Aditha would come, he knew that, but urgency pulsed through his veins rather than passion. At the start of the rebellion he'd come alive, aglow with hope and determined to win a better future for the poor commons and himself. Now he felt deflated and isolated.

Such was the force as he slammed the door behind him that a piece of timber shivered in the frame before tumbling to the floor in a pile of powdery dust. On the stairs he brightened. He could smell the odour of cooking, split ale and stale sweat and it reassured him. If nothing else the drinkers in the tavern would be a distraction whilst he considered what the next move should be.

* * *

In his chamber in the Tower, Scales was also watching the fires spreading. As fast as the night sky grew a darker charcoal colour so the explosion of red eroded it. His fury was ready to erupt too. Nothing except bad news was reaching his ears that day. Firstly the Queen's Chancellor, William, Bishop of Lichfield almost lost his life when rebels cornered him. Now fresh word recently arrived about Walter, Bishop of Norwich who was much relied on by Her Majesty as her Confessor. He too had barely escaped from the hands of more marauding rebels who travelling through East Anglia, burst into the city attacking him as he left the Cathedral. Raging at the wayward behaviour of the rebels and the inferno billowing in the distance, he muttered, "Enough! Enough."

Taking his glass of wine with him he walked the length of the chamber and back glowering into the rosy depths of the flagon. Appealing as his bed might look he was far too agitated to think of rest. Things could not continue. Those loyal to the Crown must mount a counter- attack. Even as he thought about it he felt his spirits rising. Now all he had to do was to rouse everyone else into a force which would destroy the rebellion once and for all, but who to lead it with him, who would he trust with such important task?

Several names came to mind, yet not one of them was ideal. Deep in thought, he returned to the window. The red sky was fading and turning instead into a pale orange haze. He'd seen such colours in the last hours of war, and then it came to him. Opening the door, he called down the corridor to a guard propping his inert bulk up against the oak panelling.

"You there, stir yourself. Fetch me Captain Gough and be quick about it."

When a short while later, Matthew Gough presented himself to Scales, there was nothing about him outwardly to signify the merit of the man. Ageing and grizzled, he was a little on the short side, his looks plain and his appearance inoffensive. He might seem mild-mannered with a benign expression, even apprehensive at times. Those who fought with him on the battlefields in France would tell you otherwise. Courageous, stoic and valiant, a recent knighthood added to his list of honours for exemplary service as a soldier in the King's army.

"Come in, come in Matthew," Scales greeted him warmly, ushering him towards the most comfortable chair in the room. "Good of you to come so promptly."

Pulling off his hat, Matthew bent at the knee.

"I am at your service, my lord," he replied in a rich baritone voice at odds with his slight frame.

There was raucous singing coming from a passing barge on the river and Scales hastily snapped the window shut before pouring out a fulsome glass of wine for his visitor.

"How are you finding your new position as Captain of the Tower? I hear good things about you and so soon after taking up your duties," Scales enthused.

Embarrassed by the praise the Welshman's fresh cheeks glowed red.

"Thank you, Lord Scales. After the battlefield 'tis a post I relish."

"Good, good," Scales murmured. "I expect you are wondering why I have sent for you. It can't have escaped you that Mortimer and his infernal rebellion gets out of hand. They have been in the city a week now and 'tis time they were crushed. How would you feel should I ask you to help me lead a force against them?"

Having asked the question, Scales watched closely for Matthew's reaction. He knew of his courage and skilful ways in a battle, but would he rise to this, he wondered. When Matthew bowed his head as a nod of assent, Scales sighed with relief.

"When shall we start?" Matthew enquired, draining his flask with gusto. Beads of liquor clung to his grey moustache and lodged on his pale lips which he wiped away with the back of his hand.

"At once, there can be no delays. Equip yourself with whatever you need and make sure the garrison is prepared. Tomorrow night whilst others sleep we will assemble here at the Tower."

"Will we have enough men?"

"I'll make sure of it," Scales said. "The city Aldermen must call the city to arms and I'll wager there will be no shortage. They tire of Mortimer and his men looting and brawling as much as I do."

Getting to his feet, Matthew bowed again. "Then if you will excuse me, my lord, I shall waste no time. There are preparations to be made."

"Excellent," Scales replied with an appreciative smile. With his ear to the door the guard narrowly missed detection. A stiff latch caused Matthew to fumble so delaying his exit and forewarned the guard hastily resumed his place in the corridor. Meeting Matthew's gaze as he passed him, his pale blue eyes reflected nothing whilst the wheels in his mind turned at speed. As soon as he was relieved of his post, Captain Mortimer would be pleased with the information he would pass to him.

* * *

There was so much violence on the thoroughfares, Jack doubted if anyone would notice him let alone stop him, but once he was on the street one before the *White Hart,* caution got the better of him and he had sprinted the last few yards.

First glancing over his shoulder to make sure the door was firmly shut he emptied the pockets inside his roomy coat lining of their horde of silver and gold marks. He went to the pockets on his jacket next and finally his lambskin waist bag, throwing everything onto his pallet. Annoyed his hands were still shaking, he tried hard to steady them. He was out of breath too and his gasps were painful.

What lay on the soiled coverlet represented a fortune to him and all collected in less than a few hours. The fool merchant, Alderman Malpas fought so hard to hang on to his possessions. It had begun as a friendly meal, an invitation to see if soft words could achieve a peaceful solution to the uprising and it ended in a blood-letting. Jack didn't feel any guilt. If Malpas hadn't been so reluctant to part with it, he would still be alive.

Reconciling himself with the immorality of the theft, Jack spread out the treasure before separating it into heaps. Plucking up a heavy gold chain he allowed it to slither through his fingers examining the intricately worked links as it did so. Greedy for the feel of such opulence he scrabbled through the rings like a child might through its playthings. A quail-egg sized opal was abandoned in favour of an emerald cushioned in a bed of gold and pearls, a weighty ruby tossed aside as he slipped a gold encrusted bloodstone onto his finger. It looked incongruous, but he kept it on just the same. As for the candle sticks and a small dish and salver, he had never seen such finely crafted silver. Catching his reflection in the fiercely polished surface of the salver, he barely recognised himself. His hair and beard resembled a bear, his skin laced with lines and pitted with dirt and his eyes reflected a feral expression which startled him. But there were prettier things to occupy his thoughts.

Drawn to several gold-faceted bangles he imagined them swirling around Aditha's slender wrists. A splendid pearl and vivid green peridot brooch would fasten her cloak nicely and a ring or two perhaps on her delicate fingers would not go amiss, but not yet, it was too dangerous. For now, he was content to dream of the riches they would bring to him come the day. Lost in admiration with his hoard, he barely heard the hesitant tap on the door.

Wrenching off a strip of his hoary blanket, he quickly piled the items on it and stuffed the bundle under the bolster.

Hands behind his back, he listened intently to the Tower guard. In his haste to deliver his news, the man spoke quickly to the accompaniment of showers of fine spit which spun into the air. Taking a quick step back, Jack considered the information.

"Tomorrow night, you say. Are you sure you heard them right? Any mistakes on your part could cost us dear," he said.

"I swear, Captain Mortimer, that's what Lord Scales said," the guard replied.

Anxious to depart he edged closer to the door. As if reading his mind, Jack nodded.

"Go quickly and tell nobody of this. Are you sure no one saw you come up here?"

His hand already grasping the handle, the guard jigged on the spot. Looking bemused, Jack frowned.

"Well, what are you waiting for?"

"My wages are poor, Captain," the man whined. "My wife and children need food. Is there any chance of a small reward? I took a great risk coming here."

His hand in his pocket, Jack fumbled in the lining. He made a show of it so the guard wouldn't suspect he too was as poor as a church mouse until his dreams were realised. The groat was his last and too much.

"Here take this," he said, flipping the coin casually in the guard's direction. It tumbled at his feet and he darted for it eagerly.

"God bless you, Captain Mortimer, sir. What they say about you 'tis true, you are a fine gentleman indeed," the man said, a vacuous smile spreading his plump jowls into pasty troughs.

"Speak to no one as you leave," Jack growled, but the guard was already gone.

Staring at the door his heart thudded so much he held his chest as if trying to still it. It was always the same at the thought of war, but this time there would be another edge. His destiny lay within his grasp now. *There Mammy, do you see. Fortune and fame you said. Now it is nearly mine...* He thought of all the years passed since he left Ireland. Closing his eyes he saw himself as a child on her knee by the hearth as the slow burning peat sent lazy spirals of smoke towards the thatch. The fire in his chamber didn't give out much in the way of warmth, but he felt it spreading across his face and into his belly. Only now he wasn't a little boy safe in the arms of his mother, but a grown man about to do battle. An all-consuming excitement made his hands tremble and twisted his gut. As his blood ran faster through his veins, the old wound on his arm pulsed under the puckered red skin making him grimace.

The sweat breaking out on his brow sobered him. There was no time to waste. In the poorly lit chamber he could just make out the suit of armour propped up in the corner and he contemplated whether to wear it again. Dismissing the thought with a wild laugh, he realised it was already the early hours of the morning. Encamped near the Tower the Kent men would be sleeping after hours of roistering and looting.

Elation made him heady as he ran his hand down the cold steel of his sword before buckling it to his belt then threw on his leather jerkin. Clamping his hat on his wayward curls, he left the chamber on his way to rouse them. Some forty thousand must be primed and ready to meet any force the city might care to set against them. It was an exciting prospect, he thought as he hurried down the wormy stairs.

Chapter Thirty-Three

London Bridge

CLAMPED still by the lack of wind the oily blackness of the great river of London seemed to be holding its breath. Earlier in the night it reflected boat lamps and had a generous moon to thank for its surface sheen. But a thick mist appeared consuming everything in its path like the Devil's breath, hiding the stars and devouring the moon. Rolling over the bridge it obscured the stone arches and piers before drifting ankle-level along streets. Those gathering in them could be heard cursing their luck.

"A bad omen," Richard said thoughtfully.

"I've known worse," Jack replied undaunted. "We have fortune on our side and God to protect us."

"Amen to that," muttered Merek, crossing himself. Waiting in their thousands, the rebels were gathered on the Southwark side at the North Gate end of the bridge. If the dwelling houses and shops around them contained any life, they were soundless. But anyone looking closely might have seen the shiver of a hastily closed shutter, the trembling hand extinguishing a wick and the innocence of children silenced by a nervous finger laid to their lips.

In the spindly shadows of a butcher's shop, Jack was watching anxiously for the return of Barda and Walter. As they emerged through the fog he breathed a sigh of relief.

"By God's bones, you took your time. You had me worried. What did you find out?"

Gesturing to the thick murky air, Barda laughed wryly.

"Very little in this, you'd be lucky to see your boots, but we managed to get as far as the drawbridge!"

"And then?" Richard asked.

"And then, nothing, it is quieter out there than a graveyard under snow so we went no further."

"Did you not see anyone?"

"If you mean any of the King's forces, no. A beggar or two, plump whores and a pack of dogs, that's about all." Barda smirked, but with his good humour fading, Jack said shortly.

"No sign of the garrison, are you sure? If that fat fool of a guard has told me wrong, I'll find him and feed his innards to a crow, I promise you that."

* * *

Barda and Walter may not have seen anyone of import, but hundreds of eyes were on them as they turned to go back to the Southwark end of the bridge. With muffles on his horse, Scales waited as the garrison troops emerged like spectres from their hiding places. Some yards down the street on a grey stallion, Matthew raised a scarlet cloth into the patchy fog. Once they could make out the signal, more men slipped out of dwelling houses and appeared from a multitude of shadowy places to join the soldiers. City captains, Esquires, retainers, Wyfold the mayor, a group of Aldermen led by Sutton, a goldsmith and Roger Heysant, a draper who were both well known for their prowess with maces joined the hundreds of citizens long fatigued by the rebel's presence. Every man answering the call and quietly assembling.

Well armed, the garrison troops in their dark green tunics carried a crossbow slung on their shoulder, swords to hand and poleaxes whilst others released the spiked ball and chain from their maces. At first the throng of warlike figures led by Scales and Matthew advanced slowly. Behind them followed the knights on horseback with a gentle metallic rustle and finally a host of city folk armed with any weapons they could lay their hands on.

At the same time from the other side of the bridge, Jack's rebel army were on the move too. Like lengths of pale chiffon the fog wafting round them concealed them for awhile, but inexperienced at such confrontations many of the rebels were less than careful to conceal their voices. Before Jack could send a messenger back to quieten them, the alarm sounded somewhere in front of them. Surging forward the rebels needed no encouragement. Neither would they wait for a rallying cry, but Jack gave it just the same. Waving his sword over his head, he urged.

"By the Saint's sweet deliverance for our King and his people, see to it victory is ours."

A shower of arrows discharged by the rebels flew over his head as with Richard, Merek, Barda and Walter, he charged into the attack. Never was he happier. Strategy forgotten, caution abandoned and with a devilish smile playing on his lips, Jack rode like a man possessed.

* * *

Fighting was ruthless as Scales led his men into battle. Meeting on the drawbridge neither side would give quarter, nor was it asked for or granted. At the beginning it seemed the King's men were easy prey for their opponents, but as the foot soldiers fell more instantly took their place. Directing the attack, Scales felt a momentary pang of dismay. The tenacity of the rebel army surprised him.

Perhaps he had underestimated them, rag-tag bunch as they were. He might not care for his inept ailing King and even less for Margaret, but his support for the throne of Lancaster was unshakable. The soldier in him stiffened with pride and he told himself to command his men like nothing before.

About to close his visor, he saw Matthew ahead of him. Scales smiled grimly at the skill and tenacity his captain displayed. Exposing himself to danger time and again, Matthew showed his enviable skills for which he was renowned on a battlefield. Every thrust and stab found its target as step by step he drove back his two assailants. One fell with a dagger thrust to his throat. The other suddenly off balanced gave a heinous scream and toppled off the broken bridge into the water with a loud splash. But Scales had no time for admiration and when he felt a hatchet scrape his armour he too was forced to defend his life. No sooner had he felled his attacker then another pulled roughly at his bridle. Pushing him away with his boot, the man stumbled and falling under the prancing feet of a passing horse was left with a broken head. His shrill cries stuttered and stopped.

* * *

Having just felled a man with a ferocious swirl of his sword, Jack paused. Wiping his blood spattered face on his arm he peered at the scene. It seemed the fog was lifting, but what he saw through its remnants troubled him. The only person he recognised was Merek carrying a fluttering banner from somewhere on his horse. Worse were the heaped bodies through which he navigated his way in Jack's direction.

"I thought we had the best of it," he said through gritted teeth when he managed to steady his mount beside Jack. "Now I wonder."

"This is no time for such thoughts. Look around you, the King's men don't fare well either. We shall not stop until the last of us falls," Jack countered harshly. "Beside I have a plan. Find me one of ours if you can and send him to me."

Terrible noises of moans and screams continued, but the fighting abated momentarily giving Merek his opportunity. Seizing the skinny arm of a boy rebel pausing for breath he gestured to the lad to go to Jack. At the same time, Richard broke through the melee. Before Jack could signal to him, he saw a footman grasping a poleaxe with both hands coming up behind his friend. He shouted out Richard's name, it was instinctive, yet he knew he wouldn't hear him. The war hammer rose and fell with a muffled moist thump and he saw Richard's skull explode. He went down as straight as a halberd stave with no time to crease or bend and the armour clad figure vanished back into the confusion. With no time other than to utter a dismayed groan, Jack pulled the rebel closer to him so he could be heard. He would mourn Richard later, but now was about survival.

"Find a torch and fire the bridge," he ordered.

Snatching up one of the few torches there were, the boy dodged his way across the street. In seconds the rope of the drawbridge flared, shrivelled and then fell to the ground. In fiery fragments the hemp sparkled briefly before extinguishing itself. Sudden and unexpected, huge flames erupted. At first they trembled quietly on the edge of the wooden bridge then they fired everything they could reach with crimson confidence. As the timbers burnt the remains of the bridge plunged into the cold, unquestioning river below. Those like Richard were carried with it, those still living drowned.

The same wind which carried the fog away was now the fire's willing servant. Dancing among the flames it fed them with strength and energy. In moments the nearby dwellings were alight and then quickly falling in on themselves became smouldering ruins. Women carrying babes and clutching for children ran screaming onto the cobbles before falling, only to be dashed against the dark arches of the bridge below. The fire showed no preference so soldiers, poor commons and the high born either burnt in the blazing debris or leapt to their death together.

Once he moved away from the inferno, Jack looked on with cold excitement. It reminded him of when he was on the battlefield in France; the same strength flowing through his being, the same pounding in his chest and the same satisfaction as to how easy it was to kill. It was only a rebel pursued by an axe-wielding soldier who nudged him as he ran past which woke him from his reverie and then he concentrated on the scene.

There was no doubt the royalists were being driven back, and pursued by rebels were put to death amongst the dark airless recesses of the stone slabs. All around him was the clash of metal, grinding bone and dripping swords, but Jack heard above them the shouts and cries of encouragement. Punctuated by the piercing shrieks of the wounded it only added to the terrifying spectacle. A rusty coloured light thrown onto the water from the burning buildings, illuminated the horrific scene as bobbing bodies made room for the living drowning. Vile smoke swirled into the air as stifling as any fog and he hastily pulled his tunic high to cover his nose. He had no idea how long they'd been fighting only that a pale light was emerging in the east. Pleased as he was the rebels were giving a fine display this was no time to gloat.

Sword in hand, he ventured back into the fighting trying to regroup his men to present a formidable force on what remained of the bridge. It was hazardous as more and more corpses littered the water, but seeing him the rebels rallied. Relieved to see Merek and Barda were still defending themselves with vigour, he started to cut and thrust his way toward them. A hand on his shoulder jerked him roughly round and he found himself looking into the fierce blood-shot eyes of Scales.

Gone was the upright bearing of the man, the immaculate cut of his clothes and his haughty disdain. Instead Jack saw a pale, bloody image in front of him. His breast-plate missing, his tunic cut to rusty ribbons and one side of his face a mat of congealed blood amongst the grime.

"Mortimer, I propose a truce," he gasped, his contorted lips revealing an empty blood-stained tooth socket. Unable to resist his lively humour, Jack almost managed a grin.

"Fie, sir, does that mean you will lay down your arms?" Immediately Scales spat back at him like a spirited mother cat with newly born kittens.

"No, sirrah, it does not! I intend to vanquish, not to yield, but I believe we are at an impasse and neither side seems likely to win the day. I am merely suggesting that we agree no Londoner should pass this way to Southwark, nor

Kentish man put one foot in London until the morrow. What say you?"

Thoughtfully pondering on his words, Jack passed his hand across his forehead. It came away wet with an oozing mingled with blood-stained soot and he realised at some point he must taken the point of a dagger somewhere on his scalp. Then again he hadn't noticed one leg of his hose was in gory fragments or just missing its target, an arrow tip hung from a loop of wool in his jacket.

Whist reluctant to agree, he knew Scales was right to suggest a halt. The cacophony of noise was fading and a quick glance showed him both rebel and royalists were faltering. A few dark clouds remained, but the flittering light taking their place had little success as the grey pall of smoke drifted aimlessly in the air. When a solitary ray managed to pierce the haze it briefly turned the ripples of the turgid river into shining silvery scales. Then they aimlessly changed into a drab olive colour again.

"Very well," Jack agreed. "But take heed my Lord, we are not finished yet. We shall fight the King's men and more until taxes are fair for all and all men are free."

"Brave words, my friend, but we shall see. This rising is unlawful. As you rise against the King's men so you rise against our monarch and you will be found guilty of treason," Scales replied coldly.

A disturbing light of fervour glittered in Jack's eyes and he gave a derisory laugh

"Nonsense, it is the King who will help us. Besides I know my destiny and it is told I shall triumph," he roared through spittle-ringed lips.

Looking hard at Jack, Scales wondered. Was Mortimer a madman? Or merely exhausted as he was with fatigue? Either way he had one final barb to deliver to him.

"Mortimer, I give you a word of warning. Take care who you ride with. There are some who have no interest in the lot of the poor commons. Treachery is with you. I promise you that. Now call to your men and tell them they may rest at the southern end of the bridge unhindered. It will be decided when we meet again."

Wheeling his horse he sternly saluted Jack and nodding to his Esquire who carried the white flag of truce, both rode across what remained of the bridge in the direction of the Tower. A trumpet brayed loudly followed by the sounds of beating drums and watched by Jack, the remains of the King's force stumbled doggedly behind their leader.

Dismissing the remark made by Scales as an empty threat, Jack's bravado was undiminished. With a choice of weapons strewn on the ground, he rearmed and went to look for Merek.

Chapter Thirty-Four

IT was late into the morning when the dust cleared and the fires subsided into piles of paltry ash. An evil stench corroded the nostrils of all who stood and stared, but like hungry wolves no amount of vile odour or buzzing flies could drive them from the place. London Bridge harvested so many bodies it was difficult to move. Distraught women picked their way amongst the corpses searching for a husband or son. Dragging on their skirts, grizzling children looked on with bewildered eyes too frightened to leave their mothers' side. Scales too worked diligently checking, examining, discarding one corpse after another. Alderman Sutton was missing as was Heysant, the draper and more sobering still, Matthew was also unaccounted for.

Scales knew he should be elsewhere. He'd been summoned in haste to meet the Archbishop of York and Bishop Wayneflete, without delay so the messenger told him. It was of no consequence as far as he was concerned for nothing would be so important until he found his old comrade.

Then he saw him. Crumpled up like discarded sacking beside a stone pillar, Matthew looked as if he might be sleeping except dark, congealed blood stained his red and silver tabard. His lips relaxed in a gentle smile, the pouches and lines of age had slipped away from his face leaving untroubled youthfulness. Collecting what energy he could find in his stiff shoulders and aching limbs, Scales bent down. With profound sorrow etched on his tired face he scooped the broken body into his arms. As Matthew's head lolled in the protection of his bearer's grip, Scales saw his throat wound stretching from one side to another. It was a fiendish sight and used as he was to such things, Scales couldn't prevent silent tears reach over his eyelids.

Carrying Matthew to the side of the bridge left standing, he searched for a heavy stone. Securing it using the girdle round Matthew's waist, he knelt to release him for the last time. With infinite care he rolled him toward the edge. His fingers were shaking as he laid them on the alabaster cheek. Their coldness chilled him too.

"Farewell my brave knight. May God have mercy on your soul," he murmured, with the lightest of touches. Swallowing him down with a splash and a show of bubbles, the Thames received another to hold in its watery coffin and Matthew disappeared from sight. Despondent, Scales stared at the place for a long time. It wasn't how he intended. Captain Matthew Gough, a virtuous man of such excellent renown who surpassed all others on the battlefield deserved better. Yet, as Scales watched the river carrying its vile luggage of waste and decay, he decided best his friend rested under it than be left for the crows to feast on his eyes.

* * *

"If I didn't know you, Lord Scales, I would call your tardiness impudent," one of the venerable clerics said from the gloom as Scales presented himself. Cardinal Kemp, Archbishop of York and his Bishop William Wayneflete, hovered beside a weighty stone pillar inside the door of St. Margaret's Church, firmly clutching their stout crosiers. They both looked wary.

"My apologies for my delay, My Lords," Scales replied levelly.

"I'm not sure we should even be in Southwark," Wayneflete chimed in nervously. "The hoards on the streets are mostly ruffians by the look of them and very intimidating."

"Mortimer's rebels I suppose and not to be underestimated. Which is why we are here," Kemp said briskly.

Side by side the two men made an odd physical match despite their similar clerical vestments. In their Episcopal mitres, both wore scarlet copes edged with beaver fur, Kemp's being fastened by a vast gilded brooch whilst Wayneflete's was a less ornate chain affair. Gilded cords encircled their waists above which rested gold crucifixes, so large they barely moved with each breath.

Tall, thin and haughty, Kemp cast a sidelong glance of impatience at his companion's obvious unease. Wayneflete, small with heavy jowls and a little on the plump size, shuffled his feet with a jarring scraping noise on the flagstones. His eyes were never still, searching the shadowy recesses of the nave as if he expected an unwanted visitor to spring out at any moment.

Desperately weary, Scales leant against the pillar. All he wanted was to clear his head and rest his body before his next meeting with the rebel army later that day. The look he saw on Kemp's face told him he wouldn't be doing either for awhile yet.

"So Your Grace's, what is it that brings you to London?" he asked.

Reaching into a cavernous satchel beside him, Kemp drew out handful after handful of white forms. Handing them to Wayneflete, he ignored the fact they overflowed his arms as quickly as he received them and slipping to the floor lay strewn around his feet. With a brief glance, Scales saw they were all blank.

"We have come from Kenilworth and these are on the order of the King," Kemp announced. "They are forms of pardon and His Majesty wishes them to be offered to all in the rebellion who promise to lay down their arms and return to their homes."

He gestured to Wayneflete, who with a plaintive look dropped to his knees attempting to gather up the pieces of paper. Sorry for him, Scales joined him and between them they managed to raise the forms into piles on a nearby pew.

"You have seen the King. Is he well?" Scales asked, as he brushed the dust from his knees.

Too short of breath to answer, Wayneflete simply rolled his eyes and it was left to Kemp to reply.

"Not the King exactly, the forms were issued on Queen Margaret's authority. His Majesty is indisposed. Deeply concerned for the safety of the House of Lancaster, Her Majesty desires you try kind words and reasonable pledges to Mortimer and his friends in the hope of achieving a solution to this rising."

Digesting Kemp's words, Scales was in reflective mood. It didn't much sound like the woman he knew. She would have a hidden plan, he was sure of that.

"It might be as well not to disclose the Queen's part in this. You know as I do, she lacks the support of the people whereas the King does not. Does he take to his bed?" he asked.

His fears and lack of air temporarily forgotten, Wayneflete looked excited.

"Indeed, indeed," he babbled. "It's all very delicate, but the King's melancholia is much worse this time. In fact, his apothecary fears he verges on madness."

His exasperation obvious, Kemp turned on his companion.

"Really Bishop, you are most indiscreet. It would be prudent not repeat such things about the King. If the populace get to hear their monarch is insane the outcome could spell disaster for the country. Kindly curb your tongue and get on with what you are supposed to be doing," he snapped.

The eyes rolled again as Wayneflete's cheeks flushed a shade darker than his normal puce.

"Yes of course Your Grace, at once Your Grace," he gibbered.

If he hadn't been so exhausted and grieving for Matthew, Scales might have laughed at the riposte between the two clerics. As it was the ferocious night battle left him with no zest for a repeat despite needing to secure the final part of the bridge. Bowing deeply to Kemp, he picked up a quantity of papers handing them to Wayneflete. With a heavy armful himself, Scales said gravely.

"Come, Bishop, let us find the rebels and distribute these forms of pardon.

With Wayneflete pattering after him, Scales strode down the aisle leaving the cloistered air resounding to the sound of his jingling spurs and heavy boots on the stone slabs.

"Perhaps you should go first, Lord Scales," Wayneflete said fearfully. "I come from Winchester. I am not at all familiar with the streets of Southwark."

Lowering his head so his smile wouldn't be seen, it amused Scales that the rotund little man's nervous fingers played with his Rosary as he was speaking. He could almost hear the cleric's silent prayer for Godly protection chanting inside his head.

* * *

In the yard beside the *Hart,* the stable lad held Jack's horse. Gone lame since the battle it was being examined by the smithy. Merek was there too and after running a finger down his newly sharpened axe blade, he happened to glance down the street. Watching the two horsemen warily as they rode slowly towards him, he called over his shoulder to Jack. "We have visitors, Captain."

Jack's voice had an edge to it as he laid aside the dagger he was cleaning and looked across to Merek.

"Not bearing arms I hope, otherwise we are done for. Our men are scattered all over Southwark, Barda and Walter are calling them to rally at the bridge. How many men can you see?"

"Just two, one looks like Lord Scales and the other is a fat clergyman with a white pennant raised. I see no King's men with them," Merek replied cheerfully.

"A party of peace perhaps, but we must be careful," Jack said, with no haste to his step as he joined Merek.

"Good day to you, my sons," Wyanflete called out with a benign smile. "You can see we come in peace. I'm Bishop Wyanflete of Winchester and I believe you are acquainted with Lord Scales."

Dropping his head briefly, Scales acknowledged them. He seemed content for his companion to do the speaking whilst he stared into the distance with a bland expression. A plump pigeon wouldn't have looked more important than Wyanflete when he finished rooting in his leather satchel. Pulling out a host of forms he waved them aloft.

"I have here your salvation, my sons." Still smiling broadly, he nodded his approval as Merek hastily crossed himself. "I can assure you, God has saved you from eternal damnation."

Jack laughed, loud and confident. "God, what has he to do with our struggle?"

Wyanflete's smile faded. With a pained expression he said, "It brings me sorrow to hear you say that, God is always sharing our travails. Are you not a devout man, Master Mortimer?"

The picture in Jack's mind was sharp as if the passage of years was not so. He could almost feel Mammy's precious rosary, the black beads slipping through his child's fingers, the delicate cross large in his immature hand, but tiny in her calloused palm. Her soft voice of reproach, yet tinged with laughter too.

You be careful, Jack, don't you go breaking it or else the Holy Father will chide you so he will.

Why do you hold it, Mammy?

How else do I speak to our blessed Lady? Only she will understand our sins and forgive us. Now kneel here beside me and say after me . . .

Interrupting Jack's thoughts the image vanished as quickly as it came when he heard Waynflete saying.

"I see you are slow to answer, my son. Blessed are the meek . . ."

"This is no time for a sermon, Bishop," Scales said shortly. "You had better explain what it is we have come about."

Never deflated for long, Wyanflete smiled again.

"Indeed, indeed, my Lord, you are right. Master Mortimer, I have here many thousand royal pardons for you and your followers. On the instructions of our gracious Majesties, I am to offer them freely to any who give up the rebel cause. If they abandon the rebellion and leave the city without further ado they are guaranteed a safe passage home. Now, what do you think of that?"

It was a disappointment. Not only might others consider it an easy defeat, but Jack could see his glittering future in ruins. The moving spirit of the man he was only had eyes on his Mammy's dreams, but then he knew nothing of the Yorkist influences at work and he was impulsive by nature. This was about *him*, he assured himself and it was all that mattered. Drawing himself up, his eyes locked not on the cleric but on his adversary, Scales. The other returned his gaze with the look of an iced puddle and there was a scent of rancid sweat and potent maleness in the air. A cloying musk which they all inhaled as a sudden silence prevailed. Then Jack replied, slowly and thoughtfully.

"What do I think? I think we are unwilling to abandon our fight with nothing in return. The government knows of our complaints as does the King. They have had time enough to consider them, yet we hear nothing. Tell them John Mortimer says no."

"Are that's where you are wrong," Wyanflete chuckled, deeply enjoying his role as a peacemaker. "I am to assure you all your demands will be met, is that not so, Lord Scales?"

Masking his impatience, Scales appeared civil. "The Bishop is correct. Your requests will be granted in full," he said in clipped tones.

All this time, Merek was listening. He had the look of a greedy man as he watched Waynflete shuffling the pardons back and forth in his hands. "It would be a fine outcome, Captain," he breathed in Jack's ear. "We have lost good men and some will not fight again, surely 'tis better than any more slaughter."

Remembering Simon's promise of wealth if the rising was successful, Jack deliberated. If it was true and all their demands were agreed, accolades would be his and a golden future too. Then Mammy spoke to him from the grave. *Be careful, m'aingal, my angel. Choose the right road . . . Death is final so it is.*

"God damn you, Mortimer. Haven't enough people died?" Scales said with a sour smile.

"Very well, let us go to my followers and let them decide," Jack said in his fearless manner.

Chapter Thirty-Five

Kenilworth
Warwickshire

SET free from the confines of combs and hairpins, Margaret's hair rippled over her shoulders like a winnowing wind disturbing a field of grain.

"Gold, pure gold," Catherine breathed, with a hairbrush held aloft. "Now hold still, sweet child whilst I brush it for you."

Any other time, Margaret would have allowed such a thing, closing her eyes and succumbing to the delicious sensation. Today she tossed her head ducking away from the offer.

"Enough! You brush too hard. Leave it loose. I don't care to have it touched."

It was far from her normal behaviour and brought a frown to Catherine's brow.

"My Lady?" she questioned. "Does something trouble you? If so you know you can share it with me. Let Cat carry your burden for you, for those shoulders of yours are far too slender," she crooned.

Swivelling round on her stool, Margaret gazed at her faithful servant. It surprised her to see silvery lights were appearing in Catherine's mousey brown hair and in the bright light her unremarkable brown eyes held a milky sheen. The hand which held the brush was marked with liver-spots and lost its firmness too, but the devotion in the woman's eyes was still unmarred by age.

"How old are you, Cat?" Margaret asked quietly.

"I can't tell you that my Lady, for poor Cat doesn't know herself, but ancient it seems. There are times when my bones ache and creak like a floorboard in need of a blacksmith's nail. These old eyes don't see so well either, yet never could I miss the sad expression you are wearing now. What is it, dearest child?"

This time it was Catherine's turn to stare hard at her mistress, searching her face for a sign which would tell her the cause of her beloved's poor humour. Not that she ever had much success examining those blue expressionless orbs where the light of determination never faded. Yet at the same time they were devoid of inner thoughts, of emotion, of happiness or of sorrow. Soulless eyes which were impossible to read no matter how well you knew the beautiful face which carried them.

With a heavy sigh, Catherine laid down the brush and walked away to busy herself laying out another of Margaret's exquisite day gowns.

"Don't bother, I shan't get dressed today. I don't feel well. Prepare my bed, Catherine if you please, I wish to return to it," Margaret said in a low voice.

As she stood the pain came with a terrible griping spasm which made her clutch her stomach and groan out loud. Horrified, Catherine ran across the room holding out her arms to receive the hurting child.

"Your Grace, whatever is it? Shall I fetch the apothecary?"

Margaret was hostile, pushing her away with a muttered oath.

"God's bones, don't meddle. I have no need of him. Just help me to my bed," she instructed brusquely. "It's nothing, merely the time of my moon blood."

Shaking her head, Catherine said, "Surely not, my Lady, it can't be 'tis too soon from the last, I recall . . ." Her words faltered and looking puzzled she was counting on her fingers. "No, 'twas a different month so I think we are both wrong. I do remember preparing fresh cloths, yet are you not a little delayed, my Lady?"

Margaret's sudden harsh intake of breath was at odds with her pale features and frail form clearly outlined in her voluminous silken nightgown. The tendons in her arm contorted as she gripped the edge of the bed post.

"You remember nothing, Catherine. You are clearly mistaken," she hissed. "Now help me across the chamber, oh sweet Lord, the pain . . ." Holding her stomach tightly, Margaret bent low twisting and turning as if to evade the agonizing barbs driving into her soft flesh.

Catherine's expression showed abject horror as she saw her mistress writhing in agony. Then with venomous intent the blood coursed out of Margaret onto her gown. Losing every vestige of colour, she sunk to the floor. Her blanched face crumpled when she saw the flimsy material gobbling up the crimson lake like a voracious leech.

"No," she said faintly. "No, it can't, it mustn't. Catherine, help me . . ."

"My best beloved, there is nought old Cat can do," whispered the distressed woman, holding Margaret's head, stroking away tendrils of hair stuck to her forehead, rocking her back and forth as she did so. In turn, Margaret took hold of one of Catherine's hands gripping it so tightly the woman winced. Several times more her body moved to the violent rhythm of the merciless pain, casting her up and throwing her down as a leaf is tossed in a fractious wind.

When the screams turned to whimpers, Catherine fetched a crisply laundered pillow bere pungent with the smell of rose water. Lifting Margaret's head she saw blood spots on the fine Venetian lace. For a moment she was perplexed and then looking at her hand she saw long curved lacerations running from her knuckles to her wrist and her blood beading their edges. Uncaring about her own discomfort, Catherine carefully wiped Margaret's nails so she shouldn't see the injuries she had inflicted.

"Rest for awhile, my dove," she said, covering the restless body with a fine woollen shawl. "When your strength returns, Cat will wash you just like she did when you were a baby. She'll find you sweet smelling linens and the softest of gowns. There, there, don't cry my sweeting. Cat will look after you. Things are better now, the blood is dwindling."

At first there was no response from Margaret. Her eyelids were closed, their long lashes fanning her pallid cheeks. It was an opportunity for Catherine to examine her. Very gently she lifted the hem of the sodden gown and felt her heart jolt in her chest. The evidence was there for her to see and whatever hope she might have instantly vanished. It was little more than a large jellified clot, but Catherine nursed it carefully just the same as she swaddled in cotton cloths.

"Is it a child?" Margaret asked harshly, her eyes wide open and dark with pain.

"Hardly that," Catherine replied sorrowfully.

Putting aside the bundle, she helped Margaret to her feet. Her arms encircling the slender form she led her slowly to the bedside. When she was sitting, Catherine carefully slid the soiled gown away. Bundled it up the delicate material reduced itself to nothing more than a crimson square which she quickly moved out of sight. She deftly tended to Margaret with gentle hands and a deal of pity. In a fresh gown and her braided in a thick plait, colour was returning to the wan features although Catherine noted the lack-lustre in Margaret's eyes and a tightness of her full lips. She barely spoke so Catherine chatted enough for two.

"There you are, my lovely. You mustn't grieve. You are still young and that husband of yours will plant his seed again, old Cat's sure of that," she prattled.

The reaction was short and explosive.

"You foolish old crone," Margaret said rudely. Then her lips quivered and the tears welled. "Do you think that was Henry's child, he who withers at the mere sight of me? Mon Dieu, I thought you were brighter than that. My dear Jasper, 'twas his and now it is lost."

It was Catherine's turn to pale and her eyes widened. Withdrawing quickly from the bedside, her disapproval overcame any thought of her position.

"But Your Grace, is that wise?" she said stiffly. "If word of this gets out, your poor husband will be ridiculed. You of all people must know a breath of scandal will be all your enemies need."

"You should watch your tongue old woman."

Margaret's sharp words brought a halt to Catherine's reproof and she busied herself folding up the cleaning cloths.

"The House of Lancaster is without an heir, that's all that matters. Besides have you seen my Lord Husband lately? He languishes in his bed on the verge of madness. What would he know of ridicule?" Margaret continued. Tossing herself back on the pillow bere's, she closed her eyes and her softly rounded, passionate lips were contorted into a bitter snarl. Deeply shocked, Catherine picked up the detritus of birth and went to the door.

"I'll not be long, my Lady," she assured starkly.

* * *

Margaret stared hard at the tisane which looked even more unappetising than usual. Whatever herbs were prepared for her to drink, this of all of them smelt the most pungent. In poor humour she pulled a face and asked in a tetchy voice.

"What are these foul odours? Do you intend to poison me with such vileness?" Pushing the steaming brew away from her she pulled viciously at a stray lock of hair, tucking it this way and that until she was satisfied with its position. Used to her mistress's variable moods, Catherine bore it all with her usual stoicism.

"You are not yet fully recovered, my Lady," she said evenly. "When it is all gone a sweetmeat will do away with the taste. The herbs need to be strong and there is no better than Angus-Castus and Pudding Grass. Trust old Cat, she knows her craft. There is heat in your liver and bad humors to be rid of so drink it down, there's a good girl."

Margaret raised an eyebrow. No one but Catherine would dare to speak to her in such tones. They locked eyes, one pair faded but determined the other cool, yet tinged with amusement. For the first time in a week, Margaret gave the ghost of a laugh and dutifully lifted the beaker to her lips. With a contented tilt to her mouth and a satisfied look, Catherine briskly smoothed down her bodice and skirts.

Later, when the corridor was becoming rosy with a setting sun, Margaret left her chamber to visit Henry and found him in his huge canopied bed. The curtains were drawn close and the bed almost hidden by odd rugs and coverlets. Tossed into an untidy pile on the floor were his fine linen sheets and heavily embroidered blue damask bedspread. One of his favourite books rested upside down on his chest.

When she saw the heap of bed linen she stooped, running her fingers over the spread to touch the richly woven hunting scenes and the lining of pure white miniver. Henry's pride in his bedspread had often been a source of amusement between them for he would never sleep without it. Now it was a crumpled abandoned rag.

She looked up just as the curtain parted. Henry was watching her from the bed. His pallid hand fell back from its hold on the silk drapery and he twisted it round and round the other one. Thin and bird-like, he wore a pillow bere wrapped round his head in a bizarre turban. Suddenly she felt faint and was unsure whether it was her own weakness or the sight of his decline. His chin bore a dark shadow of stubble and she thought how hollow his cheeks looked, but it was his eyes which truly dismayed her. They were nut brown and bright, too bright she thought. They were also eager, interested, questioning even following her as she moved, but what frightened her most was they were completely empty of any recognition. Sitting on the edge of the bed, she touched one of his hands. It closed round hers like a crow's claw and she saw him shiver.

"Too cold," he said, tossing it aside. "Why are you cold? Does it snow?"

"No, Lord Husband 'tis midsummer, perhaps it is because I have been indisposed."

"I am sorry to hear that," he replied politely. "Have you brought me something to eat? They keep me hungry you know. Who are you anyway?"

"My Lord Husband I am Margaret, your wife," she replied starkly.

She waited for a reaction, but Henry merely yawned. Fearing the poor light made it difficult for him to see clearly, she lent closer to him. His breath smelt sweet like new mown hay. Instantly her blatant indiscretions troubled her conscience and guilt gave way to compassion.

"I am stricken to see you so unwell, Sire," she said tearfully. "Should you like to sit in your chair for awhile? We enjoy such companionship watching the sun set behind the river on a summer's eve. Do you not remember?"

When he nodded, she felt triumphant.

"Then let me help you," she said, gently lifting the first of the covers.

She was surprised at the strength with which he wrestled it out of her hand.

"What are you doing woman? Leave me be. If anyone is to assist me it will be my sweet Lady Wife. I'm expecting her shortly so you may go."

Covering her mouth, struggling to conceal her anguished cry, she stumbled backwards away from the bed.

Henry's eyes closed and he breathed with small quivering movements which barely lifted his chest. Driven by dark clouds the last rays of the sun dipped lower turning the glass in the window to molten copper and in the shadowy room, Margaret fought back weak tears. For once it was hard to summon her inner strength; but she had more than most. Impatient for allowing herself to falter, she drew herself up and went back to the bedside.

"Forgive me Lord Husband," she whispered. "I must give you a son else the House of Lancaster will fall. No one will know any different, 'twill be your boy I promise you that." Her voice became firmer, more forceful, the way she usually conversed. "And I shall take care of everything until you are well again. I thought it time we were rid of the irritating Kentish men and their rising so I sent for Cardinal Kemp. He has been most helpful to me," she paused wondering if her words would stir Henry, but he didn't show any signs of hearing her. She tried again.

"The Cardinal spoke of royal pardons for those prepared to lay down their arms, to be revoked later of course. I thought it a splendid idea. I'm sure you would have approved. You poor man, I know how you hate any sort of violence."

How he needed her, this gentle and meek husband of hers. She attempted a sympathetic smile and then remembering he was oblivious to her presence, hurried on.

"So he is sending Bishop William of Winchester and our dear Lord Scales into Southwark to offer pardons to every man. There, don't you think your Lady Wife has done well? Now sleep peacefully and by the grace of God you will be whole again."

Kissing her finger she laid it gently on his pale brow. "Sweet Husband, I must leave you for there should soon be news from London."

She thought he smiled, but couldn't be sure. Then straight-backed with her head held high she turned and walked to the door. Nothing is beyond the reach of me, Margaret of Anjou, she told herself firmly before reaching for the doorknob.

Chapter Thirty-Six

Tower of London

RAISING his hand to the door, Pultenery lowered it again. The noises he heard coming from within the chamber warned him it would be prudent to wait. Uncomfortable at what he could hear, he moved down the corridor and stared down into the formal garden below.

Interrupting Ralph Cromwell's distinctive voice, feminine laughter was audible even from there, but as he debated on moving again the door opened. A girl emerged who looked scarcely more than a child despite the foundation to lighten her face and her smeared black kohl eye liner. Tugging her gown back on her shoulders, she smiled brazenly at Pultenery as she passed him. Declining to acknowledge her with more than a disdainful look, Pultenery hurried back to Cromwell's chamber.

"You're late," Cromwell remarked, straightening his surcoat.

"I do believe I was here on time, my Lord," Pultenery replied indignantly. "It would seem 'twas you who was otherwise engaged."

Cromwell's stony look added more chill to the austere room, but he had the grace to blush.

"If you mean the wench, she was merely bringing me refreshment," he said, waving a vague hand at the cordial nearby. He tipped up the flagon and drank from it noisily before offering it to Pultenery.

"Thank you, but no," Pultenery replied, tight lipped.

"So what is this I hear about the rebels being offered pardons," Cromwell said, wiping his mouth on his sleeve. "It's a bad idea and one that might flaw our plans. Who is responsible, would you say? Surely not the King, by all accounts he lays abed past any sensible thought."

The chamber was uncomfortably hot and airless, but it was more than Pultenery dare to suggest a casement might be opened. Instead he loosened his cape.

"It would seem Cardinal Kemp hopes kind actions and generous words might send the rebels on their way. He gained the Queen's approval and now Bishop Wyanflete of Winchester and our friend, Scales ride through Southwark this very day to present the royal pardons to all men in the rising."

Cromwell's heavy brow ridged into dark furrows and he scowled. "That woman," he fumed. "Why must she keep poking her nose into the government's affairs? As for Scales, the man is a louse on my back, but just out of reach. Best picked off and destroyed, wouldn't you say? God damn it, Pultenery, what am I to tell the *Falcon?* He is ready to slip into London unseen as soon as we give the word. It is vital attention is diverted away from his arrival and that is why, Pultenery, you are supposed to see to it this rising continues. Speak to Mortimer, do whatever is necessary, but the rising must not fail. Do you understand?"

He hammered out his words emphasising them with repeated bangs of his fist on his desktop. Pultenery flinched at his vehemence.

"Yes, my Lord," he said faintly.

"Where are those friends of yours, Simon of Kent and Richard de Courcey? I thought they were staying close to Mortimer."

"You haven't heard? De Courcy was lost at London Bridge. A bloody business by all accounts and he was a good man, he'll be missed. As for Simon, he spends time at Court keeping his ear tuned for there are some who would gladly report any word of our plans to bring back Richard of York. I for one have no wish to be found a traitor," Pultenery said grimly.

* * *

It was almost impossible for Walter to stand still as he waited for Jack. The news he wanted to impart left him agitated and he craned his neck continually for any sight of his captain. He tried concentrating on polishing his bow stave, but the nub of wax was small and crumbled in his fingers. Finally he threw down the piece of rag, hitched his bow and quiver of arrows on his shoulder and set off in search of him.

Making his way through the hoards in Southwark took him longer than he thought. More protestors from Essex now joined the men from Kent and in an atmosphere of menace and discontent the streets heaved with ever more disorder. He thought it was Merek he saw in the distance, but when he reached the place he was nowhere to be seen. After crossing the market place, Walter followed the winding path along the south bank of the river. When the cathedral came into view, Jack stood at the top of the steps with Bishop Wyanflete, his scribe and a man he recognised as Scales. They were surrounded on every side by men of the rising jostling one another to get nearer to them. The air was so lively with their voices even the noon bell sounded subdued. Wyanflete held white papers in his hand and he heard his shouts appealing to the mass.

"All in good time, there are enough for all of you," Wyanflete called, waving his bulging satchel. "You must make a line and be orderly."

Not sure what they were gathering for, Walter struggled to make a passageway through to Jack.

"Stand aside. Let me through, I have important news for Captain Mortimer," he bellowed, elbowing his way to the steps. He arrived at the top almost flung onto the stone slabs. It was then Jack saw him.

"You down there move aside," Jack called to the heaving crowds.

With Merek and Barda's help, Walter managed to right himself and follow them.

"What is it they come here for?" he called to Merek.

"The Bishop brings pardons."

"Have they listened to our requests?" Walter asked.

"They have agreed to them, everyone. It's over, we can go home," Barda chimed in, with a grin. "That's why there's so much excitement. You look grave, my friend. Cheer up. At last we have good news."

"I've heard talk which might put our Captain in danger, that's why I must speak to him," Walter replied quietly. Leaving Wyanflete and his scribe still trying to bring order, they withdrew to the stout oak doorway behind them. At least here they didn't have to raise their voices. Noticing Walter's concerned expression, they waited anxiously for him to speak. But he looked awkward and nervous. Jack rested a hand on his arm.

A Pardon Too Few

"It's alright, Walter. Whatever it is you have to say, you must speak freely. You are a good man and I trust you. What is it you would tell me?"

Walter struggled to find a smile. His Adam's apple bobbed in the baggy skin of his neck as he swallowed.

"I know nothing about you Captain, except you are a fine leader, honest with your men and worthy of every man's respect. There is no more I need to know. But I bring a warning from a friend. There is one in the crowd who seeks to bring you down."

"There are probably many more who would wish to do that," Jack replied cheerfully. "Does this man have a name?" Still cautious, Walter spoke in a low voice.

"They say he is called John Bailey and he is Squire Pultenery's man. He's been boasting how he was sent to find out things about you and paid handsomely for the information so he says. He plans to unmask you at the first opportunity, but I know no more. He could be here today."

"Squab of the Devil, I'll have his skin for a pair of boots," Merek growled.

Stepping out from the shadow of the doorway into the warmth, Walter shaded his eyes looking into the mass of men, but an arm pulled him back. Far from seeming concerned, Jack's expression remained casual as he said amiably.

"Just who are you looking for? Nigh on two thousand men stand below, would you know which one was Bailey? Whilst the Bishop hands out the pardons it could him or him or that man there," Jack said, pointing at different rebels."

"It's true, Walter," Barda chimed in. "Did your friend happen to say what he looked like?"

Walter considered for a moment then shaking his head, he said, "My friend took a great risk speaking to me and we couldn't talk for long. I'm sure he said the one who called himself Bailey was a puny figure of a man, never still he said with crafty eyes and a thin nose long enough to root out a rabbit from its burrow. Not very tall either if I have it right. I'm sorry, that's all I know."

Jack clapped him on the back to reassure him.

"No matter, you've done well. The three of you go down into the crowd. Make out you are waiting for your pardon and keep a look out for Master Bailey. He'll likely be near the front so the Bishop hears him. If you happen upon him, make sure he doesn't finish whatever it is he tries to say. There is nothing else we can do," he said, with a shrug.

They left him without question. Slipping their separate ways, they were watching keen-eyed for anyone who might speak out against their leader. Their loyalty to Jack was without question. Their affection for him evident and their disinterest in his past was one they all shared.

Outside the cathedral distribution of the pardons was going well. One by one the rebels climbed the steps, gave their name to the scribe and accepted their gleaming piece of vellum duly signed and stamped with Wyanflete's papal seal.

Whilst they waited their turn not even the sudden dismal pattering of rain could dull their spirits. Some of them pulled off their hats so they could feel the damp air cool their skulls and others turned their faces upwards to refresh their dusty sun-burnt skins. John Bailey's voice was as sudden as the change in the weather.

"So Bishop, do you have a pardon for everyone here?" he shouted out, his voice surprisingly loud for so one so scrawny. "Only I could tell you something about our leader, Mortimer which might . . ." He never finished his sentence. A ring of bodies surrounding him quickly opened. Without time for protest, Bailey vanished into it and the circle closed on him like marsh mud swallowing a boot. A little poor of hearing, Waynflete cocked his hand round his ear.

"There's too much noise. You must come and speak to me up here," he called back, looking puzzled. When nobody moved, he shrugged and picked up another handful of pardons. "Next."

Loitering far away at the back of the crowd, Pultenery sighed with relief. There was a time when he would have gladly seen the rebel leader exposed, but after Cromwell's outburst, Bailey's misplaced timing would have been unfortunate. Besides, he had a strange feeling Mortimer would bring about his own downfall before too long. No blame could be placed at his door when that happened, he told himself. As for Bailey, a pity, but he wouldn't be hard to replace. Heading in the direction of a nearby hostelry, Pultenery's crooked smile added a reptilian look to his features.

Chapter Thirty-Seven

BY dusk the *Hart* was overwhelmed with jubilant rebels. Those who couldn't get a foot in the door spilled onto the street. Jack, with Aditha on his knee, was celebrating with the rest of them. Looking on, the alewife watched as jug after jug of sweet ale vanished into the crowd inside and out. The broad smile creasing her sweaty face widened in time with the groats filling her money box.

It seemed hardly a man could believe their royal pardon so they stretched the paper this way and that, pawing it, turning it in all directions, even chewing the edges to make sure it was real. As the evening wore on the pristine surface became dotted with spittle and smudged with ale, but as few could read it was of no importance. The fine writing and impressive seal were sufficient.

Every time he moved, Jack could hear his own pardon rustling in his pocket. Not that it was easy to move with Aditha's arm wound round his neck. It was warm, comforting, as was the feel of her close to him. Inhaling the scent of her was as heady as the effect of the copious amounts of ale he'd drunk, yet behind the sparkle in his eyes a shadow of doubt dimmed their depths. He'd been the last to receive his pardon and saw Wyanflete's frown when Scales confirmed his name.

"Master John Mortimer; so my son let this be the end of your disputes with the King's government. Go home in peace and thank your Lord for the His Majesty's generosity," he said, as the scribe's quill squealed its way across the vellum.

Aditha wriggled on his lap. Pressing her head on his shoulder, watching him with fierce intensity her breathing was wild and her smile wanton. Normally it would rouse his feverish lust, but not tonight. Impatient for him, she looked puzzled.

"What is it John? Have I done something wrong?" Her fingers slipped to the tie on her gown, teasing it open, teasing him.

"Later," he said, harsh with her.

She was about to open his buckle, but stopped herself. Instead searching his face with anxious eyes, she spoke softly.

"Do I no longer please you?"

Around them the roistering was loud and coarse and the walls appeared to shudder as the stench of cooking and smoke from the hearth laid down another layer on its soiled surfaces. When Jack didn't reply, she tried again.

"I don't understand. Why are you so low? Tonight of all nights and every man with his pardon, yet you show no pleasure. Tell me John, you can trust me," she said, her plea just managing to rise above the cacophony of noise.

He met her eyes and looked away. That was it, he couldn't trust her. It wasn't her fault. There were few he ever did. Not with his secrets. Now the one which troubled him the most sat like a rock in his pocket. At the Cathedral, watching the scribe's lips carefully spell out the letters of his name as his labouring fingers shaped them on the paper, Jack knew it was John Mortimer he wrote. Now he held a royal pardon 'twas true, but what of Jack Cade?

Margaret Callow

Unpardoned, he would go to his grave as such. His gut told him it might be a grave too close, uncomfortably so. Yet who would know? Dangerous people he was sure of that, Bailey for one, whose head was attracting fish in the river. Who might the serf have told apart from Pultenery? With too many questions and no answers it was a chilling cause for concern. Absorbed in his thoughts, his expression was guarded and dark.

Disconsolate at Jack's lack of interest, Aditha slipped off his lap. With her shameless look and the roll of her body lust-filled eyes were drawn to her when she left his side. She greeted them all with a flash of smoky eyes and a toss of her mane of hair. He thought about calling her back, but didn't. Instead he sat with his head in his hands pondering.

* * *

It was how Simon found him when he managed to elbow his way across the room.

"Are you in poor humour, John or has too much ale given you a head pain. Do you want me to find you a poultice?" he asked.

Looking more closely, Simon felt uneasy. This leader of men might have the respect of his followers, but he remained a worrying entity as far as he was concerned. Struggling to appear compassionate, he laid his hand on Jack's shoulder.

"No, it's more than that. What is it?" Whatever it was, he needed to know. This rogue couldn't be allowed to run amok, not now so close to the House of York achieving its goal. The unexpected distribution of pardons had been a cause of consternation as it was. The success of the plan to bring Richard of York back to claim the throne depended on

290

a smokescreen, one which was to be achieved in warfare. It was unthinkable that now they would disperse meekly holding their pardons.

"It's not important," Jack replied shortly.

Light from the curling flame of the wall sconce danced across his face throwing the top half into shadow. It made it impossible to read his expression, but Simon was too busy scheming to notice.

Deciding he must tread with care, his jovial smile was disarming.

"Good, good so we should celebrate. Our work is done. I have just come from Parliament where they are ever more divided and now they are both back from France it seems only Edmund Beaufort and the Duke of Buckingham stand with their Majesties. Now the people rage they have a King who not only absents himself in a time of crisis but is not of sound mind."

"Perhaps our protests end too quickly," Jack said in a low voice, thinking there were still deaths to avenge. "How can we be sure our King will uphold the pardons?" It was more than Simon could have hoped for.

"You make a good point, my friend. Perhaps you would be right to seek further proof."

His face guarded, Simon left it there. The seed was planted, now he could only wait. The inn was beginning to empty as the sober dragged away the inebriated. For some it was too much and they slept where they slumped on a bed of soiled straw. Still smiling, the alewife stepped over them collecting empty flagons and tipped over jugs. In no hurry, Simon lazed back using the wall for a prop. He saw his companion searching his face and hoped he would think the flush he could feel in his cheeks was due to over warmth and not zeal.

"Be proud, John," he continued. "In a few weeks we have achieved much and you have led the rising well. The complaints of the poor commons have been listened to and the requests granted. Not only that, but they have been pardoned. I am making arrangements for you to be well rewarded, a thousand marks wasn't it? It will make you a rich man, remember that. Yes, it all ends well. Soon a certain bird will spread his wings and not before time. Of course no one would blame you should you think it necessary to investigate the pardons further."

* * *

Jack thought how grotesque Simon looked in the dim light. Hunched on his stool, his shape threw a strange shadow on the dingy wall behind him. But it was his manner which bothered him more. The warning given by Scales was still clear in his mind; and what did Simon mean when he said 'a certain bird'? What was really going on behind the laudable activities of the uprising? He knew no answers, yet good sense told him to be wary.

About to question Simon, he saw Merek at the door. Ducking under the frame, the big man came over to them.

"I'm not serving anymore ale," the alewife shrieked across the inn. "I can't shut the door as it is with that lot down there, but some of us need our rest." Pointing down to the bodies on the floor, she banged a flagon on the bar to emphasise her irritation. Merek laughed, waved a fist at her and bellowed back.

"Shut up old woman, a pox on your ale 'tis not that I want. Some of us have business to be done."

Pulling his hat from his head and ignoring Simon, he addressed Jack.

"I thought you should know, Captain. The men are scattering. Few see any reason to remain in London now. They want to go back home with their pardons and I reckon most will be gone before the rooster crows. If you are disbanding the rising then Barda and I will go too."

"What of Walter?" Jack asked.

Merek grinned. "I don't know where he is, Captain. Last we saw of him he had a wench on each arm. He had things to attend to at the whorehouse, he said."

Silence followed whilst Jack looked up at the filthy ceiling thoughtfully. He looked calm, but his mind raced. Despite his uncertainties his adventurous spirit refused to be quiet. It took effort for him to decide, but not time, never time with an impulsive nature like his. Watching him, Merek twisted his hat in his spatula shaped hands. Across the table with his eyes shut, Simon's head rested on his chest and the only noise was the heavy breathing of the drunks and the ale wife clattering somewhere in the back.

"So Merek, I've made up my mind," Jack said quietly. "The men on this rising have endured much. Our fight with the king's forces was a bloody affair and we lost many of them. Those who remain are good and worthy men, so I must be sure the pardons are true and will be honoured before I can say we are done."

"That's fair enough, Captain," Merek said firmly.

As if alone with his thoughts, Jack barely heard his henchman's comment. He spoke half under his breath making his plans.

"Before I lay down my arms, I shall ride to Rochester to seek approval. No, perhaps it would be better to take the Castle first then they will be quick enough to honour their word." He nodded to himself, a slight smile playing on his lips. *It's a fine plan so it is, don't you think Mammy . . .* There was a long pause, as though he was retracing a journey into a place where no other could go before he spoke again. Then with a start, he looked up at Merek.

"The men are leaving you said? We shall need more." He frowned. "But where . . . Southwark prison that's it, we shall free them all then they'll join us. Are you with me, my fine friend?"

"Aye Captain, that I am," Merek replied, his weathered face breaking into a broad grin. "Shall I search for Barda and Walter?"

"If you can, but we have no time to waste. Just get me a following, we shall leave at sunrise."

Turning smartly, Merek raised his hand and strode to the door. When Simon woke, both men were gone just as hoped.

Chapter Thirty-Eight

Kenilworth

GATHERED on the edge of the pristine green lawns the assembled audience of knights, courtiers and ladies of the Court hardly dare breathe. They knew better than to make a sound when the King was playing bowls. Under the shade of a walnut tree, Margaret sat watching him with Catherine at her side.

"Your Lord Husband makes a fine recovery," she whispered to Margaret.

"Seemingly recovered," Margaret replied a little tartly whilst tugging at a tangle of threads on her embroidery. "I wish I shared his love of such a game, but it bores me." When Henry's bowl set the peacock feather marker quivering it was greeted with restrained clapping. His playing companion, Edmund Beaufort however showed more enthusiasm which he knew Henry would appreciate.

"Well done, Sire. An excellent shot and one I will not be able to match. Your Majesty's eye is as true as ever." Immediately the pallor in Henry's cheeks was relieved by a hastily spreading pink and he smiled.

"Thank you, dear Edmund, a favourable shot indeed, I do dislike those who boast, but on this occasion perhaps I might be forgiven do you think?"

"Indeed you might, Sire. It is a joy to see you well again after your recent illness. I can assure you I am not alone in thanking God for your recovery."

"How kind," Henry murmured, carefully positioning the bowl in his hand for his next shot.

To an untrained eye he seemed restored to health, but Edmund noticed there was a strange urgency about his manner and a disordered look in his eyes below quivering eyelids. The peculiarity of his mental state made him look anxious and at times taking a breath seemed difficult.

"Perhaps you should rest, Sire. The apothecary warned against overtaxing yourself," Edmund said anxiously noticing the tremor in Henry's fingers was more pronounced.

"One more bowl, Edmund if you please," Henry said, in a tone more customary for a small child asking a favour. Edmund gave a short bow. "Of course, Sire."

This time the aim was poor which sent the bowl careering away from the marker. Bouncing its way into the raised ledge designed to trap the bowl it vanished into the rose beds. There it found fresh momentum and rolled gently back onto the grass. The audience clapped anyway.

Having lost interest in the game, Henry deposited himself into a chair next to Margaret. As he did so his plain gown swirled away from his thin legs exposing his hose. Even through the black silk the red blebs which covered his pallid flesh were noticeable. He scratched them irritably. Always attentive, Edmund touched his arm.

"Shall I call for the apothecary, Sire?"

"No you shall not," Henry retorted. "These are caused by his inept bungling with his leeches. The man professes to know his practices, but I somehow doubt it."

"That's a little unfair, Lord Husband. A week ago you were still confined to your bed. I believe he has done much to aid your return to good health," Margaret said briskly.

Lapsing back in his chair with a pained expression, Henry said nothing. Handing her embroidery to Catherine, Margaret turned her attention to Edmund.

"So, dear Beaufort, what news do you bring us from London? I'm anxious to return for this place stifles me." Trying hard not to meet her eyes, Edmund gathered his thoughts. He must tread carefully. He was well aware of the real reason his Queen wanted to leave Kenilworth. It was common knowledge she enjoyed the company of Jasper Tudor, too much many muttered. For once he was grateful Mortimer and his rising still occupied tongues more freely.

"If you mean the state of the uprising, Your Majesty, you'll be pleased to know your approval to issue pardons has worked well," he said smoothly. "Most of the rebels have left the city although Mortimer himself seems reluctant to disband his forces. It will only be a matter of time though."

"So this troublesome common, what does he do now?" she asked.

"Ah, Your Grace, that is more difficult to answer. I believe Lord Scales has men on the street who will report back to him as to what Mortimer intends to do next. It is rumoured he plans to increase his numbers by releasing prisoners again. Seemingly he is anxious to make sure the pardons are genuine and may well return to Kent."

"This man is more tiresome than a bug in a mattress," Margaret said, tossing her head with impatience. "What might he do should he go there, Edmund?"

Sighing heavily, Edmund shook his head.

"That I was a soothsayer, Your Grace then I might know. There is of course Queenborough Castle. One of the rebels is favoured by Lord Scales so word has passed and it is thought Mortimer intends seeking out Lord Stafford to deal with the pardons. I'm afraid I really have no sure idea."

Pacing the grass, Margaret considered the information. A patch of daisies caught her eyes and irritated she kicked at them furiously.

"Then make sure Lord Stafford is told he may expect a visit from this bunch of ruffians and shall deal with them as he sees fit," she fumed.

"Indeed I'll send a messenger right away," Edmund assured gravely. "There is one other thing which I only learnt as I was about to leave Court yesterday. It is only whispers, Your Grace, but nonetheless you should know. The rebel leader John Mortimer is not who he says he is, some are saying his real name is Jack Cade and if that is so he has no pardon."

Henry might have looked as though he was half asleep, but he was listening keenly and there was surprise in his voice.

"Pardons, what pardons? Was I consulted? If so I have no memory of such, when did you know of this, good Lady Wife?" he enquired loudly.

"Please don't make a fuss, Henry. Cardinal Kemp came to Kenilworth and I acted as I thought best. You were unable to pay any attention to affairs if you remember? I had no choice but to agree for I thought it a good idea. If what Edmund is now telling us is true, we shall deal with this matter most promptly," Margaret said with her overbearing manner at the fore. "Besides the sooner the poor are put in their place, the sooner we can return to Court. Isn't that so, Edmund?"

Before he had time to reply, Henry took Margaret's hand and looking hard at her said.

"Sometimes, my dear, I fear you act too quickly. Did Parliament agree to the demands of these people before you gave the Cardinal permission to distribute pardons? Because if they didn't and I didn't then they are of no import and all the lawbreakers remain unpardoned. What faith will our people have when they see such muddle, did you think of that?"

There was an unpleasant silence. Snatching her embroidery out of Catherine's hands, Margaret picked up the needle. Every stitch piercing the fabric with outrage she drove the silk back and forth in such untidy haste the thread knotted time and again. Edmund could see she wanted to shout out in defiance, but instead her lips tightened. Exasperated, she allowed the sampler to tumble to the ground as she rose to her feet and calling. "Catherine, come," flounced off towards the grass incline leading to the terrace. The delicate material of her skirts swirled behind her like a fast-moving grey cloud while plump Catherine struggled to keep up with her.

Edmund watched them both and then gave a polite cough. Stretching out his hand towards Henry, he said.

"You look tired, Sire. Let me walk with you to your chamber. We can talk later."

"I know you mean well, Edmund, but please stop fussing."

Pressing his hand to his high forehead, Henry looked momentarily distracted. One finger of his free hand made circles on the heavy silk covering his knee, round . . . and round . . . and round so that Edmund thought any moment he might fall into a trance. Not only that, but Henry started rocking.

"They will not be honoured, the pardons. They must be revoked at once, but it should come from me," he said in a low voice almost in time with his movements. "My mind is dark. The demons are dancing, they prance with coils of mist, too thick, too thick, I cannot see."

Alarmed, Edmund looked about him, but the lawn was deserted. A sudden and sharp wind tugged at the walnut leaves and sent them whirling wildly. Above them the broad sky was darkening and shrouded by ominous clouds, the sun faltered and slipped away. He knew it was imperative they move before a storm broke.

"Your Majesty," he implored. "We should go inside . . ." Head down, Henry addressed his knees.

"Did you hear me? I will not allow the pardons to stand. See to it at once. It is enough my Queen tries to cuckold me without her trying to rule in my place too."

His mumblings were barely audible, but Edmund knew what he was saying. Then looking up Henry smiled and said mildly. "I think we should move, eh Edmund before we get wet."

* * *

Pressed against the window, Margaret was watching Edmund supporting Henry's arm, leading him towards the terraces. When the first of the rain hit the glass with noisy violence it beaded in clear bubbles then coursed down the sill and onto the slabs below. She shivered violently.

"Oh my sweeting, you look as if you have caught a chill. Let Cat bring you hot honey and herbs to warm you," Catherine said in a soothing voice.

Margaret sounded tired. "No Catherine, 'tis my spirit is low not my body. I fear I have angered my Lord Husband. I tried to tell him, but does he not understand his moments of madness leave me with no other choice. He says I give unwise council, yet the country is in turmoil and it is no better time for the Yorkists to make their move. Do you think my lord understands how precarious his throne is? I think not for my sweet Lord Husband is helpless and at times little more than a half-wit."

She prided herself she rarely cried, but at that moment her backbone of steel failed her. The tears welled, running down her cheeks as relentlessly as the rain beat at the window glass. "Dear Lord, forgive me. I am a poor wife and a poor Queen." she whispered, her slender hands clasped in prayer.

Catherine stared at her in astonishment. "No, no Your Grace, whatever are you saying? Without you the House of Lancaster would have fallen a long time ago. The poor King can't help his insanity, it is in his bones and yours must be the voice of authority for everyone knows he's not able to help himself." Pausing, her expression was a worried one. "Pardon that I speak so freely."

A flicker of a smile appeared on Margaret's tear-streaked face and she held out both hands to her faithful retainer.

"Dear, dear Catherine, what would I do without you? Of course you can say whatever you want to me. Will the people still support us, do you think?"

The greying head shook sadly. "Ah, that I can't tell you, my Lady, your old Cat doesn't have ball to foretell such things."

She draped a fine wool cape about Margaret's slender shoulders and attentive as always re-curled some wayward strands of her hair come loose under her coif.

"There, now let me powder your face and no one will know any different," she prattled.

Margaret held more tightly onto one of Catherine's wrists and an anxious frown ridged her high brow.

"Do they speak of Richard of York behind our backs," she whispered.

Catherine's laughter was unusually shrill. "No, my Lady, why should they? I know of no one who would welcome a Yorkist on the throne of England."

Swivelling round on her stool, Margaret's eyes were like hot coals burning into the old woman's soul. "You would tell me the truth, wouldn't you?"

"Should old Cat ever lie to you, you should take out her tongue and feed it to the dogs," Catherine replied, praying to her Lord he would forgive her just this once.

Chapter Thirty-Nine

HARDLY had the wood and iron gates of Southwark prison started their trundling motion when prisoners were breaking out. Destitute and dispirited they flooded onto the streets to escape the stinking conditions. Adjusting to the light they blinked, shading their eyes whilst all the while trying to work out who had released them. Cautiously they moved slowly at first and then with the sense they were truly free, some of them prepared to sprint away, but Merek and his companions were ready for them.

"Stay where you are," Merek roared, raising his mace as a warning. "Captain Mortimer sends me to tell you he needs you. Ours is a rising for the poor commons so join us and be ready to fight with us and you will get a ration of sweet ale and all the food you can eat. Follow me and I'll take you to our Captain."

"And if we don't?" a dishevelled wretch with a stump for an arm cried out.

Merek gave a casual shrug and the spikes on his mace ball revolved in a whirl as he spun the weapon sharply.

"If it means we are free, what's there to lose?" another called with a grin. "I'm in. Where do you want me to stand?"

But others were unsure. Merek watched dismayed as many turned their backs on his offer and began to hurry away. Some would be no use to the rising, too old or emaciated to hold a weapon still, yet there were others with young blood who would serve the cause well. For a moment he wondered if he could make the offer more tempting, but those anxious to remain free were more than determined to avoid recapture. Taking to their heels they speedily disappeared down sour-smelling passageways.

Soon the street emptied of all but a few. By the time a pale orangey-glow moved up from the horizon and whilst the air was still chilled, no more than seventy souls were assembled outside the prison. Merek ran his eye over them. A sickly bunch indeed, but the best he could do. Behind him they shuffled in anticipation muttering to one another before he moved them off toward Southwark High Street.

* * *

The rebels, on meeting any but one of their own, confiscated provisions and each guarded his load well. Several carried scrawny chickens under their arm and others swung uprooted beanstalks heavy with pods. More clutched rough black bread and pocketed eggs. Whatever they saw on the journey became theirs. One even tried leading a cow, but the beast broke away in panic.

Following the course of the river the land became lonelier and bleaker. For once, Jack's expression was grim. As they made their way across the marshes outside Rochester he kept careful watch on the plump roll of blanket which was his stolen booty. At least that reassured him of future wealth if nothing else. When his horse stumbled and the roll wobbled loose, he grabbed it and pulling the cord anchored it tight then thwacked the beast on the rump to make sure it kept going.

With no proper trail to follow the terrain was difficult in the narrow passage ways between the Kentish land and Sheppey. Suddenly Merek cried out in warning. His leg was vanishing almost up to his thigh. Around it a pool of vile-smelling mud bubbled and slurped. When Jack looked down he saw he too was sinking with water creeping into his boots. Every few yards another man floundered and fell. Around them the air resonated with curses. Sounds became strangled in their throats as the ground opened to take them. Jack could do nothing. Already waist deep in the cold slime, he struggled to get free. Terror gripped him as he felt himself pulled deeper and deeper. Seeing a clump of water sedge he managed to grab it and fought desperately to free himself. With resounding gurgling noises the bog released him and he could breathe again.

One after another the rebels managed to crawl out of the mire. The plight of some of the horses was worse. Leading them became impossible and they were being abandoned. Surrounded by black pines and desolate swathes of sea pinks they screamed out their distress sinking ever deeper into the quagmire.

Jack gritted his teeth, trying to summon sufficient reserves of strength to keep going whilst beside him Merek, taller and stronger, took his arm encouraging him on. Somewhere behind them, Barda, Walter and a few hundred men fought their own battles with the inhospitable conditions.

"Almost there, Captain," Merek called cheerfully, wiping foul silt away from his eyes and spitting more back as he ploughed on to the far bank. The first to reach firm land, he waved his longbow in the air and gave an exhilarated yell to those trailing despondently knee-deep in water.

"Come on, keep going else you get left behind." Then dropping his voice he said to Jack. "Speak to them, Captain. They should hear your voice lest they give up."

Nodding, Jack hauled himself over the last of the deceptive mossy tufts.

"It's alright for you. I hardly have wind left in my body," he panted.

He thought of the bogs near his home as a child's playground. Now gathering his breath, he knew they were never as malicious as those they had just crossed.

"You do well," he managed to shout. "Soon you shall teach your sons what it is to be brave. For you who stand with me and fight by my side are my brothers'. Put your trust in our Lord and we shall be victorious, I promise you that. If you have no spirit for such things, go back now and hide behind your women."

"Three cheers for the Captain," Walter added, popping up from nowhere with an impish smile.

"Keep them for later," Jack warned. "We have no need to tell our enemy of our arrival. We shall rest here and God willing will reach Queenborough by nightfall."

* * *

Built on a motte the circular shaped castle commanded a fine view from its battlements whichever way a person faced. Its defensive cannons glinted dully in the last of the day's light and from a distance it looked peaceful enough. Below it close to the harbour, the water mill and the church were undisturbed too.

Pleased they had arrived sooner than he thought, Jack sought out a dense strip of forest. Deep in the centre the smoke from their fire wouldn't be seen. No reason to let others know of their arrival yet. With venison roasting on a spit and the women baking flatbreads in the ashes it was time for him to plan their next advance. The whole camp had an air of calm now they were in an area safer and more familiar to them. As they rested talk was kept low, but easy.

Crouched down nearby, Aditha cleared away twigs and cones fallen from the tall pine trees to fashion pits for sleeping whilst Merek, Barda and Walter were cleaning their weapons waiting for Jack to speak. He sat drumming his fingers on his satchel staring into the darkening tops of the trees.

"So this is what we do," he said finally. "The Constable of the Castle is Humphrey De Stafford. I'm told he is the King's man and should do us nicely. We take the Castle at nightfall and then we make sure the King and Parliament confirm our pardons. Rest up while you can and then make sure every man has sharpened their weapons. The moon is thin tonight, it will serve us well." Seeing Aditha about to move, he called out to her. "Woman, my belly aches for the want of food."

Then tossing down his dagger he pointed to the carcases dripping lethargic globules of fat into the crisp flames. She giggled and taking the knife, disappeared towards the fire. His henchmen said nothing at first then bolder than the rest, Merek spoke up.

"Is it wise to attack Queenborough, Captain? From what I hear 'tis difficult to storm such a place. We have a few hundred men, nothing more and some of them have little to fight with."

"Nonsense," Jack retorted. "Do you think we have come all this way to exchange pleasantries with the King's liege man? We shall take him by surprise and cannot fail." He paused as if gathering his thoughts. It was rare for him to have doubts, but on this occasion he hesitated. What was it

Mammy's friend Maeve once said? *You be watching that boy of yours, he's a hot-head alright, too hasty for his own good, so he is.* "

"Of course, if any of you have lost the will to fight then be on your way, there'll be no hard feelings," he said.

His eyes darted over all three of them. No one would argue. Heads down they worked on their weapons until it was time for them to instruct the other men. Then they formed a circle and ate in silence, each giving consideration to the coming hours. Sharing time and gossip with the other women, Aditha was nowhere to be seen. Jack knew as soon as they were gone, the women would take the children and hide until they heard them returning.

Dispatched to guard the rear of the formation, Walter and Barda crept away as soon as Jack deemed it dark enough. Taking Merek with him to lead them in and guided only by the meagre flame of a torch and a lemony strip of moonlight, they made their way to the Castle.

Rising up from the grassy slopes of its ditches, the sturdy fortification with its six circular towers looked well able to withstand any unwanted visitors by day whichever way it was approached. In the hours of darkness it appeared even more formidable. Its broad stone ramparts and triple turrets were palely visible in the clear sky and below the battlements, shaded spindles in the grey walls warned of the many arrow loops.

Halting with the rebels a short distance away, Jack could sense the unease in the air. Having looked over the men he had his own misgivings. Those from the prison were wild-eyed and unkempt, more familiar with stealing money purses or a rich man's valuables, but as for anything more than being handy with a knife he doubted. Barda and Walter had done their best arming them all with lances, longbows and a pole-axe or two, yet still their deceiving ways were more obvious than their battle skills.

Jack selected most of the old hands he recognised then left Barda and Walter to organise two smaller groups to follow up. Straightening his jerkin and brushing his breeches, he buckled his sword tighter and picked up his bow.

"Make sure you are ready when you hear the order. Until then keep your silence and your wits about you," he told them, before he beckoned to Merek to lead the front formation alongside him.

Extinguishing their torch they were left with only a blanket of pitch and as stealthy as feral cats they moved on towards the gate house. One on either side the wicks in the wall sconce burnt feeble flames so more shadow than light provided dim visibility for a stranger. Under a vaulted arch a lofty oak gate strengthened by plates of iron would lead to the bailey housing then the guardrooms, stables and storerooms. Getting his bearings, a quick glance upwards reassured Jack there were no archers stationed between the teeth of the battlements. With a sense of relief he motioned the men on, knowing somehow they must reach the lookouts in the gatehouse before they were seen.

With so much racing around in his head and expecting the alarm to sound any moment, Jack didn't think it strange the portcullis was up or else he might have been more cautious. Nor did he consider whether the ropes they carried would be long enough for them to breach such exceptionally high walls. Fired by his usual optimism, he moved fast as until they reached the last few yards then he raised his hand for them to halt. Now arrows would be notched and weapons gripped a little tighter. Each man would listen to his own heartbeat. Each would feel the sweat leaking cold onto his brow and the tight knot of muscle strangling his gut.

From the top of the keep and prominent against the studded clouds, De Stafford's standard barely moved in the stillness. Total peace prevailed. With nothing untoward, Jack couldn't know a loose mouth among his own force warned of their arrival some hours earlier so when suddenly light flooded the front of the castle he was as helpless as the rest. There was no hiding place.

"By the Saint's bones, where did they come from?" Merek breathed into his ear.

"More to the point, who told them? Methinks we have a traitor amongst us" Jack hissed.

Ten armoured knights, the first of De Stafford's retinue advanced onto the drawbridge. Following closely behind were a column of Esquires, men-at-arms dressed in doublets of coarse brown serge and wearing flat felt caps. Then astride a bay stallion, De Stafford himself appeared. Without any signal the moment his horse stepped onto the drawbridge every space along the battlements filled with archers. Looking up, Jack saw arrows poking out from the arrow loops too. Stationed at every possible vantage point, an unwanted visitor would do well to escape.

Realising they were at the mercy of De Stafford's forces, the rebel's nerves were failing them. Bunched together they fidgeted waiting for instructions, but Jack was too busy taking stock to say anything. De Stafford was a mesmerising figure. Mockingly close, he exuded a self-assurance that intimidated. Tall and well-muscled, he was wearing a rich crimson velvet mantle lined in purple taffeta, a dark doublet covered with a mail breast plate and a plumed beret. As black as a crow's breast, his facial hair almost covered his lower face, yet escaping its embrace his deep set eyes burned with a darkness all of their own.

"Welcome to Queenborough, Captain Mortimer," he said in velvety tones as more men-at-arms rumbled across the drawbridge carrying staves and lances.

"My lord Stafford," Jack murmured uneasy now the element of surprise was gone. His clenched hands the only outward sign of his discomfort, he tried to plead their cause. "We have travelled far to see you, there are certain matters to discuss," he said pleasantly.

"Do you make a habit of doing business at this late hour?" De Stafford replied, leaning forward on his lofty mount. "I hear tell you are on a different mission or perhaps I am mistaken?"

"We come to ask you to ratify our pardons on behalf of His Majesty, King Henry, nothing more I give you my word."

"Do you hear that?" asked De Stafford, looking around at his men. "The rebel asks us to trust his word. A pox on your word is what I say to you, Master Mortimer," he said, guffawing at him.

It prompted ribald laughter and jeers from his retinue which sent an angry flush to Jack's cheeks. Mastering his temper was difficult, but swallowing hard he stood his ground.

"Perhaps we should leave, Captain if the grand lord will permit it," Merek whispered uncomfortably.

"Not yet, this is not finished," Jack replied tightly. Waiting until the laughter had died down, he urged his horse closer until only the knights separated him from the grinning De Stafford.

"I think you forget we have been pardoned," he said coldly.

Trying to ignore his sense of foreboding, Jack knew all eyes were on him and his own forces likely to bolt before much longer. Determined they escape alive, he must face down his enemies. It was what he did best, that and lead his men with courage. Meeting De Stafford's scornful eyes, he drew out the pardon from under his cloak and waved it wildly at him. "There sirrah, do you see, my pardon is as good as any other."

"No, you are wrong," De Stafford replied bluntly. "You carry a pardon for John Mortimer, do you not?"

The pause was long, vibrant with anticipation and awful in its hollowness. Jack was conscious all his rebel army had drawn forward. He could almost smell their sour breaths and feel the heat from their bodies. When he darted a glance, Merek was watching at him with a questioning expression and next to him, Barda and Walter exchanged bewildered looks. De Stafford's smile was a sardonic one and his eyes like fragments of ice.

"No answer Captain *Mortimer?* Perhaps that is because you are an imposter. Should I not be addressing you as Jack *Cade*, for that is who you are, is it not? Pray show me the pardon in his name."

In the same breath De Stafford raised his hand and his command changed everything.

"Fire!"

Chapter Forty

JACK remembered Mammy like the word 'luck,' She used it a lot.

What luck we've had, she would say when they found horse mushrooms for the pot or after Maeve found him a rosy apple on her tree, *what a lucky wee boy you are, Jack.*

That he noticed the imperceptible movement of De Stafford's hand as he started to lift it and before the first arrows sang towards them, he experienced more than a little of Mammy's luck. It warned him giving him time. Wrenching at the bundle, he slid off the back of his horse. His legs powered by fear and his breath urged by terror, he started running just as the barbs began thudding home. He didn't look back.

Crying out in alarm the rebels stumbled about in the darkness. For some there was not even the time to open their mouths as wave after silver wave of arrows left the battlements. Some flew from the arrow slots others were let loose by the men-at-arms on the drawbridge. Withdrawing into the safety of the shadows, De Stafford looked on with calm disinterest as precision firing brought down a swathe of rebels. Waiting to play their role, his knights dropped their visors over their dispassionate eyes and when finally it seemed there were few left to shoot they rode out with swords raised.

His longbow pounding on his shoulder blade, Jack blundered on carrying his booty. He must draw on all his reserves, yet still he kept going. Arrows whined past him and he could hear De Stafford's voice above the mayhem bellowing his orders so the bloody rout would be settled. Something grazed the side of his face, but he didn't slow down. Finally he reached the start of the forest. With excited voices and the ugly noises of death beginning to fade, he tripped and fell panting into the bracken fronds. Their moist peaty smell filling his nose, he lay there with his painful breath rasping in his throat. There was time now to touch the rip on his cheekbone made by an arrow tip, feel the warm trickling sensation and taste the iron on his tongue.

High above him the black spectre-like fingers of the towering pines shifted gently allowing glimpses of watercolour-wash pink light to escape from fleecy clouds. Night made way for dawn. The surge of blood round his body reminded him of his old wound which almost numbed his arm with its painful throbbing. But too tired to pay it much notice he craved sleep, a closing out of the hideous sounds which still echoed in his ears and an escape from the savage brutality inflicted by De Stafford's men. Worse than that, he knew, his destiny was decided. At the realisation there would be no great future for him he might have managed to shut his eyes on his tears if it hadn't been for whispering coming closer.

Instinctively he felt for his bow. It lay a few feet away. It must have fallen as he did, sending it spinning into the undergrowth. To his relief his dagger still rested next to his water flask in his waistband and he coiled his fingers round the haft.

"Captain?" an uncertain voice asked.

Stretching out his other hand, Jack clawed his precious bundle closer to his body and wearily lifted his head. There were no more than five shocked rebels looking down at him. Any bearing they might have had as fighting men was gone and he could see them trembling. Their eyes, frightened eyes, told him of their horror whilst their physical wounds relentlessly oozed blood which quickly darkened and set stiffening their torn clothing as it did so.

"Are there no more of you?" he croaked, struggling to his feet.

"We haven't seen anyone," one grunted, his knuckles white with grasping his lance.

"Merek?" he asked hopefully. "Barda, Walter?" No one spoke, but they didn't need to. He could see by their expressions they were most likely lost. "They are dead then," he muttered.

Breathing in his pain at the thought, he felt despair. It was a rare emotion for him and he struggled to rid himself of it. He must think and quickly before De Stafford sent his forces to round up any who may have escaped.

"It isn't safe here we must move before we are discovered," he told them through dry lips.

One of the rebels stepped forward, a tall raw-boned man with a gaunt face and devious eyes who took it on himself to speak for the others.

"Where do we go? I hope you have some good ideas, 'tis your fault we were led into a trap and now we'll be hunted down like animals. Seems to me we were better off in prison," he growled, whilst his companions nodded in agreement.

"What do they call you?" Jack asked him.

"Borin son of Borin," the other replied.

Picking up his bow and with his bundle under his arm, Jack stood for a moment his head tilted and then said.

"Well, Borin son of Borin, if I'm not much mistaken those are fresh voices I hear and they are coming this way. It's up to you whether we go together. It would be safer," he said with a shrug.

They all heard them now, De Stafford the most strident of all.

"Find that dog Cade, Mortimer whatever he calls himself. I want him alive and a curse on the man who doesn't find him," he was yelling at the top of his voice. They turned then without hesitation and following Jack, moved off together into the black heart of the forest.

* * *

There was little to measure time by and none of them knew how long they walked. Fighting their way through dense thicket and tangles of undergrowth they must endure less and less light, yet neither would they stop. There were no familiar landmarks only blind instinct and an occasional shaft of sunlight to guide them before Jack finally halted.

"We should be safe enough here. Time to see to your wounds and rest then we'll move on again," he told them.

A guttural grunt or a nod was all he received in return. Distrusting of them, he watched closely as first they shovelled out loam from the forest floor with their hands to make sleeping pits. Frightened and dishevelled they took their orders from Borin. It didn't matter to Jack. He was solitary, always had been when it came down to it. He recalled Mammy's wistful look when she said more than once.

I would love it if you had someone to play with, so I would. But he didn't care for the thought. Why would he want to share any of her spoiling?

Borin sent two of them off hunting and he watched them return with a young deer.

"Keep the fire low," he reminded.

Then he sat alone with his share of the venison tearing at it hungrily and sucking on the bones un-minding of the fragments of flesh and fat which caught in his beard. Only later when he was satisfied their snuffling and snoring told him they slept, did he begin to relax. His cheek felt stiff and sore. Reluctant to use what little water he had, he tore a strip off the bottom of his shirt and spat on it. Gingerly dabbing he eased off the caked blood, then relieving himself on a pile of pine needles he pulled his cloak tightly around him. With his blanket-wrapped bundle as a pillow he lay listening for some time and then his thoughts turned to Aditha. She'd be waiting for him, waiting for all of them to return as would be all the women. Firming his resolve to get back to the camp, he imagined her until slowly his eyelids drooped and he slept.

At first he thought he imagined the tugging sensation under his head. Something was working away at the bundle which was his pillow, easing it little by little. Barely fully awake he suddenly realised what was happening. Through half-closed lids, he saw close to him dirty broken fingernails clasping the edge of the bundle and heard rough breathing.

"By the Devil's whore, what are you doing?" he snarled at the shadowy figure.

At the moment his fingers closed round the sinewy wrist, he found himself staring into eyes as dark and hard as nutshells. He was face to face with Borin. At the same time the bundle became free unrolling and scattering its contents amongst the leaf litter. The fire's dying embers turned the gemstones into sparkling orbs and cast a glow on the gold and silver. Lunging at them, Jack started clawing them towards him whilst Borin sat back on his heels watching him.

"Now I know why you held on so tight, sweeter than a harlot's tit is it, that booty of yours? Indeed 'tis fine plunder. Well thanks to you we are all wanted men so I reckon you owe us something. A share each wouldn't you say, Captain?" he rasped.

Drawn by their voices, the others were awake and crouched down besides Borin, their baleful eyes fixed on Jack. It was an uneasy gathering made more so by their inhospitable surroundings. Forest noises threatened and the hues of black and drab greens suffocating. Thinking quickly, Jack gave a ghost of a smile.

"Come now, this is no time to quarrel," he said easily. "There's plenty for all, but there'll be no sharing until we leave this damnable place. If I'm to be fair then there must be light so each of you gets no more or less than the other."

"That sounds reasonable," said one of them, older and less hasty than his companions. "What think you, Borin?"

Borin's shaggy face looked uncertain. With his heavy brows low over his eyes, he regarded Jack with a suspicious expression. Ignoring him, Jack gathered up the last of the jewellery and coins and having tied up the bundle, he stood and stretched nonchalantly.

"We should move on before the day ends. The road to Rochester can't be far now," he said, turning his back on them.

Wondering if it was a wise thing to do he steeled himself, then with his bow on his shoulder he looked for the light and struck out south. The sound of crunching footsteps behind him told him they were following and he breathed more easily.

* * *

He would never know how he managed to outwit them. Only that he was fitter and stronger than those from the prison grown weak on watery pottage once a day. He saw his moment when they were arguing as to which way to go. Then he ran, racing until his ribcage screamed for mercy and his breath threatened to burst out of his throat. When he knew he could go no farther he hid. Lying awkwardly under tall bracken he could hear them thrashing through the undergrowth and hardly dare draw breath when Borin came so close, he could see the scuffed toes of his boots.

"By Satan's bitches, he's here somewhere. Don't stop 'til we find him. The bastard will pay for this. I should have stuck him when we had him trapped on the ground," he swore.

"Shall I thrash the bushes?" one asked loudly.

"And have someone hear us? We've made enough noise as it is," Borin said, moving slowly away from Jack's hiding place. "No, by the Almighty we'll meet up with cur afore long and when we do."

There was silence then a low laugh and Jack could only imagine what gesture Borin might have made. Too afraid to move despite his lungs inhaling the acrid smell of rotting vegetation and moisture seeping through his clothes, he remained rigid. As sounds of Borin and his companions faded he was forced to shift his legs grown stiff from his position. It was then he noticed in horror should Borin cared to have looked down, most of his longbow was clearly visible. Drawing it closer, he finally raised his head.

Returned to its torpor the forest offered no threat and on his feet again, Jack eagerly breathed in the throat-easing air and felt his heart slow back into its normal rhythm. When he stepped out of the bracken and over a rotting log a shaft of sunlight threw its hazy beam onto his head turning his hair into shades of rich Titian. Looking upwards, he was left wondering if perhaps it was a sign and he felt an urgency to pray. It had been so long, he thought and guilt stopped him falling to his knees, but just the same he made the sign of the Cross and tried to remember what Mammy taught him.

'Blessed Mary, Mother of God, we ask for your protection . . .' Shaking his head he tried to recall the words and tears of frustration welled, yet he knew time was short and he must keep moving. Having abandoned the idea of returning to the camp he was at a loss as to which direction to take. Muttering "Sorry," he gathered up his bundle and bow. Without a better idea he followed the sunbeam until emerging into light he stumbled onto a rutted track.

Chapter Forty-One

Windsor

UNDER the wide boughs of an oak tree fallow deer took refuge from the heat of the day. Mouths slightly agape their speckled flanks quivered from time to time in an attempt to dislodge irritating flies. Watching them from a window, Margaret's eyes wandered over them and beyond where the rolling grass lay stretched out like an emerald carpet. The view of the Great Park never failed to soothe her although at the moment it needed to work hard as she waited alone for the arrival of four men. Two were no concern to her, but Ralph, Lord Cromwell and the doddery William Hastings twisted her lip at the mere thought of them. If she could find reason she would rid herself of them and their treacherous ways, but others advised her against such a thing.

When they presented themselves in her chamber only those standing closest would have seen her lips tighten and her grey-shadowed eyes narrowing at the sight of them. Her flinty expression vanished when she saw Lord Scales and Edmund Beaufort and her charm was obvious.

"My lords, welcome," she smiled pleasantly, making sure it was they who kissed her hand first. Turning to Cromwell and his companion she barely gave them time to skim their lips over her skin before she withdrew her hand sharply. "Pray be seated," she instructed, arranging the heavy folds of her gown meticulously as she took her place on the smaller of the Throne chairs.

"We have called you to Windsor for two reasons. Firstly we wish to know whether London is peaceful again. Have you finally rid us of Mortimer and his ruffians? The second concerns my dear . . ." Her words stumbled and fell silent. Sitting on opposite sides of the chamber, the four sat waiting for Margaret to resume. Wandering back to the window, she laid a hand on the sill and gazed out. Beaufort and Scales kept their eyes lowered whilst Cromwell exchanged the occasional word in a low voice to Hastings, making no effort to disguise the hostility in it. Annoyed at his rudeness, Margaret spun round.

"So are you able to reassure us it is safe to return to the capitol, Lord Cromwell?" she demanded, in a syrupy voice edged with hemlock.

Cromwell grimaced at the question.

"Lord Scales has dealt with this rather more than I, Your Grace. It is him you should be asking, but . . ."

Margaret's interruption was swift and brusque.
"No my lord, we choose to ask you. Kindly answer us, if you please."

Granite-eyed, Cromwell nodded.

"As you wish Majesty, I am told peace has been restored apart from their leader, Mortimer who still remains under arms despite receiving a pardon. Isn't that so, Scales?" There was a hint of indolence in the curl of his lip as he glanced across the room.

"Is this true, my lord Scales?" asked Margaret.

Unlike Cromwell, Scales stood before answering and giving a short bow said, "Lord Cromwell is right, the rebel leader has yet to be apprehended Your Grace. I can assure you there is no cause for concern since word reaches me he and his miserable little force were routed by Lord De Stafford and his men at Queenborough only a day ago."

Fiddling with the corner of his silk kerchief, Hastings suddenly became alert.

"I was told some escaped, did they not?" he said, dabbing at his lip to mop up a dribble of saliva. His age-speckled hand shook a little as he did so, a failing which did not escape Margaret's keen eye.

"Please don't overtire yourself, my lord. Others are more than capable of speaking for you. Edmund, have you nothing to say?" Margaret enquired, never taking kindly to those who appeared to day dream in her presence. Nudged by Scales, Edmund blushed deep red.

"I believe Lord Hastings is right," he said apologetically. "But no more than a handful at most although 'tis true Mortimer, who we now know is Jack Cade, is likely to be on the run."

Her lips pursed, Margaret looked at each of them in turn. It was all such a mess. A dreadful chaos which she knew gave Cromwell cause to gloat. He and old Hastings were both staunch liege men of the Duke of York. Suddenly she felt weak and her deep sigh mingled and deepened the already taut atmosphere created by a company of men so obviously on opposing sides.

Cromwell read her like a book and the feel of his contempt sent a sudden chill through her. She looked at him coldly in return.

"The remedy is simple Your Grace," he said smartly. "The King must demand the arrest of this Irish ne'er do well immediately. With a ransom of shall we say a thousand marks on his head it shouldn't take long before he is found."

"And five marks on the head of any of his followers," Hastings piped up.

"That sounds agreeable," Margaret said before turning to Scales and Edmund. "What think you, my lords?" With a quick glance at Edmund, Scales nodded. "The sooner we are rid of this outlaw the better. Then you can be sure it is safe to return to London, Your Grace."

Her patience exhausted by Cromwell's presence, Margaret was anxious to be rid of him.

"Then that is all, gentlemen, we thank you. You may leave the chamber," she said with an imperious bob of her head. "Oh Lord Scales there is one other thing. Perhaps you would remain behind."

Waiting until the door closed and she and Scales were alone, Margaret's expression and manner changed. Gliding across the floor she took his hand and he saw a frailty she rarely exposed.

"Dear Scales, what am I to do? The King lies in his bedchamber and no one must know that his health declines again. It is why I brought him to Windsor away from prying eyes. He takes few visitors and I must conduct all matters of state alone. It is so very difficult at times."

For a moment he thought she was about to weep, but she didn't. She rarely did and then alone in her chamber in the small hours where no one apart from Catherine could hear her.

"Will His Majesty be able to sign the warrant for the rebel's arrest?" he enquired quietly.

She waved an impatient hand and caught by the light the precious diamond gemstone in her ring flared into fragments of colour.

A Pardon Too Few

"He will manage a mark which I can correct if needs be."

Knowing his next question was delicate, Scales hesitated. Then in the kindest voice he could muster, he said.

"I assume it is the King's mental state which lays him low? I am saddened his bouts of mental sickness seem more regular."

Margaret's laugh sounded hollow as she struggled to conceal the truth.

"There is no mania, my lord, merely a great tiredness. He suffers a load on his mind too heavy for him to bear at times, but he will recover. I have employed minstrels to play for him and a tumbler to amuse him. Then there are some gentlemen friends who are making a pilgrimage to pray for him at this very moment. It is all very promising," she said gaily, although Scales noticed her smile failed to reach her eyes.

"Excellent," he said forlornly.

Her bright manner didn't stay long. Instead she looked disconsolate and bit down on her lip like a small child.

"Scales, what do those in the Court say about me?" she asked softly. "There are so few I can trust, but you have been most loyal and I want an honest answer."

It took several moments for Scales to reply and as she sat down on a stool beside him she watched him anxiously.

"Well," he said at last, straightening himself in his chair."There are many who admire you Your Grace. Others who feel . . ."

"Go on," she urged with a faint smile on her pale face. "I asked you to be frank, you have nothing to fear."

4

"There are some who think you lack a gentleness of nature, Majesty. That perhaps as the Queen consort you take too much upon yourself. Our country flounders at present and 'tis no fault of yours, but there are dissenting voices as to your manner and temperament."

Embarrassed by her stricken face, Scales fell silent. In a loud rustling of her heavily bejewelled gown, Margaret stood up sighing as if she were overwhelmed and her beauty was lost in a frown as deep as the gnarled branch of a tree.

"I thought as much," she said grimly. "What is it they want of me? Do I not rule with a man's hand, Scales? As for my nature, have I not founded a splendid college in Cambridge for women and do I not have courage and energy?" Her voice rising to a feverish pitch she whirled across the chamber. "Tell them this. If *they* don't, no matter, but history will remember me as a great queen who shall spare no pain to protect the House of Lancaster and if God is willing any heirs to it, so root out the unworthy ones and tell them their Queen has spoken. You may go now, Scales and you must tell no one how ailing the King is, have we your personal word on that?"

Margaret's outburst surprised Scales and for once he seemed flustered.

"Of course Majesty, my lips are sealed. And may I express my profound esteem for you," he said in a low voice. Then with his head bowed he left the chamber in silence. But Margaret was back at the window watching the dark shadow on the horizon spreading over her precious view and gave no answer. At least she hadn't revealed to the unbearable Lord Cromwell as she intended, just how unwell the king really was. It was some consolation to her as she regained her composure.

When her heartbeat settled she inhaled deeply and left her chamber to pay her husband a visit. Dismissing the servants who hovered over him she approached the bed with soft steps. He seemed to be sleeping, the merest hint of breaths so gentle she could barely discern them.

"We have come to report the day's events to you, Lord Husband."

Opening his eyes, Henry stared blankly at her. Lost in his half-witted world, he showed no sign of recognition. Undeterred she lifted his flaccid hand and pressed it to her lips. It was cold and unresponsive.

"We have entertained some of our ministers including that reptile, Cromwell," she continued. "It seems at long last the rebels cease to plague us. Now we shall revoke all the pardons and see to it a warrant is issued for the arrest of the ring leader. Good news is it not?"

She didn't expect a reply, why would she especially now the vacant eyes were closed again. Irritated, she tapped her foot on the floor. Is there one spark of intellect left in that feeble brain, she asked herself?

"I love you, my Lord Husband, but what must I do to find your spirit? You are a fine monarch, why must you leave your control of affairs to others? Do you attempt to humiliate me?" Despising herself for sounding spiteful, she hurried away from his bedside.

Back in her own, she threw herself down on the exquisite silk coverlet and despondent, she cast her mind about to brighten the rest of the day. Losing his child made Jasper no longer favoured for surely his seed was weak. Now she couldn't bear sight of him, yet another freshly arrived at Windsor had caught her eye that very morning. James Butler, Earl of Wiltshire would amuse her, she was sure of that. Filled with fresh energy, she pulled at the ivory pins to release her hair and sighed at the sensual feel of her thick curls brushing her face.

"Catherine, come here. I'm in need a fresh gown," she called, her fingers nimbly unlacing her bodice.

Chapter Forty-Two

Kent
Mid-summer

WHEN Jack finally emerged from the forest, triumph had deserted him. His hair clung to his head with wetness, leaves and twigs dangled from his clothes and his hands were bleeding from stabbing thorns. Unhealed, the wound on his cheek wept copious pus and he could feel the heat of it under his fingers.

Led by a track to a road he recognised, he cautiously he stepped out onto it. It was deserted and he breathed more freely. Continuing south would ultimately lead to Charing Heath and then Ashford. With his bravado gone he was nervous and uncertain, yet he knew keeping his wits about him was the only way he might survive.

One look at the sun told him the hour was late as its shot-silk colours blazed a fiery withdrawal just above the horizon. But more important than time was where would he go? Fear drove him forward, but also held him back. He heard noises around him and was too frightened to move, he visualised the future and saw there was none and he dithered knowing it would be fatal.

I've failed, Mammy and you were wrong. Riches beyond our dreams, you said so you did. Help me Mammy, help me.

Salty tears stung his cheek and he scrubbed them away angrily. What would she tell him to do? With his boots feeling as if they were filled with stone shot, he forced himself to start walking. Deep in thought he only saw the horse and cart at the last moment and threw himself into the ditch. The farmer driving looked as thin and weary as his horse and as the cart wobbled by, one wheel hit a flint and shook a few carrots off its load. Seeing them fall and cursing his bony beast, he took hold of his hoe and tapped it hard on its flank to chastise it.

Waiting until they were no more than a cloud of dust in the distance, Jack retrieved the thickly mudded vegetables, wiped one down his jacket and bit into it eagerly. It tasted crisp and sweet on his dry tongue. Something about its curvy shape reminded him of Aditha and it came to him. She'd told him she lived the other side of the Heath at Charing so that's where he would go. When no one returned, the camp would disband and sure she would return home he set off again with fresh hope.

Thank you, Mammy, he breathed as the opaque velvet blanket of night swaddled the round shadowy trunks of trees and melted his path into liquid pitch.

* * *

Tower of London

Watching the lights on the river coming on one by one, Cromwell felt contented. Behind him dozing uncomfortably in a hard, upright chair, the floppy head of Hastings dropped lower onto his chest muffling his plaintive snores. Turning away from the window, hands behind his back, Cromwell rose and fell on his feels contemplating his companion. Silly old fool was past it, he thought, yet with so few he could trust at Court he was still useful to him.

With a spiteful smile, Cromwell moved nearer and barked in a loud voice close to the elderly man's ear.

A Pardon Too Few

"Coming together nicely, don't you think, Hastings? Plenty of disorder now, just as the *Falcon* wanted and with the rebellion over, we in the Government will be held in great esteem. No thanks to our nincompoop king, you see. Shortly the *Falcon* will fly and be received by a most grateful populace. It's all most satisfactory wouldn't you say?"

Waking with a start, Hastings rheumy eyes flew open. Looking more bewildered than usual, he tried to collect himself whilst Cromwell gave him a piercing look.

"Did you hear what I said?" he asked suspiciously.

"Indeed I did," Hastings countered, a little uncertainly. Filling two flasks to the brim with Malmsey, Cromwell handed one to Hastings and sat down heavily in the opposite chair.

"Any word on the capture of the rebel leader yet?" Hastings ventured between careful sips. As it was the tawny amber liquid stole down the side of his flask, depositing itself on his cobalt-blue silk tunic. Fussy about such things, Cromwell watched the stain spreading with a degree of distaste before he answered.

"I saw Scales today and he assures me there is a warrant out for imposter's arrest. He has organised a considerable force to hunt him down, not that we want anything to happen too quickly. Alive or dead there is a price of a thousand marks on his head. As for his followers, any found will be hung. They are all traitors. The sooner they learn their lesson the better," he said, with a sardonic smile. One of Hastings sparse eyebrows rose almost vanishing into his thinning hairline. It was a surprising remark, he thought, coming from a man plotting to overthrow the King in favour of another, but he made no comment. Instead he drained his flask and waited hopefully for more. Choosing to ignore the direction of the old man's look, Cromwell busied himself replacing the stopper on the large flask of Malmsey he kept on a side table.

"Where might Mortimer go, I wonder?" Hastings asked, suppressing a yawn. "They say he has a wife and a house not far from Knole Park although I doubt Squire Pultenery knows of them. Married well, I heard."

"Am I concerned, Hastings? By the Saints, you prattle more than an old woman," Cromwell replied irritably.

* * *

Windsor

It was the second night in a row that James, Earl of Wiltshire moved stealthily over the glossy wooden floor from his chamber and slipped quietly into Margaret's. Too busy avoiding detection, he didn't notice a door close by was very slightly ajar. After he disappeared from view the door closed with practised dexterity. Hitching up her voluminous white night robe, Catherine padded back to her bed. As she bent to blow out the candle her silvery gray plaits dangled dangerously close to the flame whilst its flimsy light illuminated her contended smile wedged between the droop of her cheeks.

In stark contrast to Catherine's frugal surroundings every wall sconce in the Royal bedchamber was alight bouncing a glow from the opulent drapes and rich woods turning them into undulating shadows. Three of the heavily embroidered curtains were drawn round the bed. The fourth was open anchored firmly with a silk girdle round the red oak post.

A Pardon Too Few

Waiting to be called, James lifted his head from his courtly bow and looked across to the bed. Like a siren on a lake, Margaret was waiting on top of the covers. The flawless cut of her nightgown was designed to hide yet display her skin as soft and fresh as spring rain. Its neckline was cut low, yet she knew how to place her arms to look demure. She sat with her knees up to her chin allowing her lace gown to fall away, but so modestly placed not all was displayed. It was a sight to torment and his breath caught in his throat. Her cascade of unrestrained rye-gold hair glowed reminding him of an angel although her pout was more wanton than any spiritual messenger of God he'd ever seen portrayed.

Her moving threw a gross shadow on the wall and then one slender finger beckoned to him.

"Come," she said simply.

"Most gracious Queen," he murmured.

* * *

A little disconsolate, Margaret reclined languidly on the silk bed cover watching James dress. It would be pleasing to see him less nervous, she reflected. The event had been somewhat disappointing as with a foolish smile and bumbling hands he'd tried to please her. Through half-closed eyes, she took stock of her latest amour.

His looks were passable although his features were on the plain side, his hair a trifle mousey, his frame a little too lean, but thinking of her sweet Suffolk nothing would compare and James offered impeccable breeding which was paramount. All will be well she told herself. After all she had consulted her old seer first before selecting him. Shrugging the shoulders of her gown back into place, she sighed and would content herself imagining how the child would resemble her.

James was ready to take his leave of her and she nodded at his bow.

"Until another day Your Grace," he said.

"Au contraire, mon cheri. Until tomorrow," she replied, with an artful smile.

Even before the door closed behind him, her eyes hardened as her thoughts returned to state matters. The Kent rebellion might almost be over, but that afternoon news arrived of more dissatisfaction and an uprising in Sussex. It would seem like shifting sand, England was forever between peace and disorder, she thought grimly.

Hands on her stomach, she lay very still then willing herself to relax she closed her eyes tightly. She wanted to dream of her unborn baby instead it was nightmares which tormented her with awful pictures of bloodied corpses, men crying out in fright, swords of crimson and she woke screaming.

Chapter Forty-Three

DESPITE his weariness, Jack still managed to think clearly and when he reached a break in the track he didn't hesitate. Sensing the overgrown path would lead him to the river he joined it. His decision to travel across country was a desperate one, but guessing there would be a price on his head he couldn't risk being seen.

Between Queenborough and the river Swale, the plateau of heavy soil didn't lend itself to someone not only on foot, but in a hurry too. Shallow valleys offered him some relief, but under his boots the marshy ground was deceptive. He floundered time and again with vivid memories of the first journey. Crawling painfully back up on his feet, he forced himself on. At one point he was so exasperated he almost let go of his precious bundle to be free of the extra burden, but still he clung on to it finally fashioning a crude sling with a sleeve ripped from his jacket. Instead he threw away his lance so one hand was free.

Navigating his way wasn't easy, yet his soldier's instinct guided him and after all weren't the bogs of home a familiar playground, he assured himself. With only the occasional sheep for company there was nothing to break the monotony and the miles were daunting. Once he thought he saw a solitary being in the distance so pulling his hat down over his eyes, he kept low and soon the figure blurred into the ribbons of mist thrown up by the desolate landscape.

By the end of the second day he saw the winding trail of the river gleaming silver ahead of him and wading through the shallows he was on grassland. At the end of his limits it was all he could do to reach the boundary of a thick elm and hawthorn hedge and with a loud groan he tumbled under it, asleep before he could take stock of where he was.

Something nudging his foot woke him. Instinctively one hand felt for the bundle, the other for his knife, but then a piping voice said.

"It's alright Master. I don't mean you no harm."

The boy looked down at Jack with a surprised expression. With the early light behind him, his shock of fair hair and unblemished skin made him childlike and it was only when he turned his head, Jack could see the finest of down on his upper lip. It might have been difficult to judge his age accurately, but not his status. His eyes were too large for his keen-angled face, his bones stuck out of his shapeless tunic which was several sizes too small and his hands, large hands for a boy so thin were reddened and calloused.

Jack found it difficult to think clearly and saw the boy laughing as he struggled to his feet. Then the lad transferred his thorn stick to his other hand, offering help.

"Do you need a hitch up, Master? Looks like you been falling into the marsh all night," he said, nodding to the thick mud on Jack's boots and his sodden breeches.

"I lost my way," Jack muttered, catching at the boy's hand, needing every ounce of his energy to get up. In doing so, his sleeve slithered up his arm and he heard the boy gasp.

"That looks bad. Did someone do that to you?"

"It's an old war wound that's all," he said, his tone indifferent. Then cautious, he asked. "Are you alone, boy?" Curiosity replacing his benign expression, the lad nodded.

A Pardon Too Few

"I'm only out looking for something to eat." Fumbling in his small satchel slung round his neck, he opened his palm revealing the small fruits of a wild strawberry and a sprig of redcurrants. "Here you are, you can have them if you like. Why are you asking? Is someone after you?"

"You mind your questions, boy. Which way is it to Faversham?"

Swinging round the lad pointed his stick towards a steeply wooded slope whose denseness was gradually being lightened by the rising sun.

"I could show you if you like, 'tis not far if you know the short cuts," he offered with enthusiasm.

Jack hesitated. In some ways the boy reminded him of his own youth. He too would wander the land in search of a bird's egg, looking for a hapless animal who might offer a morsel of meat or snatching at a handful of early berries, anything to be rid of the numbing ache of hunger. The lad's company was tempting, yet foolhardy and dangerous. Neither was there time for reminiscing.

"Sorry," he said quickly. "I travel alone. And don't you be telling anyone you've seen me either."

The boy tried again saying with a smiling face.

"Then let me come some of the way. I could carry something for you."

"I told you no didn't I?" Jack said roughly, pushing his bundle back into its sling, anchoring it tight again.

He didn't look back until he reached the far edge of the meadow, but the boy was nowhere to be seen. Unsure whether he could trust him or not he was beset with anxiety. Whatever price had been set for his capture would be a fortune to those who scavenged for sustenance. The thought

337

spurred him on faster than ever as he tried to avoid the open land in favour of copses and dense hedgerows. When he did need to emerge from the fringes, he savoured the feel of the firm ground underfoot, of wiry grass brushing against his ankles and the ease with which he could pass over the heath land. A cloud of blue near his foot halted him. The delicate pastel flowers of a clump of harebells were a sharp reminder of Mariamne, her favourites. He couldn't remember the last time he thought of her with her bulky frame and stodgy soul. He could only imagine her father's scorn when his exploits were aired abroad and how her lip would quiver, yet loyal she'd say nothing.

After that the need to find Aditha became even more urgent. So was his hunger. In preparation he notched his bow as he walked noticing with dismay he was low on arrows. He must have lost some on one of his frequent falls. Cursing his stupidity at abandoning the lance, he stared at the quiver with a grim expression.

Veering off the heath he climbed a slope heading for woodland. Out of breath, he paused in front of the vast expanse of fir, larch and beech. From where he was standing the hamlet of Faversham, a scattering of clay and thatch cottages was spread out below him. Low in the heavens the sun no longer washed them in pale colours, instead accenting their drab facade in a blur of moving shadows. Looking to the horizon the sky looked overcast, a portent of coming rain he thought glad of the shelter the forest would offer.

When a sudden movement caught his eye he strained to make out the indistinct shapes and drew a quick breath. The column of men approaching the hamlet carried a fluttering standard. Held by a commanding knight, the King's colours were unmistakable. Gold fleur-de-lys on bold cobalt and crimson squares of gilded lions twisted and curled as the breeze caught them. Winding a steady column through the hamlet the royalist troops marched behind the Esquires. He could see householders coming out of their doors to meet them as the troops halted. Viewed from his position they presented a force of great numbers and not daring to loiter he retreated into the safety of the trees.

"God's blood," he breathed, his agitation marked by a pounding heartbeat.

Had he gone to Faversham how easily he would have been caught. Good fortune hadn't entirely deserted him. Hunger forgotten, he hitched his bow tightly on his shoulder and as Scales and his men started searching the hamlet for him, he was making his way to Charing. He chose every by-way he found, moving quickly and taking a Woodcock on his way. The bird was all feathers and took up little room in his satchel, but it was a morsel of a meal.

On his onerous journey, his feelings of despondency increased, but the thought he might soon find Aditha spurred him on. Crossing the Heath, he passed other travellers. He made a point of keeping his head low although a quick look at their pinched faces and stooped shoulders told him they had enough troubles of their own to be bothered in his. After that he followed a less worn track in the hope he wouldn't be stopped. It led him off the chalk and flint with its heather and coarse shrubs barely rooted in sparse sandy loam and down a steep hillock to a softer landscape.

He stopped, stroking his dense beard thoughtfully, to take stock of the common pasture land ahead of him supporting a sprinkling of wattle and daub cottages any one of which might be Aditha's home. It was very quiet apart from a rooster and its scabby mate picking half-heartedly at some dropped grain. On the move again, he cautiously approached the dwellings. An ox more bone than flesh was tethered behind one of them. When he was closer he saw the essence of the beast in its dark lamenting eyes before it dropped its head back to the coarse grass.

With a confidence he didn't feel, Jack passed each cottage unhurriedly. He couldn't see anyone, yet had the feeling hostility lurked behind every bleached door plank and suspicion oozed from the dark window slits. It wasn't surprising. He knew he must present a fearful spectacle with his wild appearance and tattered clothing unchanged for weeks.

A small church and a semblance of a market place with no more than a few sheds and stalls and a pen for holding animals, completed his tour of the hamlet. Disappointed, he turned to retrace his steps and that's when he saw Aditha. Half concealed by the shadow of the church, she had her back to him talking to an older woman, but he recognised her at once. Despite her coarse wool gown hers was a perfect shape enhanced by slender tanned arms and a slim neck. Her halo of hair tamed into a thick braid was held by a scrap of scarlet ribbon. He remembered it well. She used to wear it round her wrist.

He suddenly felt uncomfortable watching her and stepped back between a cart and a stack of peat turves piled high against a wall. Patiently, he waited silently rehearsing his words. Then he saw her picking up her basket. When she turned, he found it shocking. A cold chill ran down his spine when he saw the supple young girl had become an ungainly expectant woman. Advanced in her pregnancy, she seemed devoid of her youthful demeanour as she walked slowly, awkwardly towards one of the cottages and he followed her with his eyes.

Was he mistaken? He wanted to be, yet he knew he wasn't. His body sagged with despair and he needed to wait for his breathing to calm. Sudden memories, acute, painful and invading his mind made him flinch.

Dear God, Mammy, he whispered.

Until this moment he had shut away his recollections of Mary and his unborn child, his labour of duty to impregnate Mariamne which failed and his eager lusting for Aditha. Any new hope he might have was dashed, shattered just like his dreams for a rich man's future. Crumbled like the parched earth under his feet.

He couldn't go to her now. How could she provide him sanctuary? They would always be in hiding and for how long? What could he give her in return? Sweet maiden, I can only offer you a few paltry jewels and the worth of a wanted man. It wasn't enough. It could never be enough . . .

Chapter Forty-Four

SHAKING his head in bewilderment, Jack waited until he heard the soft click of her door closing. His face once alight with expectation was downcast, despairing even and as if to match his mood the sky had turned heavy. The first rain fell in driving jagged drops against his skin which bit and stung then they joined the bitter tears coursing down his cheeks. Blinded by both he came out from his place of concealment and hunched into the shoulders of his torn jacket, he stumbled away.

Once wild with power, now a fugitive both hungry and exhausted he made a miserable figure. With no direction in mind his only concern was to get away from the hamlet as quickly as possible. Distress made him less wary than usual otherwise he might have seen the man on horseback who looked down on him from the high ground. Instead Jack left a careless trail along the track the sudden cloudburst so thoughtlessly turned into sloppy mud. Alexander Iden, tall, heavily built with a mop of hair the colour of burnt ochre, watched the fugitive for several moments with a satisfied smile before wheeling his horse to ride back the way he had come. He would choose a new route to observe his man.

Huge tracts of land were recently cleared, but the great Wealden forest still offered hiding places in its dense woodland of broadleaf trees which stretched miles to the Kent border. So when Jack finally realised he had no time for grief, he re-orientated himself and sought its protection. He knew well enough a man could live indefinitely in such a place still rich in deer and wild boar and with its streams bountiful in fish.

Finding a glade which would be his refuge, Jack first scooped out a deep hole between the roots of an ancient oak notching a mark in it bark so he should remember. In the cavity he carefully deposited his bundle of booty and using his knife again filled in the soft mellow loam scattering the surface with leaves as he'd found it. His next thought was for a meal. Roasted over a fire the Woodcock was a bare mouthful, but its gamey flesh excited his taste buds and would appease his empty gut for awhile.

Later he curled up in his threadbare cloak and lay staring into the gloom. Night noises amongst the trees were strange and alarming and the events of the day put his mind in turmoil. Suddenly a rank smell drifted into his nostrils. Somewhere close, too close; he could hear something. There were no audible footsteps, but a rasping breath. Fearful, he raised his head just in time to see the grey shadow passing. The gleam from its green eyes seemed to pick him out, yet the beast didn't pause. Hardly daring to breathe, he waited, but to his relief the wolf disappeared.

After that he lay awake planning the coming day. He needed to make more arrows. There was plenty of wood for the shafts and if he sorted the Woodcock feathers they would furnish him with quills. As for tips, there would be something, he assured his fretful brain. Getting up from the pit fashioned as his bed, he relieved himself.

Starting at sudden sound of a twig snapping he hastily hoisted his breeches back into place and listened. His knife and bow were just out of reach. Trying to ignore the pounding thump of his heart, he strained to hear more.

Could he smell the foul breath of the wolf again? Or was it the tread of a deer? Or could it be something else? Were there eyes on him, yet no sign of what they might belong to? He caught his breath wondering if his eyes tricked him when he thought he saw moving shadows.

When nothing happened, he was pleased to see scraps of light appearing between the tops of the towering greenery and started to relax. Shrugging off his fears, he concentrated on making a mental list of chores to find wood and water, perhaps a trout if he was fortunate. Yet still he couldn't rid himself of the feeling of being watched.

And he was, not by the emerald eyes of a carnivore, but the insipid blue of a human. From behind a tangle of blackberry and blackthorn, Iden silently raised his bow, aimed and fired. The sing of the speeding arrow was too fast until the very last moment. Jack threw up his arm in a futile gesture to deflect the missile, but Iden was as skilled as the next man. The arrow tore through Jack's belly, its force hurling him backwards. With a surprised expression, he managed to right himself grasping the shaft before falling to his knees. Looking up, he saw Iden standing in front of him with his hands on his hips, smiling broadly.

Despite a deliberate effort, Jack couldn't get purchase on the slippery stave awash with blood. At the same time a patch of red slowly crept down the front of his jerkin. His scarlet life juice pumped rhythmically from the wound and spread out around him.

"For pity's sake, help me pull it out," he groaned in disbelief.

Iden chuckled. "Nay sirrah, would that I could assist you, but how foolish that would be on my part. Dead or alive you are worth a great deal of money and I intend to make sure the King's reward is mine."

Fighting the agony, Jack struggled to speak. "I can offer you more." Pointing a feeble finger towards the oak tree, his throat fought for air. "Over there, I buried a great treasure. You will see 'tis marked on the trunk. Dig it up for me and you shall have it all."

He felt his head too heavy to hold up and resting it back on the leaf litter, he prayed Iden's avarice would determine his fate. With his watery blue eyes full of contempt, his attacker merely mocked.

"Plundered I don't doubt. You have much to answer for, Captain of Kent. You are a thief and an imposter. Not only that you have deceived the good people of this country inciting them to rise up in rebellion against their King. So now you will answer to treason."

"There were pardons," Jack said weakly.

"You know well enough a man may only receive one pardon. John Mortimer might have gone free, but you are Jack Cade with no such forgiveness. Besides all pardons are now revoked, so whatever you might hold is worthless. I'm done with talking, I need to get you to London," Iden said with malice.

In a haze of pain, fear and blood, Jack felt hands on his ankles and then he realized Iden intended dragging him across the woodland floor. Any light there might have been was slowly being denied him and he strained to capture the last of it. Maybe he should pray, but who was there to hear him? Floating in and out of consciousness, he barely felt the flesh being flailed off his back as he was hauled over fallen wood, thorn and rough leaf litter with total disregard.

Behind him the trail was marked by a dark viscous pattern of blood splattered on the gold and bronze of dead leaves.

Iden had been careful with his preparations. Two yeomen and a hand cart stood ready on the fringe of the forest. Feeling the lump and thump through his pain as he was hauled up and thrown in, it was when his body impacted on the unrelenting wood that Jack opened his mouth to scream. His cry, *"Mammy"* went unheard for his lungs had no more strength and their final bubbles were wasted. In the moment, a myriad of white starbursts extinguished their light and only his soul uttered his last earthly plea.

* * *

At the first glimpse of day, Iden rode ahead of the cart as it appeared on the city streets. Making their way to the Tower, he was gratified to see their arrival attracted a large gathering. Once Jack's lifeless body was recognised, the air was good humoured, festive even and Iden acknowledged the cheers and waving with a dip of his head and a smug expression as the yeomen hauled the rackety conveyance over cobblestones and ruts towards Great Tower-Hill.

Word travelled fast. Hurriedly summoned, the advanced guard were approaching the entrance gateway of the White Tower. As a sign the king was in residence they were resplendent in maroon doublets embroidered with the royal crest in woven gold and striped hose. Each carried halberds with gilded staves. Their measured tread and faintly audible clank of arms were dwarfed by the stern and sombre outline of the Tower where rising turrets were still wreathed in vapours from the river. In contrast to its stark outlines the other buildings on its banks looked more hospitable in the early light with their mellow spires, tall twisted chimneys and comfortable fading facades.

Halting the cart, Iden waited. At a gesture by the Constable of the Tower, a loud trumpet-blast prepared the way for the arrival of a small group of men. Leading them Ralph, Lord Cromwell was followed more slowly by Edward Hastings and a pace behind him Thomas Scales and Edmund Beaufort walked side by side.

Giving the contents of the cart a cursory glance, Cromwell's face bore an indifferent expression.

"It would have given me more pleasure had he still been living," he said drily.

"Perhaps so, sir, but he was wanted dead or alive," Iden said timidly, fearing the possibility his reward might be lost. It was the commanding manner of Scales which eased the situation.

"We must congratulate you, Master Iden. Good riddance to a trouble maker is what I say. Whilst his health is still delicate, His Majesty has insisted he sees you personally so if you would follow me," he said pleasantly.

In the palace the party trailed through the labyrinth of passage ways leading to the royal apartments whilst the cart was taken to the Green. Awed by the splendour, Iden could only roll his eyes whilst his hands trembled in anticipation.

* * *

Dressed in a cumbersome gown of purple velvet which made him appear shrunken and frail in his chair, Henry was at least bright-eyed and more alert as he waved the visitors forward. The wood creaked plaintively underfoot when from her usual place at the window, Margaret glided across the chamber, her grey silk dress trailing behind her as if she dragged a puddle. Stationing herself behind Henry's chair, she rested one hand firmly on his shoulder.

"Majesties, this is the man who brings you the body of the rebel leader, Jack Cade," Edmund said.

"We are most grateful to you for your brave deed," Margaret replied graciously.

Then Iden felt himself pushed forward by Cromwell's hand in his back. Overcome by the occasion, he nodded uncertainly. He couldn't help seeing the steel in Margaret's eyes nor feel the strength of her spirit. Henry on the hand looked slightly bemused.

"Speak," Scales hissed.

Nervously crunching his cap up in his hand, Iden bowed.

"I am but a poor Esquire of Kent who seeks to do his duty for the King he loves," he mumbled.

Henry smiled before turning to his wife.

"What's his name, good Lady Wife?" he asked softly.

"Alexander Iden," she said prompting him. "Is that right, Scales?"

"Your Grace, it is indeed." Scales replied, not failing to notice she ignored Cromwell.

"We welcome you, Iden. Kneel down," Henry instructed gravely.

So formidable was the moment for Iden, his legs refused to move. Finally he managed to prostate himself at Henry's feet. He felt the tip of the sword brush across the harsh serge of his tunic and heard Henry's words in disbelief.

It was more than he dared hope for.

"Rise up a knight. We give thee your reward of a thousand marks for your loyal services. And we appoint you the new High Sheriff of Kent."

Flushed with pleasure, Iden replied, "Sire, I, Iden will be forever in your debt and a loving servant in return for such a gift."

Henry nodded approvingly and directed Iden away with a vague flap of his hand. Doubled up by his bow, Iden shuffled back awkwardly.

"What would you have us do with the body, Your Grace?" Cromwell said briskly.

Henry gave him a nebulous look before turning to Margaret again. Bending forward she whispered something, but he seemed reluctant to answer. With the hint of a tear in his eye he blew his nose noisily. Margaret took an abrupt step from behind Henry's chair.

"The man was a traitor. We wish his corpse to be hung and then quartered. Put his head on a pike, it is to be displayed on London Bridge and make sure others guilty of treason keep him company," she said clearly. "Then send a part each of his remains to Blackheath, Salisbury, Norwich and Gloucester as a warning." She ticked off the counties on her fingers as casually as she might be overseeing supplies in the royal kitchen, adding "the people must see the House of Lancaster is strong, mustn't they my Lord Husband?"

Already retreating into his own strange world, Henry sat nodding happily.

Chapter Forty-Five

A woman entered Margaret's bedchamber in a whirl of woollen skirts, a strong smell of camphor oil and a blast of chill air. Her face was almost concealed by the hood of her rough wool cloak, but from its depths she watched the world with button-bright eyes. Nodding low to Margaret she waited to be summoned.

It was clear from Catherine's expression she disapproved of the Soothsayer. Yet Margaret looked on her with a disarming smile. Beckoning to her, she said.

"Come forward old woman."

Carrying her hemp sack with a fierce grip, the woman shuffled across the floor.

"Is it a casting you want, Your Majesty?"

Margaret nodded and settled back in her heavy black oak chair. She was wearing a gown the colour of sage encrusted with rubies round the neckline and the skirts. Arranging them carefully around her, her eyes narrowed as she watched the Soothsayer taking off her cloak and opening her sack.

"Before we start remember this. I have summoned you twice before and both times you have failed in your predictions. I shall not be pleased if you fail again," she said tightly.

The crone rolled her eyes and there was frailty on her withered face. "Have mercy on me, Your Grace. Perhaps the castings told me wrong," she whined.

"Don't waste my time with your snivelling excuses. Just get on with it before I bore of your company," Margaret snapped.

With a watchful eye on her mistress, Catherine sat down heavily on a stool. Making more noise than she needed she was determined to show her displeasure. Ignoring her, the Soothsayer shook out the virgin white cloth, a yard square, and laid it at Margaret's feet. Ferreting through her sack again she brought out a rabbit's skin pouch and from that three vials.

"If Your Grace would hold these," she said, tipping up the first vial into the royal palm.

There was a crunching sound when Margaret's fingers curled round the dried beans. In turn the Soothsayer received them back into her shrivelled palm and started to chant in a low monotone.

A snort escaped Catherine's pursed lips, but with her eyes closed, Margaret seemed oblivious to her presence. The room was as warm as a pond in winter and Catherine shivered.

Tossed up high by the Soothsayer, the beans fell back onto the cloth. She studied them intently for a moment then whispered.

"The omens are good, Majesty, but we must look further."

Twice more she repeated the process taking first peas and then barley from the vials. Each time they scattered on the cloth, she bent over them mumbling under her breath at their portent. Margaret eagerly pressed forward in her chair.

"Well old woman, what do they say? Am I to have a child?"

The woman flinched at her tone and continued to stare at the cloth. Drawn into the atmosphere, Catherine was an unwilling listener, yet curiosity got the better of her. How could she miss the revelations made by the Soothsayer? Inclining her head, the crone attempted a pale smile, but a questioning wrinkle sat on her forehead. She sounded hesitant and Margaret sighed impatiently.

"Indeed, Majesty. The castings show me new beginnings. There will be a birth although perhaps not yet."

Margaret grimaced. Despite James's best efforts, it was disappointing news.

"Am I to believe you?" she threatened.

The Soothsayer was silent as she looked again at the peas and then the barley.

"Perhaps if Your Majesty would permit the runes, I could be more accurate," she ventured.

Margaret didn't give her the benefit of an answer merely a frosty smile. Catherine held her breath. Shaking the carved bone pieces out of their pouch, the Soothsayer sat back on her heels and studied them hard. Mastering a bland expression was a trick of hers when things were unclear. Nodding she said.

"It augurs well, Majesty. You will carry a child, of that I'm sure."

Margaret's voice was hopeful.

"Are you certain, old woman? Will it be a son?"

The Soothsayer made a thing of squinting at the rune stones again. She managed a pleasant expression, but her eyes were shadowed.

"Yes Majesty, it will be a boy," she said emphatically. Catherine's sharp intake of breath was lost in Margaret's loud cry of joy. Tilting her head back, she screwed up her eyes as her vision momentarily blurred. Dabbing at them she said in a low voice, "Then all is not lost. My son will be born to greatness. I will make sure of that."

When Catherine showed the Soothsayer out of the chamber, they exchanged glances.

"For your sake, we must hope you are right," Catherine hissed.

Holding her sack tightly the Soothsayer looked agitated and wasting no time scurried down the corridor. From one of the windows she caught sight of Traitors Gate and hastily averted her eyes.

* * *

In another corridor in the Tower, Cromwell, anxious to be rid of Scales and Edmund, walked hurriedly ahead of them taking Hastings by the arm. When the two of them were safely in his chamber, he wiped his brow in relief and flopped heavily into his chair.

"So Hastings, it went well don't you think? We shall put abroad that our incompetent sovereign continues to be unable to make a single decision. The populace won't be pleased and even less so when they know the Queen continues to meddle in such matters. Never has our land faced such poor leadership. Now we can be sure the people will want the *Falcon* returned from exile." At the door he called to a passing servant. "Find me someone to take a message to Knole."

"Pultenery is a good man, he knows what must be done," Hastings affirmed when they were alone again.

Walking across to his mantle shelf, Cromwell mused aloud.

"There is only one man who can put right the state of the government and this country of ours which labours under such disarray. That is Richard Plantagenet. Our supporters will be relieved the waiting is over. Sweet Heavens, I can already taste victory. What think you, Hastings?"

"I can only see war," Hastings replied gloomily . . .

* * *

Bibliography

Middle-ages.org, Jack Cade: The Middle Ages Website

Miller, Michael D, *The Wars of the Roses*

Sommerville, JP, *Henry VI and The Wars of the Roses*

Wikipedia, Jack Cade

Ross David, *Jack Cade's Rebellion,* britainexpress.com

Brockhampton Reference, *Chronology of British History,* Brockhampton Press 1995

Ainsworth William Harrison, *The Tower of London,* Bradbury and Evans 1840

About the Author

Margaret Callow lives in a village to the north of Norwich with her family. Working for most of her life as a health professional, she has always found time to write poetry, much of which has been published.

An interest in her ancestors plus a growing fascination for social history, particularly in the lives of working people developed and her first novel, *A Rebellious Oak* was written and published in 2012. Two more novels set in the 14th and 15th century have followed. Margaret is currently working on her next book, also set in Norfolk, but in the later period of the 19th century.

Printed in Germany
by Amazon Distribution
GmbH, Leipzig

5173019R00210